PENGUIN BOOKS

Making Hay

Veronica Henry is a scriptwriter who has written for *The Archers*, *Boon*, *Heartbeat* and, most recently, *Doctors*. She has written two novels, *Honeycote* and *Making Hay*, both of which are published by Penguin. She lives in Worcestershire with her husband and three sons.

www.veronicahenry.co.uk

D1392045

Making Hay

VERONICA HENRY

PENGUIN BOOKS

PENGUIN BOOKS

Published by the Penguin Group
Penguin Books Ltd, 80 Strand, London WC2R ORL, England
Penguin Putnam Inc., 375 Hudson Street, New York, New York 10014, USA
Penguin Books Australia Ltd, 250 Camberwell Road,
Camberwell, Victoria 3124, Australia
Penguin Books Canada Ltd, 10 Alcorn Avenue, Toronto, Ontario, Canada M4V 3B2
Penguin Books India (P) Ltd, 11 Community Centre,
Panchsheel Park, New Delhi – 110 017, India
Penguin Books (NZ) Ltd, Cnr Rosedale and Airborne Roads,
Albany, Auckland, New Zealand
Penguin Books (South Africa) (Pty) Ltd, 24 Sturdee Avenue,
Rosebank 2196, South Africa

Penguin Books Ltd, Registered Offices: 80 Strand, London WC2R ORL, England

www.penguin.com

First published 2003
5

Copyright © Veronica Henry, 2003
All rights reserved

The moral right of the author has been asserted

Set in 11/13.25 pt Monotype Garamond
Typeset by Rowland Phototypesetting Ltd, Bury St Edmunds, Suffolk
Printed in England by Clays Ltd, St Ives plc

Except in the United States of America, this book is sold subject
to the condition that it shall not, by way of trade or otherwise, be lent,
re-sold, hired out, or otherwise circulated without the publisher's
prior consent in any form of binding or cover other than that in
which it is published and without a similar condition including this
condition being imposed on the subsequent purchaser

ISBN 0–14–100307–3

To my parents, Miles and Jennifer

Acknowledgements

Special thanks to Matt Batham, of Batham's Brewery, for insight into running a village pub.

Making Hay

Honeycote Ales

———◆———

Small family-run brewery in the Cotswolds
seeks management couple
(preferably chef/partner)
with exciting ideas but traditional values
to put village pub on the map.

Contact Keith Sherwyn
Honeycote Ales, Honeycote
Nr Eldenbury, Glos.

I

Suzanna stood back from her handiwork and eyed it objectively. The frustrating thing was that she knew perfectly well half of the food she'd prepared wouldn't be touched. The women it was destined for were all bound to be on a diet: Parmesan shortbread with roasted cherry tomatoes and feta cheese would be mentally converted into points and instantly dismissed as having far too high a fat content. Perhaps she should stick a little flag into each canapé indicating its calorie count? She popped one into her own mouth defiantly and gave it her approval: the base was crisp and buttery, the tomato roasted in a low oven overnight to a rich depth, the tiny sprig of rosemary offsetting the combination perfectly. Satisfied that the price she was charging was worth it, she was just about to snap the lid on the last container ready to transfer them to her car when the doorbell rang.

Damn. Her schedule was tight enough, and she had to have a shower yet. Her hair was lank and her skin oily from the fug she'd created in her tiny kitchen. She flew into the hallway, where baskets of snowy-white cloths and napkins were waiting, and opened the door.

'Katie?' Suzanna frowned in puzzlement. 'Why aren't you at work?'

Her oldest friend stood on the doorstep, looking stricken. It was eleven o'clock; normally by now Katie would have done what was for most people a full day's work. Suzanna had never really got to the bottom of what exactly it was she did – something to do with environmental law – but it was certainly more high-flying than running an upmarket catering company, and made her a great deal more money. Suzanna secretly marvelled at the fact she was still allowed to be Katie's friend. But she knew she always would be. They'd been through so much together. And it was obvious Katie had some kind of a crisis now. She'd double-parked her BMW outside, recklessly abandoning it to the whims of the Twickenham traffic wardens.

'Suzanna.' Katie, who never cried, threw her long, rangy arms round Suzanna's neck and sobbed. 'I had to tell you first.'

All sorts of things ran through Suzanna's head. Breast cancer? The sack? Dead parent?

'What is it?'

Katie looked at her. Tears had soaked the understated pearl grey silk of her Nicole Fahri blouse. She'd have to go and change if she was going into work. Though she was bound to have a rail of suitable clothes at the office.

Katie managed the revelation in a whisper.

'I'm pregnant.'

For a moment, Suzanna felt emotionally winded, and it was all she could do not to step back with the shock. She'd prepared herself hundreds of times for this eventuality, but it was one of those things you could never really be ready for. Despite her inner turmoil, she managed a bright smile.

'That's fantastic. I'm so proud of you.'

She gave her friend a huge hug, hanging on as if to give her reassurance, but really in order to compose herself, to shut her eyes tight for a moment to squeeze back the tears. Katie was crying even more than ever, but laughing at the same time.

'I thought you'd be upset. I was so worried . . .'

'Don't be silly. You're my best friend. I'm thrilled,' Suzanna lied.

Katie wiped her face.

'Will you be godmum?' she croaked.

'I'd be livid if you didn't ask. Of course I will.'

'Thank God. I haven't slept all night. As soon as I found out, I wanted to tell you. And I couldn't just phone . . .'

Suzanna squeezed her friend's hand reassuringly, then looked at her watch.

'I'm going to have to kick you out, I'm afraid. I'm doing a lunch for Sybilla.'

Katie wrinkled her nose.

'Do us all a favour. Stick arsenic in her Kir Royale.'

Suzanna laughed. 'I'm not killing her off till I get paid. You know how tight she is despite her squillions.'

Suzanna, Katie and Sybilla had all met in Oxford, where they'd shared a grotty little terraced house in Jericho. Katie had been in her third year of law at the university, Sybilla was at the Oxford and County secretarial college and Suzanna was waitressing at Browns and cooking at lunchtimes in a smart-ish restaurant. They'd lived together for a year, fighting over clothes, men and whose food was whose in the fridge, before going their separate ways. Suzanna had bumped into Sybilla in Richmond High Street nearly ten years later, to find that she'd bagged herself a millionaire and a much-coveted house on Richmond Hill, where she lived with her two children, Hamish and Aurelia, a Filipino housekeeper and a Czech au pair. Katie and Suzanna had always kept in touch, but Katie refused to have anything too much to do with Sybilla nowadays, considering her vain, lazy, shallow and tight-fisted – which of course she was. Suzanna, however, maintained their friendship because Sybilla did a lot of entertaining but couldn't cook for toffee. She knew Sybilla only used her company, Decadent Dining, because she expected a hefty discount. Which she duly gave her, after hiking up the quote in the first place. They had an unspoken agreement that they would pretend not to know each other when Suzanna catered for her: it meant the boundaries didn't blur and kept their relationship businesslike. They both preferred it that way: the thought of socializing with Sybilla's friends filled Suzanna with horror and Sybilla didn't really like to be seen fraternizing with staff. Today was her birthday lunch, her thirtieth, she'd reminded Suzanna breathily, so she wanted it to be special, though she didn't actually want anyone to know she was thirty so no candles.

When Katie had gone, Suzanna took a deep breath. She looked at her watch: eleven thirty-five. Absolutely no time to have a nervous breakdown. She sped up the stairs and hurled herself in and out of the shower, then opened the armoire on the landing where her freshly washed and ironed work clothes were neatly stacked. A lunch party dictated casual, so she chose a white T-shirt off one pile, black jeans off another and a monogrammed chef's apron off a third. She had crisp white blouses and black velvet skirts for more formal occasions. Her black suede loafers went with either option. The key was to look smart and discreet, but definitely not sexy – men inevitably made passes at the catering staff after they'd had a few, and the

4

last thing they needed was a hint of leg or cleavage to encourage them.

She hung her head upside down and dried her hair quickly. Her long, straight, dark brown hair might be boring, but it was thick, shiny and obedient, and she twisted it deftly into a plait that would stop the ends dangling in the pesto. She sat at her dressing table for a moment, gazing in the mirror, wondering if what she felt showed in her reflection. She decided not: she'd become adept at disguising her feelings. The face that stared back at her was serene and impassive. A blank canvas. Her eyes were a sludgy greeny-brown, like the mossy flat stones at the bottom of a river. Deep chocolate brown freckles were scattered across the bridge of her nose, as if applied carefully by a child doing a drawing. The skin underneath was porcelain pale; her generous mouth punctuated by a single dimple in her right cheek when she smiled – though there was no evidence of that now. Suzanna didn't feel like smiling; she wanted to hurl herself on to the bed and cry her eyes out. But business was business and Sybilla was unquestionably one of her best clients. Swiftly, she applied a flick of charcoal grey eyeliner to her upper lids, a slick of matt pinky-beige lipstick to her mouth, then popped two drops of Bach's Rescue Remedy on to her tongue, praying it would get her through the next few hours.

Sybilla answered the door looking fresh as a daisy in baby-pink Chanel, which set off her baby-blonde hair and her baby-blue eyes. Suzanna was ushered into the kitchen, thirty grand's worth of bespoke beech and stainless steel that she now knew her way round better than Sybilla, who seemed oblivious to its charms. They exchanged ritual kisses – the only indication that they were friends. Suzanna instinctively put up a hand to brush off the sugary lipstick mark she knew would be left on her cheek.

'Happy birthday.'

'Don't! God! Thirty! I don't look it, do I?'

'No,' said Suzanna truthfully. She looked thirty-four, which was what she was. Sybilla seemed to have forgotten that thirteen years ago, together with Katie, they'd celebrated her twenty-first in the little house they'd shared. They'd lined up twenty-one of Mr Kipling's French Fancies, each with a candle stuck in it, and drunk four litre-bottles of Lambrusco between them. Suzanna distinctly remembered holding back Sybilla's hair while she was sick, but she wasn't going to remind her. Instead, she hustled her out of the way, not wanting her inane babble to distract her while she plated up.

She laid out the food on huge white serving dishes and put them on the dining table, while the gaggle of stick insects that made up Sybilla's closest friends swigged champagne in the drawing room. She'd devised a pretty, girly menu: her own modern-day version of coronation chicken, with lime and coriander and Greek yogurt, followed by a sinful concoction of white chocolate and raspberries which she hoped wouldn't go to waste. Hopefully after a few drinks the stick insects would all lose their willpower and dig in. There was nothing Suzanna loved more than seeing people enjoying her food. She wasn't called Decadent Dining for nothing.

Half an hour later, the stick insects had helped themselves then carried their plates – their tiny wrists barely supporting the weight – out into Sybilla's exquisite conservatory. Their jaws worked furiously, but no one really ate; they just talked. As ever, Sybilla managed to turn the conversation round to herself with a shock announcement.

'I'm preggers again.'

'Oh my God!' There was a collective gasp of sympathy.

'Bloody Piers just can't keep it in his trousers.' Sybilla lit a cigarette, with total disregard for both her foetus and the fact that some of her guests were still pretending to eat.

'You should send him for the snip.'

'It's a bit late, isn't it? Talk about shutting the barn door.'

'What are you going to do?'

'Get rid, of course. I'm not going through that nightmare again. Aurelia was bad enough, but Hamish . . .' Sybilla shuddered at the memory. 'No, I've made up my mind. I'm booked in for next Friday. I can be in and out by lunch – it's quicker than having your highlights done.'

She smiled brilliantly, but the smile faded as she realized Suzanna was standing behind her, hands trembling as she gripped the sides of a porcelain plate bearing a selection of tiny petits fours.

Suddenly the plate fell to the floor, smashing and scattering tiny crumbs of meringue and pate sucre all over the Fired Earth tiles.

'Suzanna – I'm so sorry. I didn't know you were there.'

'Obviously. Otherwise you wouldn't have discussed infanticide in so casual a manner.'

'I'm sorry. I'd never have said anything if I'd realized.' Sybilla paused, before plunging recklessly on. Champagne made her more tactless and insensitive than ever. 'But actually – I would have thought you'd have got over it by now.'

'What?'

'It's been more than a year –'

'Fourteen months, three weeks and two days,' Suzanna informed her flatly. The rest of the room was silent, as wide eyes set in Botoxed foreheads watched the drama unfold.

'I mean, I know it was awful – ghastly – and you'll never really get over it. But –'

Sybilla paused, in order to find the right words. Suzanna fought the urge to shake her hard, until her bulging, baby-blue eyes popped out of her head.

'Life goes on, Suzanna.'

Suzanna gave her a long, level stare while she decided what to do. Slap her. Stab her. In the end she just walked out.

Sybilla turned back to her friends defensively.

'Someone had to tell her.'

They all nodded wisely in unison. None of them had a clue what was going on.

'She had a baby. About two years ago. It – he – died when he was six months old.' Sybilla couldn't actually bring herself to say the words out loud so she mouthed them exaggeratedly. 'Cot Death.'

Everyone recoiled in synchronized shock. Sybilla looked round at them defiantly.

'But I was right. Life does go on. Doesn't it?'

As Barney cycled out of Richmond back over the bridge towards Twickenham he remembered Suzanna had been doing a lunch for Sybilla today, and wondered how it had gone. Sometimes she saw the funny side of Sybilla and sometimes she didn't. Either way, it was good bread-and-butter money for her. And, more to the point, gave her something to think about.

He thought about the weekend ahead, started etching out plans in his head. Definitely a lie-in, with John Peel and *Home Truths* – he still wasn't sure which was more bizarre, that John Peel was on Radio Four or that he was listening to it. Then perhaps the gym, because even though he cycled to and from work every day his abs needed attention and he could never be bothered to do his crunches at home. Suzanna could do the Pilates class, then they could ruin all their hard work by going somewhere on the river for lunch.

He thought about the cutting that was burning a hole in his briefcase. Suzanna had left last week's *Caterer and Hotelkeeper* in the bathroom, and he'd leafed through it in the bath one night. The advert had leaped out at him: perhaps it was meant to be. He decided he'd show it to Suzanna over lunch tomorrow; soften her up first with a nice bottle of something crisp and white. Whatever happened, he couldn't carry on what he was doing. It was destroying what was left of his soul. And if he didn't cut the apron strings soon, it would be too late. He knew it would cause havoc and uproar if he left, but he'd never wanted to be a bloody accountant in the first place.

He'd wanted to be a rock and roll star. And he'd nearly done it. He and his mates from sixth-form college had been the hottest thing on the student circuit in 1985, with their little-boy-lost looks and their bitter-sweet lyrics, the melodies that got under your skin and wouldn't go away. Girls had swooned over their tousled hair, the jumpers with too-long sleeves and ripped-up jeans. With his huge brown eyes and blond hair, his near-perfect torso peeping through his torn T-shirt, Barney knew he was in danger of stealing the thunder from Tim, the lead singer, and suspected that his days were numbered. It was a game of egos, and Tim was a manipulative, paranoid little shit whose agenda was to divide and rule.

Two days after they'd been signed up as support for a chart-topping act, Barney had contracted pleurisy, exacerbated by too many late nights rehearsing. He'd been wracked with guilt as he lay in his hospital bed gasping for breath, worrying they'd have to pull out of the tour. But Jez, their manager, had soon put his mind at rest. They weren't pulling out. Barney was being sacked, replaced by an older, more experienced and definitely uglier bass player.

His only consolation was that without him the band sank without trace and had split up within six months. Unquestionably, it had been Barney that had held them together; Barney who had given their music the depth it needed, who'd added the hidden extra to each song that made it memorable rather than ordinary. He'd had the talent but not the wherewithal or the political nous to survive the bitchy, cruel world of rock and roll. He'd taken his betrayal lying down, and it had hurt like hell.

He'd gone home to Richmond to convalesce and lick his wounds, found himself skint and taken up his father's offer of a summer job at his accountancy practice while he sorted out what he wanted to do with his future. He realized now that his father had made it easy for him, made his life very comfortable and paid him more than was realistic, so that any alternative would seem less attractive. And eventually he'd agreed to sit his accountancy exams at evening classes, which he'd passed. He'd then taken on his own clients, and before he knew it there he was, at the age of thirty, earning a good salary with a down payment on a house in Twickenham.

It had been a strange metamorphosis. One minute he'd been there on stage, in a world of sweat and booze and gob and fags and adrenalin, an object of lust, preening and strutting. The next he was in a suit, wearing aftershave, carrying a briefcase and paying into a pension plan. He'd always assumed that he would return to the former, shake off his dull, grey chrysalis and become a butterfly again, but the years had slipped by. Now he was thirty-six and it was too late. He was too old to get away with the little-boy-lost look any more. But if he wasn't going to turn into his father, he needed to take evasive action and quickly. So much had happened to make him realize life was too short.

Barney wheeled his bike into the hallway and halted. Something was wrong: the house had a sense of foreboding. His stomach clenched with dread. It had been nearly two months since Suzanna's last relapse. He'd thought they might be coming out of the woods.

He opened the door of the living room and saw that they were right in the middle of the bloody forest with no hope of escape. Suzanna was sitting on the sofa, staring into space, an ashtray full of half-smoked cigarettes in front of her and a bottle of red wine, decidedly empty, at her side. Her eyes slid round to the door as Barney entered, and she looked at him dully.

'Katie's pregnant. And so's Sybilla. But *she's* having a fucking abortion.'

Barney winced. He loved her husky voice, with its cut-glass English enunciation. But he hated it when she swore. It grated on his ears.

He rushed to her side and held her tight, this beautiful woman who'd had his baby, whose hand he'd clung on to at the graveside as the tiny coffin was lowered into the ground. He breathed in the smell of her, pressed his lips to her skin, her hair, offering her comfort for the thousandth, millionth, infinite time, wishing he could suck out her pain like poison from a snake bite. She lay crumpled in his arms, almost unconscious with the grief and the guilt she still felt, even after more than a year. She couldn't carry on like this, haunted by reminders and tortured by ironies. Barney's deepest fear was that Suzanna's grief might kill her, for surely death would be preferable to the pain she was suffering. He couldn't bear the thought of losing her too.

He'd met her when she'd done the catering for one of his clients' Christmas parties. He admired her from afar – her cool professionalism, how she was utterly charming yet detached. And her food was sublime; nothing startlingly original or self-consciously different, but perfectly executed. He'd cornered her after the party and got her card. Not that he often had need of a caterer, but because she was the first person to have remotely fascinated him for years. He'd gallantly carried her paraphernalia out to the car at the end of the evening, and persuaded her into a quick drink.

She was astonished to hear he was an accountant. Even

after more than ten years, he still didn't dress like one, favouring Paul Smith and Hacketts. She'd admitted to him, half embarrassed, half defiant, that she hadn't filled in a tax return since she'd started up her business. Horrified, he'd offered to come and sort out her books. She'd looked a bit blank and said she didn't think she had any.

It took Barney nearly two weeks to plough his way through the mess, piecing together five years of scrappy receipts, credit-card slips, bank statements and diary entries until he had established some kind of order. She'd kept no proper records, had no concept of profit and loss, or how to price a job. It seemed that she gave a rough estimate, without working out the costs, then as soon as she had the money, spent it. On clothes, shoes, CDs . . . stuff. She certainly hadn't saved a penny. Barney was astounded that someone who seemed so organized in the kitchen could be so chaotic in their business life.

He filed her return to the Inland Revenue, praying they would be lenient. Then he went through her various bank accounts, credit cards and store cards, added up all her debts and marched her down to the bank, where he negotiated a loan on her behalf spread out over five years that would pay off all her debts and, hopefully, cover her tax bill. Then he sat her down and made her snip up all her plastic, leaving her with just two cards: one for business and one, with a very low credit limit, for pleasure. He followed this with a lesson in book-keeping, showing her how to log everything neatly and efficiently. He didn't even begin to try and computerize it – she had no idea how to turn on a computer, yet alone fill out a spreadsheet. But he hoped by the end of it she'd got at least a vague idea.

He thought she must think him insufferably boring, banging on about annual percentage rates and the importance of keeping her receipts in order. But she'd been hugely grateful, and insisted on cooking him a meal to say thank you. They drank four bottles of wine between them, by which time he was totally relaxed, and he spent the evening regaling her with tales of his misspent, albeit brief, youth. She, in turn, told him tales about her ghastlier clients and how she dealt with them. She was funny, irreverent and unbelievably sexy. Barney didn't think he was in with a chance. Not many girls wanted to screw their accountant, after all. So he was surprised when she leaned over and kissed him, her lips tasting of the orange-scented dessert wine they were finishing. It was only a short walk to the bedroom, and not a much longer walk up the aisle six months later.

They'd had a small but perfect wedding at the Petersham Hotel, and his father had given Barney a substantial raise in recognition of his responsibilities. And as Barney felt the prison doors clang shut, he thought it was a small price to pay for having such a beautiful wife.

That had been nearly five years ago. So much had happened in between. As he cradled and rocked Suzanna in his arms, Barney made up his mind. He was going to put his foot down. He was going to have to take control, ditch the softly-softly approach. They needed a change, a new beginning, a chance to start again. And he thought he'd got the answer.

Three days later Suzanna answered the door to find an enormous bunch of flowers with Sybilla hiding sheepishly behind it.

'I've come to say sorry. I should never have said what I said. But you know me – Mrs Gobby. Speak first, think afterwards.'

She thrust the flowers into Suzanna's hands.

'Please. Let's be friends again. I can't bear it.'

Suzanna smiled. It was so Sybilla, to cover up her crime with an ostentatious gesture. For every time she was stingy, she made up for it on another occasion with a display of generosity. And she knew she wasn't going to get rid of her until she'd accepted her apology. She took the flowers.

'These are divine. Thank you.' She buried her nose in the bouquet. Sybilla was impatiently pawing the ground like a racehorse at the starting gate. Suzanna decided to put her out of her misery and stood back to let her past. 'Coffee?'

Sybilla didn't need asking twice. She charged through the hall, scraping the tiles with the razor heels of her Russell & Bromley boots, and tripped into the kitchen. It was tiny, about ten foot by eight, simply fitted with pale blue Shaker-style units, a four-ring gas hob and an eye-level oven. A large picture window overlooked the garden, and the sill was crammed with pots and pots of fresh herbs that miraculously seemed to flourish. Apart from a large year-planner on one wall, covered in bookings for christenings and cocktail parties and directors' lunches, there was no real evidence that the kitchen belonged to a professional cook. Sybilla could never believe that Suzanna created the sublime dishes she did in such a restricted space, with so few appliances, and without help – except for a few casual waitresses and a very camp butler she employed for grander occasions, she managed Decadent Dining all on her own. Suzanna insisted it was just a question of being organized and knowing what you were doing. Besides, she had a huge fridge-freezer in the garage and a massive store cupboard where unusually shaped cake tins sat beside madeleine moulds and tagines and any number of gadgets that weren't needed on a day-to-day basis, as well as all her serving dishes and accessories – empty oyster shells for serving sea salt, Japanese-style espresso cups for chocolate mousse . . .

Sybilla perched on the stool by the table that was squashed up against the wall, and started rooting through Suzanna's post. She was shamelessly nosy – a trait you could either deal with or not, but Suzanna had learned not to mind. She soon pounced with glee on an A4 brochure with an enticing photo of a Cotswold pub on the front.

'What's this? The Honeycote Arms? Are you going for a romantic weekend away or something?'

'No.' Suzanna didn't elaborate. Sybilla would work it out for herself any minute. She'd opened the brochure and was perusing it with rapacious eyes.

'Oh my God! You're going to buy a pub! I would so love to own a pub! I'll invest, if you need money. I'll ask Piers. I'm sure he could turn it into some sort of tax dodge . . .'

'Calm down, Sibs. We're not buying it.'

'Well, I think you should. It's a brilliant idea. The Cotswolds are di-vine. And you've always wanted your own restaurant.'

That was true. Suzanna and Barney had often talked about it in the past, but had inevitably concluded that they couldn't afford the sky-high rents and the initial investment.

'We're not buying it because it's not for sale. They're looking for tenants.'

Sybilla did not look impressed. Suzanna went on to explain.

'It belongs to a small local brewery. They were just about to go to the wall, when they got this new bloke in. He's investing a load of money, apparently. They want a total revamp. The Honeycote Arms is their first project – their flagship. They're looking for a couple to run it.'

'But you two would be ideal. You're just the best cook ever, and Barney is so boring about numbers, it couldn't fail. My God, I can't wait . . .'

Suzanna had to laugh. She could see that in Sybilla's head it was already up and running. She was practically going to book a table for lunch. Today.

'I don't know. The competition is pretty fierce round there. And we don't really have relevant experience. And it would be bloody hard work.'

'Like you don't work hard at the moment?'

'True.'

She did. More often than not she was on her way out of the door to cater for something just as Barney walked in. And she inevitably had a job on at the weekends. It wasn't that they needed the money, or that she needed to keep the bookings up to keep the business afloat. It was just that it stopped her thinking . . .

'I think you should do it.'

'Why?'

'Because it's the first time I've seen your eyes light up since Ollie died.'

17

There was a long pause. Sybilla looked at her defiantly. Sybilla had a certain honesty that was refreshing, even though you might not always want to hear it.

When Barney had first run the idea past her, Suzanna had been very dubious. But gradually, as they talked it through, they both realized they had nothing to lose. It was the opportunity they'd long wanted, without the risk of a huge investment. By the end of a long, boozy lunch, they'd talked themselves into it.

'I have to admit, I am quite excited about the idea. But I'm scared, too. It would be a whole new life. We'd be leaving everyone we know behind –'

'Oh, come on. It's not as if you're emigrating to Australia. It's an hour and a half away max –'

'Only if you drive like Piers.'

'Look at it this way. You're both bloody miserable here. Barney hates being an accountant. You go round with a face like a wet weekend. No one wants to ask you to dinner parties because everyone's sprogging like mad and they don't want to upset you –'

Suzanna put her head in her hands.

'Stop! I don't want to hear any more.'

'It's true. Everyone loves you both, but . . .'

'I know. I'm a miserable cow. I'm on the edge. You don't know how dark it gets in my head sometimes.'

'It's totally understandable. I'm sure I'd be the same. Worse, probably. But you can't go on like you are.' Sybilla leaned forward to emphasize her point. 'Nobody's had the guts to tell you before. Barney treats you like china. His mum is too uptight and middle class to discuss emotions. Your mum doesn't even know what planet she's on. But I stick by what I said the other day. Life goes on. It's got to.'

'I know. I've been totally self-indulgent. Wallowing round in self-pity –'

Sybilla shook her head in violent disagreement.

'No, no – don't ever belittle what you've been through. None of us are fit to judge. But for your own good . . . You need a change. A change and a challenge. You can cater bloody cocktail parties standing on your head. You've turned into a Stepford chef. It's no wonder you spend half of your life moping.'

It was amazing how much sense Sybilla talked some-times, considering the amount of crap she was capable of coming out with at other times. Suzanna picked up the details and looked at the pub. It certainly looked idyllic, with its mellowing, crumbling Cotswold stone, smothered in a tangle of wisteria.

'It's probably horrible. It's probably on some ghastly main road with huge lorries thundering past every two minutes.'

'I bet it isn't. I think it's got your name on it. I think it was meant to be.'

'OK. If it makes you happy, we'll go and have a look at it. A look, mind.'

Sybilla sat back, a smile of smug satisfaction on her face. She never gave up till she got what she wanted, and Suzanna plunged the cafetière to pour them both a coffee to toast her capitulation. When Sybilla sheepishly asked for camomile tea, she sensed something was up. Sybilla ran on strong black coffee. What the hell was the matter with her? She realized something else – she hadn't had a fag yet. She looked at Sybilla suspiciously.

'I've got a confession to make.' Sybilla looked un-characteristically nervous. 'I'm not going to have an abortion. I'm going to have the baby.'

There were tears in her eyes as she looked at Suzanna. Whether they were tears of joy, or guilt, or just a defence mechanism Suzanna couldn't be sure. She touched her on the arm reassuringly.

'That's not a confession. That's fantastic. I'm really glad, Sib.'

It was the second time in a week she'd lied through her teeth to a friend. She certainly couldn't express her real feelings. Her absolute mad, insane jealousy that both Katie and Sybilla could go ahead and have a baby without a deep-rooted terror of it being snatched away from her. It wasn't an irrational fear, she knew that. But she had been told time and again that just because it had happened once, it didn't mean it would happen again. Nevertheless, at this moment in time it was still a fear she couldn't, wouldn't, confront. And Sybilla's confession somehow cemented the decision she'd already made. She couldn't bear her two best friends giving birth within weeks of each other. It would be too much like rubbing her nose in it. Not that she wanted to cut herself off from them. But as she gave Sybilla a hug of congratulations, she decided that putting some distance between them might make things easier to bear.

As soon as Sybilla left, she picked up the phone and called Honeycote Ales. She made an appointment for her and Barney to visit the pub that weekend. Then she went into the dining room, turned on Barney's computer and started to draft a proposal – now she'd conquered her fear of the word processor, she didn't know how she'd lived without it. She worked late on into the afternoon. And when she hit the print button as she heard Barney come in through the door, she flew into the hallway and gave him a huge hug that took his breath away and lifted his heart.

2

The car nosed its way down the centre of Honeycote, silent and self-important, defying so much as a speck of dust to land on its shiny body. It was impossible to identify its passengers, as the windows were as black as night, totally impenetrable, but the inhabitants of Honeycote rolled their eyes nevertheless: another bloody pop star, no doubt, scouring the Cotswold countryside for a bijou, twenty-four bedroom hideaway.

Inside, Damien Wood kept a shrewd eye on his newly-appointed driver, noting with approval how he kept just within the speed limit. Damien himself had been stopped for speeding three times lately, and twice for talking on his mobile – a car like his inevitably attracted police attention – so he'd thought it better to employ someone to drive him round while he was on business, as the points on his licence were mounting up. Rick Bradley had fitted the bill nicely. Damien made it clear that as long as he was punctual, made sure the car was always immaculate and kept anything he saw or heard to himself, he would be handsomely remunerated. He bought him a black suit to wear when he was on duty – not designer, only from Next, but the lad wore it well and looked the part. And to Damien, appearance was everything.

He'd spent most of the morning deciding whether Rick was gay. He was incredibly pretty, with long lashes and a cherubic mouth that gave him the look of a Botticelli angel, and dishevelled locks that he continually brushed out of his eyes with a casual gesture that came from years of practice in front of a mirror. But when they'd stopped earlier at a zebra crossing, and a young girl tottered across the road in her too-short skirt and her too-high heels, Damien had his answer. Rick's eyes followed her progress, idly but with an unmistakable interest. No doubt about it, his beguiling androgyny was the type used by only the most male of men: Jim Morrison before he got fat; Michael Hutchence before he got buried. Not that Damien minded either way what Rick's sexual persuasion was – but when you were putting your trust in someone, you needed to know their preferences.

He was going to be relying heavily on Rick over the next few months. When he wasn't needed as a driver, he'd do maintenance around the house, mow the lawns, that sort of thing. Not that the house needed much maintenance yet, as it was brand spanking new.

The moment Damien had set foot in Honeycote, he knew it was the perfect place for him and his daughter Anastasia. It was the last place anyone would look for him, a committed urban dweller, a penthouse prince. He couldn't remember the last time he'd set foot in the countryside, but found he was rather looking forward to being part of a community. He imagined legions of villagers trooping to his door – apple-cheeked old ladies with tins of welcoming home-made shortbread, an absent-minded vicar touching him up for donations to the church roof fund (who would subsequently be speechless with the generosity of his cheque), comely young wenches offering to do his cleaning – until it occurred to him that none of them would actually be able to get to his door.

For Honeycote Grove was a gated development nestling just outside the village: five luxury houses – or rather, 'homes' – contained within an eight-foot-high brick wall armed with discreet razor wire, remote-control gates, hidden cameras and security lighting, impenetrable to unwanted visitors. Each house stood in its own half-acre plot and was styled as a mini-castle, built out of authentic Cotswold stone with castellated roofs and pointy turrets and mullioned windows and studded oak doors. Inside, by contrast, they were the height of modernity, kitted out with the ultimate in gadgets. Every bedroom had an en suite with a power shower and spa bath, there was a study with a mezzanine library, fully geared up for working from home and bursting with the latest in telecommunication, and a kitchen that would gratify the most demanding chef. The garden was beautifully landscaped, already filled with mature trees and shrubs, with a fountain and a terrace and a built-in gas barbecue and floodlights and outdoor heaters. With each house came a share of five acres adjoining the estate, a swimming pool, a small gym and a tennis court. Damien had bought off plan, so he'd been able to choose all the paint finishes and the tiles and the curtains to his liking. And he knew just what he wanted. Damien always did.

The pièce de résistance was Anastasia's bedroom. It was every little girl's dream, contained in the very top of the turret, and was painted in sugared almond shades of lilac and pink, with silver stars on the ceiling and a princess bed with white toile curtains all around, like Sleeping Beauty. He couldn't wait till Sunday, when he was going to fetch her from his mother's in Weston-super-Mare, so he could show her everything. It was all for her, after all.

If it hadn't been for Anastasia . . . She lit up what was otherwise a rather dark life. It was why he called her Star for short.

He supposed that to an outsider, theirs was a peculiar set-up. A thirty-two-year-old entrepreneur, ensconced with his three-year-old daughter in the lap of luxury, in one of the most beautiful villages he'd ever seen. Yet they would be, essentially, prisoners in their own home. Paranoia was one of Damien's weaknesses, even though he constantly told himself to chill out and relax. It was one of his favourite sayings: just because you're paranoid, it doesn't mean they're not out to get you.

She couldn't possibly know where they were. He'd covered his tracks very, very carefully. But you never knew with Nicole. He didn't trust her an inch.

As the car left the outskirts of Honeycote and sped towards the neighbouring town of Eldenbury, it occurred to Damien that he ought to fill Rick in. Not with all the gruesome details, of course. But just enough so he could be on his guard, make sure they weren't being followed. And to let Damien know if he saw or heard anything suspicious. It was, after all, only a matter of time . . .

Single fatherhood hadn't been on Damien's wish-list, but it had turned out to be the one thing that gave him true satisfaction. He often wondered who it was up there, moving the chess pieces around the board, when he'd met Nicole in Bristol four years before. She was the head waitress in a flashy restaurant he'd taken a business client to, and he'd been knocked sideways by her efficiency. It was notoriously difficult to get good staff who knew how to treat the clientele, and she handled it beautifully. He watched as the neighbouring table, a trio of braying PR guys, guzzled the best part of a bottle of wine priced at seventy-five pounds and then sent it back, claiming it was corked. She didn't bat an eyelid. She took the bottle with charming apologies and without demur. As a result they went on to order an even more expensive bottle, and left her a huge tip. Damien was quietly impressed. He was changing direction, and thought she was the ideal figurehead for his next venture: a bar in Cheltenham, upmarket, no funny stuff. Nicole had got balls and beauty; the class and style needed to run it. She could go places under his direction. They could go places.

When he slipped her his card and told her to give him a call, he was surprised when she did that very evening. He took her out to dinner to discuss her prospects; how they could help each other. They'd hardly touched the terms and conditions before they ended up in bed, and Damien realized he'd made a fatal error. He couldn't employ her now, not when he'd fallen in love with her. He never, ever, mixed business with pleasure. It was his golden rule from the day he'd first got into the skin trade.

He didn't know at the time he'd been duped. Nicole had actually been sacked from her job that very afternoon, after failing a random drugs test by the militant company who owned the restaurant where she worked. She might look the part on the surface, but underneath she was a party animal, spiralling out of control with her insatiable hunger for sex, drugs and shopping, two of which Damien was willing and able to satisfy. The drugs he didn't know about. He was surprisingly blind to her faults, dazzled by her beauty and magnetic personality, but then she was a mistress of deception.

At first she'd made him happy. He never felt prouder than when they went out together. They made a stunning couple: he was fair, with a sheet of blond hair falling over his eyes that was cut by a top stylist every two weeks and conditioned every day; she had exquisite bone structure, flashing dark eyes and a mass of lustrous black curls. They were style icons, always dressed in the most cutting-edge designer clothing, never seen in the same thing twice; by the time everyone else had caught up with the latest must-have item, they were on to the next. They took last-minute deals and shopped in New York, to be sure that they were the leaders of the pack, that no one else could be seen in what they were wearing. They were big fish in the small pond that was Bristol, and it was, for a year or so, immensely gratifying.

In time, though, Nicole turned out to be dangerously flawed: behind her immaculate facade was a bundle of neurotic hang-ups, an evil temper and a monstrous ego that was heightened by her drug abuse. Nothing Damien did for her was enough. She was like a vampire, preying on his pocket, his heart and his soul. The baby of her Irish family, she'd been spoilt and cosseted, indulged in her every whim, and she expected the same level of attention from Damien. Gradually, however, his patience wore thin, and he began to express irritation at the fact that she couldn't even begin to keep their riverside apartment tidy, or get food in. When she refused one day point-blank to pick up his dry-cleaning, he lost his temper. Nicole had panicked, seen that she was in danger of losing her own personal cashpoint machine and realized that Damien had meant it when he'd told her to shape up or ship out. In the following few weeks, her housekeeping would have put Martha Stewart to shame. Damien came home to lovingly prepared (even if it was by supermarkets) meals, and he got the full benefit of the hundreds of pounds' worth of Italian underwear he'd bought for her. The result of which was Nicole became pregnant. Damien had felt a growing sense of unease when she'd announced this over a particularly intimate supper (Waitrose duck à l'orange and lemon mousse) and couldn't help feeling that he'd been hoodwinked. It was the oldest trick in the bloody book, after all.

The wedding was lavish; a candlelit winter ceremony held at a country house hotel just outside Bristol. Nicole wore a white velvet dress trimmed with marabou at the neck and cuffs, cleverly cut to hide her bump but maximize her cleavage, a coronet of blood-red roses and ivy entwined in her curls. She looked the picture of fairy-tale innocence, Snow White or Rose Red. But Damien could tell, by the way that no one could quite meet his eye, that the congregation held out little hope for the success of his marriage. He'd worn a green velvet frock coat and the Irish contingent had been horrified. It was bad luck to marry in green, they said. Damien often wondered what would have happened had he gone for the red silk Nehru jacket that had been his second choice.

The remaining months of Nicole's pregnancy were calm and trouble free. She still managed to spend money, but Damien felt it was all in a good cause as he watched the room put aside as the nursery fill with exquisite French babywear and the latest gadgets to make the new mother's life a breeze.

When Anastasia was born, he realized what love was. Sadly, Nicole didn't feel the same bond, but almost seemed to resent the baby. She'd demanded a maternity nurse, followed by a nanny, and Damien put his foot down. What was the point, he'd demanded, when Nicole didn't have anything else to do? A baby should be looked after by its own mother. The tantrums and hysterics were hideous, and in the end Nicole had effectively gone on strike, completely unable to face up to the responsibilities of motherhood. She let her mother look after Anastasia while she went out shopping, to the gym, to the nail bar, out partying and clubbing every night. Damien, weighted down with work, hadn't been able to do much about it. He couldn't stand Nicole's mother, a self-centred, opinionated witch from County Cork, with dyed black hair and far too much cheap gold jewellery that Damien suspected he financed. His own mother was sweet-natured but seventy-six and crippled with arthritis. He'd moved her into a nice bungalow at Weston, but there was no way she could look after a tiny baby full-time, much as she would have loved to help. And much as he hated the idea of Kathleen O'Connor being in charge of his daughter, at least she was blood, which was more than a nanny would be. He'd read too many horror stories in the tabloids to trust Anastasia with an eighteen-year-old who had no loyalty but her pay cheque at the end of the week. And so the status quo had remained as it was, with him working all hours and Nicole pleasing herself, until Anastasia was nearly three.

He'd come home unexpectedly early one evening to find a small party lolling about in his lounge as high as kites, drinking champagne. He recognized Sarita, a friend of Nicole's who claimed to be a model, but who Damien was pretty sure was a high-class hooker. The other member of their little coterie confirmed his suspicions. It was Sebastian Chadwick, who fancied himself as a bit of a Mr Big in Bristol. An obnoxious individual who'd reaped none of the benefits but all of the disadvantages of a minor public school education and had never really grown up, Sebastian brown-nosed the city's wealthy and successful, earning his place amongst them by selling recreational substances, which he delivered to their elegant Georgian town houses by courier. He charged handsomely for this service, but as he was saving his clients precious time and a risky trip to the dodgy side of town, no one seemed to mind. Deeply unattractive, being overweight and piggy pink, Sebastian notoriously spent most of his profits paying for slightly depraved sexual favours. Damien knew all of this. What he didn't know, and was about to witness, was who he was paying for those sexual favours.

The trio were so engrossed in their revelry they hadn't even noticed him in the doorway. He watched as Nicole, eyes glittering with whatever Sebastian had pumped her full of, sashayed over to the sound system and flicked on Donna Summer, 'Love to Love You, Baby'. Then she held out her hand for a partner. Damien expected Sebastian to lumber on to his little pig's trotters but no – it was Sarita who took Nicole's hand. Sarita who slid into her arms. He watched, horrified and entranced, as Sarita and Nicole proceeded to perform a double act for Sebastian. A professionally choreographed lesbian twosome. It was pretty impressive. Every man's fantasy, allegedly. Damien might have enjoyed it if it hadn't been his own wife in the spotlight, and he hadn't been distracted by the repulsive sight of Sebastian fondling a rather pathetic little chipolata that poked out from amongst the folds of fat.

He was shaken from his trance by the sound of a whimper further down the corridor. Anastasia! Anastasia had been in the house all along, asleep in her little bed, no doubt woken by the pounding, throbbing bass. Nicole would never hear her cry, as the baby monitor had been switched off. He'd crept into her room, gathered up a few of her belongings and a packet of nappies, and scooped her up in his arms. Before he left, he checked the monitor of the CCTV that was housed in the utility room off the hallway. Sick to his stomach, Damien had taken the videotape out of the closed circuit television that was installed throughout the apartment, knowing full well his wife's sordid performance would have been recorded for posterity. He didn't know if it would be permissible evidence in a court of law, but he was pretty sure he could make some use of it. He didn't know if Nicole was doing what she was doing for cash or kicks, but it didn't matter either way. She was an unfit mother.

Damien had called Nicole an hour later from his mother's house. She still hadn't realized Anastasia was missing, taking her silence for sleep. He'd phoned her again at ten, to find her in a state of hysterically high paranoia, not even able to remember what arrangements she'd made for her daughter. Damien had taped that phone call as well. He'd need plenty of evidence if he was filing for custody.

As soon as Nicole clocked that without custody she didn't stand much chance of a decent settlement either, things had turned ugly. Astoundingly, she claimed un-diagnosed post-natal depression as a defence for her behaviour, and pointed the finger at Damien for being unsympathetic to her plight, and indeed worsening it. Without her mother's support, she declared, her situation would have been intolerable. Although now, of course, she was cured and ready to take on her responsibilities. And the best place for Anastasia was with her mother. Not with her father, who worked around the clock.

Damien had been granted temporary custody, claiming that Nicole was unfit. The court case was looming, pending doctor's reports. Damien knew that Nicole had enough tricks up her sleeve and enough dodgy contacts to be able to trump up a fake medical history. He also knew that she had enough knowledge of his business interests to be able to fight back, that it was going to descend into mutual mud-slinging.

The whole incident made him take stock of his life. OK, so he'd made a massive amount of money out of what a pedant would call vice. He'd always justified it by telling himself that it would still go on even if he himself didn't profit. And although he benefited from earnings that were verging on the immoral, he didn't carry that through into his personal life. He'd always remained faithful to his girlfriends in the past. He'd never sampled the goods himself. In fact, he was bordering on puritanical. But now, that squeaky cleanness was going to have to go across the board.

Basically, the further down the M5 you got, the more disreputable his business interests became. Cheltenham was bars and clubs, nothing seedy – yet. Gloucester was lap-dancing. And Bristol, his home town, was massage parlours, deep down and dirty. The bottom line was the massage parlours had to go. And the lap-dancing clubs, for good measure: they weren't illegal, but they wouldn't look too good in front of a judge. Anyway, he was feeling increasingly uneasy about them. Ever since he'd become a father, his conscience had begun pricking. Every time he auditioned a dancer, he couldn't look them in the eye, knowing that somewhere they had a father just like him, someone who had had hopes and dreams for his daughter just like he had for Anastasia. The thought of her ending up writhing round a pole for the gratification of a load of dirty old men filled him with disgust. So how on earth could he expect someone else's daughter to line his pockets?

Added to this was his greatest fear: Anastasia not being invited round to anyone's house for tea, because word had got out that her daddy traded in flesh. Naked, female flesh. It would only be a matter of time before he got found out, he was sure. Damien knew better than anyone how very, very small the world was. You only had to look at the playbacks of the CCTVs he had in his clubs to know – familiar faces popped up all the time, people whose worst nightmare would be news of their visit to 'Faster Pussycat' or 'Diamondlife' getting out.

So he'd started putting out feelers for a buyer and found one almost immediately: Marco Dinari, who had a variety of pasta and pizza restaurants scattered around Bristol. Marco and he began negotiations; they'd done business before, and trusted each other. It was just a question of arriving at a figure that was satisfactory to both of them.

Meanwhile, he also decided that the dirty city was no

place for Anastasia. No child should be brought up in an apartment, even if it was a luxury one. As the more salubrious and less incriminating of his business interests were in Cheltenham, which he intended to keep, he decided to settle in that area. He'd contacted all the local estate agents and demanded they find him a suitable home.

So here they were in Honeycote; the quintessential English village that was to be their haven, the idyllic setting for their new life. Damien had got the keys two days before, and supervised the move of his furniture from Bristol. He'd deliberately omitted to leave a forwarding address; hadn't even told Nicole he was moving. It would probably be weeks before she realized they'd flown the coop. She wasn't really interested in her daughter, except as a meal ticket, so it would only be when she came calling for cash that the penny would drop. Damien smiled contentedly: life was going to be so much easier without her malevolent presence in close proximity . . .

The car drove on into Eldenbury, a small market town on the Oxford to Evesham Road, which had originally sprung up from the profits of the local wool trade. It shared the golden glowing stone and shambolic, rather random architecture of Honeycote, but on a slightly larger scale: it boasted a decent-sized hotel, an off-licence, a deli, some decent shops, a small supermarket. And a train station with its magical link to London, just ninety minutes away.

Rick pointed out the Chinese takeaway he lived over – disconcertingly named the Golden Swallow – and the beauty salon his sister Kelly ran.

'She's moving into the flat with me this weekend.' He grinned a trifle ruefully. 'Farewell, bachelor life. Hello, Marigolds and empty ashtrays. But I don't mind. She'll look after me.'

Damien felt a momentary flash of envy. He had no one to look after him. Well, only people he paid.

The Mercedes ground to a halt at the far end of the town. Half the road had been dug up and there was a queue of traffic waiting in front of a man with a lollipop that read STOP. The traffic from the other end had just filtered through, the lollipop was twizelled to read GO, and Rick was about to put his foot down when another car decided to whizz through from the other side.

'Wanker!' swore Rick.

Damien looked up to see a dark-haired young man in an open-top Austin Healey car roar past and up the high street.

'Nice car,' he remarked.

'The bloke's a tit,' reiterated Rick.

'Who is he?' Damien was always curious about people. And their relationships with other people. He was intrigued to see that Rick's face was thunderous. Definitely no love lost here.

'Patrick Liddiard. His family own Honeycote Ales. He's an arsehole.'

'Why?'

Rick explained. His own parents had been tenants at the Honeycote Arms for over twenty years. The brewery had as good as run the place into the ground over the past twelve months. And now that Ted and Eileen had taken early retirement, were in fact leaving that very weekend, Honeycote Ales had announced they were doing the pub up and completely relaunching it. They hadn't allowed his mum so much as a new deep fat fryer, and now they were spending thousands.

'Patrick's overseeing the revamp. God knows why they're letting him get his hands on it. He'll completely fuck it up.' Rick changed gear viciously, bitter resentment clouding his features.

There was obviously more to the story, but Damien left it at that for the moment, satisfied he'd found Rick's Achilles heel. He was glad about that. He prided himself on being able to divine people's weaknesses. It was the only way you could really control them and use them for your own ends. He'd noticed the brewery, of course – it was at the other end of the village from Honeycote Grove, and you could smell the brew if the wind was blowing in the right direction. Damien wasn't a real ale man, but he thought Honeycote Ales was worth investigating. He knew small breweries struggled to keep afloat these days. And that large ones were predatory, always on the lookout for another niche, another novelty. He wasn't entirely sure how this suited his own ends, but Damien was nothing if not an opportunist. If there was a deal to be had, he could find it.

But before he started thinking about the future, he had to get today out of the way. He was meeting Marco Dinari to finalize a price, before signing the papers the following week. Damien wouldn't be able to relax until the money was actually in the bank. So as they sped towards Bristol, he put the brewery to the back of his mind, in a file marked 'pending'.

3

Ginny Tait debated the wisdom of trying to reverse the Shogun into the driveway and decided against it. The parking space was only marginally bigger than the car, the gateposts were decidedly close together, and she couldn't see out of the back over the pile of boxes and paraphernalia. Instead she pulled up on the road outside Tinker's Barn and went round the back to open the boot.

Her twin daughters slid out of the back. Kitty, who loved dressing up for any occasion, was wearing a pair of workman's overalls and a Hermes scarf tied pirate style round her head. Sasha, still in denial about the move, sported white jeans and a pristine pair of Dunlop Green Flash. Ginny herself had on baggy tracksuit bottoms, a bleach-stained sweatshirt and her hair tied back in a scrunchie, face already red and shiny from the anticipated exertion. She caught her reflection in one of the windows of the barn and shuddered with revulsion. It was no wonder her husband had left her. She summoned up her brightest, most enthusiastic voice.

'Shall we get started? Or shall we make a cup of tea first?'

'You two start. I'll make tea.' Sasha wandered up the path without taking her nose out of *Now* magazine, totally uninterested in her new home. Kitty smiled sympathetically at her mother.

'It looks . . . sweet.'

For sweet read tiny, thought Ginny. She didn't know how the three of them were going to manage. She'd only found the house three days before, and taken it on in desperation. Four hundred and fifty pounds per calendar month. Which left five hundred and fifty for them to live on, going by the budget she'd worked out for herself. Interesting times, she thought. Interesting times.

Most of her friends had been appalled when they learned she'd agreed to sell the family home and move out before she'd even contacted a solicitor. But she thought there was no point in being difficult. David had made up his mind. And she wanted a fresh start. Though looking at it now, Tinker's Barn didn't look quite as appealing as it had done when she'd looked round three days before. Now she noticed the weeds peeping through the cracks in the path, the dirty windows, the broken rotary dryer making a half-hearted attempt to rotate. Never mind, she told herself. It was all cosmetic. A bit of elbow grease and the place would be fit to move in to tomorrow. And Ginny was good at elbow grease.

Sasha walked back out of the house looking thunderous.

'I suppose,' she demanded, 'two bedrooms mean that we're going to have to bloody share?'

'Yes,' said Ginny defiantly. 'You bloody are.'

'Well, I hope you're going to let us have the big room.'

Ginny sighed. Of course she'd have to. You couldn't get two beds in the other room. Nine foot by eight. Smaller than her walk-in wardrobe in the other house. She shut out the memory.

She should have suspected an impending mid-life crisis when David had bought an MGF, which he insisted on driving with the roof down in all but the most appalling weather conditions. The Oakley sunglasses had been the next give-away, especially when he started wearing them on top of his head. Extra long sideburns had been the third sign. Ginny had itched to shave them off. They made him looked completely ridiculous.

He was a dentist, and he'd run off with his hygienist. What an unbelievable cliché. What was so tempting about someone who scraped plaque off people's teeth for a living? Though she supposed you only had to look at Faith Bywater to get the answer. With her long shiny (dyed) auburn bob and bulbous green eyes – Ginny thought she looked like a fish – she was all crisp white coats with a hint of stocking underneath. Efficiency combined with repressed sexuality. She could imagine her thrusting her cleavage towards her more attractive male clients, and chastising them for not flossing. She was any middle-aged man's fantasy, including, it seemed, David's. Ginny had been beyond reasonable when it had all come out. No plate-throwing hysterics or bitter recriminations. She'd swallowed hard and asked him, just once, if they could make a go of it. Surely he owed it to her and the twins to try and overcome this overwhelming passion? He hadn't quite looked her in the eye when he'd replied.

'I can't. She's pregnant.'

Fish-face was obviously cleverer than she'd given her credit for. They had a plan, evidently. A plan that didn't bode well for Ginny. They had already put an offer in on a big wedding-cake house in Cheltenham. The bottom half was going to be converted to a surgery. David was going to move his practice there. And of course, once Faith had the baby, she would recommence her plaque-scraping. The upper half of the house would contain their living accommodation – they were going to convert the attic into a suite for the live-in nanny.

Meanwhile, the Tait family home would have to be sold, so he could realize some capital. Fish-face had done very well on her own property, apparently, and had put down a substantial deposit on the house itself, but David needed money to kit the place out, get new equipment for the surgery – he was going massively upmarket, concentrating more on cosmetic dentistry, so the place needed to be decorated accordingly.

David wanted to be fair, he insisted, but the truth was there wasn't going to be much cash left, what with setting up a new business and the baby arriving . . . He was, he insisted, going to find it as hard as Ginny. He wished as much as she did that it had never happened, but you couldn't argue with fate. The sooner he got the new business up and running, the sooner he'd be able to reap the profits and pass them on to Ginny and the girls by way of a settlement. So they'd sold the house and split it fifty-fifty for the time being, which didn't actually leave a lot once the mortgage had been paid off. Ginny was left with a hundred and ten thousand in the bank. Not enough to buy anything decent, unless they moved to the Outer Hebrides. Or France. Now that was tempting . . .

She tried very hard to be positive. Think about this as a new start. She was wiping the slate clean and being given the chance to be whoever she wanted to be. She was only just forty-three, after all. But then she laughed – she had nothing but a very out-of-date clutch of nursing qualifications which, even though the country was crying out for nurses, wouldn't get her a decent job. Plus she had the twins to worry about. David had offered them a room in the wedding-cake house, if they liked, and as much emotional support as he could give them, but, as he pointed out, they were eighteen now. Ginny had been very touched that they had rejected his offer, and wanted to stay with her. But sometimes she suspected that was because she was such a soft touch, picking up after them and making their clothes smell of delicious fabric softener, cooking them meals uncomplainingly at whatever time their appetites or their social lives dictated and providing a twenty-four-hour taxi service. She didn't think Fish-face would be happy to wait on them, and David would be far too busy bleaching teeth to be much help.

All in all, rented accommodation seemed the only answer, until she knew for definite what capital sum she was going to be left with, and had worked out what she might do for a living, because whatever she got it wasn't going to sustain her for the rest of her life, that was for sure.

She'd found the barn at Honeycote by a stroke of luck. One of her friends worked for a company that rented out upmarket holiday cottages. Tinker's Barn had been rejected by them recently as the facilities didn't match their exacting requirements, although she'd insisted to Ginny that it was perfectly habitable. Ginny had whizzed over to have a look and decided that, although it was tiny, it gave her a strong feeling of reassurance.

It was part of a small courtyard development just off the high street in Honeycote, which was only six miles away from their old house in Evesham. There was a small kitchen separated from the living area by a breakfast bar, and the entire downstairs wasn't more than twenty foot by fifteen. But it was light and airy because of the floor to ceiling windows, with a dinky wood-burning stove and a sea-grass carpet and two 'shabby chic' sofas – admittedly more shabby than chic. Upstairs, tucked into the roof space, were a bathroom and the two bedrooms with wooden floors and Velux skylights. If you sat up in bed too quickly in either of them you'd crack your head open on the ceiling. But they were warm and cosy. Yes, they were definitely cosy all right.

Ginny surveyed the contents of her boot thoughtfully, and decided it was going to take at least three more trips back to Evesham before all their stuff was safely transferred over. It was already getting gloomy and it was going to take them all evening to clean the old house. She knew she needn't be quite so meticulous about the cleaning – she didn't suppose the next incumbents would actually thank her for rigorously bleaching every single kitchen shelf – but she couldn't bear the thought of leaving even a trace of dirt for them to wrinkle their noses at. The irony of it was she knew the last tenants of Tinker's Barn had had no such conscience.

She put on her best ward sister voice, the no-nonsense one that had always struck fear into even the most irascible of her patients, and began to supervise the unloading of the car. The twins knew better than to argue with her in this mood. Their mum might be a pushover in some circumstances but they knew when she meant business.

Damien lay back in his whirlpool bath, enjoying the force of the water jets as they massaged his weary muscles. It was unusual for him to be tired from physical labour: it was usually mental gymnastics that wore him out. But he'd spent all day arranging and rearranging the furniture in his house, until it was just to his liking. At his side was a chilled bottle of Smirnoff Ice. Moby was playing through the hidden speakers that the developers had so thoughtfully installed in every room.

For most people, this would be bliss. But instead of being relaxed, Damien was on edge. He felt like a little boy who'd been expecting a bicycle for his birthday and been given a geometry set instead. For his reception from the inhabitants of Honeycote over the last couple of days had been lukewarm, to say the least. He'd been treated with, if not outright hostility, then at best suspicion. He didn't expect a red carpet, or for people to prostrate themselves in front of him. But he would have thought they could have managed to be polite.

The woman in the post office, for example: Coral, with her apricot poodle perm and her badly applied lipstick, which hardly made her fit to judge. He'd gone to put an ad up for a cleaning lady, and she'd practically split her sides laughing. She pointed out, rather patronizingly, that no one in Honeycote got out of bed for the sort of money he was offering. The reason for that being that *outsiders* (accompanied by a meaningful glare) had pushed the house prices up so high that locals of the type who would be prepared to skivvy for him could no longer afford to live in the village. Damien had been rather hurt. He thought eight quid an hour was more than generous, and he could hardly be blamed for the rocketing property market. He hadn't set the price; just paid it. She'd also remarked on the apparent need for security at Honeycote Grove. Until the arrival of *outsiders* (again that look), she claimed it had never been necessary to lock one's back door, or one's car, or indeed anything. The implication being that the likes of Damien were to blame for the upsurge in crime.

The local dairy, too, had been difficult. How were they supposed to deliver his milk when they were ostensibly locked out? They refused to leave his bottles outside the gates, because if they were pinched they would have no proof they'd been delivered. Damien had run out of patience and told them to forget it.

He couldn't compare notes with his neighbours, because he didn't have any yet. His house had been the first to be finished: carpenters and plumbers and decorators were still filing in and out of Honeycote Grove finishing off the other four dwellings. At least when the other residents moved in he might have some allies, and wouldn't feel single-handedly responsible for upsetting the locals. So for the time being he was living in splendid isolation and getting all the flak for what was obviously a local bone of contention; a planning scandal; a blot on the landscape of the picture-postcard perfection that was Honeycote. He consoled himself that it was jealousy, because they would know he could afford to pay eight hundred grand for his house, and because some property developer had obviously done very well out of the whole deal when they probably couldn't get permission to erect a garden shed, hoist by their own petards.

Perhaps the locals would be nicer to him when they saw Anastasia. Children were a great ice-breaker; they melted the stoniest of hearts. He was collecting her from his mum's tomorrow. Maybe once she arrived, he'd be on the road to acceptance. No one had made him feel welcome at all. In fact, the only person to extend an invitation had been Rick. Damien hadn't been sure whether to accept when he'd asked him along to his parents' farewell party at the Honeycote Arms. He didn't want to get too close to his employee; it didn't do to blur the edges. But he was curious. And lonely. He didn't want to sit alone in his castle on a Saturday night. So he'd said yes. He could always leave if he didn't like it.

Rick stubbed out his fifth Camel of the evening and thought regretfully of his mates gathering at their favourite haunt on their motorbikes for a Saturday night out. It was too late to join them now. He had hoped the speeches would be over early and he'd be able to slip away, but things were dragging on a bit. It didn't matter. His parents obviously appreciated him and his sister Kelly being there for their leaving party, and he supposed it was for them, too, in a way. After all, the Bradley family had been part of the fixtures and fittings here at the Honeycote Arms for twenty years. It was certainly the only home he could remember. OK, so he'd moved out two years earlier, to his flat over the Chinese takeaway in Eldenbury, because he wanted the freedom to shag a different girl every night if he wanted to without getting a reproachful look from his mum. But nevertheless, it was going to be strange not having her nearby, to rustle him up a proper meal when he tired of chicken fried rice, and to do his washing. He visited the pub at least twice a week – and not just when he wanted something. They were close. He loved his parents.

He took a look around the lounge bar, wondering if he would miss the pub too. It was so familiar. It had hardly changed in all the time they'd been there: the green and gold patterned carpet, the horse brasses, the rickety tables covered in ring marks and fag burns; the dartboard; the dark red velvet curtains that had been faded by the sun; the smell of disinfectant that never quite disguised the underlying hint of stale wee that wafted in every time the toilet door was opened; his mum's writing on the menu board, with its spelling mistakes – 'lasagna, chili con carn, chicken curry all served with jack pots or rice'. He knew the builders were coming in to gut the place on Monday, because one of his mates was in the gang. Rick and him had already done a deal with a local salvage yard: all the baths in the en suites upstairs had claw feet behind the formica that was boxing them in. They should get a couple of hundred quid out of it between them. Every cloud, it seemed, had a silver lining.

He looked over at his parents. It was strange seeing them the wrong side of the bar. His mum had been self-conscious at first, but she'd had a few by now and looked more relaxed. His dad was getting louder and louder, inviting all and sundry down to the place they'd bought in the Forest of Dean. They were going to do Bed and Breakfast, though privately Rick thought it was time his mum had a rest. She'd insisted, however, that giving up just like that would be the death of her, and B&B wasn't a twenty-four-hour job like running a pub. Just a few sheets to change and a plate of bacon and egg, then you had the rest of the day to yourself. Rick supposed they'd thought it over and were happy with what they were doing. His dad was determined he was going to spend the rest of his life fishing, and his mum was chuntering about taking up bowls.

Rick pushed his way to the bar for another pint. He

was gratified at how full the pub was, though the free beer probably had something to do with it. He looked at all the punters crowding round the bar and wished they'd bloody well put in an appearance more regularly over the past few years, or perhaps things wouldn't have come to a head like they had.

The story he'd given Damien the day before had only been the tip of the iceberg. About eighteen months ago, his parents had been threatened with eviction by the brewery, who'd been planning to sell the Honeycote Arms to raise some much-needed capital. At the eleventh hour they'd got an investor, Keith Sherwyn, and the pub was saved. But by then Ted and Eileen, having had the fright of their lives, had resigned themselves to a life elsewhere. They'd clung on for another twelve months while they found their ideal retirement home, but now the time had come: they were moving out the next day. And Honeycote Ales had had the grace to throw a farewell party for them. Guilt, no doubt. They were bloody lucky Ted hadn't had a heart attack when they'd told him he'd be out on his ear. His mother had been bitter – she was the one who had insisted on moving even though they'd been given a reprieve. She couldn't live with the fear of it happening again, she said. She wanted to be a free agent, not live out her days at someone else's beck and call.

Rick sat back down, and was distracted by a loud banging on a table top. The speech was about to start. He tilted back in his chair to get a better view, and took a sip out of his pint as he watched Mickey Liddiard, managing director of Honeycote Ales, take his place in the middle of the room. Though he had to be in his mid forties, he still attracted admiring glances from women, with his eyes that were simultaneously smiling but suggestive. Rick knew from his own experience that eyes were a man's greatest weapon, and Mickey had definitely used his over the years to get him in and out of trouble.

When Mickey had the attention of the room, he smiled round.

'I haven't been looking forward to this day one bit. Losing loyal tenants is every brewery's nightmare, and you can't get much more loyal than Ted and Eileen –'

Pity they hadn't received loyalty in return, thought Rick.

'– but I know they've made the right decision for them, if not for us. Twenty years is a long time in one place, and they deserve to put their feet up. To say they will be sorely missed is an understatement. The Honeycote Arms has been the heart of the village for so long, and Ted and Eileen have provided so many of you with a warm welcome and a well-earned pint, that it's hard to imagine someone else taking their place. We tussled long and hard about what to give them to mark our appreciation, but finally chose something that we hope will always remind them of their time here.'

The door opened and Mickey's son Patrick entered bearing a huge, awkwardly wrapped parcel which he deposited on the table. Ted and Eileen opened it, somewhat self-consciously, to a round of applause. It was a barometer; antique, expensive. Rick thought it was a bloody stupid idea. If you wanted to know what the weather was doing you just had to look out of the window. They'd have been better off with the cash.

His gaze followed Patrick Liddiard round the room.

Like his father, he was a good-looking bastard. But while Mickey's eyes were warm, Patrick's were like chips of blue ice. He looked more arrogant than ever, leaning against the wall, one hand curled round a glass, the other holding a cigarette. Rick thought he looked like a posey git, like he was auditioning for the next James Bond. He could barely hide the sneer that curled his lip whenever Patrick came under his scrutiny.

He turned his attention to Patrick's girlfriend, Mandy. Sleek camel-coloured trousers and a short-sleeved cashmere jumper. High-heeled pale suede boots. French polished nails and gleaming dark hair. She looked decidedly out of place – she belonged in a chic city bar or restaurant, not in a grotty country pub – but as head of PR for the brewery no doubt she had to be here. She was taking pictures with a flashy little digital camera, probably for the newsletter that was now distributed amongst all the pubs belonging to Honeycote Ales. Rick guessed she and Patrick would be going somewhere else after this, now they'd done their duty, patted their tenants on the head and given them a fucking useless present to salve their conscience.

He looked over at his sister Kelly, to compare her. She'd got on a little bustier top and her fake Burberry trousers, and she'd put her hair up – she looked very glamorous. Just as good as Mandy, Rick thought. He was very proud of Kelly: she'd done all right for herself. She was only twenty-two and she'd got her own beauty salon in Eldenbury. Some rich bloke had backed her, apparently. Rick didn't know what she'd done to deserve it, but he was sure Kelly wouldn't have compromised herself. She had her pride, did Kelly, and her code. And she was very good at what she did. She was booked up months in advance.

He hadn't missed Kelly looking at Patrick wistfully earlier in the evening, and felt the knot of disdain in his stomach contract even tighter. It was strange to think that Kelly and Patrick had once been an item – the heir to the brewery and the publican's daughter – but they'd seemed to get on well enough at the time, even though they could have had little in common. She'd insisted that she hadn't minded when Patrick had finished with her the Christmas before last, even when he'd taken up with Mandy indecently soon after. It was no coincidence, thought Rick, that Mandy's father had ended up pumping a vast amount of money into the brewery. But that was the Liddiards all over. They used people to their own end. They were prepared to sacrifice anyone in order to save their own skin. Patrick had dropped Kelly like a hot potato when something better had come along.

No one had told Rick about it at the time, because they knew how hot-headed he was, and his mum had been worried he'd get someone to do Patrick over; rearrange those smug, pretty-boy features. But Rick knew beating Patrick up wouldn't hurt him in the long term. He'd have walloped him ages ago if that had been the case. No, with people like Patrick it was a question of biding your time, waiting for the perfect moment. And Rick had been waiting for years . . .

It was dark in the cupboard under the stairs, horribly dark, and Rick knew that because there were cobwebs there would be spiders and he hated spiders, but he tried his very best not to think about them. He had no idea how long he would have to suffer his incarceration. He wasn't sure what time the party was ending, and there was no way, absolutely no way, he was going to start banging on the door so that everyone would know what a fool he'd been made of.

It was Patrick Liddiard's seventh birthday, and Lucy, his stepmother (not that you'd know, for she treated Patrick like her own) had hired out the games room at the Honeycote Arms for him and a dozen of his friends. As the Liddiards arrived to set up, Rick had been loitering in the pub garden on his bike. He was the same age as Patrick, and Lucy had insisted that he be allowed to join the party. He protested volubly to his mother, Eileen, but she'd marched him up to his bedroom to be washed and brushed up, and made him put on the dickie bow he'd worn earlier that year to his aunt's wedding. He'd been mortified when the other guests had arrived in cords and jumpers; wanted to die when Patrick had mockingly referred to him as 'Prick' – well out of Lucy's earshot, of course.

And after skittles, while his mother was cooking the sausages for their hotdogs and they'd played hide and seek, Rick knew it was Patrick who'd slid the bolt across the outside of the cupboard he'd chosen to hide in. Panic was rising in him now, as he suddenly wondered whether there would be enough air in the cupboard, or if he'd be found by his anxious parents, blue and lifeless, in a couple of hours' time. He choked back a sob, then suppressed it in case it used up too much of the precious air he was convinced was running out.

It was Ned Walsh who let him out. Kind-hearted, red-faced Ned, who for some inexplicable reason was

Patrick's best friend, and who'd noticed that Rick had gone missing. He'd given Rick his clean handkerchief to wipe the tears and snot off his face, and enough time to compose himself before rejoining the party. Patrick had given Rick a scornful glance from the top of the table, where he reigned over his guests like a little prince, as Lucy brought in an enormous cake, decorated with plastic cowboys and indians.

There'd barely been any time to celebrate Rick's birthday a couple of weeks before. It was Cheltenham Gold Cup week, and the pub was full to bursting with Irish. His mum and dad were rushed off their feet, serving their rumbustious guests into the small hours. Apart from Christmas, it was their best week. There'd only been time for a hastily opened card before school, as Eileen had been turning out infinite cooked breakfasts for the hungover. At teatime, there was a hastily prepared birthday tea of sausage and chips, and an Arctic roll from the pub freezer which his mum had stuck some candles in, the same ones she'd used on Kelly's cake. There was no party, no banner strewn across the room pronouncing HAPPY BIRTHDAY, no balloons, no party bags . . . Lucy had made sure Rick got a party bag. He'd watched her remonstrate with a scowling Patrick, who'd had to sacrifice his.

Later in his room, he'd tipped out his booty. Refreshers and Black Jacks, a plastic yo-yo, a slice of the cowboy and indian cake and a magic slate. Rick had picked up the sharp red stick with a purpose, inscribing on the carbon 'Patrick Liddiard must suffer', swearing that one day he'd feel the same sweaty panic that Rick had undergone in the cupboard, the same humiliation . . .

*

Rick had found the magic slate two weeks ago, when he'd cleared out his room, ready for the next incumbents of the Honeycote Arms. The letters had long faded, but the fury and the sense of injustice came flooding back as he remembered the untidily scrawled letters: the vow of a wronged seven-year-old.

Now, Rick knew that the long-awaited day was getting closer. The stakes were nicely high. And Patrick would have no inkling that there was a vendetta in the offing. There was no way he would remember locking Rick in the cupboard. He'd have no idea of the turmoil his family had unleashed on poor Ted and Eileen, or how he had trampled over Kelly's finer feelings when he'd dumped her. The bastard simply didn't have a conscience. It was time to knock him off his perch.

Rick hadn't quite decided which way to play it, but he knew there were only two ways to get to someone like Patrick: by hitting them in the pocket or in the balls. Or – and this was bordering on the realms of fantasy – both.

4

Suzanna stood at the door of what had been Oliver's nursery, and hesitated. Barney was downstairs, taping up the last of the boxes to load into the car next morning. The past few weeks had gone by in a blur as they'd prepared to pack away their old life and embark upon their new one. They'd spent most of their time contacting clients to tell them of their move – Barney passed his over to a colleague at his father's practice, Suzanna recommended a girl she knew who lived in Wandsworth. She'd also done a whistle-stop tour of all the influential gastro-pubs in London to glean as much inspiration as she could – the Eagle in Farringdon, the Atlas in Barons Court – and had taken copious notes which she'd typed up conscientiously on Barney's computer, thinking that if things got really tough she could always write a recipe book or a guide to eating out in London. They'd also decided, after much agonizing, to keep the Twickenham house and let it out, so they'd always have something to come back to if things went wrong. And if they made a success of it, well – maybe then would be the time to think about going out on their own, finding a backer. Sybilla had made them promise they would come to her first if that was the case.

Suzanna smiled as she thought about what a brick Sybilla had turned out to be. Several times her courage had left her, but Sybilla had been behind her, driving her on, giving her moral support. She'd helped in practical ways, too. Not least by selling them her Jeep at a ridiculously low price, arguing that it was a totally impractical car for her to have when all she had to do was drive from the top of Richmond Hill to the bottom twice a day to take the children to nursery. It was far better suited to the rigours of the Cotswold countryside. It had taken Barney days to clear it out, as it was full of sweet papers and crisp packets and biscuit crumbs and fag ends, because despite her groomed exterior Sybilla was an appalling slut. It was in the garage now, loaded up with everything they needed for their new life. They'd had a monumental clear-out that had been therapeutic and cathartic, agreeing to take only the absolute necessities and one indulgence each. Which in Barney's case was his sound system and two hundred CDs, and in Suzanna's was her massive collection of cookery books which, she had pointed out, were the tools of her trade and therefore didn't really count as an indulgence.

Now the time had come. They were actually leaving the house first thing next morning, and Suzanna found it hard to believe that this was it. She hovered at the door, not sure what she was expecting to find inside, but wanting to say some sort of goodbye. It was silly, really, because it wasn't even the nursery any more. Six months after the funeral she'd braced herself and emptied it out with her mother, who'd packed all Oliver's little things away in a trunk and taken them home with her. Suzanna couldn't live with them, but she couldn't have thrown them away either. Her mother would be the perfect curator. If she ever wanted to look at his things, she only need ask, and there'd be no questions. All she kept in the house was a photo album and his blue bunny rabbit. Although it wasn't actually his blue bunny rabbit. It had been Suzanna's greatest dilemma, whether to bury Oliver with his cuddly. She couldn't bear to think of him without it, but it was her comforter too. In the end, she'd compromised. The blue bunny was readily available in Mothercare. She'd bought herself a replacement, and handed the original over to the undertaker . . .

Once the room was emptied, she'd painted the walls magnolia, neutralizing the room completely. It was now a sterile, anodyne space with slatted wooden blinds and a set of Ikea shelving all along one wall. But Suzanna couldn't help feeling that there was still a little bit of Oliver in there, little pockets of air that he'd once breathed, and she wanted to say goodbye.

She opened the door and stepped inside, flicking on the light, waiting for the familiar wave of despair to rise up and engulf her. Usually she gave in, surrendered to the grief and collapsed in racking sobs. But this time she resisted it. She couldn't break down. She didn't think Barney could bear it. And she didn't want to spoil their last night. She swallowed hard to get rid of the lump in her throat. For once it didn't choke her, but went back down obediently. Then she put up a hand to touch the wall, stroked it and said her own private farewell, just in case something of Ollie was lingering. She wasn't sure what. His soul, or his spirit, maybe – she imagined it to be something like the cartoon of Caspar the friendly ghost, lurking in the shadows. She expected hot tears to prick the insides of her lids, but surprisingly they didn't. She felt calm. And strong.

Then she turned off the light, shut the door firmly and went downstairs.

Barney was in the kitchen, taping up the last box containing the essentials they'd left to the last minute – favourite mugs and knives, a few provisions – before putting it in the hallway ready to pack up first thing in the morning. He mused that this was actually only the second time in his life that he'd moved. He'd lived with his parents in their handsome Edwardian villa until he'd bought the house in Twickenham – apart from a summer interlude squatting in a friend's flat in Westbourne Grove, when he'd been in the band. But he wasn't daunted. It was definitely time for a change, if he wasn't going to become Mr Boring Man in a Suit who mowed his lawn on Saturday and washed his car on Sunday.

Not that there was any real danger of that, because Barney still had a rebellious streak in him that refused to let him conform. The streak that made him play Iggy Pop at full blast on a Sunday morning and habitually test drive unsuitable sports cars for the thrill of it. And anyway, Suzanna wouldn't ever allow him to metamorphose into a middle-aged, middle-class cliché.

He wondered what his life would be like now if he'd never met her. He supposed he would probably be married to someone else; a nice, local girl, no doubt, perhaps the daughter of one of his father's clients. An aspirational blonde who would want to give up her job in order to chintz up the house and produce babies who she'd insist had to go to private school. And Barney would be chained to his desk for the rest of his life, to pay for the Colefax and Fowler and the school fees. He shuddered. Whatever hell he and Suzanna had been through, at least they allowed each other the freedom to be themselves and didn't make unreasonable demands. Neither would have wanted something at the expense of the other.

Suzanna came down the stairs, just as the pizza delivery boy rang on the bell. Barney answered the door.

'Here's your usual.' The boy proffered the still-warm cardboard box. Suzanna felt a surge of sentiment: he'd been part of their lives for the past couple of years. They ordered in at least once a week.

'It's our last for some time,' said Suzanna sadly.

'What – you going on a diet?' he asked cheekily, as Barney rootled in his pocket for money to pay him.

'We're moving. To the Cotswolds. To run a pub.'

'Cool,' said the boy, slightly overwhelmed as Barney gave him a fiver tip and Suzanna gave him an impulsive hug.

They sat down at the kitchen table, eating the pizza straight from the box. It was split down the middle – pepperoni and mushroom on Barney's side, olives and red onions on Suzanna's. It was what they always had. They didn't even have to stipulate their order any more.

'I bet they don't deliver pizza in Honeycote,' mused Suzanna.

'No,' said Barney. 'I bet they don't get Channel Five either.'

'Oh dear,' said Suzanna. 'No more late-night mucky films for you.'

Barney grinned.

'As if,' he countered. 'Anyway, I'll be slaving away behind the bar till midnight every night.'

When they'd finished, Barney put the empty box in a black bin liner and tied it up. Everything bar their toothbrushes and pyjamas was packed up and ready to go. The house was gleaming, ready for the tenants to arrive the following week. Their furniture was staying; all their bits and pieces were in the car or safely stored in the attic.

There was nothing to do but go to bed and wait till morning.

At the Honeycote Arms, half an hour after Mickey Liddiard had announced free drinks for the rest of the evening, Rick looked over and saw Damien standing rather awkwardly in the doorway. He stood up and made his way through the rabble that was queuing up at the bar to greet his new employer.

En route, he bumped into Mandy. She had her head down, fiddling with her camera, so their collision was inevitable. She looked up, startled, and he put his hands out to steady her.

'Sorry, love,' he apologized, insolent yet charming.

He gave her a couple of seconds' eye contact, then walked on, confident that the warmth of his fingertips on her bare arms had had a physical effect on her. He'd seen her shiver ever so slightly. He turned and caught Mandy gazing after him. He knew that look. He sometimes drove a vintage wedding car on Saturdays for extra cash, and the brides always looked at him longingly before they trotted off down the aisle. He'd actually screwed one of them once – what a laugh that had been. It had taken all his powers of persuasion to stop her from running off with him. He gave Mandy a wink of acknowledgement and she turned away, blushing furiously. Rick grinned to himself as he walked over to greet Damien, his hand outstretched.

Damien was amazed at how much he enjoyed himself that evening. He couldn't actually remember the last time he'd been in a pub as such, but the atmosphere in the Honeycote Arms was infectious. Something to do with the free booze, no doubt. Damien couldn't help feeling a bitter sense of irony that the one place where he'd felt comfortable since his arrival in Honeycote was closing down that very night. Rick's dad Ted welcomed him with open arms, forced a pint of beer into his hand, took him to one side at one point and confidentially asked him to keep an eye on his son ('His mum's worried sick. We've always been on hand to help him out, but we're going to be miles away . . .') and Damien assured him he would, though privately he thought Rick was more than capable of looking after himself.

He was forcing down the unfamiliar brew, which to him tasted foul and flat, but he thought it would be rude to leave it, when his attention was drawn to a young girl flitting round the room like a butterfly. A bubbly blonde with wide, innocent blue eyes, Damien noted how she worked her way round the guests, chatting to people, sharing a laugh, a joke, a hug. She was obviously part of the fixtures and fittings; she knew everyone and everyone knew her. When he saw her hugging Rick's mum, he surmised it must be Rick's sister Kelly, the one he'd spoken about, the one who was moving in with him.

He was right. Eventually, Rick introduced them. Kelly greeted Damien warmly, just as her parents had done, and chattered away, grilling him openly and unashamedly about Honeycote Grove. She was the first person he had met who seemed to be impressed.

'Is it true they've all got hot tubs?' she asked, wide-eyed.

Damien smiled. 'They were optional extras. I didn't have one. I was a bit worried about my daughter falling in, to be honest.' Seeing Kelly's disappointment, he suddenly wanted to make it up to her. 'But I could always get one put in.'

'I think they're fantastic. Just imagine, sitting in there on Christmas morning with a cup of hot chocolate!'

Despite himself, Damien had an image of Kelly in a hot tub with a Father Christmas hat over her curls, firm breasts just visible beneath the waterline. Just as they were in the gravity-defying top she was wearing. Fucking pervert, he chided himself fiercely, and tried to concentrate on her eyes instead. She went on to ask about exactly what he did, because Rick was being annoying and wouldn't tell them.

'We thought maybe record producer or an agent.'

'Nothing so exciting, I'm afraid.' Flattered to have been awarded such glamorous possibilities, he went on to give her a sanitized version of what he did, the one he'd been rehearsing, the one that focussed on the future rather than the past. When he explained about his plans to expand his restaurants and bars, she gave him a gleeful nudge.

'You should buy this place.'

'I thought it was being done up. I thought they were getting someone new in to run it.'

Kelly gave a little pout and a shrug.

'Apparently the couple who are taking over have never run a pub. They won't last five minutes. People know when you haven't got a clue. Word's already out that they're going to be a disaster.'

Kelly spoke with the authority of one who had insider knowledge. It was surprising what people would tell you

61

when you were waxing their legs or painting their toenails. Elspeth, the receptionist at Honeycote Ales, had given her the lowdown the other day, knowing that the Bradleys could take some comfort in the knowledge that their successors were destined to fail.

Armed with Kelly's information, Damien looked round the pub with interest. It wasn't an appealing prospect as it stood: most of the clientele looked as if they might be popping out for a bit of badger-baiting or a cock fight any minute. But Damien knew as well as anyone that making a silk purse out of a sow's ear was often a question of cash. And if everything went to plan, he was going to have plenty.

Half an hour later, Damien was about to take his leave. He'd had an intriguing evening, and was gratified to find that some, if not all, of the locals had their feet on the ground. He caught up with Rick at the bar, just as Kelly came over.

'I've taken Mum upstairs. She's going to start crying any minute and I don't want her embarrassed. We'll leave Dad to get out of his head.'

Rick nodded. Kelly smiled sadly.

'It's going to be weird, isn't it, Mum and Dad not being here?'

'They won't be far. It's only an hour to Ross-on-Wye.'

'I know but . . . I'm going to miss them.'

'Never mind. You've got me to look after you. Your big bruv.'

The two of them shared a hug. Damien looked away, a trifle embarrassed, unused to open displays of sibling affection. For a moment he felt like an outsider again.

Just then the door opened and Patrick Liddiard strode back into the bar, his jacket slung over one shoulder and his keys jiggling in the other hand. He interrupted rudely, looking round accusingly.

'Some bloody pimp in a black limo's blocking me in.'

Damien flushed and stood up, extricating his car keys from his pocket.

'Sorry – I'll move it. The car park was full by the time I arrived. I had to double-park.'

Patrick didn't listen, just nodded curtly and swept out of the pub, assuming Damien was in his wake. Damien swallowed his fury. He'd trained himself for years not to get riled when people insulted him, otherwise he'd have spent half his life in casualty given his line of business and the fact that most of his clients were half-cut. But he'd nearly made an exception for Patrick. Who did the arrogant little shit think he was, calling him a pimp?

He moved his car without demur, and watched impassively as Patrick roared out of the car park, Mandy at his side – although at least she had the manners to raise her hand in a gesture of thanks. As he manoeuvred his Merc into the space left by the Healey, Damien decided that Patrick Liddiard definitely needed bringing down a peg or two.

5

Over at Keeper's Cottage, Keith Sherwyn was roused by the sound of his daughter's car arriving back. He'd fallen asleep in front of the telly for the tenth Saturday night in a row. Most people would think him a bit of a sad bastard because of that, but he found it a luxury. It had been nearly eighteen months since he and his wife Sandra had split up, but he still remembered with a shudder how he would be route-marched out of the house every Saturday night to some hideous social function or another that she had organized. And he would always have to drive, because Sandra had no off-button when it came to knocking back the gin and tonics, and even if she had agreed to drive she always got pissed anyway, so Keith had learned the hard way to stick to his two units.

He smiled at Mandy as she came in and gave him a kiss on the head.

'You're back early.'

'We were going to go out but I feel a bit fluey.'

Keith looked at her suspiciously. She didn't look remotely ill.

'Is everything all right?' He didn't add 'between you and Patrick', but that's what he meant. He'd sensed a bit of tension between them lately, perhaps because they were working so closely together.

'Of course it is.' Mandy smiled brightly at her dad and

flopped down on the sofa next to him. 'What are you watching?'

'Um – I don't know. I was asleep.' He grinned ruefully at her. She picked up the remote and started flicking through the channels. 'How did it go?'

'Great. They loved the barometer. I think. I got some nice pictures for the newsletter. It was all getting pretty wild when we left.'

Keith nodded approvingly. He hadn't gone to the Bradleys' leaving do because he felt he represented the new regime, and although he had pressed them to stay at the Honeycote Arms for as long as they liked, he couldn't help feeling that most people saw him as a new broom and the Bradleys had been part of his initial sweep. And he wanted them to enjoy their leaving do and let their hair down. They couldn't do that with the new boss breathing down their necks.

He felt a little tremor of excitement. With the Bradleys gone, what he called Phase One was well and truly imminent. It was time to get creative. He'd spent the first year at Honeycote Ales shoring everything up, weeding out dead wood, paying off unnecessary debts, putting systems in place – and not least having everything computerized. He'd found a freelance chap in the next village who'd worked out a program and hadn't charged the earth. Each pub had its own computer linked into the brewery for orders, which meant everything was now frighteningly efficient. It was incredible how a bit of common sense and a bit of vision had made for a tighter ship. The most difficult thing had been implementing his new ideas without offending the old regime – Keith had long since come to the conclusion that Mickey Liddiard was neither

65

a rocket scientist nor a grafter, and had lived with his head in the clouds for the past twenty years. But he was a nice bloke and he did what he was told, and he looked better in the publicity photos than Keith did.

So now, happy that the brewery had been dragged into the twenty-first century without sacrificing any of its inherent charms and was underpinned with a streamlined system and efficient, motivated staff, Keith felt ready to broaden their horizons. He was a firm believer in not running before you could walk – he'd seen many a business expand too quickly only to collapse. But now he was ready to enjoy the fruits of what had been a gruelling, tedious, nit-picking year, when he hadn't really been able to exercise his creative flair.

His only distraction from the brewery had been the house. It hadn't taken him long to find Keeper's Cottage and decide it was the perfect home for him and Mandy. It was snug, but well-proportioned, in need of refurbishment but nothing too drastic – no soul-destroying rewiring or damp courses. The house had been stripped right back down to its basics, the original features exposed. It had taken nearly a year to complete the renovations, but they'd finally moved in just after Christmas. Having a pristine new house fitted in nicely with the clean slate a new year always brought.

Keith had, however, resisted the urge to go running out to buy everything that it needed to make it a home. Instead, he'd asked Mandy to oversee the decoration, giving her free rein. He wouldn't have a clue where to start, and she had a good eye. And he had to admit that he was bowled over with the results.

She'd left the living room to speak for itself. It had a

huge inglenook fireplace, French windows looking out on to the back lawn and stripped and polished elm floorboards, so she'd furnished it simply with a couple of kelim rugs, an enormous squashy sofa covered in a mossy-green corded fabric and three architectural drawings in thick black frames to hang on the walls, which she'd had painted in a neutral but warm sandy colour. She'd had very simple drapes made of heraldic chenille, hung on wrought-iron poles. When he'd first stood back to study the effect, he'd been amazed at what good taste she had, and had to admit he didn't know where she'd got it from. Sandra had always chosen everything in their house in Solihull: a visual cacophony of green studded leather furniture, swagging and smoked glass. All he'd had to do was sign the cheques. He'd never really taken any notice of his environment. But now he luxuriated in it. He adored this house. He loved the kitchen best – it had been hand-built in reclaimed oak, very rustic and unstructured, with chunky handles. And although he wasn't a great cook, he was taking pleasure in finding his way round; was becoming quite experimental. Mandy had bought him the latest Jamie Oliver for Christmas, and he was pleasantly surprised to find most of the recipes within his grasp.

Occasionally he worried that perhaps the house was a bit masculine, that she'd gone a bit overboard in her attempt to give him what he wanted, but Mandy assured him she liked it. And the few things that were in it were definitely comfortable, because he'd made sure she bought the best when it came to chairs and sofas and appliances. And she'd decorated her bedroom, so she had her own space exactly as she wanted it.

All in all, Keith was very happy with his life. It certainly couldn't have been more different than the one he'd been living eighteen months ago. When he looked out of the window now, he saw a pretty, albeit slightly overgrown, garden, with gnarled apples trees and a huge horse chestnut, instead of stifling surburbia with its towering Leylandii that attempted to hide the immediacy of one's neighbours. He loved the fact that when you listened, all you could hear was birds or the wind rustling in the trees, or perhaps the distant drone of some piece of farm machinery, instead of the dull roar of traffic buzzing in and out of Solihull.

He'd changed so much in such a short space of time. His marital status, his living, his house – even his appearance. He'd lost over a stone in the past six months, a result of eating more healthily and doing more exercise. He'd also had his hair cut shorter, which surprisingly had taken years off him, and his dress was more casual. Whereas once he'd always worn suits in order to stamp his authority on his workforce, now he found he gained more respect by dressing down, so that he could be hands-on where necessary. Keith didn't mind helping out on the 'shop floor' – in fact, he loved it. He loved the entire process of making beer, from the arrival of the hops to the ritualistic pouring from the pump. He couldn't ask for a more fulfilling lifestyle.

However, very, very occasionally, he felt a little pang that he ought to be sharing his good fortune with someone. Sometimes, he wanted to wax lyrical about what he'd done that day, but there was no one to speak to. Sometimes, when he opened his wonderful American fridge to extract a bottle of wine, it felt wrong that he was only filling one glass.

He hadn't told a soul, but he'd actually joined a dating agency a few months earlier, the day his decree absolute had finally arrived. It had felt like the right thing to do at the time. The agency he chose was supposedly upmarket, as you had to have a certain annual income to join, though Keith knew in his heart of hearts that love wasn't about money. But he supposed it would keep out the gold-diggers.

He'd been interviewed by a hideously self-satisfied woman who'd set up an office in a barn conversion adjoining her house. She grilled him unashamedly for an hour and a half before congratulating him on passing the stringent tests she set to allow him on to her books. Keith had wondered if he was supposed to be grateful as he wrote out a cheque for seven hundred and fifty pounds, which entitled him to an initial three introductions.

It was a horrendous process. Contrived. Unnatural. He'd had three dates before deciding that he wasn't going to humiliate himself any longer. His first date had got outrageously drunk, then banged on and on about all the things she would do to her first husband if she got the chance. The second invited him to a spiritualist meeting. The third talked to him in urgent undertones about how everyone had needs, then showed him her stocking top during dessert. They'd all oozed desperation. Keith had wanted to run a mile.

If he wanted someone to share his life, he was prepared to give it time. Choosing a partner needed care – especially when he'd clearly made such a shocking choice first time round. He certainly wasn't going to go touting himself about. If it was meant to be, then someone would appear, he felt sure. In the meantime, he was quite content.

Because in the meantime, he didn't have to answer to anyone else.

Back home at Honeycote House, Patrick spent ten minutes over a glass of red wine in the kitchen with his father and stepmother, Lucy. Just to be polite. Then he went upstairs to be alone with his thoughts for the first time that day. Mandy hadn't been very pleased when he'd dropped her off earlier: they had been going on to a friend's party in Winchcombe, but Patrick had known he'd be lousy company. He was tense, nervous, and he didn't like to admit it. Which made him even more tense. He was best off on his own, and didn't want to inflict his brooding and glowering on anyone else. Least of all Mandy. The last thing he wanted was for his worries and insecurities to get in the way of their relationship.

He flopped back on his bed and lit a spliff, to fast-track his way into relaxation. Drink had never done it for him, unlike his father. As the mellow smoke softened the edges of reality, Patrick thought back over the past eighteen months and the extraordinary events that had brought him to where he was.

It seemed a lifetime ago now, but only the Christmas before last his father Mickey had been having a raging affair with Kay Oakley, the wife of a local millionaire. Patrick had tried to intervene and persuade Kay to drop his father, but by then Kay had found out she was pregnant. In the ensuing mayhem, Mickey had managed to drive Patrick's beloved Austin Healey into a brick wall and nearly kill himself: rather a drastic distraction from his misdemeanours. Because there were more – and the affair rather paled into insignificance next to the fact that the brewery was nearly bankrupt.

It had, thank goodness, been happy endings all round. Kay had her baby, and she and her husband Lawrence had undergone a whirlwind reconciliation. Lawrence had sold his business, a thriving garden centre, for a massive profit, and they were now apparently living in Portugal in contented bliss and unashamed luxury. And Keith Sherwyn had appeared like a knight in shining armour, at a time of his life when he needed a new challenge, and had fallen in love with Honeycote Ales. If he hadn't intervened when he did, Patrick felt sure they'd have been in the hands of the official receiver by now. Their ten tied pubs would have been sold off and the brewery itself would have been put on the market as an 'interesting development project'. And Honeycote House would have gone too, no doubt – Patrick shivered at how close they had been to losing their entire legacy. But Keith never rubbed it in that it was his cash that had saved the brewery. He had respect for the fact that it was Patrick's own great-great-grandfather who'd founded Honeycote Ales, that it had been in the Liddiard family for a century and a half, and he was adamant that it should retain its image as a family-run business. He was diplomatic and considerate, and made sure that every decision made was a joint one. But there was no doubt that he was in the driving seat, and it wasn't just because he'd invested a large amount of capital. He had vision, knew there were risks to be taken and was more than prepared to take them.

When Keith had come on board they'd divided up the responsibilities between them. Mickey was made production director, overseeing the day-to-day practicalities of brewing as much beer as they needed and making sure it reached its destinations in perfect condition. He was the best man for the job, as it took experience and know-how that couldn't be learned overnight, and Mickey knew the workforce, their little foibles and hang-ups and how to handle them. Also, it was plain to everyone that he wasn't firing on all four cylinders since his accident. He tired easily; still had headaches that forced him to take time off work. Plus he'd had his driving licence taken off him for two years – so all in all, he was best left to his own devices. Keith became marketing director, hunting out new sales outlets and looking into the possibility of new product developments – they were debating an organic range. And Patrick was estate manager, responsible for the ten tied houses and the people that ran them. Which, Keith had just announced, included overseeing the relaunch of the Honeycote Arms.

He'd told Patrick over lunch in the Horse and Groom at Eldenbury the week before. He explained that he thought he was ready for the responsibility and had made it quite clear to him that he was to steer the entire project from beginning to end – not without Keith's support, of course, but he didn't want him to come running to him for advice on what colour napkins to have.

So, Patrick had a budget to control and a deadline to meet. Forty grand to refurbish the Honeycote Arms. And four weeks to do it in. It was a pretty tall order, especially for someone who hadn't always been known for his work ethic. Though to be fair, Patrick had changed over the past year, and had learned a lot from Keith. He was surprised to find that he enjoyed work.

But this increase in responsibility represented something new. Patrick felt sure Keith was putting him to some sort of test. He liked and respected Keith enormously, but his bluff geniality and the vulnerability card he liked to play every now and again didn't fool him in the least. Keith was ruthless, he knew what he wanted and he didn't suffer fools. Now it was up to Patrick to show him what he was made of. And he knew why: he had to prove to Keith that he was good enough for his daughter.

Patrick adored Mandy. He knew, in his heart of hearts, that she was the girl he was going to marry. They'd had a wonderful time together over the past year, once things had calmed down and Keith had taken over at the brewery. The Sherwyns had moved to nearby Kiplington, and Patrick and Mandy spent hours together, days together, nights together. He'd been proud to show her the countryside he'd been born and brought up in, either in the Healey or on horses, riding through the tangled woods and open fields and down the lanes dappled with sunlight. And even though she'd been brought up in the suburbs of Birmingham, she was quick to adapt to life in the country. Not that it was all green wellies and horse muck. Sometimes they sneaked off for a weekend somewhere resolutely urban – London or Bath, usually – and Mandy made him shop, which he pretended not to enjoy, and they wallowed in the spas of expensive hotels then were inevitably late for dinner, as the effects of the first bottle of champagne of the evening took hold. And they'd shared high-spirited evenings with Patrick's sister Sophie – who'd been Mandy's friend at school – and her boyfriend Ned, whose parents' farm lay next to Honeycote

House. The four of them went bowling and ice-skating and to the races and the movies . . .

And one day he had woken up to realize that he was truly in love for the first time in his life. Up until Mandy, every girlfriend or lover he'd had was disposable, or had been for an ulterior motive. Kay had been his lover, but only so he could lure her away from his father. Kelly had been his girlfriend, but only because she was sex with no strings – and great sex at that. Even his friend Mayday recognized a sea change in Patrick. Mayday, the Gothic barmaid in the Horse and Groom, who'd taught Patrick everything he knew, had been shocked when he'd turned down her offer of a quick roll in the proverbial one night.

'Well, well, well,' she said. 'You have got it bad.' She'd grinned, but Patrick knew she was a tiny bit hurt and a tiny bit sad that their relationship had moved on, that they weren't going to have their ritual, unconditional bonks any longer.

Because Mandy was the girl for him. Mandy was going to be the next Mrs Liddiard, was going to stand at the Aga where Lucy had stood all these years, was going to fill the beds at Honeycote House with beautiful babies – because how could they not be beautiful? And Patrick, when Mickey and Keith were grizzled and elderly, would take over as managing director of the brewery, and the next generation would be established.

But first, like a knight, he had to win his spurs. It was up to him to put the Honeycote Arms on the map. And Patrick didn't like to admit, even to himself, that he found the prospect rather daunting.

*

Rick decided that it would be best if he stayed to keep an eye on his father, who was definitely making the most of his last night and the drinks that were being pressed on him now the free bar was over. So he asked Damien if he would mind taking Kelly home. Damien didn't mind at all – in fact, he was dying for the chance to be alone in her company. He'd fallen completely under her spell: her bubbly, effusive nature, her forthright manner, not to mention the fact that she actually seemed to like him for who he was and what he'd done. Not that he craved approval, but he was still in shock that people seemed to be sneering at him, and the fact that Kelly didn't made him warm to her.

Kelly went into ecstasies over Damien's car. She breathed in the smell of the leather, ran her hands over it admiringly, sank into its cushioned comfort. Damien smiled at her pleasure and fiddled with the in-car entertainment centre until he got his acid jazz at just the right volume: enough to provide atmosphere but still be able to have a conversation.

She was a little bit emotional on the way home, worrying about her parents and how they were going to manage in Ross-on-Wye without Rick and Kelly to keep an eye on them. Damien was alarmed when she wiped away a tear – what was he supposed to do? Stop the car and comfort her? But she pulled herself together and apologized, laughing through her tears.

'Sorry – one too many, I think. I don't usually drink much.'

'That's OK. You're bound to be worried. But I'm sure they'll be fine.'

'I know. But I can't help worrying. About all of them.

Especially Rick. I'm glad you've given him a job.' She looked sideways at Damien. 'He's a good bloke.'

'Don't worry. I wouldn't have taken him on if I didn't think he was up to it.'

'A lot of people think he's a bit of a waster. But he's true to himself, do you know what I mean? Doesn't do things because he thinks he ought to.'

Damien nodded. It was an admirable quality in the right person. He was about to ask Kelly more about herself – he wasn't actually all that interested in Rick at this precise moment – when he realized they were already heading down Eldenbury high street. Curbing his disappointment, he drew up outside the Golden Swallow. The town was quiet now, though the air was still rich from the scent of frying chips that had been provided to late-night revellers.

Kelly rewarded him with a polite but firm kiss on the cheek that signified affection, but no invitation, which was something of a relief.

'Thanks so much for the lift.'

'That's OK.'

'And if you ever want a sitter for your little one . . .'

Damien had told her all about Anastasia. Probably bored her, in fact, as he always went on about his daughter given half the chance.

'Thanks. That's very kind.'

He watched until she'd unlocked the door to her flat and was safely inside. She gave him a little wave as she shut it behind her, and he smiled through his window, even though she couldn't possibly see him.

He leaned back in his seat for a moment, overwhelmed and not a little startled by the effect she'd had on him.

She was warm, genuine, open, big-hearted, unaffected, unpretentious. And, thought Damien, she had a fabulous pair of tits. He felt slightly ashamed of this last observation, but he was a bloke, after all. A bloke that hadn't seen any action for longer than he cared to admit.

Damien told himself to stop being ridiculous. It was far, far too early. The wounds inflicted by Nicole hadn't even begun to heal over yet. Not to mention the fact that his divorce was the other side of a hideously bloody battle that they were yet to have. Each side was still gathering their weapons and putting on their armour. He couldn't possibly drag Kelly into that. But on the way back to Honeycote Grove, he couldn't get her out of his mind. And as he pressed the remote that opened the gates, he realized what it was he found so attractive about her.

She was about as unlike Nicole as you could possibly get.

Nicole was as subversive and seductive and addictive as the narcotics she was hooked on. A deadly poison that insinuated its way into your system; a drug that was hell bent on destroying everything in its path.

Kelly was fresh air, a summer breeze, a butterfly: warm, open, uncalculating, uncomplicated. At least, that's how she seemed. Damien warned himself to be careful and not to rush into anything. Not to make the same mistake twice. He had more than himself to worry about now, after all.

But as he slid between his sheets later that night, he imagined a soft, warm body behind him, and blonde curls spread out on his pillow. And he allowed himself the ultimate fantasy: to be able to reach out and scoop that soft, warm body into his arms and hold it in a companion-able embrace for the whole of the night: nothing more, nothing less.

6

Sunday morning dawned, rain-free with a light breeze and the odd patch of watery sunshine. Suzanna woke up with butterflies, and realized that it was the first time since Oliver had died she hadn't felt the cold lump of dread descend upon her heart as she slid into consciousness.

Next to her Barney woke too, feeling an initial wild panic – it was he who had initiated the move after all. What if it was a huge mistake? But when he looked over and saw Suzanna had already got up, and was dressing excitedly, he knew it was all worthwhile. If only for that. Usually she lay for at least ten minutes staring dully at the ceiling before she moved. He didn't know what she thought during that time, and he'd given up offering her sympathy or support. But today she had beaten him to it, was pulling on her cargo pants and the lavender mohair hooded top he'd got for her birthday. She looked over to him and grinned.

'Tea?'

Barney was flooded with a mixture of relief, jubilation and excitement. He felt like champagne, but it was a long drive to Honeycote. They could have champagne when they got there.

An hour later, a small crowd gathered on the pavement outside 19 Burcot Road, as Barney and Suzanna emerged with the very last of their luggage. Sybilla was there, excited and emotional, clad in a faux leopard-skin coat and matching hat. So was Barney's father Gerald, for which he was very grateful. There had been uproar when he had revealed his plans to his parents, and he could tell they'd felt betrayed in some way, but in the end his father had given him his blessing, if a little grudgingly, and had told him there would always be a place for him back at the practice if things went wrong. Barney hadn't liked to say that he would go back to accountancy over his dead body, but he was glad he had his parents' good wishes. His mother hadn't come this morning because she wouldn't have been able to stop herself trying to dissuade him at the last minute. And she would have probably cried, which would have embarrassed her beyond belief. Instead she'd sent a card with Gerald – 'Good Luck in your New Home' – and a potted plant that Barney knew they would kill within a week but that still touched him.

Suzanna's mother Iris hovered on the sidelines, dressed in a rust velvet cape and sheepskin boots, her heavy amber earrings stretching the holes in her lobes. And as Suzanna hugged the fragile bag of bones, she felt a twinge of regret. She was going to miss her so much. The wonderful thing about Iris was she never interfered but she was always there for her; she never questioned the wisdom of what Suzanna was doing, but would always have an opinion that Suzanna valued. They were close, but not in each other's pockets. They'd only had each other when Suzanna was growing up, after all.

Iris had been a single mother, a drama teacher – well, speech and elocution. Eccentric and self-sufficient, her holiday romance with a violinist from a BBC orchestra at the age of forty had produced a baby, which had been a shock and a delight. She'd coped marvellously, carrying on with her work, teaching the middle-class children of south-west London how to enunciate clearly while Suzanna slept soundly in a basket for the first few months, then played in a playpen, then scribbled carefully at a tiny little desk and never interrupted the lesson.

Iris's only flaw, as far as Suzanna could see, was that she cared very little about food. Tiny and bird-like, she would often forget to eat herself, though she never neglected her daughter. But by the age of twelve Suzanna had tired of fishfingers, spaghetti hoops and tinned peaches. One day she discovered a battered and well-used copy of Elizabeth David in amongst a box of books Iris, a voracious reader, had picked up at a jumble sale. She'd found the descriptive recipes fascinating and mouth-watering, and resolved to try one a day. The first night's omelette was barely edible, but by the end of three weeks Suzanna had a repertoire that made her realize food was to be enjoyed, not just used as a fuel.

From then on, she was hooked. She trawled second-hand bookshops for recipe books and read them avidly from cover to cover. Constance Spry, Prue Leith, Jane Grigson, Robert Carrier, Marguerite Patten, even Mrs Beeton – between them she gleaned all the basics of formal cookery. Veloutés, béchamels, reductions, hollandaise, roux: her repertoire expanded day by day. Trial and error in their glorified bedsit kitchen produced some spectacular successes as well as some dismal failures, but Suzanna knew that you learned more by your mistakes than anything, and she wasn't one to give up. Iris found her taste buds assaulted on a nightly basis, and her slight seven-stone frame gradually expanding. And her daughter became an accomplished self-taught cook.

At eighteen, the obvious option was catering college, but Suzanna had looked through the prospectuses and concluded she had little to learn, and besides she couldn't afford the time or the money. So she took jobs in restaurants – as many different restaurants as she could find, to gain as much experience as she could. The one thing she decided was that if she was going to cook for a living, she wanted freedom and few overheads. She'd moved to Oxford for a short time, as Iris insisted that she needed to mix with young people and learn to stand on her own two feet: living with her dotty mother wasn't going to teach her much about the ways of the world. Though Oxford had been fun, Suzanna craved her own space and found she missed her mother more than she thought she would. But Iris refused to let her move back into their tiny flat, as she didn't think it was healthy, so Suzanna found a flat in Richmond and set up Decadent Dining.

Now, with the prospect of Iris at least an hour and a half's drive away, Suzanna felt a sudden rush of panic. Iris had been there for her, a mere five minutes away in the car, throughout the last eighteen months of hell. She'd always been able to howl on her shoulder without having to explain anything. In Honeycote there would only be Barney, and Suzanna felt that he'd had a basinful of her wobblies. Would she be able to survive without her? Iris assured her repeatedly that there was always the telephone, but that was no replacement for an unconditional shoulder to cry on.

There was nothing she could do now. The car was packed up, the new tenants for their house were arriving tomorrow. If she changed her mind, there was nowhere they could go. So she steeled herself, promised to ring as soon as they got there and slid into the front seat. And once Barney had started up the engine, and they'd roared off down the road, and the farewell party became tiny little figures waving frantically in the rear-view mirror, Suzanna felt excited again. If she could have chosen a destiny for her and Barney, surely this was it?

Fickle April had arranged a bitter wind and relentless drizzle that was in total contrast to the sunshine they had left behind in Twickenham as Suzanna and Barney drove into the empty car park of the Honeycote Arms. It looked most unwelcoming. The faded sign swung in the breeze and seemed almost to mock them; the boarded-up windows glared out. The stone had none of the warmth they remembered from their visit; the paintwork seemed to have peeled away in the intervening weeks. The gate to the garden swung back and forth on rusty hinges; the garden itself was muddy and overgrown, with a broken-down set of swings that screamed litigation, a few empty metal bins and some rotting garden chairs. Suzanna looked at Barney and shivered. It was almost like some-thing out of a horror film. She expected a hunched figure to appear from somewhere with a warning not to stray off the path.

At three o'clock, as arranged, Keith Sherwyn arrived with the keys, and gave them a warm welcome along with a hamper of Cotswold goodies. But he didn't want to get down to business – he wanted them to spend the afternoon on their own, getting their bearings, settling in.

'There's time enough for business tomorrow. We're

meeting at the brewery at ten, if that's OK? The builders should be here at eight, ready to start ripping out the interior.'

He smiled warmly at the pair of them.

'I can't tell you how excited we all are. I hope you feel the same. I know it looks a bit grim at the moment . . . but then the weather's not doing us any favours.'

Moments later he was gone. Barney and Suzanna looked at each other, then back at the pub. Neither of them wanted to voice to the other what they were thinking.

The Honeycote Arms was a two-storey building, wider than it was high, and only one room deep. At right angles to the main body of the pub ran a large games room. Housing a skittle alley, pool tables and dartboards, it formed an L-shape into which further parking was tucked around the back, flanked by an assortment of ramshackle outbuildings. The bed and breakfast accommodation was over the pub itself – four bedrooms, two with en suite shower, the others sharing a bathroom. The staff accommodation was over the games room, and comprised a tiny kitchen and three bedrooms, with a private snug area downstairs. Oozing potential, one might say. Although at the moment it just looked ripe for demolition. An empty crisp packet scudded across the car park, driven by a bitchy little breeze.

Barney tried to inject some enthusiasm into his voice.

'Well, shall we go and have a look inside?'

Inside, the empty pub looked even less inviting. The Bradleys had been winding it down when they had visited, but there had been some feeling that there was life within the walls. Now all the furniture had gone, it looked neglected and shabby. The air smelled of stale beer, cigarettes and chip fat. Barney swallowed hard. How could they ever have thought they could turn this around? It was beyond hope. Dark, dingy and dismal.

They had four weeks to work their magic. Four weeks and a tight budget.

To his amazement, Suzanna didn't seem phased. She was pulling up the carpet, which was so rotten in places from years of spilt drinks that it disintegrated in her hands. She smiled up at him with glee.

'Flagstones underneath. I thought so. They must have been mad to cover these up!'

The toilets were a nightmare. They needed condemning. Ghastly formica cubicles, the floors and walls covered in cigarette burns. Cracked sinks. Stained floor tiles. Barney reckoned sorting them out could take up most of their budget. You had to have decent loos these days. People might not mind things being a bit rough round the edges, but not when it came to toilets.

He didn't even want to go into the kitchen. He knew without looking that it would be covered in a thick layer of grease. It was beyond filthy. For the first time Suzanna looked daunted.

'Shit. That's going to take more than a squirt of Mr Muscle.'

She pulled open a cupboard door and it came off in her hand. She looked at Barney and started to laugh.

'What have we done?'

Barney didn't really think it was all that funny, but if Suzanna was prepared to put a brave face on it, he decided to go along with it. Hesitantly, they ventured upstairs. Neither of them had paid much attention to the living accommodation on their visits.

It was hideous. The Bradleys had obviously let their Alsatian sleep in their bedroom, as there was a thick coating of dog hairs, and deep scratches on the door. The furniture was beyond salvage – fit only for the bonfire. Suzanna took one look at the bed and shuddered.

They'd insisted on staying at the pub, even though Keith had offered them B&B accommodation elsewhere while the renovations were taking place. But Barney didn't see the point in spending unnecessary money, and he wanted to be on site. Suzanna had agreed with him. But now, as the light faded and the single naked bulb swung over their heads, the peeling wallpaper and worn carpet seemed squalid.

'Bed bugs,' said Suzanna.

'Don't!' said Barney, who'd actually been wondering about mice. They looked in the other bedrooms, which had belonged to the Bradleys' children, Kelly and Rick. Kelly's was tiny, but seemed to have been decorated more recently. Although it was predominantly pink, with a shaggy acrylic carpet, it seemed cleaner than the master bedroom, and they decided to squat in there for the time being.

They went down to the car to get their things. Suzanna opened the boot and was puzzled to find two large shoeboxes on top of their luggage, one tied with a pink ribbon, the other with a blue. She certainly hadn't put them there.

Puzzled, she and Barney ripped them open. Inside they found a pair of Hunter wellies each, in the appropriate size. Suzanna smiled: the gesture had Sybilla written all over it. Suddenly, it occurred to her just what they were leaving behind. People who understood them, people

86

who knew them; people who cared. People who knew their shoe sizes, for God's sake . . .

Here, they were all on their own.

Down the road at Tinker's Barn, having spent their last night in Evesham, Ginny and the twins had scrubbed and polished frantically all morning while their worldly goods lay waiting to be unpacked, before Ginny deemed the house fit for habitation. They had then argued for the rest of the afternoon about what should go where, and the sad conclusion by six o'clock was that there wasn't nearly enough room for any of it. Battered boxes of clothes were piled up on the landing as the wardrobe space was minimal. The twins were bickering: Ginny could hear that Sasha was tired and on the verge of tears, which meant she became incredibly spiteful.

She decided to make an early supper with the few groceries she'd brought with them. She'd tried to empty out her cupboards completely at the old house – there was no point in transporting things unnecessarily. And there was something quite therapeutic about the thought of restocking all the kitchen cupboards. So her basic ingredients were pretty uninspiring. She made spaghetti with a tin of chopped tomatoes, a tin of tuna and a tin of sweetcorn thrown in. Not particularly edifying, but Ginny had had rather a lot on her plate this weekend.

'Is this organic?' Kitty poked suspiciously at her sauce.

'No, it isn't. We can't afford organic any more. We've been relegated to the world of blue and white stripes: Tesco's value for money. If you want organic, you'll have to get out there and dig yourself a garden.'

Kitty looked mortified, whether because she was

risking slow poisoning by pesticides or because her mother had been uncharacteristically sharp, she didn't know. Ginny was instantly sorry, and smiled round brightly as she tried to sprinkle Parmesan on her pasta. A solid block of dried cheese thumped vainly against the lid. Ginny put the drum down hastily before anyone started examining the sell-by date.

'Shall we explore the village later?'

Sasha looked up witheringly.

'What, in the pitch dark? Anyway, what are you expecting to find, exactly? Fatboy Slim hosting an all-nighter? I can tell you exactly what there'll be. A post office that doesn't even sell Tampax – the one thing we're likely to run out of. And a pub full of sad, pissed old farmers. And that'll be it.'

Sasha shoved her plate out of the way, got up and stomped out of the room. Kitty looked at her mum, rolling her eyes at her sister's outburst.

'She's such a bitch.'

'She's upset. She's bound to be. We all are, I'm sure.'

'I don't know why you're so reasonable, Mum. I don't know why you give her the benefit of the doubt. You're too nice.'

Which was why her husband had left her, thought Ginny. She'd been a total doormat, made it easy for him. Maybe it was time to get tough. Only she didn't have a clue how. And with who? She couldn't start on her daughters. They'd had just as hard a time as she had. If not worse.

Despite being technically identical, the twins were quite different. With their high cheekbones and their dainty noses and their wide grey eyes, they looked like little kittens. The only superficial difference was their hair. They each had corkscrew ringlets, white blonde at birth that had now, sadly Ginny thought, darkened to a tawny brown. But while Kitty revelled in the abandon of her curls, leaving them wild and loose past her shoulders, or twisted into a big clip on the top of her head, Sasha utterly loathed them, and spent fortunes and hours straightening her hair with any number of conditioners and de-frizzers and medieval-looking instruments of torture until it was dead, Jennifer-Aniston straight.

Personality-wise, however, they were living proof that horoscopes were total bollocks. In their dress alone, they were poles apart. Kitty's look was grungy, eclectic, eccentric and exotic – she usually wore things she'd customized herself. She was never happier than when scrabbling through jumble sales where she'd manage to find the dinkiest pink woolly cardigan on to which she'd sew big silver star buttons, or an army jacket which she'd embellish with scraps of lace and glittery gold ricrac. Sasha, on the other hand, wouldn't touch second-hand clothes with a barge pole – everything had to be pristine, up to the minute and preferably designer. She spent as much on magazines as Kitty spent on clothes, and moaned for hours about what she couldn't afford.

And while Kitty was easygoing and supportive, Sasha was highly strung and demanding, and Ginny found herself wishing, only slightly and very occasionally, that Sasha had chosen to live with David. Ginny once, in absolute desperation, told her that she loved her very much but sometimes found it very hard to like her. And Sasha just shrugged and said that was OK, she didn't need to be liked, nobody got through this bitch of a life by being liked – did she, for example, think Madonna was liked . . . ?

As she gloomily stacked the barely-touched supper plates, then scraped the leftovers into the bin, Ginny realized that the twins were obviously taking the upheaval harder than she thought. After all, it was the first time they'd moved. They'd lived in the big Victorian semi in Evesham all of their life, and although it hadn't been luxurious it had been large, with plenty of room for them to have their friends back. It had always been a lively, happy house. Any hopes Ginny had of recreating that atmosphere here were rapidly diminishing. It wasn't home, by any stretch of the imagination.

She decided to have a bath. She tiptoed past the twins' bedroom, where she could hear Sasha complaining and Kitty telling her to shut up. Ten minutes later, she was lying up to her neck in bubbles – thank God there was plenty of hot water – with Sasha's Discman playing *Led Zeppelin's Greatest Hits* to drown out the noise of their carping.

Big mistake. Or, as Sasha would say, bi-i-i-i-ig mistake. By the time Robert Plant had started crooning that he was going to have to leave, there were big fat tears rolling down Ginny's cheeks. She didn't know if it was the pertinence of the lyrics that triggered her sobbing, or the memories the music unleashed: memories of her and David in their flat in Birmingham, where he was finishing his dental training and she was a nurse at the Queen Elizabeth hospital. The turntable was always spinning, music turned up full volume till the neighbours complained; friends spilled in and out; David cooked his special curries with a dentist's precision and attention to detail, using mysterious spices and unrecognizable vegetables from the ethnic shops down the road. There was endless beer and wine and everyone danced and sang. Nothing really mattered back then, before they were married. They worked hard and they played hard.

Real life had only kicked in once they had moved to Evesham, where David joined a practice and Ginny had the twins. The emergency hysterectomy when she began haemorrhaging after the birth had come as a shock, but they both agreed they should be grateful to have two beautiful daughters, and not to dwell on it. Ginny also felt that it had been a warning to her, that she should concentrate on her girls and not her career, and so they had agreed that she wouldn't work again till the girls had grown up. Besides, David was going to need a lot of support, both moral and practical, as he wanted to start his own practice.

So why had he chosen to leave her now, when she'd given him so much and given up so much? Had he deliberately waited for the moment when the twins had essentially reached adulthood, thinking that would some-how make it better for her? When in reality it made it so much worse. Because without David and the twins, she was nothing. And why had he left her? They had very rarely argued, because their roles were so defined – the edges of their responsibilities had never blurred; they were both happy with who and what they were and what they were supposed to be doing.

After much internal agonizing and analysis, Ginny had decided it was because she was boring. She got through life by being efficient and organized. It wasn't that she didn't know how to have fun – she knew people enjoyed her company; she had a wry sense of humour and a caustic wit when she felt like it. But she was frighteningly sensible. She always had paracetamol and plasters in her handbag in case of an emergency. She took people's car keys off them when they were too drunk to drive. David must have been bored to death. She tried to remember the last time she'd done anything spontaneous, out of the ordinary or naughty. Even her clothes were safe and dull. Jeans. Fleeces – grey or navy. She had some nice clothes for dressing up, but realized there was little occasion to do that. Should she really be blaming herself for that? What had been stopping David organizing a night out? They usually had friends over or went to their houses, where they all indulged in an Indian takeaway – David had long since given up showing off his culinary skills, complaining that you couldn't get the ingredients in Evesham – with cans of beer for the blokes and cheap white wine for the women while the kids fought or sulked or listened to loud music upstairs.

Ginny gritted her teeth. Don't look back. Look forward. She could do what the bloody hell she liked from this day on. She turned off the Discman, wiped away her tears, turned the hot tap back on to heat up the water and concentrated on making a list: a list that would make her life bearable and give her back a sense of self.

NUMBER ONE: Get a dog. She had always wanted a dog. Had always had one when she was growing up. But once she'd got married, it was out of the question. David was allergic to them, he said. Badly allergic. He only had to sit in the same room as a dog and his eyes puffed out and his skin came out in hives. Ginny had never actually seen any evidence of this, but a dog had been a complete no-no for the last twenty years. Now she could have one – hell, she could have a hundred and one if she wanted. It had been the first thing she'd checked on the lease of the barn, that pets were allowed. They were. She was off to the NCDL as soon as was feasible. Apart from anything, three women living alone needed some sort of protection, even if it was just a warning bark when a stranger came to the door. She'd sleep easier in her bed with a dog roaming round.

NUMBER TWO: Get a job. Money was the last reason. Although it was a pretty good one. She didn't want to spoil the twins, but there were things they needed, things she couldn't afford at the moment, and some extra cash would mean she could give them those things without feeling resentful, without feeling that it was her having to make sacrifices in order to provide for them. No, the main reason for getting a job was because she wanted to feel like a person in her own right again. She'd adored nursing and been bloody good at it, and she'd enjoyed the life. But she didn't think she wanted to go back to that now. It was too big a commitment, even with the twins the age they were. She certainly didn't want to work nights. And things had changed. Morale had plummeted. Conditions in nursing were at best frustrating, at worst impossible. She didn't need to feel any more undervalued than she already did. If it was an ego boost she was looking for, nursing was probably the last thing she should consider. So what instead? Ginny didn't have a clue. Perhaps she'd look in the local paper. That would give her an idea of what to aspire to.

NUMBER THREE (and this was the most scary): Get a bloke. A chap. An escort. A companion. Ginny realized that she'd never been without a man in her life since she was fourteen. She'd had her first serious boyfriend then. It wasn't that she was sexually precocious, just mature for her age. And she liked the company of men, liked the deal that went with a partnership. And she utterly loathed her own company. She'd always waited anxiously for the sound of David's key in the lock, had welcomed him eagerly at six, seven, eight o'clock, whenever he'd got home, so she could talk to him, compare notes on the day, debate what to watch on television. To Ginny, life was for sharing. There was absolutely no point in seeing a film on your own, eating a meal on your own, going to bed on your own . . . Not that she was a raving sex maniac. But she'd found over the past couple of months that there was nothing bigger than a double bed with one person in it.

Therefore, she needed a man. Whether she'd find one in a place like Honeycote she couldn't be sure. Eligible bachelors hadn't been part of her criteria when she'd started house-hunting. All she'd wanted then was a roof over her head. Furthermore, she had a strong suspicion that not-quite divorcees were not always made particularly welcome in the English countryside. There was always the fear that they were predatory and ruthless, if not utterly desperate, and would make off with your husband without a by-your-leave.

Perhaps she could meet someone through tennis? She was quite good, even though she hadn't played for a few months. She didn't want to go back to her club in Evesham – too many tongues and prying eyes and too many friends of David. But there was bound to be a country club round here. Maybe she could have some lessons to sharpen up her game. Maybe she could have an affair with her coach! She imagined a strong, athletic young man who would find her irresistible, a woman of the world, experienced and mysterious — then she remembered that she couldn't possibly afford tennis lessons. Or membership of a club, for that matter. Or a dinky little skirt for flashing her knickers.

OK. So the order was: dog, so she'd feel safe, and job, so she'd feel valued and to boost her self-esteem. Then, and only then, she might feel strong enough to embark on the Great Bloke Hunt.

Filled with resolve after her soak in the bath, Ginny went downstairs and found that Sasha had made them all mugs of hot chocolate topped with marshmallows, a Tait ritual when things weren't quite going to plan.

Sasha came and gave her a big hug.

'I'm sorry I was such a cow.'

Ginny was instantly mollified and nearly started crying again. It was typical Sasha, to go flying off at the deep end so that you reached the end of your tether and decided you wouldn't care if you never saw her again. Then when she made it up to you, you were filled with love and remorse. It was exhausting, but it was Sasha.

Ginny had always felt a stab of guilt deep down that it was her fault that Sasha could be so difficult. She'd breastfed both the twins for six weeks and then, weak with exhaustion and lack of sleep, been told by the midwife that she should give up feeding one, or preferably both, and get her husband to share in the chore. Reluctantly, she had put Sasha on the bottle and handed her over to David, and carried on feeding Kitty herself, often pulling her into bed and leaving her snuggled up in the crook of her arm till morning. Perhaps it was the continuation of this mother love that had made Kitty so relaxed and happy, while Sasha had felt spurned, made to suck on a hard plastic teat and thrust back into her cot by a firm and disciplined father who did, after all, need his sleep in order to be sure of extracting the correct teeth the next day.

Of the two girls, it was definitely Sasha she worried about most, in terms of the effect the split would have on her. In spite of her protests that everyone's parents were divorced, and that it was really uncool to have a happy family, Ginny knew that she minded very much indeed. Her only consolation was that there really wasn't much Sasha could get up to in a place like Honeycote.

It took Barney nearly two hours to get to sleep that night. The windows didn't fit properly and there was a draught that seemed to whistle right past his ear, and even their goose-down duvet didn't go all the way to keeping out the cold. And he was panicking. He felt sure they'd made the wrong decision, and he felt guilty, because he worried that he'd sold the move to Suzanna by playing on her weaknesses and vulnerabilities. Not because he was selfish and because it was what he wanted to do, but because he truly believed it was the only way they were going to save their marriage. He supposed they could go on for years in their parallel universes, because they never actually rowed. They just existed for periods of time until Suzanna had a wobbly, then he picked her up and put her back on track.

He knew he was having to be the stronger. Some

people would argue that the death of a child was worse for a mother, that the guilt was greater, but Barney didn't believe it could be measured. To him too the feeling of your own child in your arms was the most precious gift one could be given, an invaluable high, the ultimate gratification. The paternal bond, the need to protect and provide, was surely as powerful as the umbilical cord that connected mother and baby. As for guilt, how many times had he gone back over Oliver's short life, wondering if decisions he'd made were to blame for his death, wondering if there could have been something he could have done. When he'd woken up earlier that night wanting a pee, why had he chosen to ignore it and gone back to sleep? If he'd got up to go to the loo, he would have looked in on Oliver; he always did. And maybe that would have been the moment he'd been drawing his last breath; maybe he could have saved him . . .

After eighteen months, and a few counselling sessions, Barney knew that thoughts like these weren't going to help anyone. Definitely not Oliver, and not him and Suzanna either. Guilt was destructive; a poison that gnawed at your insides and would ultimately drive you mad. He knew Suzanna felt guilty too – she went back over the cigarettes she'd smoked before she knew she was pregnant; the odd fag she'd had with friends after Oliver was born; the fact that she'd stopped breastfeeding too early; had left him with a childminder two days a week; hadn't bought a thermometer for the bedroom – he'd heard every ramification of every possible cause, and even though they'd been told time and time again not to blame themselves, what the fuck else were you supposed to think when you found your own child cold in his cot?

There wasn't anyone else to point the finger at – they were his parents. They had the ultimate responsibility.

Barney hoped that moving to Honeycote would help Suzanna, give her the courage to blossom and grow again back into the creature he'd married, the creature who had, despite all her subsequent self-doubt, been a brilliant and wonderful mother. For he was convinced that the only way they were going to survive was to have another baby, otherwise they would live out the rest of their lives with Oliver's ghost always there in the background. He hadn't dared broach the subject yet – it lay unspoken but obvious between them – but Suzanna was too emotionally fragile to discuss it as a reality, and he felt it was a waste of time just speculating.

Life in Honeycote would be so different, such a new beginning, so free of any reminders, that perhaps she would turn the corner. And if not, perhaps it would give each of them the courage to let each other go – although Barney hoped desperately that this wouldn't be the outcome.

Now, however, he was terrified that they had bitten off more than they could chew, that running the Honeycote Arms was going to be daunting and stressful and exhausting and hardly conducive to the repair of a marriage that had been ripped apart by tragedy. If they were going to be constantly working and struggling to meet targets and deadlines, what time and energy would there be left over for each other? He must have been mad to think they could do it. Four weeks to rip the guts out of this dump and turn it round? He felt his bowels turn liquid with panic. There was nothing they could do about it now. They were committed.

Barney sighed. Half of him was desperate for sleep so he could stop the fears going round his head; the other half knew that the sooner he slept the sooner morning, and therefore reality, would arrive, and the longer he put off the moment of reckoning the better.

He put out an arm to curl round Suzanna. She was fast asleep and therefore didn't resist. He knew if she had been awake she would have stiffened involuntarily; moved imperceptibly away from him. The only time she wanted close physical contact was when she was in need of comfort, as she knew that Barney was too much of a gentleman to take advantage of a woman in distress. Then she craved his arms around her. But in the cold of a newly-entered bed, where it was natural for a man and a woman to turn to each other, she was an island, frosty and remote. On the few occasions he had tried to touch her, he could feel her teeth clench, hear her willing him to leave her alone and go to sleep. She was never actually cruel enough to tell him to go away. But her silence spoke volumes and made Barney feel ashamed, which he knew was unfair, but he certainly wasn't going to confront her, demand his conjugal rights, tell her that more than twelve months without sex was totally unreasonable. He loved her more than that. So he put up with it, and occasionally snuggled up to her while she was sleeping and hoped that one day the ice maiden would thaw . . .

7

The next morning Barney woke before Suzanna, light-headed from only a few hours' sleep but in a more optimistic mood. He dressed quickly and crept down the wooden stairs that led from the staff accommodation to the games room and went through the connecting door into the pub itself. He wanted to have another good look round, with the copious notes he'd made over the past couple of weeks, before they went to their meeting at the brewery. He didn't want to be caught out by something obvious and for Honeycote Ales to think they'd made a mistake.

Barney wasn't a great one for politics, but he was enough of a realist to know that even if you didn't play dirty, you needed to understand the rules and who the key players were. He could tell Keith Sherwyn was a man capable of making ruthless decisions: if he thought they weren't up to it, he'd have them out before you could say best bitter. Mickey Liddiard was a softer touch, he'd decided. He'd also worked out that Keith probably knew Mickey was the weak link. Therefore if he needed an ally it was Keith. He'd been impressed with his line of questioning at their interview, his perceptiveness, enough to know that little would escape him.

Before Barney could embark on his tour, he was distracted by an unearthly grinding and clanking that sounded like the chains of Marley's ghost. He padded outside to find a skip being manoeuvred on to the driveway and a trio of builders watching with crossed arms. He picked out who he thought must be the gaffer and walked across with his hand outstretched:

'Barney Blake. I'm going to be the new landlord, for my sins.'

Minutes later he found himself making tea, which he knew was a mistake, a precedent he shouldn't have set, but he wanted a blokey chat, to get on the right side of these men so that when he wanted something doing that wasn't on the agenda they wouldn't tut and shake their heads sorrowfully, weighed down by the impossibility of whatever task he might be suggesting. He also knew that there were any number of horrors likely to be uncovered in the next couple of weeks, and he didn't want to be strung along or have the wool pulled over his eyes. He wanted them to think he was a good bloke – though why shouldn't they; he was! – and if that meant making endless cups of sugary tea, so be it. Barney didn't actually know an RSJ from a JCB, so he was at their mercy.

The gaffer, Tony, reckoned that by the end of the week the whole place would be stripped out ready to be put back together again. They agreed to use the games room to store anything that might need putting back, such as whatever of the kitchen equipment was reusable, though from first viewing Barney suspected that would be very little. In general, the plan was to keep much of the original building intact – they couldn't afford either the time or the money to start knocking out walls. Anyway, it worked structurally, and it was important to retain the spirit of the place, not rip out its heart, mainly because they didn't want to alienate what regulars they already had. Because although the Honeycote Arms was in for a total revamp, it was vitally important that it should maintain its status as a village local and not become intimidating to the clientele that had frequented it in the past. They didn't want accusations of commercialization and inflated prices hurled at them. Therefore the lounge bar, with a few cosmetic alterations, was to retain its down-to-earth image: darts matches and quiz nights would continue; the TV screen that broadcast the more important sporting fixtures would still be wheeled out; well-behaved dogs and dirty Wellington boots were to be made welcome. After all, the primary object of a tied house was to sell beer, otherwise there wasn't much point in keeping the brewery running. That was the side of the pub that was to be Barney's domain – the innovative side was to be Suzanna's – so it was going to be important for him to ingratiate himself with the locals: the lads who might come in after football training, the farmers who wanted to quench their thirst at eleven o'clock in the morning when they'd already effectively done a day's work. Barney smiled as he looked forward to the prospect of being a vital cog in the wheel that was a village community. He wondered if there was a village cricket team, and if there wasn't might he start one . . .

Then he laughed at himself as he sugared the teas. His imagination was running riot already. There was an awful lot of hard work to be done before he could even begin to contemplate the thwack of leather against willow and chewing on a cucumber sandwich.

Upstairs in Kelly's pink bedroom, Suzanna was steeling herself to throw back the duvet and get up. Having spent half the night freezing to death she was now snug and warm. She'd woken when Barney got up, but lay snuggled under the covers, allowing herself the luxury of falling back into a semi-doze. She'd spent the last fifteen minutes giving herself a pep talk. There was no point, she told herself, uprooting themselves and throwing themselves into this new project if she was going to fall at the first fence. She wasn't going to allow herself any histrionics, any mini breakdowns. They weren't going to have time for it. They were going to need nerves of steel as it was.

Barney came in with a cup of tea, thick and strong, just as she liked it. He sat on the edge of the bed and watched his wife with amusement as she struggled to sit up and look alert. She wasn't a morning person. He never gave her any important information until she'd been up at least an hour, had showered and drunk at least three cups of something containing caffeine. She smiled dopily at him from under her fringe. Her thick brown hair was always like a bird's nest first thing. He brushed it carefully out of her eyes, handed her the tea and urged her to drink up.

'Come on. We've got to be at the brewery at ten, firing on all cylinders.'

'It's only eight, Barns.'

'I know. But the builders are here already. And I want us to go through all the paperwork again before the meeting –'

'I've been thinking.'

She cut him off in mid diatribe, her mind clearly on another agenda. He looked at her, mildly annoyed.

'What?'

'Let's do this for Oliver. A sort of . . . memorial to him.'

Barney was puzzled, not at all sure what she meant,

but she explained. They should make the Honeycote Arms a tribute to Oliver. They were to make it a success in memory of him and the happiness he'd brought them in his short little life. Barney thought it was a wonderful idea. They clanked tea cups to toast their allegiance to it.

Suzanna finished her tea, full of smug satisfaction that she'd been able to dupe herself so easily. Now she'd put such high emotional stakes on the pub's success, she couldn't let it fail, because then she'd be failing Ollie.

Barney too was relieved. It was the first time Suzanna had used Ollie's death as something positive; a reason to move on. And somehow he felt they'd turned a corner.

Damien stalked through the corridor of Hazlehurst Preparatory School, his Oliver Sweeney heels clipping authoritatively on the polished wooden floorboards. He left behind him a trail of aftershave that matched his suit. His aftershave always matched his suits – Gabbana with Gabbana, Armani with Armani. Damien was a perfectionist. It was what had got him where he was today.

By the time he reached the stout red door that led out on to Eldenbury high street, his resolve deserted him. He felt sure he could hear her crying. He hovered, hesitating, not sure what to do, which was very unusual for him. He looked round. Further up the corridor, two mums were chatting, both wearing the local uniform of faded jeans, loafers, Sloppy Joe sweatshirts and pearls. He approached them, coughing nervously.

'Excuse me – could you do me a favour?'

They looked up at him, polite but startled, two clones, same blonde hair, same English rose skin tone. He ploughed on, praying that the stress of the situation wouldn't allow any twang of Bristol to pop unwelcome into his speech.

'I've just left my little girl in the kindergarten. It's her first day. Could you have a look through the window and see if she's all right?'

One of the clones smiled obligingly.

'It's a nightmare, isn't it? Leaving them for the first time. But they're absolute poppets here. I'm sure she'll be fine.' She walked towards the door of Reception. Damien hung back, not wanting to see Anastasia or, worse, for her to see him. 'What does she look like?'

He wanted to shout that she was beautiful, the most beautiful child in the class, probably the world. But that would make him sound like a wanker.

'She's got dark hair. Curly. With a red bow in it.'

The clone peeped through the glass at the top of the door.

'Zebra-skin boots?'

Damien nodded proudly. They'd chosen the boots together, he and Anastasia. The clone smiled reassuringly.

'She's fine. She's at the play-dough table. Just go. There's no point in torturing yourself.'

The other clone chipped in. 'They only scream because they can. The minute your back's turned they're as right as rain.'

God, they were hard, these woman. Didn't they have a maternal bone in their bodies? He was finding it incredibly difficult to leave Anastasia that morning. He'd scoured every nursery and every school in a ten-mile radius to find the right place for her, even though nowhere would ever really be good enough. But Hazlehurst seemed to have most of the ticks in most of the boxes, the staff really seemed to care, the atmosphere was warm and jolly and, best of all, the children were treated like children. The kindergarten teacher was a big, cuddly, happy-go-lucky woman who had done her very best to reassure him that morning. She had obviously seen legions of anxious parents leaving their children for the first time, though it was probably unusual for it to be a father on his own. Nevertheless, now it was time to go, Damien wanted to burst the door down, scoop Anastasia up in his arms and take her off for the day to some magical fairyland where they could both live out their dreams.

But he couldn't. He'd got two lap-dancers to audition, a barmaid to sack and sixteen grand's worth of cash to put in the bank before midday, when he had the vitally important meeting with Marco Dinari which meant never having to do any of those things again. So instead he smiled his thanks and hurried away before he could change his mind. He'd phone in an hour or so and make sure she was still OK. He'd bought an extra phone specially so that the school could contact him if necessary; he spent so much time on his mobile that he didn't want the line to be blocked if there was an emergency.

The two clones looked at each other and dissolved into giggles as soon as he was out of sight.

'My God – they're letting anybody into this place these days.'

'Could you smell it?'

They both waved their hands in front of their noses and grinned conspiratorially.

'New money,' they chorused.

Damien, who was hovering round the corner just to make sure he couldn't hear his daughter crying, clenched his fists with fury. He was gutted. Absolutely gutted. It had taken him at least three-quarters of an hour to decide what to wear that morning, and he'd thought he was the epitome of good taste. Apparently not, according to those fat-arsed, self-satisfied cows he'd been talking to.

'What do you suppose he does?' The one's voice could have been heard in the next county.

'God knows,' replied the other. 'Bound to be something dodgy. Or maybe he's a lottery winner.'

She made it sound one up from mass murder. Damien pushed his way angrily out into the road, praying that Anastasia's classmates weren't as snotty as their mothers. He hurried to his car, where Rick was waiting to drive him to Bristol, and tried to push the unpleasant scenario to the back of his mind. After all, he'd got a lot to get through if he was going to be back in time to pick Anastasia up at three.

Keith arrived earlier than usual at work that morning. Elspeth, the brewery's receptionist-cum-secretary, smiled brightly at him and leaped up straight away to get him a cup of coffee. He was impressed to see that she'd already opened the post and had laid it out in four piles – urgent, non-urgent, file and bin. He liked to see everything, even junk mail, before anyone else dealt with it.

He took a cup of coffee and walked through into the heart of the brewery. He watched as one of the men slashed through the top of a sack of malt. Keith dipped his hand in and took out a grain, nibbling it to test the quality, and nodded his approval. He loved the sweet, Ovaltine taste that would provide the beer with much of its flavour. Up tipped the sack and the grain fell through into the crusher, a steady stream of rich carbohydrate that would soon be ground into a fine powder.

He walked through past gleaming copper-lined vats, big enough to hold ten men, that would have been scrupulously scrubbed out the night before. The rich smell of yeast hung in the air as the latest brew fermented, awaiting the moment of perfection before it would be deemed fit for the barrel. Keith prided himself on the fact that he sampled every brew, because that was the only way he was going to become an expert. He had a lot of catching up to do. A year ago he could probably have counted the pints of real ale he'd had on the fingers of one hand. And Mickey and Patrick had been brought up on the stuff – they could tell in an instant if the balance wasn't right, if the sugar level was too high or too low, if the malt or the hops weren't of the best quality.

He went through into the room that he'd designated as a general meeting room not long after he arrived. It had once been a storage area for the sacks of hops and malt, but those had been moved to one of the out-buildings. The bare brick walls had been whitewashed, and a large table moved in which sat eight at the most. It wasn't exactly equipped with the latest in conference facilities, but there was a coffee machine bubbling merrily in the corner and a flip chart, and Keith had had all the facts and figures that were going to be relevant to the morning's meeting collated and put in individual folders at each place. One day, maybe, there would be a purpose-built room with soft carpets and designer lighting and PowerPoint facilities, but that was a long way off. There were many more important things to spend money on before that eventuality.

Keith tried out the head of the table for size, wondering if he was usurping Mickey's position, then salved his conscience. Someone had to lead from the front and it was never going to be either of the Liddiards, who always seemed to have other preoccupations. It came from having a more exciting life than he did, he supposed. He had to admit that he had nothing much else to think about but work.

Keith wasn't a superstitious man, but he did wonder if there was a patron saint of pubs, and if so whether he should offer up a quick prayer, just for luck. Only he knew just how precariously the brewery's finances were balanced. It didn't actually frighten him – not most of the time, anyway – because he knew a good percentage of successful businesses were equally precarious. There was no such thing as a dead cert, there was no profit without risk and you had to spend money to make money. The trouble was, they were spending it like water at the moment, and it was his.

Keith knew exactly what they had to achieve over the next twelve months and there was nothing out of the ordinary about any of the targets he had set. But there was little margin for error. Very, very occasionally, in his more pessimistic moments – which as a good businessman he had to have: you needed to work out your Armageddon in order to make a contingency plan – he wondered what would happen if Barney Blake turned out to be a drunk, or if Suzanna had a penchant for gambling, or if some hideous bacteria crept into the labyrinth of pipes in the brewery and contaminated the whole system, bringing production to a halt. Or, on a more universal level, what if there was another outbreak of foot and mouth, or another September the eleventh. Any of these eventualities could have a serious effect on their profit margins, and they couldn't afford to just break even. They needed a significant profit in order to continue the brewery's across-the-board investment.

Keith had worked out a five-year plan. There was a perfect equation whereby the brewery's maximum capacity – the amount of barrels they brewed per week – would exactly match the number of pints drunk throughout their ten tied houses, with a bit left over for the small amount of free trade they supplied: the odd working man's and sporting club and a few free houses. At the moment the brewery was running at about two-thirds of its potential output, so they had to kick the pubs into touch in order to increase the barrelage. Between him and Patrick, they had worked out that they could afford the time and the money (all things going to plan) to upgrade one pub every six months for the next five years, thereby achieving, hopefully, a concomitant upsurge in profit and beer consumption. The refurbishments would encompass a fine balance between maintaining each pub's image as a traditional local, while simultaneously increasing its appeal to a wider, more affluent market. It was hardly an original formula, but as country pubs were closing at an alarming rate if they chose to remain complacent and didn't seek means of diversification, it was the only option open that didn't involve massive risk.

The Honeycote Arms was to be the template. It would lead the way and establish some sense of house style, though Keith was determined that each landlord should have their own influence, allowing for a sense of individuality. The last thing he wanted to establish was a chain of identikit pubs, yet at the same time if he could exploit the idea of a brand – or at least the idea that a Honeycote Ales pub upheld certain standards – then so be it.

He had very high hopes of Barney and Suzanna. He knew that though neither of them was a landlord or a restaurateur or had any actual experience of running a pub, between the three of them they had expertise and acumen in other areas. And the Liddiards had generations of the experience they didn't have. Keith was pretty confident they couldn't fail, that the way ahead would provide a good living for himself, the Liddiards and the Blakes. But he knew that the road wasn't necessarily going to be a smooth one and prayed that there was no eventuality he hadn't thought of.

An hour and a half later, Barney and Suzanna walked arm-in-arm down through the village. Honeycote looked like every tourist-board's dream. Spring flowers were peeping shyly though the wide grass verges that were just on the point of becoming unruly, thanks to the alternating April sun and showers. The biting wind of the day before had blown itself out and the sun had emerged rather self-consciously, looking as if it might nip back behind a cloud at the first sign of trouble. The local stone that had looked rather grey and forbidding yesterday had warmed to a mellow ginger. There seemed to be no continuity of style amongst the buildings: some were handsome, steadfast, perfectly proportioned; others were rambling and slightly shambolic, with Gothic arched door and window frames – Georgian symmetry versus gingerbread chaos. It was saved from total twee-ness by the rugged stone, the alarming dip in some of the rooflines, the bowing of some of the ancient windows and the splodges of bright yellow lichen that liberally studded every available surface. Moreover, most of the houses seemed to be owned by people happy to let their gardens run free as nature intended: there were no severely manicured lawns and hedges, no regimented displays of bedding plants, just a soft verdance throughout – an effect which probably took as much maintenance as a formal garden.

No one could have walked through Honeycote for the first time and not be utterly enchanted. Even the inhabitants looked hand-picked for their authenticity. A lady in a green quilted jacket walked an elegant pair of Dalmatians. A rosy-cheeked postman cycled his way up the road with a bulging sack of letters. There was even a milkman delivering milk in bottles – a novelty indeed, as for as long as they could remember, Barney and Suzanna had only ever seen milk in cartons. A fat tortoiseshell cat lay on top of a wall observing them shrewdly from between half-closed eyes, as if waiting to report back to the rest of the village that he'd seen the new incumbents of the pub.

'It's like a film set,' observed Barney, as the ting of the bell over the door of the post office heralded the exit of the local vicar. A white sports car roared past, its driver clearly in a hurry. Suzanna caught a glimpse of a darkly handsome young man at the wheel, and smiled.

'Right down to the drop-dead gorgeous lord of the manor?'

'So where's the femme fatale?' countered Barney.

'Isn't that me?' Suzanna grinned. Barney tapped the heel of his hand against his forehead as if feigning forgetfulness.

'Of course. Stupid me. Stunningly attractive girl from London moves to the village and breaks everyone's heart for miles.'

Suzanna fell against him, laughing, and he felt his heart skip a beat with joy. He'd just caught a glimpse of the old Suzanna, the one that made up stories about people they'd seen on the Tube, the one that wove elaborate fantasies for them and sometimes pretended to act them out. And already she looked different, her eyes sparkling and colour in her cheeks from the fresh country air and the exhilarating walk, as she made up stories for the rest of the inhabitants.

Gradually the hotchpotch of houses and cottages that made up the village became fewer and farther between, and they turned down the little lane that led to Honeycote Ales. Soon the magnificent Victorian tower of the brewery itself became visible, topped by the weathervane that always proclaimed the wind to be blowing from the east, as it had rusted up years ago. And underneath the tower sprawled the rest of the buildings clustered round a cobbled courtyard: the offices, the storerooms, the old stables that used to house the dray and the horses – all utterly unspoilt with no sign of extensions or additions, sympathetic or otherwise.

It was a hive of activity. They could hear the thump of the steam engine that drove the whole brewing process, the barrels being rolled down the long tunnel to the trucks that were waiting to be loaded up, the shouts of men giving each other instructions. Barney breathed in the malty fug that filled the air appreciatively; Suzanna wrinkled her nose slightly, not quite as enamoured, though it was a smell she was going to come to love in time. The whole scene was like stepping back a hundred years. Only a smattering of modern-day vehicles in the car park and a lorry driver chattering into a mobile phone spoiled the illusion; they seemed anachronistic, continuity errors that the director should have spotted.

They passed the white sports car that had roared past them earlier. Its driver had abandoned it as close to the building as he could, blatantly ignoring the carefully painted lines that indicated designated parking spaces.

'Do you think he's going to be an arrogant, ruthless bastard who goes round exercising his droit de seigneur?' Suzanna grinned, continuing the fantasy she'd started.

'No,' said Barney. 'He's probably an ineffectual fop with a weak chin and a speech impediment.'

'God, I hope not,' said Suzanna fervently. Barney looked at her sideways, amused. He'd forgotten how wrapped up she used to get in the stories she wove; how she used to almost believe them. But before she could elaborate on the tale any further, Keith Sherwyn hurried out with an outstretched hand to greet them and led them inside to the reality of the boardroom.

In Mandy's makeshift little office, which had been the object of much resentment amongst some of the other staff, particularly Elspeth, the tiny mobile on her desk chirruped into life, ringing out the tune to 'Viva España'. Mandy sighed. It was her mother's ring-tone. Was she up to a phone call from Sandra? She'd have to answer. She'd ring incessantly every five minutes otherwise.

'Hi, Mum,' she said warily.

Sandra launched into her diatribe without drawing breath. She and Leon, her boyfriend (how could you call a fifty-five-year-old a boyfriend? wondered Mandy), had apparently hit a *gold mine*. A veritable *gold mine*. They were setting up Botox clinics up and down the Costa del Sol, raking it in. They needed more people to help. And Sandra had thought of Mandy straight away. When you hit a gold mine, it was most important to keep it in the family; let your nearest and dearest get the first share of the spoils. Mandy pictured her mother in a white coat, bearing down on her patients with a hypodermic full of neat botulism, and shuddered.

'Sorry, Mum. It's not really my scene.'

'How do you know? You haven't even been out here to see me.' The voice dripped reproach. 'It's a very good life here, Mandy. Constant sunshine, unashamed luxury. Wonderful people.'

Privately, Mandy doubted that.

'And it's about time you found your nitch. You're not going to find it there, stuck in the depths of the dreary old countryside, working for your father.'

Mandy wondered what on earth her nitch was. Was it like a G-spot? Sandra droned on relentlessly.

'You're falling into the same trap that I did. I spent the best years of my life working for my father at the garage.' She pronounced garage to rhyme with marriage. 'Then I met your father. That, of course, was my really big mistake. Nearly twenty years I was virtually a prisoner, a slave to the household, making sure everything was just so. It's a good job I came to my senses. It's only now I've really bloomed. Blossomed. I've found my nitch, Mandy, and I want you to find yours.'

It suddenly dawned on Mandy that what her mother was on about was finding her *niche*. Ironic, really, because if it was anyone's fault she hadn't found her niche, it was Sandra's. From the moment Mandy had decided to live with Keith when her parents had split up, Sandra had been trying to lure her back, regain her sympathy, and had used every trick in the book that she knew. For months, Mandy had dealt with her mother's drunken sobbing, tantrums and empty suicide threats when she realized Keith was going to divorce her, that he'd called her bluff and there was no going back.

Eventually, half a million quid had shut her up. By which time Mandy was drained, had no energy left to decide what she wanted to do now she had finished her A levels, couldn't even think about going off to university. The last year had been such an upheaval, all she wanted was some stability. Keith had told her to take her time, not rush into anything, and had given her a job in the meantime looking after PR at the brewery. Life thereafter had fallen into a pleasant little rhythm: she'd done up the house for her dad, enjoyed Patrick's company and was conscientious about her work. But now everyone else had been sorted, she felt it was time to think about her future and what she wanted to do. It was strange that Sandra, who had for so many years been oblivious to her needs, should have put her finger so firmly on the spot.

Sandra was still babbling on, garrulous, ebullient, effervescent. Mandy didn't know which was worse: Sandra up or Sandra down.

'Why don't you come over for a little holiday? It's glorious. I'm lying here now by the pool on my sun-lounger.'

Mandy could just see Sandra in a tiger-skin sarong, skin slick with sun oil, admiring her airbrushed toes through the biggest Versace sunglasses she'd been able to find at Marbella airport.

Mandy might need to find her niche, but she knew it wasn't in Puerto Banus.

She looked up and saw Patrick standing in the doorway.

'Look, Mum. I'll think about it, OK? I've got to go.'

She hung up and smiled at Patrick, who said 'Listen, Mandy' in a tone that made her realize he was going to say something she didn't want to hear.

He told her, as gently and kindly as he could, that her input wasn't going to be needed at that morning's meeting. Suzanna and Barney had enough on their plate; he didn't want them overwhelmed by having too many people there and there was plenty of time to discuss PR at a later date. And even then, he added, Suzanna and Barney were going to have their own ideas about how to handle the publicity. Of course they'd need her help with the administration – which Mandy knew meant stuffing envelopes. She was effectively being relegated to general dogsbody.

She took the news quietly, without making a fuss, because she knew there wasn't any point. She'd already had a knock-back the week before. She'd desperately wanted to be in charge of decorating the pub. She'd known exactly what she'd like to do with it and had given it a great deal of thought. She'd done her research, reading *Caterer and Hotelkeeper* avidly, looking for trends, what worked and what didn't. She'd even drawn up a design on a large piece of board, and attached samples of paint and curtain fabric and floor tiles. Patrick had listened patiently to her proposal. So had her father. Then they had both as good as patted her on the head and told her renovating a pub was hard work and that she'd hate it. The implication being that she was some sort of princess who, once she'd chosen the wallpaper, wouldn't be interested in the rest of it. Anyway, the Blakes had strong ideas about what they wanted to do, and Patrick and Keith didn't want to tread on their toes.

Mandy wondered to herself who was in charge here. If they'd wanted to tread on the Blakes' toes, they were perfectly entitled to. They were the ones paying the bills. If they'd wanted to put Mandy in charge of the refurb, they could have done. But nobody took her seriously. They treated her like a silly little nineteen-year-old with A levels in Art and Classical Civilization and a rich daddy who'd put her in charge of PR, just to keep her quiet. And they as good as ignored her. She'd been sidelined, marginalized. But there was no point in behaving like a spoilt brat about it.

With this second piece of news, everything became perfectly clear. No matter how good she was at her job, there just wasn't room for her. It wasn't personal, or political, she was pretty sure of that. And it wasn't a judgement on her talent or capability. To put it in a nutshell, she was in the way.

Compounding this problem was her relationship with Patrick. It was pretty simple. Whenever they were away from work, if they went out for a meal or to a film or to a bar, they got on like a house on fire. The chemistry between them still crackled, they made each other laugh, they enjoyed a lot of the same things and had respect for each other's opinions. And the sex was amazing. Patrick had been Mandy's first lover, but she was under no illusion that he had returned the compliment. Often when they were out they'd be accosted by some girl or other who Mandy could tell had been a previous conquest. And you didn't learn the tricks Patrick could pull in bed out of a book.

But get them in the confines of Honeycote Ales and the atmosphere was awkward and strained. Patrick seemed almost intimidated by her presence. Mandy could only conclude that he felt threatened by her, perhaps because it was her father who'd rescued the brewery, but she couldn't imagine what he was actually afraid of. Her being made managing director and sacking him? It was ridiculous that they couldn't find a way of working together side by side. It was clearly an ego thing, decided Mandy. She was glad she was able to rationalize it, but at the same time felt hurt that Patrick didn't feel their relationship was strong enough to be able to rise above it. Surely they were a team? They were all in it together. It wasn't a competition. There wasn't going to be a winner. In fact, if they didn't pull together, they would all end up losing.

Mandy sighed and, opening her file, tried to concentrate on composing a blurb for the new labels that had been designed for their bottled range. They didn't sell many, as they had decided not to go down the supermarket route – there were too many people doing it – but a lot of free houses and restaurants liked to stock a locally bottled ale. As she tried to encapsulate the spirit of Honeycote Ales in less than fifty words, the same thought came to her again and again.

They'd all be better off without her here. She'd have her own identity; Keith couldn't be accused of favouritism; Patrick wouldn't feel compromised. And Elspeth would probably throw a party.

*

In the boardroom, still waiting for everyone to arrive, Suzanna was getting increasingly nervous. She wasn't used to formal meetings. She was used to being her own boss. And the sheaf of pie charts and diagrams and targets on the sheets of paper in front of her were disconcerting. It all seemed horribly grown up and serious. When Keith disappeared off to get coffee cups, she turned to Barney, panic-stricken.

'God, Barney – do you think we've done the right thing? What's a GPM?'

'Gross Profit Margin. And don't take any notice – it's all jargon and bollocks. You don't have to worry your pretty little head about any of it.'

Actually, she did, but Barney thought she'd probably bolt if she knew the reality at this point. He was banking on her picking up most of it as she went along. Suzanna was pretty quick on the uptake, as long as she didn't think she was being forced to take something on board. It was going to be up to him to guide her. And one thing he was sure of: she was the one person that was going to make this whole project work, even if she didn't quite realize it.

'I'm having second thoughts. I'm never going to be able to do this!'

Shit, thought Barney. She really was panicking. But before he could say anything to calm her down, there was a discreet cough in the doorway and they both looked up to see a dark-haired young man in a four-button moleskin suit lounging in the doorway. He smiled at them disarmingly.

'Sorry to interrupt.' He came into the room, holding out his hand first to Suzanna, his manners impeccable.

'Patrick Liddiard. We're going to be working together on this.'

It was the boy who'd whizzed past in the sports car. A bit up himself, thought Barney. Fucking gorgeous, thought Suzanna.

Five minutes later, Barney had to eat his words, as Patrick charmingly put them at their ease and Suzanna visibly relaxed, all her worries seemingly evaporating into thin air.

Ginny woke up that morning and decided she couldn't possibly feel depressed. The first thing she saw through her Velux was a periwinkle blue sky with the odd cloud scudding across. This was, in effect, the first day of her new life. She didn't count yesterday, which had been too fraught and difficult. And today she'd have the luxury of being by herself to gather her thoughts, as soon as she'd got the twins to college. They were studying for their A level retakes, as neither of them had got the grades they'd needed in order to go to the universities they wanted. It was the one thing Ginny had held against David, that the trauma of him leaving had meant a dismal trio of D grades each the summer before. The only up-side was they seemed to enjoy the social life at the college, though Ginny was worried that their life was becoming *too* social and they'd only repeat their performance in the upcoming exams. But both girls protested they were working hard, and their grades seemed to prove that.

She dropped them, moaning and groaning, at the train station in Eldenbury which was only ten minutes from Evesham. They could walk or catch a bus at the other end. They'd spent all of breakfast trying to persuade her that they were too traumatized after the move to go to college, but she'd been firm. She promised if it was raining that evening to come and pick them up.

She got back, had a shower and found something to wear. Her favourite old jeans and the indigo-blue cotton cable-knit sweater that covered her bum, and her trainers. She decided to walk down to the shop to get a paper, then read it over a cup of coffee. Then she'd go about putting some homely touches to the barn. Go to the supermarket and stock up on everything. Somehow she thought that once the fridge was full and there was a bowl of fruit on the side, and perhaps a vase of fresh flowers, the place would feel more lived in. Less transient. They might feel less like tenants.

As she walked down to the heart of Honeycote, she remembered what it was that had drawn her here in the first place. For years she'd wanted to move to the country. She'd been brought up there, after all, at the foot of the Malvern Hills in a small Worcestershire village. But it had been out of the question while she was married. David had needed to be within ten minutes of the surgery in case of emergencies. Of course, now she realized that of all those out-of-hours root-canal treatments and agonizing abscesses, fifty per cent had probably been bogus. He'd been filling Faith, not teeth. So now she was going to have what she wanted, even though the twins had moaned that Honeycote was the back end of nowhere. It would do them good – she didn't really want them hanging out in the pubs of Evesham anyway. There were decent buses and trains, and she'd never complained about dropping them off or picking them up from anywhere. And anyway, they were supposed to be spending every other weekend with David – Cheltenham, with its trendier bars and clubs, and a better selection of shops, should keep them happy.

She'd wanted a break from her immediate past, as she felt that was the only way she was going to be able to forge a new existence for herself. She didn't want to go to the same supermarket where she'd once bought family suppers; she didn't want to pass people in the street who knew her and David as a couple. Honeycote was like another world, yet it was only fifteen minutes in the car from her old life. And with its olde-worlde chocolate-box perfection, she could surely live out any fantasy she liked. She knew, of course, that she was being whimsical; that bad things happened in places like Honeycote just as they did in an inner-city slum. But for the time being, as she walked down the village high street, its total charm gave her a spring in her step.

She passed the Honeycote Arms and saw a posse of builders having their first brew of the day, looking at the pub and eyeing up the task ahead warily. There was a skip waiting in readiness. She wondered what was going on: whether it was going to be demolished or just renovated. She hoped it was the latter – half the fun of moving to a village was to have a local. Ginny wasn't a great drinker, but she was looking forward to being part of a community.

She went into the post office and was greeted with a glorious smell: a fresh delivery of croissants, Danish pastries and doughnuts was being loaded on to the shelves. Ginny had a sweet tooth, and eyed up a pain au chocolat – could she resist? She didn't want it to become a habit, but she thought she deserved it. It had been the weekend from hell after all. And the walk there and back would have given her some exercise – her early-morning branflakes seemed a long way off.

She slid her choice into a paper bag and picked up a copy of the local paper. She could have a look and see what the local job market was like. The prospect gave her butterflies, and she waited rather impatiently in the queue, anxious to get home in order to see what her future might hold. There was a girl in front of her, in cream jodhpurs and a pair of tobacco-brown suede chaps. Ginny felt a stab of envy. Perhaps if her bottom had looked like that, David wouldn't have gone rushing into Faith's thighs.

The girl turned and Ginny saw it was in fact a woman – and that she recognized her. Ginny racked her brains – she prided herself on always being able to remember names – and realized it was Lucy Liddiard. She'd made up a foursome with her for tennis a few times, at a mutual friend's house near Broadway. She gave a hesitant smile, not wanting to make a fool of herself in case Lucy didn't have a clue who she was, but Lucy smiled back. She was unashamedly open about recognizing Ginny but not being able to remember her name.

'I know you from tennis, I'm sure. But I'm so sorry – I'm hopeless with names. Completely useless –'

'Ginny. Ginny Tait.'

'Of course. Lucy Liddiard. I didn't realize you lived round here.'

'I don't. I mean, I didn't. I do now. We moved in yesterday.'

'Really? Where to?'

Ginny could see Lucy racking her brain, wondering which house she could have moved to.

'Tinker's Barn. We're only renting.'

'Oh yes. It's sweet.'

Ginny could see Lucy was a bit puzzled. With the best will in the world, Tinker's Barn wasn't a family home. She went on to explain.

'I've just separated from my husband.'

'Oh. You poor thing. I'm sorry.'

Ginny tilted up her chin defiantly.

'I'm not. He was behaving like a prat.'

She was amazed to hear herself say it. But it was true. She gave a rueful grin, to show that she wasn't really bitter, then was horrified to feel her lip tremble and her eyes fill with tears. It was the first time she'd actually voiced her position out loud, in public, and it hurt like hell. Lucy touched her arm sympathetically.

'Why don't you come and have a coffee? If you're not busy, that is.'

'No. I'm not busy. I've got nothing to do for the rest of my life . . .'

My God, she really did sound resentful and twisted. She'd been kidding herself for the past four months. In a way it had been easy to pretend everything was as normal while they still lived in the Evesham house; when David stopped by regularly on his way home from the practice. But now she'd burnt her bridges, she was on her own and she was responsible for her future happiness. And she wasn't going to turn down an offer of friendship.

Lucy gave her a lift up to her house. Ginny felt a stab of envy as they went up the drive: Honeycote House was an idyll, a sprawling Cotswold family home that belonged in the pages of a magazine. Just walking through the door made her realize what she was missing, as the Liddiards' mad Irish wolfhound leaped up to greet her and Lucy scooped up the post from the doormat. Even her post looked more interesting than Ginny's ever was: there was a postcard from Australia, what looked like an exciting invitation in a thick white envelope, two subscription magazines and nothing that looked like a boring bill.

Lucy settled her in the garden room while she went to make coffee. A glorified conservatory tacked on to the back of the house at the turn of the last century, it had a red quarry tiled floor, shabby Lloyd Loom chairs and a chaise longue covered in faded gold velvet and a profusion of cushions. An ancient bookcase held stacks of magazines, trashy novels and a couple of dozen orange Penguin novels. It smelled slightly damp and earthy. It was a room for relaxing, lounging around reading a book or writing a letter. The doors looked out on to a Cotswold stone terrace with steps down to a sunken lawn. Ginny opened one and breathed in the April air – there was still a stiff breeze that made it too cold to sit outside, but the freshness was invigorating. The wolfhound had flopped at her side and Ginny scratched it under the chin, enjoying her surroundings and wondering what the rest of the day would bring. Lucy came back in with a tray of coffee.

'You've got a friend for life there. Pokey thrives on attention.'

'She's gorgeous. I'd love a dog myself,' said Ginny wistfully, remembering her wish-list of the night before.

'What sort?'

'Anything, really. I just want a companion.'

'My brother-in-law's Labrador bitch has just had a litter. Not pure-breds, I'm afraid. In fact, nobody's too sure what they are. Lola escaped one dark night and produced six black bundles. I know James is desperate to get rid of them. I'll give you his number.'

'That sounds ideal,' said Ginny happily.

Lucy poured coffee out of a French enamel pot. It was fresh and strong and far more reviving than the instant Ginny would have brewed herself at the barn. For a few minutes they talked about nothing of consequence. Lucy told her of her plans to revive the old grass tennis court and about how much she missed her older daughter Sophie, who was spending a year in Australia, before she took the bull by the horns quite unashamedly.

'So – tell me what happened. He's a dentist, isn't he? Your husband.'

Lucy was refreshingly direct and honest, and so Ginny found herself telling her the whole sorry tale. She had a feeling that if she was going to make anything of her life in Honeycote, then Lucy was going to be a good ally, and she might as well give her the gory details before people started filling in the gaps for themselves. It might have been years since Ginny lived in a village, but she had no illusions about what people might think about a woman on her own.

Ginny had wondered ever since the day David had come home and told her he was leaving how she could possibly have been so thick. There hadn't been any signs that she could pick up on – not of dissent or dissatisfaction or any breakdown in communication between them. Of course, she could see the signs logistically when she looked back. But dentistry allowed for any number of absences, not just for work, but for conferences and golf tournaments which all involved overnight stays and which

Ginny had always given a wide berth. So in a way she'd left the field wide open for Faith.

Faith was nearly twenty years younger than him, much closer in age to the twins than himself. Ginny couldn't see how they could possibly have anything to talk about, what they had in common, what their relationship was based upon. David had tried, rather shamefacedly, to explain.

'Faith makes me feel like a new man. She makes me feel as if I could conquer the world. She's made me realize I'm capable of things I never even dreamed of –'

'Such as?'

'Moving the surgery, for example. I never had time to have any vision before. And she's made me realize there're so many things in life I've never done and I should do. Skiing, for example. I've never been skiing.'

Ginny was indignant. 'I'd like to go skiing.'

'But you've never said so. And you've never done anything about it. Faith's a doer. She makes life exciting. I feel as if I'm living life, not just running to stand still.'

Well, thought Ginny. That had told her. That would teach her to be supportive; to be what she considered a good wife and mother, when what she should have been doing was booking two weeks in Courchevel with little or no regard to the state of their bank account.

David had gone on to ask if she wanted to meet Faith and talk about things, and Ginny had looked at him as if he was mad.

'I think you'd like her, Ginny.' He was desperately trying to be open and grown up about it, as if that made it somehow better, which Ginny found rather insulting.

'Please, David. Don't ask for my approval, on top of

everything else. I'm sure she's perfectly charming – in fact, I hope she is. Because if she isn't, it's a waste of a bloody good marriage. And if she's the key to your future happiness, just go.'

So he did. He'd moved out and into Faith's 'apartment', which Ginny had found a rather pretentious name for a couple of hundred square feet divided up by plasterboard in an old mill by the river. She'd been shellshocked and dumbfounded that he'd taken up her challenge; that nearly twenty years of devotion could end in rejection. And it wasn't as if he hated her. But what Faith had to offer was so much better. Ginny had given up her career – quite willingly, admittedly – to run the family home, bring up the twins and give David all the practical support he needed to build up his practice. Now all that counted for nothing. The practice was a success, finally. The twins were practically grown up. And he was off, in his yellow MGF.

You only had to look at Faith to know why. She was young, firm, gorgeous – she'd got him between her nutcracker thighs and fucked the sense out of him. Ginny had toyed with the idea of trying to seduce him back, but the prospect of donning slinky underwear and coming on to him was rather humiliating. If that was what it was all about, it was too late. If all those years of devotion counted for nothing, and it was just down to sex, then she was sunk.

She wondered what Faith wanted out of it. David was quite good-looking, quite fit, quite successful, quite well off – but not *very* any of those things. Chemistry, perhaps, had a lot to answer for. Doing something you shouldn't be doing probably had a bit to do with it as well. Maybe now it was bona fide, and David had had permission to move in with her, things wouldn't seem so exciting.

David wasn't pushing for divorce. So Ginny didn't either – the thought of a divorce filled her with horror and failure. And anyway, what if he changed his mind? She'd have him back, she knew she would, because she had a strong sense of family. And she wasn't one of those people who snipped the crotches out of their husband's best trousers. She was stoical, passive, and wanted to get through the whole scenario with a minimum amount of pain.

Little Polly Positive, that's who she was. And secretly she quite liked the fact that it obviously annoyed David she was being so calm, because it made him look worse. And she bet it annoyed Faith, because she wouldn't be able to understand Ginny's reaction, or rather lack of it. In fact, she rather thought she was in the driving seat at the moment. He'd played all his cards and she'd played none. Only because she didn't have any, but he wasn't to know that.

By the time she'd finished outlining the horrors of the past few months, Ginny felt drained. Unusually, Lucy didn't offer mounds of sympathy or advice. Ginny was used to friends exclaiming what a bastard David was, or how she was mad for letting him walk all over her, or how she should get herself straight to the best divorce lawyer in town. She found it insulting – it was all right for her to brand her husband a swine, but she really didn't want anyone else pointing it out to her as it made her feel worse, not better. And she was perfectly capable of picking up the *Yellow Pages* and finding a lawyer if she needed one.

Lucy was in fact the first person to offer anything Ginny considered remotely constructive. An invitation.

'Come for supper – next Saturday. I've asked the people who are taking over the Honeycote Arms. And my brother- and sister-in-law. And our partner, Keith.'

'I'd love to.'

As Ginny left, insisting that she could walk home, it would do her good, Lucy watched after her thoughtfully. It really was about time Keith came out of his shell. And Ginny was perfect. Kind, gentle, quite pretty in a natural sort of way, not money-grabbing – the complete antithesis of Keith's ex-wife, in fact. She wasn't sure if Ginny was ready for any romantic involvement. She suspected that despite the brave face she was putting on things her wounds were probably still quite raw. But that didn't mean she couldn't enjoy the company of another man. And Keith was a gentleman. Having spent more than a year now with him in close proximity, of that Lucy was quite certain.

As she walked back to what she didn't quite yet consider home, but was hoping she soon would, Ginny had a spring in her step. Her morning with Lucy had restored her faith in human nature and had given her the strength to realize that after all that had happened she was entitled to a bit of fun. She decided she was going to reinvent herself, make a few changes – and not be afraid of them. She had a blank canvas after all. The twins were pretty self-sufficient and she'd got if not money then all the time in the world to do whatever she wanted.

The meeting at the brewery went better than anyone could have expected. Its primary purpose was to make sure that everyone was singing from the same song sheet, and it was clear they were. They all agreed that, while the builders were ripping the place apart, it was probably best if they stayed out of the pub. In the meantime, Keith and Barney would be based at the brewery setting up the nuts and bolts of the operation, while Patrick and Suzanna, as the creative team, were to go out and source furniture, fixtures and fittings, as well as suppliers for the restaurant.

The longest debate they had had was finalizing the philosophy behind the food. Suzanna stood up to speak, and Barney felt proud as she voiced her feelings, knowing that this sort of thing was anathema to her.

She was adamant that quality and consistency came before novelty, and felt the formula was quite simple: rustic English fare, simply prepared, with the flavours speaking largely for themselves, with as much produce sourced locally as possible and preferably organic. As a premise it was not startlingly original, as more and more restaurants were taking up these very principles. But it seemed a logical brief to follow in what was, after all, a typical English country pub, and was in keeping with the legacy of Honeycote Ales as well. Pacific Rim, Thai fusion and Caliterranean wouldn't really sit that easily with most of their target customers – though Suzanna wasn't averse to the odd influence creeping into a dish here and there if she felt it appropriate.

She spoke passionately, her eyes shining as she described a sample menu: a rough game terrine served with onion chutney followed by a simple, pink rack of lamb or a fresh pea risotto paired with corn-fed chicken and wild mushrooms. The emphasis, if anything, was to be on vegetables. She felt that too many places knocked themselves out devising enticing main courses, only to offer garlic-infused mash and green beans as an accompaniment. Suzanna wanted to exploit the fact that they were perched on the borders of the Vale of Evesham, with its cornucopia of fresh fruit and vegetables. Every meal should automatically be served with at least five different side dishes that were included in the price: dishes whose colours and flavours would be bold, robust and daring, yet at the same time subtle. Sweet potato purée clashing with ruby-red chard. Bright orange Vichy carrots and deep emerald spring greens. Purple sprouting broccoli and chunks of yellow pumpkin. And fruit inspired puddings: cider apple crumble, cherry crème brûlée, pear and almond tart. And a local cheeseboard.

By now, everyone's mouth was watering, and so it was agreed: Modern English Rustic, if they were pressed to describe it in three words. But otherwise, Suzanna insisted on the freedom to serve whatever she felt was appropriate given whatever local produce was seasonal and available. A market-driven menu that was chalked up daily. Nothing pre-prepared, nothing frozen, nothing out of season imported from foreign climes.

Keith closed the session with warm thanks.

'I feel as if I should take everyone out for lunch,' he said, 'but unfortunately there isn't anywhere decent to eat round here.' He beamed. 'Yet.'

Patrick came out of the meeting feeling as if a great weight had fallen off his shoulders. He'd been nervous about meeting the Blakes. It had been Keith and Mickey who had interviewed them, and although they had each individually reassured Patrick that the couple were spot on,

Patrick had had his doubts. People from London could be so snotty, so patronizing, and were perfectly capable of going off on a tangent with ideas that might work in Notting Hill or Soho but just didn't cut the mustard in the depths of the Cotswold countryside. It was a fine balance, introducing sophistication whilst retaining the rough edges that provided a certain charm. He'd hoped he wasn't going to have a battle on his hands. Now, he felt reassured. Suzanna was an absolute honey and Barney seemed like a good bloke. He should have trusted Mickey and Keith's judgement.

He decided to find Mandy and see if she was all right. She'd been very quiet at their meeting this morning and Patrick wanted to reassure her. And apologize if he'd been a bit curt. Nerves always made him brusque. He knew he'd been a bit on edge over the past couple of weeks, since Keith had told him what was on the cards. But now he was feeling more confident. He wanted to make it up to her.

She wasn't in her office. Elspeth looked at him with wide innocent eyes and said, in her little girl's voice that didn't fool Patrick one bit:

'I don't know where she's gone. She was here earlier.'

Elspeth knew perfectly well Mandy had gone to take the artwork for the bottle labels to the printers, but she relished any chance to dump her in it. If anyone should have been in charge of PR, it should have been her. She'd been at Honeycote Ales for five years, not five bloody minutes.

Damien was elated as Rick drove him back up the motorway that afternoon. The signing of the contracts with

134

Marco Dinari had been at twelve and, to his surprise, Marco hadn't tried to reduce the price at the last minute. He knew there was probably a reason for this, that Marco knew something that he didn't, or perhaps he was trying to legitimize wads of dirty cash and this was the quickest way to launder it. But he didn't care. He was finally shot of his grubby little empire. And it felt good: as if he'd undergone some financial colonic irrigation. He was cleansed. Legit.

The car slid into Eldenbury at about half past two. Another half an hour before Anastasia's first day at school would be finished. Rick parked up on the side of the road and Damien decided to kill the time by exploring the little town. He hadn't really had a chance to get to know his neighbourhood yet.

He came to rest outside an imposing square building with a dark green sign proclaiming JAMES LIDDIARD ANTIQUES. In the window was something that quite took his breath away. A rocking horse. A stunningly beautiful dapple-grey rocking horse with a real horse-hair mane and tail, flared nostrils and a red leather saddle and bridle.

He pressed down the brass latch with his thumb and pushed open the door. There was a discreet buzz as he entered the hallowed surroundings. This was a proper antique shop; not a shop full of people's unwanted junk. There was silence apart from the reassuring tick of an exquisite grandmother clock, cavorting shepherdesses depicted on its face. Damien gave a muffled cough, in case the buzz hadn't alerted the shop's owner to his presence, then went over to examine the horse. It was a triumph of craftsmanship, intricately detailed. Damien imagined it would only take the tiniest grain of magic dust to bring it to life, then laughed at himself for being fanciful. He was soon brought back to reality. Attached to the horse's bridle was a price tag, boldly demanding the sum of four thousand pounds in thick-nibbed black ink.

'Beautiful, isn't she?'

He turned to find a man, presumably the owner, standing behind him. Damien reckoned he was about ten years older than he was, immaculately dressed in a window-pane check suit and silk tie. The man held out his hand.

'James Liddiard. Please feel free to browse. I'm here if you've got any questions.'

Damien shook James's hand. It was obvious that this was the sort of bloke people in Honeycote looked up to. He screamed good taste and understatement. Well, thought Damien. He couldn't go wrong if he furnished the rest of his house in here. You could mix modern with antiques. He knew that, because he read *World of Interiors* at his hairdressers.

Damien carried on looking. He chose a beautiful writing desk with lots of little drawers. A painting of Venice, shining with golds and blues. And a round oak table, which would look fantastic in his hallway with nothing but a simple vase of lilies, just like the ones James had on his desk.

He wandered back over to the desk, where James was leafing through a Christie's catalogue. On the wall behind him was a colour photocopy of what looked to Damien like a basket full of Anastasia's Beanie Babies – ridiculously furry, fat-pawed little creatures. The sign indicated they were free to good homes.

'What are they?' he enquired politely.

'Bitsers,' answered James, and when Damien frowned, not recognizing the breed, he laughingly explained. 'Bits o' this, bits o' that. My Labrador bitch got out one night.'

Damien thought about it. A dog might be fun. Anastasia would certainly love a puppy. And more to the point, Nicole hated dogs with a passion. Was terrified of them, in fact, after an unfortunate childhood incident with a neighbour's Doberman. If anything was going to keep her away, it was a dog. More than locks and bolts and intruder alarms or remote-controlled gates.

Then he thought no. Dogs needed care and attention. He didn't know what the immediate future was going to bring. He didn't want to have to worry about getting back in time before the dog had crapped everywhere. The rocking horse was a much better option. It wouldn't need any attention at all.

'No, thank you,' he said decisively. 'But I would like the rocking horse. And there's a few other things.'

James tried not to blink in amazement as Damien coolly pointed out the desk, the painting and the table, then took out his chequebook, wrote the full sum in the box and asked, politely, if it was possible to have it all delivered at the weekend, once the cheque had cleared.

'Are you local?'

'I've just moved into Honeycote Grange.'

James gave a knowing nod. 'No problem.'

Damien noted that James didn't flicker, gave no indication that Damien's address meant that he had more money than sense or taste, just promised to have it all delivered to him on Saturday morning.

In fact, James was rather nonplussed at not having to negotiate. He'd have put any money on this fashion victim in the Dolce and Gabbana (he only knew because the label was stitched to the outside of his sleeve) trying to knock him down. Never mind. That was certainly the easiest twenty grand he'd made in a long time.

James had taken the decision not to follow his brother into the family business before he'd even left school. He never wanted to be in a position to have to undermine or overrule the somewhat wayward Mickey. It would only end in tears. He'd gone into antiques instead and done astonishingly well. Proper antiques, not the junk that masqueraded as such these days. He mostly dealt with a list of regular, private clients, many from abroad. The shop was really just a glorified showroom, serviced by an insatiable supply of tourists who usually only bought glass or china.

It was rare that a walk-in dropped such a huge amount of money like that. James was delighted. He'd never before had to worry about money, only having to please himself. Not that he worried now, as such, but he'd recently married and had a new baby. And his wife, Caroline, a one-time career girl, showed no signs of wanting to go back to work. So he bent over backwards to be charming to Damien. Nothing was too much trouble. Christ, thought James, I'll carry the rocking horse up there on my own back if I have to.

Now that, thought Damien as he left the shop, was a true gentleman. James Liddiard hadn't looked down his nose and thought he was any better than him. He'd treated him like an equal. He looked at his watch and realized there was only five minutes before Anastasia finished. He slipped into the bakery, bought a gingerbread man and went to wait amongst the cluster of mothers outside the red door of Hazlehurst, hoping against hope that Anastasia hadn't been marginalized by her classmates like their parents had marginalized him.

He needn't have worried. As Rick drove them back home, Damien listened with a smile on his face as Anastasia excitedly recounted her day to him. She told him about finger-painting and learning to count to three in French and a story about a mouse that was a ballerina and a girl called Phoebe who was sick at lunch and yucky macaroni cheese and yummy jam sponge and managing her first forward roll in the gym. Any fears he might have had about Hazlehurst being the right choice were soon dispelled. She'd had a wonderful day, and finished off by asking if her friend Emily could come for tea. Damien agreed that Emily could come that very weekend if her mummy said yes, and had a warm feeling in his heart as he thought about Anastasia and Emily clambering over the rocking horse.

Later, Rick came in from hosing down the Merc. Damien offered him a Bud Ice, which he gratefully accepted, and the two of them sat on the decking outside the French windows while Anastasia collapsed on to her beanbag in front of the telly, chewing on her gingerbread man.

Damien had decided he was going to have to take Rick into his confidence. He had nothing to lose by confiding in him, and he could control how much information he gave him. And the lad had just the right amount of discretion, just the right quota of initiative, to make him useful, but not a threat. Kelly had hinted that he was a bit of a drifter, but that was down to his age and the fact that he was devastatingly attractive to women. After all, why spend your best years slogging your guts out when you could waft around picking up casual jobs and equally casual fucks? It had never been an option for Damien, as he wasn't blessed with the same raw ingredients as Rick, but he could see how tempting it would be to rest on one's aesthetic laurels.

Damien was slightly concerned that he felt the need for a confidante. To him it indicated a sign of weakness. But he was on unfamiliar territory. He'd been cock of the roost on his previous patch, he'd known the rules and the key players. Now he was in uncharted waters, and he needed someone to guide him. He also felt certain Rick could be instrumental in the next phase of his master plan.

For Damien, buoyed up by the success of the day's deal, had a dream. He wanted to open a hotel, a countryside playground, but not one of those genteel and gentle sprawling country hotels that the Cotswolds was already so good at. He wanted to create something funkier and more stylish, where relaxation and stimulation went hand in hand, where one could indulge one's fantasies and get a quick fix. Somewhere that combined buzz with bliss. Not somewhere traditional, staid and stuffy, where one did battle with obsequious staff and silver service, but somewhere that encompassed chic, clubby élan with decadent luxury. Somewhere that successful young entrepreneurs like himself could recharge their batteries; somewhere celebrities could escape to safe in the knowledge they could relax and be pampered away from the cameras;

a hotel that was on the 'must visit' list of everyone who was anyone.

He'd quickly come to the conclusion that the area around Honeycote was a perfect location. It was only an hour and a half away from London, yet surrounded by exquisite countryside that would yield great opportunities for sport: golf, hunting, shooting, even polo. Inside the hotel would be a spa, a library, a cinema, a casino, a nightclub. Maybe even one day a recording studio and edit suites.

It was to be an amalgamation of different influences. The Hotel du Vin in Bristol had the right feel, a stunningly eclectic mix of old and new. Babington House in Somerset had the right philosophy and client base, being beloved by the arts and media crowd. Damien wanted to take all of these ingredients, put them in a pot and create something even more ambitious. There was only one thing holding him back. Money. He might be a success, but this was without doubt a multi million-pound venture. And he didn't want a partner. Damien hated compromise and was unflinchingly focussed and single-minded.

The only partner he would ever have considered was Nicole. If things had gone smoothly, they could have had a great partnership. When things had gone well between them, they'd understood each other perfectly. They had the same tastes, same drives, same appreciation for the beautiful things in life. He imagined for a moment a picture of them in the press release, smiling at the bottom of a sweeping staircase, welcoming a posse of A- and B-list faces to the dream they had created between them. It would have been so gratifying; a million miles away from the back streets of Bristol they had been dragged up in. They would be living proof that you could do whatever you wanted in this life, as long as you had the drive and the determination.

Annoyed with himself, Damien shook himself out of his reverie. He was never going to get anywhere if he kept dwelling on the past. Nicole was beyond redemption; she'd pushed the self-destruct button. There was no point in looking back. He had to look forward. And he could do it on his own. He knew he could. He'd doubled his turnover every year for the past five years. And now, thanks to Marco Dinari, he had money burning a hole in his pocket. What he needed, if he wasn't going to pay hideous amounts of capital gains tax, was a stepping stone. All he needed to do was to make that money work for him. And to that end he had an idea.

He was going to drive the revamped Honeycote Arms into the ground. Make a hostile takeover bid. Fatten it up a little bit and add it to his portfolio, which he would then use to attract investors safe in the knowledge that it was underpinned and that he had collateral to keep the bank happy.

Of course, there were hundreds of other places he could have chosen to fatten up. Cheltenham was full of propositions. But after just a short time in Honeycote, Damien was burning to do something that would make all those snotty locals sit up and take notice. Everyone loved a restaurateur, regardless of their background. Everyone wanted to walk into their local and be acknowledged by the owner. It would give him no end of pleasure to watch all those people who had sneered at him over the past few days grovel for recognition, for a table, for a kind word from their host . . .

Although, Damien thought, he didn't actually want to lord it over them. He'd be no better than they were if he did. He just wanted to belong, to feel wanted, to feel respected. He wouldn't treat them in the same way he'd been treated. He wanted to create a hub of warmth; a focal point for the village first and foremost, but also a 'destination' pub, somewhere that was spoken of in hallowed tones. Somewhere that got write-ups in the Sunday papers and was booked up for months . . . He wanted to apologize charmingly to Coral from the post office when she came in to find the place fully booked, then magic her a table from nowhere and enjoy her grovelling to him for evermore.

But first, he needed to know more about Honeycote Ales. With no local knowledge, he wasn't sure where to start asking questions, and besides, he didn't want to arouse anyone's suspicions. Rick, with his background and contacts, was the perfect spy, and Damien knew for sure he had no loyalty to the Liddiards.

He outlined his proposition casually, as if it was a mere fancy. Which at this stage, it was.

'Can you find out the state of play for me? How things are fixed financially? Who's in the driving seat? Who holds the purse strings?' He paused. 'I'm just curious, really. Quite fancy myself as the landlord of the local.'

He grinned disarmingly, knowing he wasn't fooling Rick for a moment.

Rick surveyed Damien thoughtfully. He'd seen the sort of joints he was running; seen the people he was dealing with. Damien might look like a ponce in designer clothing, but he was tough. He was big league. And while Rick fancied himself as a bit of a ducker and diver, he was small-time in comparison. He had the odd mate who dealt in dope and Es; knew people who could get you a dodgy MOT or some knocked-off Quiksilver gear. But Damien was potential cement overcoat territory. Did he want to get involved?

Then he remembered his parents' devastation when they thought they were being faced with eviction. How his mother had had to go to the doctor for sleeping tablets because she hadn't had a wink since the day Mickey Liddiard had dropped his bombshell. How he'd had to carry his dad upstairs after he'd pumped dry the huge bottle of Bells that hung at the end of the bar. How Kelly's face had crumpled when she hadn't realized he was looking, when she'd seen Mandy Sherwyn in the front of Patrick Liddiard's car – the place that had once been hers. And surely this would be the perfect revenge on Patrick? If he could be instrumental in engineering his downfall . . . The trouble was, Rick wasn't quite sure how he was going to go about getting the information Damien wanted.

Suddenly the memory of Mandy at his parents' leaving party came back to him. How she'd shivered involuntarily under his touch. Surely she was the key? My God – it was perfect! He could use her to get the information he needed, then Patrick would lose the Honeycote Arms *and* be made to look a fool in front of his family and his prospective father-in-law into the bargain. Talk about an eye for an eye!

Rick turned to Damien with a smile.

'Sure – I can find that out for you. No problem.'

Damien told him that he didn't care what it cost him; that if he had to spend any money in the process, just to keep his receipts and he would be reimbursed.

8

From her office window the next morning, Mandy watched Suzanna Blake slide into the front seat of Patrick's car. She didn't look too much of a threat. Skinny, yeah, but not glamorous – she was wearing khaki carpenter cords, a denim jacket and a baseball cap. With her she had a battered old leather satchel that presumably contained her plans for the pub. As Patrick got in beside her and put the key in the ignition, she began talking animatedly, using her hands to describe something. Patrick listened intently, with a smile on his face, nodding in what looked like agreement.

Mandy swallowed hard to get rid of the lump in her throat. Whenever he was with her these days there always seemed to be a crease between his brows. He never seemed to laugh. He was laughing now, at something Suzanna had said. He threw the car into reverse, backed up and roared out of the car park.

Mandy burst into tears.

She turned away from the window, hurt, frustration and humiliation welling up inside her. She must be premenstrual. It wasn't like her to feel so defeatist. But she wanted it to be *her* in the car with Patrick, not some husky-voiced creature from London who she'd already heard the lads in the brewery describe as a 'fit bit'. Not that she was threatened by Suzanna. She was old, for a start. Well over thirty. And she didn't think Patrick was the type to go for an older woman. But she wanted to be making plans with him, throwing ideas around, stopping off for lunch and inspiration at some out-of-the-way little country pub.

There was someone coming up the corridor. Mandy quickly ran a finger under each eye, praying her tears hadn't smudged her mascara, and turned to see Elspeth, with her smug little smirk, holding out a letter Mandy had given her to be posted.

'There's a couple of spelling mistakes. I wondered if you'd noticed? And if you wanted them changed?'

Mandy gritted her teeth and smiled.

'Thanks. If you don't mind.'

Maybe she *was* useless. Maybe they would be better off without her and her silly little ideas. Maybe all they needed was Elspeth the Human Spellchecker. She should have gone with Sophie to Australia after all.

She'd had an e-mail from Sophie and Ned this morning. They'd gone out to Australia just after Christmas, and had pleaded with Mandy and Patrick to go with them. Of course, it was out of the question for Patrick to go – there were too many changes afoot at the brewery. But Mandy could have . . . her dad had told her it would do her good. But she didn't want to be a gooseberry. She looked at the photo they'd e-mailed, the two of them standing laughing on a beach, nut brown and hair bleached from the sun and the salt of the sea.

Mandy slammed down the lid of her laptop and picked up her bag. She didn't know where she was going, but she needed some time to think. No one would notice. Her father was waxing lyrical somewhere in the bowels of the brewery, showing Barney Blake the wonders of beermaking. And Patrick certainly wouldn't be worried where she was. He hadn't even bothered to come and say hello to her that morning. For a moment she thought about taking her mother up on her offer then shuddered. Things weren't that bad, but she needed some space to get her life into perspective; try and put a finger on where it had all gone wrong and maybe find a way to get things back on track.

She whisked past Elspeth.

'If anyone wants me, I'm on my mobile.'

She knew that would annoy her. Elspeth liked to know everything that was going on.

Suzanna felt bubbles of excitement rising up in her throat. She couldn't believe what was happening: that she was being whizzed along a country lane in an open-topped sports car on a beautiful spring morning, and that it could actually be classified as work. Today Patrick was taking Suzanna 'off-piste' in order to start tracking down suitable suppliers. First stop was a nearby dairy farmer who was diversifying into local cheeses, and who'd had the initiative to contact Patrick with an invitation to come and taste.

They came out on a long, narrow road that stretched as far as the eye could see, flanked on both sides by enormous fields topped at the very edges by ancient trees. Patrick grinned, dropped the car down a gear and put his foot down. Suzanna screamed with excitement. She felt sure they were going to take off any moment. They could go so fast because the road ahead was totally clear – the only remote danger was if a foolhardy rabbit rushed out. Eventually they slowed and came to a crossroads. Patrick looked sideways, a trifle sheepish.

'Sorry. I always have to do that.'

'That was amazing. It's a wonderful car.'

'It was my grandfather's. Dad's not really into cars, so he gave it to me for my eighteenth.'

Suzanna hid a little smile. Patrick said it so casually, as if people were always given vintage motorcars for their milestone birthdays. But somehow, he managed to get away with it. Suzanna had had a basinful of young men born with silver spoons in their mouths when she'd lived in Oxford, and had never found them an attractive proposition. But Patrick seemed different. She was sure he could be an arrogant and patronizing little sod if he felt like it, but at the moment he seemed charm personified. Even Barney, who was usually very wary of public-school types, seemed to think he was a good bloke. She was glad they were to be a team. She knew she sometimes needed the voice of reason when she got carried away, and she couldn't always take it from Barney. Patrick could provide her with an objective opinion if she became over-enthusiastic. Suzanna knew her weak spots were her passion and her complete inability to budget. It was only Barney's tight control over her pricing policies, and the fact that he rigorously checked every quote before she sent it out, that she'd managed to make a profit from Decadent Dining.

As wide and flat and uncluttered as the scenery had been, now it became twisty and windy and hilly and dotted with exquisite cottages and manor houses and farm buildings. Again, Suzanna felt filled with disbelief that anyone actually lived here, and exclaimed how lucky they were. She was surprised that Patrick disagreed.

'The grass is always greener. I'm sure if you asked half

the people round here, they'd give their eye-teeth to live in London.'

Suzanna wrinkled her nose.

'I don't miss it. Not a bit.'

'So why *did* you decide to move to the darkest depths of the countryside? Really?'

Suzanna looked at him, startled by the line of fire. He carried on smoothly.

'I know the official party line. The bollocks you gave on your application form. Lifelong ambition to run a pub blah blah blah.'

Suzanna swallowed. She hated lying. But she supposed it was only by omission.

'It was for Barney, really. He hated working for his father. I suppose it was a question of now or never. He didn't want to die an accountant.'

'Understandable.' Patrick nodded. 'And you were happy to drop everything and go with him?'

'Isn't that what marriage is all about?' said Suzanna lightly.

'It's a pretty drastic move.'

'It's a challenge. Anyway, I've done every canapé in the book six times over. A hundred and one ways with flaky pastry. I was getting stale.'

They'd pulled into the farmyard by now, and Patrick turned to look at her. Suzanna didn't meet his gaze. He had interrogator's eyes, clear blue and perspicacious and piercing, eyes that would make you confess to things you'd never even thought of. Instead she jumped out of the car, eager to christen her wellies before Patrick could dig any deeper.

*

Mandy was batting along the back lane that would eventually come out on the road home. She felt better already now she was free of the claustrophobic confines of her office. She fished about on the passenger seat for a CD. Destiny's Child – 'Survivor'. It was her current battle hymn.

She only looked down for a second, to press the right track number. When she looked back again at the road ahead, she saw a car had come to a halt in front of her. She slammed on the brakes, gripped the steering wheel and prayed.

It was funny. Bashing into a car didn't sound like it did on the movies. It was a flat thump, with no melodramatic crashing noises that went on for several seconds after impact.

Mandy slumped over her steering wheel and wept. She'd only had the car five months. It was a second-hand VW Beetle, the new kind, silver, and she'd borrowed the money off her father. She was paying him back two hundred pounds a month out of her salary. It was her pride and joy; her personal space. And now, not only had she ruined that, but God knows what damage she'd done to the car in front. Someone was getting out of the driver's seat. She braced herself for a confrontation, winding down the window, and looked into a pair of smiling grey eyes.

'I'm so sorry – I didn't see you,' she stammered.

The bloke shrugged. He was only young, dressed in a black suit with a white T-shirt underneath.

'It's only a car. Are you hurt?'

Mandy, who'd been prepared for a haranguing, was surprised he was bothered about her and not what she now saw was a Mercedes. Shit. Why couldn't she have gone into the back of a Nissan Micra?

'I'm fine.'

'Why don't you reverse it up so we can look at the damage?'

Mandy's hands were shaking so much she couldn't start the ignition, so she let the bloke do it. She stood helplessly by, clutching her handbag, feeling like a total girl.

The front of her car was crumpled. The Mercedes was untouched. Mandy burst into tears for the third time that day.

'My dad's going to kill me.'

'It's not as bad as it looks.' He ran an expert hand over the front. 'You could get that bashed out, no problem.'

'Do you think so?'

'I've got a mate who could probably sort it out for you. He works at a garage in Evesham. It'd probably cost you fifty quid.' He grinned. 'It saves the bother of filling out insurance forms. And you won't lose your no-claims.'

Mandy looked at him, frowning. His face seemed familiar. That slightly-too-long hair that touched his collar and should have looked effeminate, but only made him look more masculine. That mouth.

'I'm sure I know you from somewhere . . .'

'My parents used to run the Honeycote Arms.'

'Oh yes.' She smiled. 'How are they?'

Like you give a fuck, thought Rick. 'Very well. Glad to be out of it, really. They've settled into the B&B; Dad's got his fishing rod out . . .'

Mandy wasn't really listening. She was looking at her car, worried.

'Will you phone your friend?'

'Sure. In fact, why don't you get in your car and follow me? He should be able to do it on the spot. No one will ever know.'

Mandy followed the Mercedes carefully into Evesham, making sure that she kept well back from his bumper so as not to repeat her earlier performance. They eventually pulled into an industrial estate, finally drawing to a halt outside an enormous car workshop. There was noise and smells everywhere: oil, exhaust fumes, Virgin radio, bashing and hammering, fag smoke, engines being thraped, jokes and insults being exchanged. Men in blue boiler suits ran hither and thither. Mandy hung back, shy and embarrassed, while Rick sought out his mate and showed him the damage.

There was much umming and aahing and sucking in of teeth and shaking of heads before they finally shook hands and Rick came over to Mandy.

'He's got a couple of other urgent jobs on, but he owes me a favour. He says give him two hours.'

Mandy looked at her watch. Two hours in Evesham didn't fill her with inspiration. It wasn't exactly a shopper's paradise.

'Why don't we go and have a drink on the river?'

She hesitated for a moment. It was very kind of him, after all he'd done, but she wasn't sure she was in the mood for company. It had been the worst kind of morning. But what was the alternative? Browsing in Poundstretcher?

'Haven't you got to be at work?'

'Nah. I'm not on duty till three this afternoon. I was on my way to the gym.'

'If you're sure . . .' Mandy was obviously anxious not to lead him astray.

'Course I am. Come on.'

Rick led her to the Mercedes and opened the passenger door for her. He could barely keep the grin off his face as he walked round to the driver's side. Like a lamb to the bloody slaughter.

It was a pretty grotty pub, but the garden went down to the river and they found a table without too much bird pooh on the seat. Rick brought out glasses of cloudy local cider and ham sandwiches and salt and vinegar crisps. They sat in the sunshine and watched two swans glide silently past. It was strangely idyllic. The combination of the scrumpy and the warmth and the peculiar novelty of the situation made Mandy feel quite light-headed. Rick took off his jacket and her eyes were drawn to a Celtic circle tattooed around his bicep, just visible under his T-shirt sleeve.

'Did it hurt?'

He shook his head. 'About —' he picked up her arm and pinched, gently — 'that much.'

She giggled. 'You're lying.'

'Honestly. Well, maybe just a bit, but it's over pretty quickly. You should get one.'

She put out a finger to touch it, to see if it had made any indent on his skin, but it was smooth. Incredibly smooth, and soft, like golden velvet, the muscles underneath rock hard. Mandy swallowed. Rick picked up their glasses and got up.

'Another drink?'

'I shouldn't . . .'

'We've got at least another hour. Kipper said he'd phone me on my mobile when he was finished.'

'OK then.'

What Mandy didn't realize was the potency of the brew they were drinking. It was known locally as a guaranteed entry into any girl's knickers. But Rick didn't want to get into her knickers. Not yet, anyway. He wanted to get into her mind. Another glass and her tongue would be loose; she'd be totally suggestible.

By the time another glass had slipped down, Mandy found herself confiding in Rick. It was nice to have someone to talk to about her frustration. She explained how hurt she was at being left out of relaunching the Honeycote Arms. It didn't occur to her that she was being indiscreet. She was too absorbed in her own resentment.

'It's really important to Honeycote Ales. Dad's pouring everything he's got into it. But they obviously don't trust me. Though I don't know why they think the Blakes are going to have all the answers. They've never run a pub before. And it's not that easy, is it, running a pub? I mean, you should know that.'

Rick nodded in agreement.

'You've got to be pretty tough. You've got to learn not to take any crap from anyone.'

'Anyway, I don't know why I'm worried. It's obviously nothing to do with me, is it?' She swallowed the last drop of cider in her glass. Rick leaned forward.

'You know what I think? I think you need to get away from it all.'

Mandy stared at him.

'What do you mean?'

'It's all a bit incestuous, isn't it? Your life? Claustropho-bic. I mean, you live with your dad. You work for your dad. Your boyfriend works for your dad. You never move out of Honeycote.'

'We live in Kiplington.'

'You know what I mean. When's the last time you went to a gig? Or out with your mates? Your own mates, I mean.'

Mandy didn't like to say that she didn't have any of her own mates. There were girls she used to go to school with, but apart from the odd postcard she hadn't really kept in touch. Now Ned and Sophie were gone, the only people she socialized with these days were in Patrick's social circle.

'I don't know,' she said lamely.

'When's the last time you went out without your boyfriend or your dad? You need to get out – get some head space.' He realized he sounded a bit hippy dippy, and rolled his eyes self-mockingly. 'Find yourself, man. There's loads going on out there and you're not going to fall over it living in a bloody one-horse village. I should know. I lived there long enough.' He leaned forward again. 'OK, maybe you have nice clothes and champagne for tea every night and drive round in posh cars. But you're not happy, are you?' He pointed at her to empha-size what he was saying. 'Because you're missing out on the simple pleasures.'

Many couldn't help feeling a bit defensive.

'Like what? What am I missing out on?'

'Well . . .' Rick thought about it. 'You ever been surfing?'

Mandy shook her head.

'I'm going down to North Devon with some mates in a couple of weeks. You should come. It would get you away. Give you a chance to think. And surfing's wild. You'd probably be good . . .'

He looked her up and down appraisingly, then grinned.

'You'd have the best teacher.'

Mandy swallowed, flustered, not sure if he was teasing or meant it. The next moment he was serious again.

'I'd better get us some coffee if we're going to be driving. That cider's stronger than it looks.'

Afterwards, they went back to the garage to fetch her car. Mandy felt a bit self-conscious. A gaggle of boiler-suited mechanics were sitting round drinking tea and they teased her gently about her prang. Typical woman driver, they'd said, and Rick had gallantly come to her rescue and told them it was his fault. Even though, strangely, she hadn't minded their jibes.

She thanked him, and tried to give him some money, but he wouldn't hear of it.

'Like I said, Kipper owes me.'

'I've got to give you something for it.'

He looked at her with a smile on his face.

'OK. Here's the deal. You come out for a drink. With me and my mates. That's your payment.'

He picked up her mobile and programmed his number in, then held it out to show her.

'There – I've put it in as Car Repairs. So no one will get suspicious.' He smiled. 'I'll text you. There's a load of us going to the pub on Saturday. It'll be a laugh.'

Afterwards, Mandy wondered if she should have been quite so frank with him. But he'd been such a good listener, so sympathetic, and had seemed to understand her dilemmas. And anyway, it didn't really matter what she told him. His parents didn't work for the brewery any more. He probably wasn't remotely interested in anything she'd got to say.

She also realized with a stab of guilt that she hadn't asked him anything about himself. Why he was driving around in a big, swanky Merc, for a start. He must think she was a self-centred little madam. And maybe she was. But it had been so nice to have someone who had time for her, unlike Patrick, who only seemed to be interested in himself these days.

And what Rick had said was right. On the surface, she'd got everything. But what did it all mean? She was trapped. Trapped in a gilded cage.

At Honeycote Grove, Damien reimbursed Mandy's garage bill without a murmur and lapped up everything Rick had to tell him.

'It's all pretty tight. They've spent a fortune on the brewery since her dad took over, and they haven't been doing much business. Sherwyn holds the purse strings. The Liddiards have got no cash to their name. I know that for a fact.'

'So this relaunch is vital?'

'If it fails, they're completely fucked.'

'It doesn't take much to screw up a new restaurant. Quickest way of losing money, if you don't get it exactly right.' Damien's voice was one of experience. He'd seen more start-ups in Bristol vanish within six months than he could remember. And he had observed them all, where they had made their mistakes, so that he could be sure never to make them himself. He carried on questioning Rick.

'Do you reckon Sherwyn's got enough money to keep them going? If it does fail?'

Rick shrugged.

'I don't know exactly. Though according to Mandy, his ex-wife's managed to get a good chunk of his capital. I think he was just glad to get rid of her.'

I know the feeling, thought Damien.

'But if I could split up Mandy and Patrick, that would cause a huge rift. There's no doubt she's got daddy wrapped round her finger. If she spits her dummy out, he'd probably bail out at the first sign of trouble.'

'Do you reckon you could split them up?'

Rick tipped back in his chair and took a swig of his beer.

'It would be my pleasure.'

Damien nodded in satisfaction. His mind was ticking over, doing calculations, working out timescales, wondering just how long he'd have to wait. Patience had always been one of his virtues.

It wasn't one of Rick's, however. He leaned forward eagerly.

'So what are you going to do? Wait until they've spent all their money doing the place up, then send the boys round?'

Damien gave a tight smile.

'Something like that, yes.'

He was anxious not to come across as too much of a cheapskate gangster. It wouldn't do for Rick to know too much. For his own good, as much as anything else. He suspected that despite his tough exterior, Rick was quite naive underneath it all, and he didn't want to give him a glimpse of what he was capable of.

To Damien, what he was planning was normal; it was common practice in the world he came from, to circle round a business you fancied like a carrion crow until it died on its feet, then swoop in on the carcass. And if a little industrial sabotage was necessary to hasten the procedure, that wasn't frowned upon. It was all part of the game; something that you had to put up with yourself from time to time. At the end of the day, it was all about the survival of the fittest. You had to fight your corner.

That had always been Damien's life. Ever since he was tiny, he'd contended with protection rackets, men demanding money with menaces, loan sharks, people calling in favours at inopportune moments, people happy to smash up your success if it intruded on theirs. Even now, he shuddered at some of the memories. The man who gave his mother the paltry sum she was able to keep secret from his dad. He didn't like to think what she might have had to do for those few measly coppers . . .

He was shaken out of his reverie by Rick peering at him, puzzled.

'Why are you doing this, anyway?'

Damien smiled.

'Because it's easy. Because it's there. Because I can.'

9

The following Saturday, Keith got ready for his evening at the Liddiards' with a well-deserved but delicious sense of anticipation. He loved going to Honeycote House. It was the one place, apart from his own home, where he could truly relax and be himself. It was all down to Lucy, of course. Keith absolutely idolized her. Not in anything resembling a romantic or sexual way. He simply thought she was quite the most wonderful person to walk the earth. She'd single-handedly helped restore his self-confidence when his wife had left him by welcoming him into her home, introducing him to other people, feeding him, listening to him – being something that was rather out of fashion these days: a good friend. And he was eternally grateful. In some ways he thought that he'd come to the rescue of Honeycote Ales because of her. Of course, it hadn't been a total act of altruism, but she had been a motivating force. He would never have felt moved to step in merely on Mickey's behalf, or Patrick's. But there had been something of the white knight in him that had come to the aid of the damsel in distress, because he so valued Lucy's loyalty. And it was the thought of her that had kept him going in the darker hours when he'd panicked that he'd been mad to take on such a white elephant.

He showered and doused himself with Polo, then put on a pair of nut-brown cords and a black cashmere roll-neck. A year ago he wouldn't have dared wear something so snug-fitting, but the incipient paunch he'd once sported had diminished and his stomach was relatively flat now. He towelled dry his hair, which he'd had cut that morning at the barbers in Eldenbury – much shorter than he used to wear it. He checked over his appearance in the mirror and nodded with approval. Definitely a vast improvement – not exactly a babe magnet, but not bad for a man speeding towards his fiftieth year. He laced up his suede brogues and checked his watch. He wondered if Mandy would give him a lift. There was no point in kidding himself that he was going to be in a fit state to drive back. It just wasn't possible when you went to the Liddiards'. The welcoming gin and tonic alone would be enough to give you a twelve-month ban.

He decided against asking her. He was sure she'd say yes, but a gut feeling told him that perhaps Mandy wouldn't want to go near Honeycote House tonight. The rift between her and Patrick was increasing, and the last thing he wanted to do was humiliate her by thrusting her into his territory.

Keith was very worried about his daughter. She looked pale and drawn and terribly thin. And when you thought about it, it wasn't really surprising, thought Keith. She was only nineteen, but she was holding down a responsible job which had, by her own engineering and ingenuity, become quite pressurized. Moreover, she had taken over the role as woman of the house; even though Keith had hired a reliable cleaning lady, she still took it all far too seriously for a girl her age. He supposed it was instinct, combined with her perfectionism, that made her house-proud. He had himself to blame as well. He'd cursed himself three weeks before, when he'd found her struggling in with a week's worth of grocery shopping. He'd never really considered how time-consuming and exhausting it might be organizing provisions even just for two. He'd taken matters into his own hands at that point. He'd got straight on to the Internet, found the nearest supermarket that did home deliveries and set up an account. He compiled a weekly shopping list so that every week a supply of bread, milk, cheeses, fruit, fresh soups and pasta with sauces was delivered first thing on a Saturday morning. It was one less thing for Mandy to worry about.

Though Keith felt at the moment that if he took away every single source of worry from her, she would find something else. She looked as if she had the weight of the world on her shoulders. And that wasn't what he wanted for his little girl. She should be enjoying the best years of her life – her youth, her beauty, her freedom. What she probably needed was a holiday, but Keith could ill-afford the time to whisk her off to some Mediterranean hotspot for a bit of rest and relaxation. In fact, he couldn't risk any time off until the Honeycote Arms was up and running smoothly, which was going to be well into the autumn by the time they'd sorted out all the teething troubles.

Perhaps he'd have a chat with her. Even better, perhaps he'd have a chat with Patrick. He'd pay for them to go somewhere for a nice weekend. Barcelona. Great weather, good food, easy to get to. Nice shops. In his experience, most women blossomed given a temperate climate and a bit of retail therapy.

He decided to drive himself. He could leave the car and fetch it the next morning. He'd call Jim the Taxi from the village. Jim did a roaring trade – he could name his price on a Saturday night between twelve and two, as no one in the countryside seemed capable of abstaining from alcohol and people were increasingly reluctant to risk their licences. This gave Keith a flash of inspiration – perhaps he could hire someone to drive their customers home from the Honeycote Arms at the weekends. He was sure the resulting rise in alcohol consumption would more than cover the costs, for he had often observed that there was an equation which said the more people that were drinking, the more was drunk per capita. For example, a table of four, two driving, two drinking, might get through two bottles of wine, tops. But a table of four who were all drinking would demolish five bottles easily, plus aperitifs, plus liqueurs, as they all egged each other on in their cups . . .

Pleased with this brainwave, Keith made a note in the Mulberry filofax Mandy had bought him for Christmas and, hoicking a bottle of St Joseph from the wine rack, headed out the door.

Mandy waited until she heard the front door go before rolling off the bed and pulling open the wardrobe door.

She kept telling herself that there was absolutely nothing wrong in what she was about to do. It was what normal nineteen-year-old girls were doing all over the country – going out with a load of mates. Never mind that she didn't actually know any of the people who were going. Only Rick. She told herself it had just been a casual invitation. Not a date. And she was only going because she was bored. Fancied a change of scene and company. And because Patrick had gone to some boring black-tie cricket dinner that she hadn't been invited to because she was a girl.

She wasn't sure what to wear. She didn't want to look too dressy or too tarty. She put on a pair of distressed Diesel jeans, boots and a broderie anglaise top, and put her hair in two plaits. Happy that she looked cool, but not threatening, she picked up her mobile and texted Rick. Her finger hovered over the send button before jabbing it defiantly.

A minute later her phone squawked, indicating she had a message. It was Rick, asking if she wanted a lift. She thought about it – she wouldn't have to worry about where to park or how much to drink. She texted him back, giving her address. 'CU AT 8' came the reply.

She wondered what sort of a car he'd have. The Merc apparently belonged to his boss. An old Ford Fiesta, she decided, with an overflowing ashtray and hundreds of parking tickets.

A throaty roar outside the front door twenty minutes later made her rush to the window and look out. She gulped. She couldn't have been more wrong.

Rick was sitting astride a Harley-Davidson in faded jeans ripped at the knee, a Che Guevara T-shirt and a black leather jacket. He looked like every father's nightmare: a devil in angel's disguise whose hobby was defiling innocent young middle-class virgins and turning them into drug-crazed biker chicks overnight.

'Wow.' Mandy ran her hands admiringly over the gleaming chrome.

He grinned ruefully.

'I'm probably going to spend the rest of my life paying it off. Have you been on a bike before?'

Mandy shook her head. There was no point in pretending.

'It's no problem. Just put your hands round my waist. And relax. Go with it.'

It was all very well saying relax, but every horror story Mandy had ever heard about motorbikes raced through her mind. Yet she knew she couldn't bottle out; she didn't want to look like a wuss and, besides, she had a feeling it was one of those things you had to experience once, even if you never did it again. Her heart was hammering wildly as she put on the helmet Rick held out to her and climbed on behind him. Thank God her Diesel jeans were low-slung and quite baggy and she hadn't put on high heels. She slid her arms round his waist and breathed in the smell of his jacket. Leather and oil and eucalyptus.

She felt reckless, rebellious and quite, quite wicked. And she hadn't even done anything wrong yet. A mixture of fear and elation rose in her throat as he started the bike and accelerated out of the drive, gravel spraying everywhere.

She felt as if her stomach had been left behind, fought the urge to scream at him to stop. She shut her eyes but that was worse. He took a bend, leaning the bike to the left, and she felt sure they were going to hit the road, but no sooner had she braced herself for the impact than they were upright again. Trees, gates and houses flashed past. Heads turned.

Eventually, Rick pulled into the car park of a country pub. It wasn't one Mandy recognized – it wasn't one of theirs – but there were half a dozen other bikes parked up and a crowd of people sitting at tables outside, drinking beer.

Rick pulled off his helmet and turned to her with a smile.

'How was it?'

Barely able to speak with exhilaration, Mandy smiled back at him, eyes shining.

'Fantastic.'

She was hooked.

At Tinker's Barn, Ginny was regretting having had such a hot bath because she was now rather red in the face. Putting foundation over the top had resulted in a ridiculously clown-like mask which she'd then had to scrub off. She resisted the temptation to glug down a glass of white wine to calm her rising panic because drink always made her cheeks flush and would therefore worsen her plight. She wondered if either of the twins had any of that green stuff that was supposed to calm down your complexion, but decided not to call upon either of them for advice, because it wouldn't stop there. She would put off doing her face for another ten minutes, and get dressed instead.

She'd chosen her clothes for their safety, if nothing else. Lucy had said casual dress, which Ginny knew could mean anything, so she opted for semi-smart-but-not-dressy. A black velvet shirt, which had a hint of Lycra in it to make it clingy. It was supposed to be fitted, only she'd bought it two sizes too big because she didn't quite have the nerve for fitted; what she really wanted was baggy. Underneath she had a long grey jersey skirt, which she thought swirled quite nicely around the top of her black suede ankle boots, which were for her quite high.

Once dressed, she spent five minutes with a round brush blow-drying her hair, something she never usually did. She'd also conditioned it for once. There hadn't been time to snip off her split ends with the kitchen scissors, but when she'd finished it hung straight and quite shiny to her shoulders. Her face was still a bit flushed, but she couldn't wait for ever, so she put on her make-up. Only when she'd finished did she open her wardrobe door to gauge the final effect in the mirror.

She gave a wail of despair. The twins came bursting in immediately. They'd obviously been hovering like vultures outside the door, waiting to see what she'd put on. They were very excited about her evening out.

'I look like a total frump. I look like a librarian.'

Kitty and Sasha glanced appraisingly at their mother, then at each other.

'Look, Mum. You look lovely. You just need . . . sexing up a bit.'

'Sexing up? Sounds like something from one of those awful rap records.'

The twins looked at each other again. Ginny suspected a plot.

'We've been dying to do this for ages,' said Kitty.

'It's OK – we won't do anything outrageous. You can trust us,' added Sasha.

And so Ginny found herself at the hands of her daughters. They ordered her to strip right down to her underwear. Even that made them shudder. Sasha marched back in with a black lacy bra with a bright pink bow at the cleavage and matching G-string.

'I bought these in a sale, but they're too big. They should be just right for you.'

Ginny picked them up reluctantly. She'd never been comfortable with a thong – she'd bought a three-pack from Marks & Spencer once, but it was rather like sitting on a barbed wire fence all day. Sasha, however, insisted.

'If you feel sexy underneath, it'll shine through.'

'I don't want to look sexy. I just want to look . . . nice,' grumbled Ginny, but did as she was told. She looked at herself in the mirror and couldn't resist a smile. Actually, she didn't look at all bad. She still had a good figure, if a tiny bit thicker round the middle than she might have liked, but at least she didn't look like a sumo wrestler from behind.

Kitty was telling her off.

'You could have shaved your legs.'

'I didn't need to. I had a long skirt on.'

'Well, you can't wear fishnets now. All the hairs will poke through. Never mind – you'll have to make do with opaques.'

Ginny thought that was probably for the best. At this rate she was going to look as if she was touting for business, she mused, as Sasha manoeuvred her into a tight, black, long-sleeved lacy T-shirt. Shored up by the bra underneath, it gave her an impressive, but not too revealing, cleavage. Kitty produced a dark red silk skirt cut on the bias, which was teamed with a pair of knee-length black suede boots. The girls then attacked her hair, teasing it and backcombing it until she feared it would look like a bird's nest, but then it was smoothed and pinned up with just a few chosen strands escaping. Then they re-did her make-up: daubs of charcoal grey and taupe that went on with the addition of tinted moisturizer, light-deflecting powder and highlighting blusher. The finishing touches were a three-stranded jet choker, matching dangly earrings and red, red lipstick.

Ginny looked in the mirror for the second time that evening and screamed. She didn't recognize the person standing there. She looked positively glamorous. The knee-length boots made her calves look incredibly slim and elegant. The make-up combined with her hairstyle gave her usually round face a semblance of bone structure. The fitted top and flirty skirt looked fluid and streamlined. She looked like a sexy, confident woman who knew what suited her. Which couldn't in fact be further from the truth.

Suddenly there was a knock on the door downstairs.

'Dad's here to pick us up.'

There was a flurry of activity as the girls went to get their stuff. They were going to supper at David's. She walked to the door to see them off, hoping that he wouldn't get out of the car, but he did. He looked at her with an expression she couldn't define, but she felt sure was distaste.

'What on earth are you wearing?'

'Doesn't she look fantastic? Give him a twirl, Mum.'

Feeling horribly self-conscious, Ginny held her arms out to her sides for a second so David could see her in all her glory, and felt hot mortification at the horror on his face.

'Very nice. Very . . . Moulin Rouge.'

He obviously thought she looked like a tart.

As soon as they'd gone, she rushed back to the mirror for a second appraisal. David was right. She looked like mutton. She couldn't possibly, possibly turn up to a dinner party looking like that. She didn't have the confidence. She wouldn't tell the twins. They'd been so sweet, and were so excited and proud of their handiwork.

Once she was quite sure the coast was clear she put the velvet shirt on over the tight T-shirt, took off the choker and scrubbed off the red lipstick, replacing it with her usual neutral, barely-there, boring nothing colour. She still felt like another person, though, and her tummy was churning. She was slightly turned on by her disguise, but also apprehensive about this evening. It had been years since she'd gone to a social event on her own.

Barney lay on the bed, waiting for Suzanna to finish her bath and come in to get dressed. It had taken him hours in the shower to wash away the brick and plaster dust and grime earlier on. Even his teeth seemed coated in the stuff – he'd brushed them twice this evening. But they'd done it. Everything they didn't want was gone – the last skip had been lowered on to the lorry that afternoon.

He and Suzanna had cheered as the hideous carpet that was spread throughout the pub was finally rolled up and taken away. They'd spent the day scrubbing at the flagstones underneath. Barney had gone to the local reclamation yard for advice and come away with several tins of solvent designed to remove the sticky residue left by the mixture of glue and underlay. It was hard work; their knuckles were red and raw and the best manicurist in the world would have no effect on the state of their nails. But when they'd sat back to survey their efforts, the results had filled them with glee. Already the interior of the pub had a different atmosphere – just by removing the heavy, gloomy carpets and curtains, and stripping off the hideous brown veneer on the bar, it had a lighter feel.

Now they had a blank canvas, the fun was about to

start. As was the really hard work. Demolition was easy. Now they had three weeks to pull everything together: a kitchen, a restaurant, staff, a menu, the bedrooms, an image. Barney tried to blank it all out as he invariably felt overwhelmed when he considered what they had to achieve. He was going to enjoy tonight, relax and get to know the people he was working for – or should that be with? It was probably the last evening he was going to be able to unwind for some time.

He caught his breath as Suzanna came in from the bathroom wrapped in a towel. He could smell the Laura Mercier bath foam she'd been using: the scent of warm honey radiated off her skin. From half-closed eyes he watched her get dressed. She slipped on a pink lace-edged cardigan with tiny mother of pearl buttons. With it went a grey silk ruffled gypsy skirt with an asymmetric hem and delicate strappy sandals of the same pink as her cardigan. She pulled her hair up into a ponytail on top of her head, teasing the ends and spritzing them with spray, before fixing it all in place with a pink silk flower. She scooped up her lipstick, a comb and a packet of cigarettes and stuck them in a little raffia bag that was decorated with brightly coloured straw flowers. It could have been pilfered from a little girl's dressing-up box or it could have cost a fortune from some exclusive backstreet boutique in Richmond. You never knew with Suzanna.

Barney thought she looked gorgeous. Not at all tarty – even though she'd left the top few buttons of her cardigan undone, and her heels were quite dangerously high – but fresh, young and incredibly sexy. He wanted to pull her into his arms and kiss her. That's what he would have done years ago. They'd often made love before they went out, she still damp from the shower, he freshly shaven and half dressed. But it had been a long time since those days.

He reached out an arm lazily from the bed and grinned. 'Come here.'

She walked over to him, half smiling. He caressed the side of her thigh; a gentle gesture, not, he hoped, a lecherous grope. He could feel the warmth of her skin through the silk.

'You look gorgeous.'

She smiled. 'Thank you.' She didn't physically edge away, but he sensed her reluctance to succumb to his touch. It was an infinitesimal tension. Maybe he was hypersensitive to it; maybe he had anticipated it. Maybe he should just pull her to him and hang the consequences? They didn't need to be at the Liddiards' for another half an hour. It was what they should be doing, for God's sake, a beautiful married couple on a warm spring evening that was balmy with promise. Making love. Because they did still love each other, after all that had happened.

But Barney was too afraid that the moment would be spoiled. He was terrified of rejection, of the shutters coming down. If he didn't try it on, then he couldn't be rejected.

He swung his legs decisively over the edge of the bed and stood up.

'Shall we walk? It's a lovely evening. We can get a cab back later if we're tired.'

He thought he could see the relief in her eyes. He turned away so she couldn't see the hurt in his, and grabbed his jacket off the back of the bedroom door.

*

As David drove back towards Cheltenham, he pondered over what he had seen. If he hadn't heard her speak, he wouldn't have believed it was Ginny. How could she have changed so much in such a short space of time? Was it the country air? He thought she looked ... fantastic. Sophisticated and knowing, slightly exotic. Younger, but at the same time more experienced. Annoyingly, he felt a tinge of regret. He wished he was taking her out tonight, instead of taking the twins back to the hellhole that Marlborough Crescent was becoming.

They'd managed to complete the surgery, and it was now up and running and looking very smart. He was gratified that most of his private patients from Evesham had followed him there, as he had a faultless chairside manner. He'd taken out extensive advertising in the local lifestyle magazine, done leaflet drops in all the best roads, and his client list was gradually building up.

But the surgery had eaten voraciously into their budget. There was nothing left over to do up the house and Faith was becoming increasingly hysterical as she realized that the underfloor heating, wall-to-wall carpeting and state-of-the-art kitchen she'd set her heart on were not going to appear before the baby was born. David had had to put his foot down. The house might not be *House and Garden*, but it was perfectly habitable – the kitchen was only five years old, maybe not to their taste but service-able. Faith continually ranted about the nursery suite on the top floor – a bedroom for the baby, adjoining bathroom, a 'day' nursery and a room for the au pair. David put her straight – the baby would have to go in the boxroom next to theirs and the au pair would have to wait. Until he'd made the money needed to convert things to her liking. He certainly wasn't going to put himself into any more debt. Faith had had a panic attack and David had fought the urge to slap her – it was what she needed, but he knew walloping a pregnant woman was indefensible.

There was no doubt about it: the honeymoon was over. He couldn't believe that Faith was the same woman who'd made him feel like a god. Who had, as she called it, empowered him to achieve his potential. Who'd made him reach for the stars. And did things to him that only girls who subscribed to *Cosmopolitan* could know about.

Now all he had was a monstrous mortgage and less sex than ever in his life. Gone was the cosy little dream he'd envisaged for himself, the utopia he had described to Ginny when he'd tried to defend his decision to leave her. Ginny, who had put up with their own rather grotty melamine kitchen without a word of complaint. In fact, she'd got off her arse and had a go at painting it after she'd watched one of those make-over programmes, and bought new handles for the doors. It had looked, if anything, worse, as the paint hadn't gone on very smoothly, but she'd just laughed. David felt a nasty stab of guilt as he remembered promising her that a new kitchen was top of the list next time he had any spare cash. But Faith had come along before then. Faith, who wasn't happy with the kitchen that was ten times better than the one Ginny had put up with for years. Faith, who wanted stainless-steel pyrolitic ovens and an electric wok. And a dual cyclone washing machine because of all the laundry she'd be doing when the baby arrived. He had a flashback to Ginny bent over a twin tub, pulling out reams of terry nappies like a conjurer pulling handkerchiefs from his pocket. He didn't suppose Faith had ever seen a twin tub.

He put Craig David on the CD and thought he caught the twins exchanging amused glances in the rear-view mirror. He immediately felt defensive.

'What? What's wrong with it?'

'Nothing, Dad. Very groovy.'

What were they complaining about? Surely it was good to have a father who had his finger on the pulse and knew about the latest music? Or would they prefer him to listen to Barbra bloody Streisand? David defiantly turned up the volume and put his foot down so they sped through the back lanes to Cheltenham. Though in fact he wasn't in any hurry to get home. He was going to have to cook supper, as Faith still insisted that preparing food made her nauseous, even though she was well into her third trimester. She'd enlightened him with the fact that morning sickness could last well beyond the magic three-month cut-off point, had proven it by showing him the paragraph in her *Mother and Baby* manual, but David was convinced it was some sort of plot by women to avoid doing what they didn't like doing when they were pregnant. Supper was going to be a logistical nightmare – Faith had a long list of foods that apparently gave her heartburn (morning sickness and heartburn weren't mutually exclusive, apparently), Kitty still insisted on everything that passed her lips being organic and was a demi-vegetarian, whatever that meant, and Sasha was just plain fussy and didn't eat anything with bones or fat or that looked like what it was.

What he fancied was a big fat juicy steak, cooked rare, with chips and a spinach and watercress salad, but that was off everyone's menu except his own. Ginny loved steak. It was the one thing she cooked to perfection. She always used to buy them a sirloin each on birthdays and anniversaries. David's mouth watered at the thought, then with a sigh he resigned himself to pasta. Again. He'd start shitting penne at this rate.

Ginny needn't have been nervous about going to supper at Honeycote House, as Lucy and Mickey were the most natural hosts in the world and instantly put guests at their ease. There was no ceremony, no formality. Mickey led her out on to the terrace to enjoy the last few fingers of sunlight and pressed a glass of champagne into her hand – no need to ask what she wanted to drink, who would refuse vintage bubbles?

Already enjoying the view was Keith Sherwyn. Mickey introduced them and excused himself for a moment – a judicious withdrawal so they could break the ice together. Both Mickey and Keith were dressed down in a sweater and cords; Ginny had panicked when she'd seen how casual the men were, but was relieved to see Lucy was more dressed up, in an orange silk skirt and a wrap-around cashmere cardigan.

Keith and Ginny chatted idly for ten minutes or so, about neutral subjects. Keith was very careful to avoid anything too personal. His heart had gone out to Ginny as soon as he saw her. Lucy had filled him in briefly on her background before she got there and he knew just how vulnerable she was probably feeling. He tried to hit the right balance in his chatter – enough so he wouldn't sound like a self-centred bore and leaving enough room for her to contribute to the conversation without feeling obliged to tell him anything that left an open wound. He could see she was nervous – she was gulping back her champagne and she obviously wasn't used to it, as her cheeks quickly became flushed. Keith made a note to himself to make sure she drank enough water at dinner. The Liddiards were useless at supplying water – he'd been a victim of dehydration after one of their dos often enough.

Inspired by the view they were looking out on, they discussed gardening, which they both confessed was an unknown area they would like to know more about, then moved on to the incredible diversity and immense usefulness of the village post office. Halfway through their conversation, Keith found himself quite smitten. She was sweet! The rather severe black and red outfit she wore was stunning, though he could tell by the way she kept pulling the velvet shirt across her chest that she didn't really feel comfortable in it. Her face was soft and round, its slight plumpness disallowing the onset of wrinkles. She would once have been quite fair, guessed Keith, but her hair had now darkened to slightly lighter than mouse. It was her eyes that made her so pretty. They were large, round orbs lit up by millions of tiny blue prisms; fragmented chips of deep sapphire that sparkled like sunlight dancing on the Mediterranean sea. They were eyes that said you were fascinating. Eyes that laughed at all of your jokes, but not at you. Eyes that understood all your woes and promised to take them away –

Keith realized that he was in danger of gawping and tried to regain his concentration, bringing the conver-sation round to the point-to-point that was due to take place the following weekend in Kiplington, the village where he lived. Ginny admitted being terrified of horses, but Keith assured her that point-to-points were less about horses than drinking, gambling and socializing.

'Honeycote Ales are sponsoring the last race, in fact. We always have.'

'Wow.' Ginny looked impressed.

'It sounds very grand, but it's only a couple of hundred quid prize money. We're using it as an excuse to bung up a hospitality tent. Pimms and canapés. Basically it's a bit of a PR jolly to advertise the fact we're doing up the local pub.'

'I saw it was being demolished.'

'Not entirely, I hope. We're due to open again in three weeks. Anyway, you must come on Saturday. Come as my guest.'

Ginny looked a little flustered, a little unsure, and Keith did his best to reassure her.

'It's all very informal. And great fun, I promise you. And we'll picnic afterwards.'

Shit, thought Keith. I've done it. I've asked someone I genuinely fancy on a date. He prayed that he hadn't pressured her into saying yes; he knew Mickey had filled up his glass twice while he'd been talking, so he was filled with Dutch courage. She'd seemed pleased enough with the invitation, though he hoped he hadn't come across as a pompous git, waffling on about point-to-points when he'd only been to his first last year. And referring to Honeycote Ales as 'us'. Was he entitled to do that? It wasn't his great-grandfather that had hit upon the idea after all. Bloody hell, thought Keith. Who do I think I am? Bloody landed gentry?

*

In the kitchen, Lucy emptied a bag of Kettle Chips into a bowl and looked out of the window as an Aston Martin insinuated its way up the drive and drew to a halt next to Keith's Land Cruiser. James, Mickey's brother, and his wife Caroline had arrived. Lucy smiled as Caroline got out of the front seat, eager as ever to party, her post-natal curves defiantly poured into what was clearly a pre-natal dress. James was immaculate in a pale blue shirt and cream chinos. Then her mouth dropped open in horror as a tall figure emerged from the back seat, clutching a magnum of champagne.

'Shit!' wailed Lucy. 'James has brought Tall, Dark and Hands. I'll kill him . . .'

Tall, Dark and Hands was so called because of his height, looks and his inability to keep his hands to himself. Otherwise known as the Dishonourable Bertie, he was six foot three, with impossibly long legs clad in steel-grey velvet trousers, shiny black Chelsea boots and a voluminous white cotton shirt untucked at the back and undone at the cuffs. His mane of dark hair was swept back off his face. He looked like a pirate; a pirate that would have his very wicked way with you before making you walk the plank.

James apologized very prettily to his hostess for the gatecrasher.

'I'm sorry. He came over this afternoon with a load of stuff for the shop, then we had a few drinks and . . . well, I didn't think you'd mind, to be honest.'

'That's where you're wrong. He's the last thing I need,' she hissed. 'I've got a guest for Keith. I was trying to set them up.'

'I'll tell him to keep his hands to himself.'

'You'll have to bloody chop them off first. You know Bertie – anything with a pulse is fair game. And poor Ginny won't be able to cope.'

'Who's Ginny? Another one of your lame ducks?'

'She's not a lame duck. She's very sweet. And she's had a rotten time from her husband so the last thing I want is bloody Bertie abusing her.'

'Who can't I abuse? I promise to keep my hands off your daughters.' Bertie slid an arm round Lucy's waist and dropped a nonchalant kiss on her cheek. Lucy looked at him, as strictly as she could, because the most frustrating thing about Bertie was he made you laugh. You just couldn't be cross with him. She thrust the bowl of Kettle Chips at him and told him to be useful. At least if his hands were full he couldn't do anything else with them.

A few minutes later, Barney and Suzanna arrived, heralding the opening of even more champagne. Ginny had been nibbling at the Kettle Chips in a vain attempt to line her stomach, but it was a bit like shutting the barn door after the horse had bolted. She was relieved to see Suzanna was carrying three Tupperware boxes of canapés, which she'd brought by previous arrangement with Lucy.

'I've been experimenting all week. If I don't bring them, Barney and I will have to eat them all ourselves.'

Barney patted his stomach.

'Thank God there's a lot of hard physical work to be done, otherwise I'd be the size of a house. She makes me try out something new every day – puddings as well!'

Lucy arranged the canapés on a huge willow-pattern

plate and led them through into the living room, where Mickey promptly filled up everyone's glasses again and proposed a toast.

'I can tell you, we're not the only ones excited about the Honeycote Arms. The whole village is waiting with bated breath. So good luck!'

Suzanna and Barney fielded questions from everyone about how things were going, until Lucy intervened, protesting that it was their night off. Suzanna begged for a tour of the house and the gardens, so they were led off clutching their champagne.

Like everyone, the Blakes both fell in love with Honeycote House. It was so English, so uncontrived, so right.

'Oh, Barney,' sighed Suzanna, as she stood on the terrace, breathing in the scent of early roses. 'Maybe one day we'll have a place like this . . .'

Barney raised an eyebrow. This wasn't the sort of house you bought, not in this day and age.

'If this is what you want, you'd have to marry Patrick,' he joked. Suzanna jabbed him in the ribs with her elbow, grinning.

'Not this big, maybe. Just a little one.' She held up her thumb and forefinger to indicate how small.

Barney took another swig of his champagne. He could definitely get used to this new lifestyle. It felt about a million miles away from Twickenham. As Suzanna and Lucy plundered the herb garden for cuttings, he took in the view. After an exhausting week, it put everything into perspective. They'd definitely done the right thing, he thought.

*

In the living room, Keith had left Ginny to go and talk to James, and she panicked as the vulpine Bertie descended on her. His presence was most disconcerting. He smelled utterly delicious, making her feel quite faint. Her eyes were on a level with his chest, despite the two-inch heels on her boots, and she had to crane her neck to look up at him.

'Tell me three interesting facts about yourself.' The command would have seemed obnoxious coming from anyone else, but somehow he had an air of mischief that made this a perfectly acceptable opening gambit. All the same, she couldn't think of a single one. He lit a cigarette and blew out a plume of smoke. As she grasped around for something to say, he apologized. 'Sorry. I'm being my usual aggressively over-the-top confrontational self. It's because deep down I'm actually hideously shy. And I've never mastered the art of polite conversation. Just three facts will do. They don't necessarily have to be interesting. Name, rank, serial number, that sort of thing.'

Ginny could tell that he'd realized his request had been an impossible one, that she couldn't possibly have anything interesting to tell him about herself, so she rallied and did her very best.

'OK. My husband's run off with a woman half his age who's about to give birth to his baby. I'm sharing a house that's a glorified stable with my twin daughters. And this week I've discovered that I am officially unemployable.'

Bertie tutted as he surveyed her. 'Has he realized his mistake yet?'

'What?'

'Your imbecile of a husband. If he's gone for a younger model he's only going to be in for GBH of the earhole.

He'd have been much better sticking with you, I'm sure. You look fairly placid.' He peered at her more closely, as if he was examining a racehorse for signs of bad temper before buying it.

'Placid, but dull.'

'Well, that's his fault, entirely. It's a man's responsibility to bring out the best in a woman.'

Ginny's eyebrows nearly shot through the roof. She wasn't sure if Bertie was winding her up or not. He carried on regardless.

'And I can't believe you're unemployable.'

Bertie was looking at her as if he'd happily pay her to undertake certain tasks. It was an unfamiliar feeling to Ginny, but she began to see what he meant about bringing out the best in a woman. She explained how she'd been scouring the local papers for gainful employment.

'I could be a care assistant in a local nursing home, for a pittance. Or I could train to become a driving instructor, but I imagine that means I'd have to part with large sums of money at some point, as I presume I'd need a car. I could be a panel beater, only I'm not sure what one of those is. I could pack eggs or stuff chickens. Other than that, I am either too old, overqualified or underqualified.'

'Who says you've got to work for somebody else? Start your own business.'

'Doing what? I wouldn't know where to start.'

'What are you good at?'

Ginny had to think long and hard.

'Ironing. I'm fantastic at ironing.'

Bertie looked baffled.

'No one likes ironing, surely?'

'I do.' Her third glass of champagne made Ginny

passionately emphatic. 'I love the entire process: taking a crumpled bit of rag and transforming it into a crisp, pristine item of clothing that looks like new. I love the smell of fresh laundry, the noise of the steam, the sense of achievement. And all the time you can be doing something else in your head —'

God, she must be pissed. How boring could you get, lecturing somebody on the joys of ironing? But Bertie seemed interested.

'There you are, then. I'm telling you, you could charge outrageous amounts for taking in people's ironing round here.'

Ginny laughed.

'Don't be ridiculous.'

'It's not. You could do mine for a start. I love the thought of you running your iron over my wrinkled shirts, lost in a fantasy.'

Ginny could sense he was about to expand on his theory, but just then Lucy called them through into the dining room and the moment was lost.

10

At Honeycote Grove, Damien looked out into his garden gloomily. The outside lighting turned itself on automatically as soon as the sun began to fade from the sky, lighting up the ferns and the lilies that the landscape team had planted for instant effect. He could go and have a drink outside, he supposed. The heater blasted out enough warmth to heat the entire tenement block he'd been brought up in. But he couldn't see the point.

He was in agony. For the first time in his life, he didn't have a clue what move to make next. Ever since the night he had met her at the Honeycote Arms, he'd wanted to see Kelly again, but wasn't sure how to go about it. Common sense told him to grasp the nettle, make a cold call, ask her out, but he couldn't bear the thought of rejection, however polite.

What alternatives were there? Take her up on her offer to babysit? But then what? Drive round for hours? He supposed he could wait till she got here, then say his arrangements had been cancelled. But what if she then just wanted to go home?

He poured himself a vodka and knocked it back, then gave himself a stern talking to. He'd ring her up – her number must be the same as Rick's – and be spontaneous.

'I've got the new George Clooney DVD. Pirate copy from the States. Why don't you bring round a Chinese and we'll watch it together?'

No matter which way he said it, he sounded like a dork.

Lucy had cooked an enormous leg of spring lamb, served with dauphinois potatoes and roasted baby carrots with their green tops left on. Then a Moroccan almond cake scented with orange flower water, and caramelized clementines and thick dollops of crème fraîche. And a magnificent cheeseboard served at the same time, because she knew some people didn't bother with pudding, some didn't bother with cheese, and some would want both. There was a ripe Chaumes, unctuous under its velvety orange crust, a slab of Torte di Dolcelatte and a rather forbidding mature Cheddar.

It was simple food, thoughtfully prepared, but most importantly the serving of it was relaxed – there was no tension from the kitchen, no mad scramble to synchronize the dishes, it all just seemed to happen under Lucy's vaguely languorous direction. Suzanna thought if she managed to impart some of this atmosphere into the dining room at the Honeycote Arms, she'd be well on her way.

Everyone was drinking furiously, except James, who was driving and seemed to be able to keep his head while everyone around him was losing theirs. In fact, he was very amusing, and kept them all in stitches with his description of marriage and fatherhood with the addition of six incontinent puppies thrown in.

'I've got rid of three, through the shop. I sometimes wonder if I should go into dog-breeding, not antiques. Only three more to go.'

Caroline protested volubly. She thought they should

keep one, but James put his foot down. Ginny, daring after her fair share of Gavi di Gavi, spoke up.

'I'll have one. You'll have to tell me how to train it, because I haven't a clue. But I've always wanted a dog.'

'Come round and have a look. You can have the choice of what's left and I'll issue you with a full set of instructions. Anyway, there's an old bat that does puppy-training in the village hall every Wednesday. She'll soon put you straight.'

Ginny felt a surge of excitement. It was ridiculous, really, that the prospect of a puppy could be so thrilling. Or perhaps it was the whole evening that was making her feel the way she did. Everyone was so charming – witty and interesting without being intimidating. The food was the best meal she'd had for – well, months, if you didn't count her evening out with David when he'd taken her to the Petit Blanc to 'discuss things', when she hadn't really noticed what she was eating because she'd been concentrating so hard on what she should say. She was actually getting a social life!

The meal finished with big lumps of home-made fudge that Lucy's daughter Georgina had made, which they drank with heart-racingly dark, bitter coffee. Lucy made all the men move round a place and Ginny found Bertie sitting next to her. He'd been openly flirting with Caroline all evening, unashamedly trying to throw grapes down her cleavage, and she'd retaliated by retrieving the grapes and then feeding them to him. It was outrageous behaviour in Ginny's eyes, but obviously par for the course, as nobody batted an eyelid and James didn't seem remotely threatened. Ginny thought Bertie would be bored by the prospect of sitting next to her – she surreptitiously buttoned up her shirt in case he got any ideas about tableside netball – but he seemed genuinely pleased to be next to her.

'Hello, Mrs Tiggywinkle.'

She felt sure she was being teased, but found she rather liked it. David had never, ever, teased her. He took life and himself and other people very seriously indeed.

Caroline was waxing lyrical over the joys of mother-hood.

'I thought I'd hate it. I thought I'd want to be back at my desk after six weeks, but the thought of work is horrendous. I love being a mum! I love having an excuse not to get dressed till midday. I love snuggling up with the baby in front of *This Morning* and giving him his feed. I want at least three more.'

She gave James a mischievous smile, but he refused to react, used as he was to Caroline's drunken rambling fantasies. He knew as well as the next person she'd be grumbling like fury the next morning. Mickey passed round the port.

'You're not the only one set on whelping. Lucy keeps banging on about having another.'

Everyone turned to Lucy in amazement, who shrugged, embarrassed.

'Empty-nest syndrome, I suppose. I'm just panicking at the thought of Honeycote House being empty.'

'Bit bloody drastic, having another baby, isn't it? Why don't we take in paying guests?' Mickey clearly wasn't enamoured of the idea.

'Rubbish,' slurred Caroline. 'Go for it, Lucy. If we time it right we could have our next ones together.' She poured a slug of port into her glass, ignoring James's protestations

189

about how she would feel the next morning, and turned her attentions to Suzanna.

'What about you? Don't you want children? Or are you married to your career?'

There was a silence that seemed cavernous to Barney, whose heart had leaped into his mouth. All attention turned to Suzanna, who looked round, her head resting lazily on her hand, with a nonchalant smile.

'I've got years yet. I'm only thirty-two. Plenty of time to worry about that after the Honeycote Arms has got a Michelin star.'

Everyone laughed as she mentioned the elusive holy grail of awards so coveted by ambitious chefs. There were only three pubs in the country that had been awarded one. Keith smiled approvingly at her.

'I'm very glad to hear you've got your priorities right.'

Caroline waved an admonishing finger at her.

'You wait. Your body-clock will suddenly kick in and you won't be able to do a thing about it.'

Suzanna fixed her with a firm gaze.

'I'll cross that bridge when I come to it.'

At that moment, Caroline knocked her port glass over and in the ensuing chaos the subject was forgotten. Barney touched Suzanna on the back of the neck, just to let her know he understood, but she ignored him, so she obviously wasn't unduly perturbed.

Not long after, Suzanna and Barney pleaded utter exhaustion and they left, with many kisses and thanks and offers of help with the pub. Lucy lent Suzanna a pair of trainers for the walk home. Barney was carrying a cardboard box full of cuttings for the pub garden.

As they turned out of the drive, Barney mused on what a great time they'd had.

'That was a fantastic evening. Wasn't it?'

'Lovely,' said Suzanna. 'Lucy's a fantastic cook. And a lovely person . . .'

She trailed off and leaned against Barney for support, hoping he would think she'd just had too much to drink. As they made their way back down the high street, Suzanna prayed that she would be able to contain her misery. The lump was there, the panicky lump, and no matter how hard she swallowed, it wouldn't go back down.

She didn't know how she hadn't lost it at the dinner table. Hadn't broken down when Caroline had grilled her about her body-clock. Hadn't screamed at the unfairness when Caroline had banged on about cuddling up in front of the telly with Henry. It had been one of Suzanna's favourite things, staying defiantly in her pyjamas till eleven o'clock, watching *This Morning* and sharing digestives with Ollie. Instead she'd put on that act, the one that had them all utterly fooled and totally oblivious to her agony.

Barney had known. Barney had understood. She'd felt his sympathy but hadn't been able to look at him, because she would have broken down. She had to be brave. She couldn't spoil things. Not when they were doing so well.

She desperately wanted to turn and hug him, but once she started crying she knew she wouldn't be able to stop.

Back at Honeycote House, Caroline insisted on more champagne, because it was her first night out since Henry had been born. James warned her yet again that she would feel like death the next day, as she wasn't used to drinking, but she didn't care and refused to touch the Malvern water he was trying to foist on her. Her mother was babysitting for the first time and she was determined to enjoy herself, and Bertie egged her on. Keith and Ginny didn't protest either; everyone was very relaxed, so Mickey popped another cork. When their glasses were all charged, Bertie made a suggestion.

'Let's play "I Have Never".'

Lucy groaned. Bertie always wanted to play 'I Have Never' because he loved showing off, and no one had ever found anything he hadn't done.

The rules were simple. Each person took it in turns to stand up and state something they had never done. Anyone else who had never done it either stood up and joined them; the ones that had, stayed seated. It was a pointless game, but endlessly fascinating. The only real rule was that you weren't allowed to lie. It always started innocently enough – 'I have never eaten oysters', 'I have never been to Blackpool' – but invariably turned before long to sex. That was when things became interesting.

Once the rules had been explained to Keith and Ginny, the game began. Ginny felt nervous as her turn arrived. She felt it was a test of some sort; as if whatever she said would be an indication of how interesting she was. What the hell was she going to say? The truth was the list was endless – she had never done an awful lot of things. But what could she admit to that didn't make her sound wet? She stood up.

'I have never . . .'

Everyone looked at her expectantly, and she took a gulp of champagne to give her courage.

'Slept with a man apart from my husband.'

There was a silence. Ginny felt that somehow she'd said utterly the wrong thing.

'Do you mean before or after marriage?' demanded Caroline.

'Ever,' replied Ginny emphatically.

'Oh, well then. In that case, I'm not budging,' said Caroline happily. 'Everyone knows I was a complete slapper until I met James.'

Round the table Keith and Lucy were the only ones to stand up with Ginny. Keith was pink with mortification, but took it in good spirit. Lucy looked very coy.

And rightly so, thought Caroline at the other end of the table. She thought it was very interesting who broke the rules in this game. She knew for a fact that Lucy had slept with James, only months before they'd got married. Lucy and Mickey had hit a rough patch in their marriage, when the brewery was in trouble and he was drinking too much. It was almost inevitable that Lucy had turned to her brother-in-law for consolation.

James was such a gentleman. He'd told Caroline all about his indiscretion before he proposed. And now, armed with the information, she decided to play devil's advocate. She didn't want to cause trouble; just make Lucy squirm a bit because everyone thought she was such an angel. Drink always made Caroline provocative.

'What – you mean you've only ever slept with Mickey? I don't believe you, Lucy! No fumblings with a stable lad when you were seventeen?'

'Absolutely not,' said Lucy, smiling. 'Anyway, it's nothing to be ashamed of, is it?'

'I think it was probably my biggest mistake,' said Ginny.

All eyes were suddenly upon her. 'If I'd had a bit more experience, maybe he'd never have gone off.'

She couldn't believe she'd said it. She must be completely gone.

'Well, it's not too late,' said Bertie kindly.

At his cricket dinner, Patrick watched with distaste as most of his companions started behaving like absolute buffoons. He didn't feel like behaving like an idiot without Ned around. He missed his partner in crime. Not that he ever got as out-of-control as this lot.

Maybe he'd go round to Keeper's Cottage and see Mandy. They could do with some quality time together. Not to mention a shag.

He tried texting her, but there was no response. She must be in bed. If he really broke his neck to get home, he might just be back at Honeycote House in time for port and the last of the cheeseboard. But maybe not.

He looked round in despair and pulled a nearby bottle of wine towards him, thinking if he couldn't beat them, he might as well join them.

Half an hour later Caroline nearly fell asleep, knocked out by the unaccustomed amount of alcohol, and James apologized for breaking up the party. He offered Bertie and Ginny a lift home, both of whom accepted gratefully. Keith looked a bit disappointed, as he'd been hoping to offer Ginny a ride in his car, but he didn't have the nerve to butt in and change the arrangements. Instead he took his leave, safe in the knowledge that he would see Ginny the following Saturday.

Bertie insisted on seeing Ginny to her front door.

James rolled his eyes – this was a ritual with Bertie; he knew there'd be a ten-minute wait while he tried to charm the pants off her, literally. Caroline was asleep in the front seat, out for the count. He smiled fondly, remembering the days when she would have partied all night and been the last one standing. Motherhood did extraordinary things to one's stamina.

Bertie guided Ginny up the path. As they reached the front door, he turned to face her, picked up her hand and stroked the inside of her wrist.

'I didn't get to know you properly this evening. Will you come out for dinner with me one night?'

'That would be lovely.'

My God. Two invitations in one night. She wasn't doing badly. She was also aware that Bertie was very close. She breathed in Acqua di Parma, closing her eyes involuntarily as he leaned in to kiss her goodnight just on the very corner of her mouth where her smile started. She opened her eyes and found him staring straight at her. She met his gaze, willing him to kiss her again, properly this time. Bertie was excellent at reading body language.

As their lips met, Ginny leaned weakly against the wall. He was doing things to her insides that she'd never dreamed possible. She felt as if there was a tub of Ben and Jerry's ice cream melting inside her, a delicious puddle dissolving into her knickers. Correction, Sasha's knickers. Oh God – what was happening to her? Now his hands were on her waist and he was brushing her ear lobe with his lips. She shuddered as he whispered to her:

'Why don't I come and tuck you in?'

My God – what was she thinking of? She must be mad, snogging a virtual stranger on her own doorstep.

And she could hear James's engine ticking over on the road outside. What if he could see? What would he think of her?

She tried to look stern, but the smile wouldn't leave her lips.

'No. Absolutely no way.'

He was kissing her jawline, her neck, imperceptible butterfly kisses that made her want to scream. She tilted her head back and dug her teeth into her bottom lip – half of her wanting to abandon herself, the other half desperate to keep control.

Two faces at the window brought her to her senses. Shit – it was the twins. What were they doing back?

'Sorry – I've got to go.' She had her hand on the latch to let herself in. He made to follow her, but the look she gave him stopped him in his tracks – it was her strictest ward sister glare.

'I'm serious.'

He held up his hands in aggrieved surrender.

'OK. But you're not getting away for ever. I don't give up that easily.'

'I'm sure you don't,' she replied tartly, and disappeared inside.

She found both Kitty and Sasha staring at her, arms akimbo.

'*Who* was that?' they chorused.

Ginny grinned. 'The Dishonourable Bertie. I think I might have pulled.'

The twins exchanged shocked glances, before turning back to smile at their mother.

'Result,' said Sasha.

'Respect,' said Kitty.

Ginny wagged a warning finger in the air.

'I'm absolutely definitely one hundred per cent not interested. He's trouble with a capital T. You can see it a mile off.'

The twins folded their arms simultaneously and shook their heads.

'You've got to give him a go, Mum.'

'He's completely gorgeous.'

'No. I'm not going near him with a barge pole.' She looked sharply at them. 'And neither, I hasten to add, are either of you.'

That was a thought. She mustn't let Bertie clap his eyes on the twins. They'd be prime fodder for a predator like him.

She went up to bed, took off her party clothes and folded them neatly, as if to remind herself that she was a sensible, grown woman and very much in control. Then she took off her make-up, scrubbed her teeth, put on her pyjamas and slid into bed. Thankfully one of the girls had put on her electric blanket, so she felt safe and warm and cocooned as she drifted off to sleep.

At the Honeycote Arms, Barney had just dropped off into a contented, wine-sodden slumber, when he was woken by a noise. Startled, he sat up, and his heart plummeted when he realized it was the sound of Suzanna sobbing into her pillow.

Immediately, he put out an arm to comfort her but she pushed him away.

'It's OK. I'm OK. Honestly. I'm just having a bit of a moment –'

But no sooner were the words out than her sobs redoubled and she threw herself into his embrace.

'I'm sorry!'

'I know, I know.'

He patted her hair, helpless as ever, despairing himself. He'd been so relieved that life in Honeycote seemed to be working. He thought they were moving forward, leaving the ghost behind. Healing. But oh no. It had only been a temporary reprieve. As he held her to him and felt the grief pour out of her, shoulders juddering, it was like standing on the edge of a very dark abyss.

The ghost was back.

I I

Barney prayed that a night's sleep would dissipate the despair of the night before, but he knew instinctively the next morning when he woke that Suzanna, too, was awake, but pretending not to be. The gloom within her was palpable. She'd slipped into one of her 'black clouds', those insidious and indestructible bouts of depression he had come to dread. There was no cure; it was impossible to snap her out of them. A multimillion-pound win on the lottery would leave her unmoved.

On several occasions, he'd tried to persuade her to take some sort of medication, something to get her on an even keel, but she'd refused. She needed to feel the feelings, she said, not have them blanked out by happy pills. It was all part of the grieving process. Barney felt she was torturing herself unnecessarily, but she remained stubborn. For some reason she'd always steered clear of prescribed drugs. It was strange, when she was happy to indulge in alcohol and tobacco, which were proven to do damage, but avoided the very things that were supposed to be healing. She'd insisted on a drug-free birth, which Barney had found bizarre. Why suffer the agonies of childbirth when there was relief available? Nobody gave you a medal for it. And now, why tolerate the depression when there was bound to be a pharmaceutical solution? It was almost as if she had a slightly masochistic streak. Or – and this was Barney's private theory – as if she was punishing herself for Oliver's death, as if by suffering she was atoning in some way.

He wondered what had brought this particular bout on. Whether it was hormonal, whether she was exhausted from the week's hard labour, whether it was the upheaval from the move suddenly kicking in or whether it had been over-indulgence the night before. Caroline's tactless questions had only been the catalyst. In a more robust mood, Suzanna might have been able to brush them off without a care.

There was no point in analysing the cause. The black cloud was here and Barney had to try and get her out from under it as quickly as possible. The moods could, he knew from experience, go on for days, weeks, and they had no time to spare. For a moment he felt a surge of annoyance. He didn't need this. Fuck it – he didn't allow himself the indulgence of bloody depression, and he'd been through the same trauma. He'd never voice that, of course, didn't even like it when the thought popped into his head. But he was already overwhelmed at the thought of the work he had to get through in the next week and he needed to be firing on all four cylinders to get through it. And Suzanna needed to be on top of it as well – of the two of them, in fact, she was the linchpin, the one with the creative drive, the one that was going to give the Honeycote Arms its soul. If he got run over by a bus, he was eminently replaceable, but she wasn't.

Barney had never kidded himself that he had anything to do with getting them where they were. He'd seen it in both Mickey's and Keith's eyes when Suzanna had spoken at their interviews: she was the one who had sparkled with ideas, creative energy, enthusiasm, had breathed life into their dream. She was passionate, driven, focussed yet at the same time totally open-minded, receptive to suggestions, happy to take other people's ideas on board. Though somehow she always managed to incorporate a change that would give it her own stamp, a twist that was indicative of her own inimitable style. It had been Suzanna that had convinced them to take the Blakes on, not Barney's reassurances that he had a handle on profit and loss, portion control and the minutiae of licensing laws.

In fact, Barney was undermining himself by making this assumption, because at the end of the day, what they were was a team. Neither could operate without the other: they were yin and yang, two halves of a whole, they each had qualities which when combined made up the complete package. But put the black cloud into the picture and that package was in danger of collapse. Barney remembered a time eight months ago when Suzanna hadn't got out of bed for three days. He'd had to cancel a christening she was supposed to be catering for. He'd had to plead shingles, as it was indefensible to bail out at the eleventh hour and her reputation would have been in tatters had the excuse been any less serious.

Barney lay still for a few minutes, trying to work out his next tactic. He had to shut his eyes. Kelly's bedroom was doing his head in: the pink walls made him feel like he was living inside a Barbie world. He groped round for a solution. Iris, Suzanna's mother, sometimes managed to resuscitate her, but that meant driving up to Richmond to fetch her and then where would she stay? They were only coping with the accommodation because it had been their choice. A seventy-two-year-old couldn't be expected to put up with it.

Suddenly he had a brainwave. The perfect diversionary tactic! Sometimes, just sometimes, it was possible to snap her out of her gloom with a totally new thought, a novelty. He slipped out of bed, picking up his clothes and shutting the door very gently so as not to disturb her.

He hoped that the diesel-stoked roar of the Jeep's engine wouldn't rouse her, but then reasoned that she'd assume he was going for the papers. They always had the *Independent* and the *Mail* – one to stimulate the brain cells, the other to catch up on gossip and for the recipes and fashion in *You* magazine. But he sailed straight past the post office, which opened for two hours on a Sunday morning to flog papers and croissants, and straight on into Eldenbury, where he sought out James's and Caroline's house. There it was – a magnificent building fronting on to the tail-end of the high street. It was split into two, one half shop, one half residence. So carried away was he by his spontaneity that it was only when he was on the doorstep banging on the knocker that he wondered if ten o'clock was too early, but then he remembered they had a baby. They were bound to have been up for hours.

Caroline answered the door. Barney looked apologetic. 'I'm sorry to disturb you –'

She waved him in gaily, seemingly unperturbed and not needing any explanation for his arrival.

'Come in, come in. James is up and out already – he's gone to value some old bat's paintings. Left me holding my head and the baby. Why didn't anybody tell me to stop drinking last night?'

She looked at him in mock outrage. She didn't seem to be in too much agony, but he would hardly have recognized her as the vampish sex kitten from the night before. Gone were the plunging neckline and the wild red curls. Her hair was scraped back in a scrunchy, she was wearing a pale blue sweatshirt, regulation post-natal black leggings and a pair of sheepskin slippers. There were suspicious stains on her left shoulder. She grinned as she clocked Barney eyeing them up warily.

'Excuse the designer vomit. Henry still insists on chucking up half his bottle.' She led him through into the kitchen, which looked as if a bomb had recently been dropped. Breakfast things were strewn everywhere; last night's saucepans – or, presumably, the night before's, as they had been out to supper – were soaking in the sink. The *Sunday Telegraph* was spread over the table. A row of empty Avent bottles waited on the draining board. Caroline grimaced. 'James will kill me if I don't get this cleaned up before he gets back. His woman that does says she won't do any more unless I get my act into gear. But it's like wading through bloody treacle, trying to get anything done with a baby. Henry hardly sleeps at all during the day. Mind you, he goes through the night, so I can't complain. He's an angel, really. Aren't you?'

She made a squeaky kissing noise in the direction of the floor. Barney looked down and what he saw made his heart jump into his mouth. A brightly-coloured ring that formed a baby nest. Just like the one Oliver had had. And in it, a gorgeous, fat baby with ginger curls, gurgling happily.

He staggered back as if he'd had the wind knocked out of him. He could barely breathe for the shock. He'd never got used to how it could hit you, suddenly and unexpectedly. He'd thought he was over it. Well, not over – you never got over something like that. But he thought he could cope. In public, at least. He still had the odd private moment, but he'd really thought he was able to function. It seemed not. It would teach him to be complacent, and judgemental . . .

Caroline was looking at him, concerned.

'Barney? What's the matter?'

Barney couldn't speak. A choking noise came from the back of his throat.

'Are you all right?'

Barney passed a hand over his face. He wasn't all right. Not at all. He was engulfed in a mixture of misery, self-pity and despair. Half of him wanted to scoop up Caroline's baby and have once more the feeling of a soft, warm, wriggly bundle in his arms. The other wanted to bolt out of the door and never come back.

At the sound of his choking, Caroline had rushed to the sink to get him a glass of water. She handed it to him, concerned, then watched in appalled horror as Barney broke down in sobs.

He pointed.

'We had one like that.'

'A baby?'

'A nest. For our baby.'

Caroline looked utterly baffled. Barney tried to compose himself.

'Shit – I'm sorry. You must think I'm a complete idiot.'

'What baby?'

Their agreement not to mention Oliver to anyone now seemed like a terrible idea. But the cat was out of the bag, and Barney found that he wanted to tell her. He took a deep juddering breath in.

'We had a little boy. Oliver. He died when he was six months old.'

'Oh my God.'

'It was a cot death. They said he wouldn't have felt anything. Just like going to sleep and not waking up . . .'

He said it to convince himself as much as anything. Many was the time he'd tortured himself over Oliver's last moments. For a second, Barney thought he was going to break down again, but with a supreme effort of will he managed to keep control. By now Caroline's own eyes were filled with tears.

'That's terrible. I can't think of anything more terrible.' She touched his arm; squeezed it compassionately. 'I'm so sorry.'

Barney smiled his thanks, feeling a complete berk. He couldn't believe he'd blown it like that. He thought the best thing was to say no more about it. A sudden thought occurred to Caroline, and she put a hand to her mouth in alarm.

'Shit — after everything I said last night. I had a go at Suzanna about her body-clock. Oh my God . . . why didn't anyone tell me to shut up?'

She sat down in a chair next to him, stricken with guilt.

'It's OK. How were you to know?'

Caroline looked at him.

'Nobody at the brewery knows about this, do they?'

Barney realized that Caroline wasn't the dippy mother come party animal she liked to pretend to be. She was sharp and shrewd, and he could tell the brewery's interests were very close to her heart. He gave a helpless shrug.

'Suzanna and I agreed we wouldn't mention it. It just seemed easier, somehow. We could start again with a clean slate.'

'Pretend it never happened?'

'Well, no, we can't do that. It was for Suzanna, really. She took it very hard.'

Caroline gave a little shudder.

'Who wouldn't?'

'I think she wanted the chance to start again. Be a new person. Not be branded as some tragic figure. I think she thought people would be analysing her for a nervous breakdown if they knew about Oliver. Either that or making allowances all the time.'

'I see your point. But don't you think it's a bit . . . duplicitous? Keith and Mickey not having the full picture?' Caroline sounded concerned.

'I'd be grateful if we could keep it to ourselves. Just for the time being. I don't think Suzanna would be able to cope with it being out in the open – not just at the moment. The move and everything – it's been quite stressful.'

Caroline agreed, albeit reluctantly. She also offered Barney a shoulder to cry on, if he ever felt the need. Barney was incredibly touched by the generosity of her spirit; it had been good to talk. And while Caroline might come across as a bit of a nightmare at first, she was honest and spoke her mind, which he liked, because he felt he could trust her.

He was about to go, when he remembered what he'd come for.

'I forgot! I wanted a puppy.'

'No problem. James will be delighted.'

'You can't move to the country and not have a dog. And it will be good security for the pub.'

'I'm not promising they'll make very effective guard

dogs. Their mother would lick you to death. But come and have a look. See what you think.'

She led him through into the backyard and into a garage, where a sheepish chocolate Labrador nursed a pile of squirming, splodgy fur.

Barney picked out the one he wanted. It was all one colour, the colour of Marmite. Which seemed like the perfect name.

'Marmite,' he murmured, and buried his face in the little bundle.

'You'd better take him today,' said Caroline. 'One less thing to pooh and wee about the place.'

Barney stopped off at the feed merchants on the way home and bought a smart wicker basket, a dog duvet, two stainless-steel bowls, a collar and lead, and a supply of the food that Caroline had recommended. The dog might have been free, but he'd managed to spend more than a hundred quid, he realized ruefully as he popped the puppy in its basket in the boot for the drive home.

When he got back he was surprised to find that Suzanna was actually up. She was in the games room, which they had decided to convert into a temporary headquarters and makeshift office. They'd been offered space at the brewery, but Barney was insistent that at least one of them should be on the premises at all times now that the demolition was over and things were being put back together. Builders and decorators could not be trusted to get on with the job in hand without someone breathing down their necks; there would be deliveries that needed checking; decisions to be made. So everything that had been dumped in the games room had been moved to the outbuildings and a phone line and computer had been installed, as well as a big table for meetings. Suzanna was sitting there now, surrounded by recipes and menus from rival pubs and price lists from suppliers. She eyed Barney warily.

He stood in the doorway, the puppy squirming in his arms.

'What's that?' she asked.

Barney walked over and bent down. The puppy wriggled happily on to the floor.

'It's for you. His name's Marmite.'

Suzanna looked up at him, her face a mask of hostility.

'I don't want a baby replacement,' she said.

There was an ominous silence, while they both considered the harshness of what she'd said, each of them shocked.

'It's not a baby replacement,' said Barney. 'It's a fucking puppy. I thought it would give you something to think about. Other than yourself.'

He turned on his heel and marched out of the room.

Suzanna flushed hot with shame. She was a bitch; an utter bitch. But no one seemed to understand how easy it was to be defensive; her reactions were knee-jerk, to protect her. If she didn't put up that barrier, she'd collapse.

The puppy looked up at her. His paws were ridiculously large, like a little boy wearing his father's slippers. He waddled over to her, sat down and did a defiant wee, not taking his gaze from hers.

'You little sod,' she chided, utterly charmed. She scooped him up in one hand and rubbed her nose against his.

'Hello, Marmite,' she whispered.

How could she have been so cruel to Barney? His face when he'd put Marmite on the floor had been so full of hope, and she'd slapped him down because she'd been taken unawares, because she was still labouring under the trauma of the night before. It had been all she could do to get up that morning, but she'd forced herself, telling herself that she had to struggle on against the odds. And then she'd ruined her resolution with a cheap jibe.

She didn't blame Barney for being sharp with her. In fact, it frightened her, because he was always so patient.

She went to find him, Marmite in her arms. He was in the cellar, surrounded by pipes and barrels and buckets and bottles of bleach. Suzanna swallowed.

'I . . . don't know what to say to apologize. He's the most gorgeous puppy and I don't deserve him and I don't deserve you and . . . you don't deserve me. I was appalling.'

Barney looked at her gravely. His expression was very serious and her heart thumped. What if this what it? What if she'd pushed him too far this time?

He handed her a big red bucket full of disinfectant and a huge scrubbing brush.

'Get scrubbing,' he grinned, and Suzanna nearly dropped the puppy in relief.

The night after the Liddiards' dinner party, Ginny had very disturbed dreams. Several times she thought she'd imagined a dark head on the pillow next to her, a pair of glittering eyes staring into hers and a deep, husky laugh. She woke the next morning exhausted, telling herself it was the rich food and the unusual amount of wine she'd consumed playing havoc with her digestion, because the bed was decidedly empty and she had on her grey flannel pyjamas. There was no way she could have got up to what she'd dreamed about wearing those. But it had seemed very real, and the images flashed through her head all day. What really worried her was – if it was her imagination, where on earth had she got all those ideas? She thought she was bewitched, that somehow Bertie had transposed his wicked thoughts into her head.

At ten o'clock she staggered downstairs to find the twins had been down to the post office for croissants. A thought suddenly occurred to her: what were they doing back? They were supposed to have stayed over at David's the night before. Sasha looked mutinous as Kitty explained.

'Sasha said something to Faith and she freaked. Dad thought it was best if he brought us home.'

'Poor sod. Imagine having to live with that neurotic cow.' Sasha spread raspberry jam defiantly on her croissant. Ginny tried to look strict.

'What did you say to her, Sasha?'

'I only asked her if she was sure it wasn't twins. She's enormous.'

'She's not that big,' protested Kitty.

'It was only a joke! Does anyone round here remember jokes? God!'

Ginny smothered a smile. Anyone not as neurotic about their weight as Faith could have taken the jibe. But she chastized Sasha none the less, because she knew that her mischief could come across as spite, and she didn't always realize how people took her remarks to heart.

Having devoured two croissants in the hope of soaking

up whatever alcohol was left in her stomach, washed down by an Alka-Seltzer and three cups of tea, Ginny felt fit to broach something that had been playing on her mind since she got up. It was a fragmented snatch of conversation from the night before – something she was trying to focus on to eradicate the images of Bertie kissing her, memories that threatened to turn her into a quivering jelly.

'You know I've been looking for a job and I haven't been able to find anything suitable? Well, someone suggested setting up an ironing service. What do you think?'

There was a small silence.

'I'd rather screw someone for money than do their ironing.' Sasha was emphatic.

'Thank you for sharing that with us, Sasha. Sadly that's not an option.' Ginny was brisk. She scribbled down some figures on a piece of paper.

'I reckon I could charge twenty pounds for a basket of ironing. Each basket would take me an hour, an hour and a half max. Two baskets a day is two hundred quid a week. I'd be my own boss. I could have the days to myself and do it in the evenings. Or if I got my skates on I could finish it all by eleven . . . it doesn't matter. The point is I can please myself. Do as much or as little as I want.'

Kitty frowned. 'It doesn't seem fair that you've got to work.'

Ginny was touched.

'I want to. I'd like a bit of independence. A bit of my own money so I don't have to go grovelling to your father if I want something.'

She noticed she'd slipped into divorce-speak, even though they weren't officially. 'Your father.' She used to refer to him as 'dad'. Sasha waved her knife in solidarity.

'Don't talk to me about grovelling. He is such a tight-arse. And do you know how much Faith has spent on her new pram? Six hundred quid!! I told him, he could have bought us a car for that.'

'Sasha, shut up. This is about Mum, not us.' Kitty turned to Ginny. 'Why don't you give it a go? You've got nothing to lose. And if you don't like it, you can give it up.'

Kitty was right. She had nothing to lose. She smiled at her daughter, grateful for the support. Sasha chipped in.

'I'll do you a poster. You can put it up in the post office.'

Ginny raised an arch eyebrow. 'I thought you thought it was a bad idea?'

'I only meant *I* wouldn't do it. No one would want me anywhere near their ironing. But you're fantastic at it.'

Ginny grinned ruefully. Sasha had always been the mistress of backhanded compliments.

'Come on, then.'

Galvanized into action, Ginny freshened herself up with a shower and got dressed, eager to get on with her new project. Remembering what Bertie had called her, she got Kitty to look out their old Beatrix Potter books and found the *Tale of Mrs Tiggywinkle*. She found a picture of the old hedgehog with a basket of washing under her arm and scanned it into the computer. Sasha messed around with some fonts and colours until they had a striking A4 poster advertising her services. Later, she went to a DIY superstore and bought half a dozen square wicker laundry baskets which she planned to issue to her prospective clients. That way she could control the amount of clothing they gave her: she was sure people's definition of a basket would vary enormously. They also went nicely with the image she wanted to portray – of a traditional, old-fashioned service. At the same time, she would guarantee to turn the clothes round in forty-eight hours. There was no point in giving someone your ironing to do if it just lingered in their house for weeks on end.

She also bought a new iron – she needed one anyway – and a new ironing board. She saved the receipts, putting them in a file marked 'Business', even though she probably wouldn't make enough in the first year to have to pay tax. But you never knew. She might not be Anita Roddick, but everybody had to start somewhere. Who knows, she might have a multimillion-pound franchise by the end of the year.

'You seem very chirpy.'

Keith beamed.

'Yes.'

He and Mandy were sharing mushrooms on toast, a sort of brunch as neither of them had surfaced until gone eleven. Keith had been lying in bed, having opened his curtains to the glorious April sunshine, trying to read the Sunday papers, but every now and again his thoughts had strayed to Ginny. He'd never warmed to anyone so instantly before. And Keith thought she needed looking after. He remembered the gory details Lucy had given him of her husband's desertion; having been through a similar experience, he sympathized.

Keith told himself not to get his hopes up. There would probably be a queue of people lining up to console her, not least the Dishonourable Bertie. Keith had watched him surveying Ginny with predatory interest, and he didn't trust him an inch. Bertie had sold him some bricks when he was doing up his house: quite a few had been unusable. This was, apparently, par for the course when you bought reclaimed bricks, Bertie had assured him, and the price reflected that. But Keith hadn't been taken in. That distrait, floppy-haired English gentleman act didn't fool him for a second.

'Do you fancy coming to Barton Court with me? Get a few things for the garden?'

Mandy shook her head.

'No thanks. I think I'll have a bath.'

Keith frowned. She seemed tired, which was strange, given that he'd left her lying on her bed last night flipping through a magazine. He didn't press it, knowing that he risked having his head bitten off if he showed too much concern. She'd been very moody lately. He wondered if it was late-onset adolescence: she'd never been a particularly stroppy teenager. And he didn't feel it was quite his place to go barging in, questioning her. For a moment he felt a stab of guilt that she was lacking a mother figure, a gentle, feminine presence in the house. Though he supposed that what she'd never had she didn't miss: his ex-wife Sandra hadn't had a maternal bone in her body.

The thought brought Ginny into his mind again. She seemed to be the archetypal mother figure: soft, understanding, but without being *too* mumsy – just someone that would always be there for you. Then he reprimanded himself. He was running before he could walk. And he was quite sure that Ginny, with a pair of twin daughters on her hands, wouldn't be chafing at the bit for another addition to the brood.

He picked up his keys. A mooch round the local garden centre would take his mind off things. He was going to look at furniture, now the weather was getting warm enough to sit outside in the evenings. He wanted a nice table and chairs, and perhaps one of those swinging sofa things with a canopy over the top.

Mandy breathed a sigh of relief as soon as Keith had gone. She wanted to be alone with her thoughts; pick over the events of the night before without being disturbed. She'd woken early, at about half seven, but had stayed resolutely under the duvet, clinging on to the residue of dreams from the night before, until she'd heard her father pottering about downstairs, dragging her reluctantly into the real world.

She'd got back last night just before her father – she didn't want to give him a heart attack, turning up on the back of a motorbike at three in the morning. Rick had been happy to drop her off, and just before she went in the house he kissed her on the cheek, touched her lightly on the arm and told her to take care, before driving away into the darkness.

He left her feeling bereft. And she wasn't sure why. Because in his presence half of her felt on the edge of danger, with a fluttering sensation that charged through her veins and arteries, like a deranged butterfly rushing from her heart to her stomach making her feel quite faint with longing. But the other half of her felt incredibly safe with him, as if he'd always be there to scoop her up and care for her. It was almost a fairy tale, as if she was a distressed damsel and he a valiant prince that was going to protect her from some evil. Mandy knew this was ridiculous, that there was no evil, and that if there were any both her father and Patrick would be first in the queue to fend it off. But even though she told herself this repeatedly, it didn't stop her fantasizing. She was haunted, possessed.

Not that Rick had made any overtures to her. Far from it. He'd treated her purely platonically, as a friend, introducing her casually to all his mates who hadn't made any assumptions, just accepted her as one of the gang. They all seemed to muck in together. And the girls had been as friendly as the blokes. They hadn't treated her as a threat, an interloper. They hadn't looked her up and down to check out her clothes. And Mandy wasn't used to that.

Over the past eighteen months, she had become used to being an object of jealousy, either because of her looks, or because she was with Patrick, or because she had a wealthy father, or because of her position. She never tried to rub people's noses in it, but she couldn't help it if she had so many of the things people wanted. And because of it she felt they treated her with suspicion and kept her at arm's length. As if you couldn't be rich and pretty *and* nice. And although she had security, Mandy often felt as if she didn't belong. It had made her withdraw into herself a little bit, which she knew probably made her seem standoffish. But she didn't know how to break down the barrier.

Sophie had been her one true ally; the person who she

could confide in, who understood her. She missed her dreadfully, because she could be frank and open and honest with her. For even though Sophie had been born into the very society that made Mandy slightly on edge, she had her own hang-ups, about clothes and her weight and boys, and sought Mandy's reassurance in return. And now, even though they e-mailed each other constantly, they couldn't share their fears and worries in the anonymity of cyber space. It was the sort of conversation you needed to have holed up in someone's bedroom while you painted each other's toenails; a cosy, sisterly sort of chat. And try as she might, Mandy hadn't found anyone else to fill Sophie's void.

The girls at the brewery, for example. They went and ate their lunch in the staffroom – Pot Noodles or Slimfasts – and compared notes on sex and weight loss. But if Mandy ever went in, a frosty silence fell. The unspoken assumption was that she didn't have to worry about excess pounds or keeping a bloke, so she wasn't part of the club. When she'd mentioned it to Patrick, he hadn't understood why she'd wanted to be friends with them in the first place. But Mandy wanted to be liked by everyone and was shocked when she wasn't, for no apparent reason.

She'd been thrown into a completely new world and wasn't at all sure of her place. By dint of her father and boyfriend, she was at the top of the pecking order, yet her position at the brewery wasn't powerful enough for her to feel accepted at their level. She was out on a limb, floundering, trying to establish herself and nine times out of ten finding herself chewing on a sandwich alone in her office.

And when she went out with Patrick, with friends or

acquaintances of his, people he had known for years, she felt a little bit like a fish out of water. They were perfectly pleasant and polite, of course, but they all had so much in common, had known each other for so long, that she didn't know what to talk about. Meanwhile, they all fell about laughing at in-jokes and talked about people she'd never heard of. She found herself sitting mutely at tables with a fixed smile on her face, trying desperately to find it all amusing and sparkle herself, but often people just talked over her or at her. Either that or the blokes tried to feel her up while Patrick wasn't looking. But apparently you weren't supposed to get upset about it, just give as good as you got. When a decidedly married friend of Patrick's father had propositioned her at a dinner party once, she'd been horrified. Patrick had just laughed and said, 'Typical Nigel.' If that was typical, thought Mandy, she didn't want anything to do with them.

The only one of Patrick's friends she'd felt really comfortable with was Ned. Big, solid, jolly, happy Ned, who would never have made a pass at her in a hundred years, and would have planted a huge fist on the nose of anyone who'd tried it on. But he was thousands of miles away with Sophie . . .

So meeting Rick's mates last night had been a revelation. They were different. They weren't bothered about money or what you were wearing. They just wanted to have a good time. Sure, they asked her questions, but not because they were nosy, because they were interested. And they included her in their conversations, valued her opinion. She was accepted for herself, not because her dad was loaded. And when they discussed their upcoming trip to Devon for a weekend's surfing, they begged her to come with them. Mandy had laughingly said she'd think about it.

All day Sunday, she couldn't think about anything else.

At six o'clock that night Ginny phoned Lucy to thank her for a lovely evening.

'How did you get on with Keith?'

Ginny realized guiltily that she hadn't given Keith a single thought all day.

'I thought he was lovely. He asked me to the point-to-point next weekend.'

Lucy sounded pleased.

'That's great. I'd have asked you anyway, but I'm glad you're going with Keith. He's . . . a very good friend of ours.'

She wasn't going to say any more. There was nothing worse than pressuring people into a relationship. She carried smoothly on.

'Which is more than I can say for Bertie. I'm so sorry – he can be such a nuisance. He's like a badly trained dog – you just need to give him a good whack on the nose.'

Ginny managed to laugh it off.

'Don't worry – I coped. I think I'm probably far too old for him, anyway.'

'Don't be fooled by those boyish good looks. Bertie's nearly forty and old enough to know better.'

'Hasn't he ever married?' Ginny tried desperately to sound casual, rather than delighted that Bertie was closer to her in age than she'd thought.

'He was engaged to the sweetest girl ever. Tor Lynd-hurst. She was worth about twenty of him – an absolute saint. But they didn't go through with it.'

It suddenly occurred to Lucy that that was who Ginny reminded her of. An older, slightly plumper Tor. Although in fact Tor would be nearly Ginny's age by now ... But she thought she'd better not mention it. She changed the subject hastily.

'Anyway, so you're coming next weekend. Fantastic. We're doing drinks and nibbles in the hospitality tent.'

'Should I bring anything?'

'No, no – it's a Honeycote Ales corporate thingy – everything's laid on. God knows why we're doing it, because I'm sure we can't afford it. But never mind – just bring yourself and a waterproof. It's bound to pour; it always does.'

Lucy rang off. Ginny hung up, wishing that she could have asked the one question she couldn't possibly. Was Bertie going?

Lucy bit her lip as she came off the phone. She was still furious with James for bringing Bertie the night before, even though the evening had gone well. But now the penny had dropped about Tor, she was worried.

Bertie had been a shadow of his former self for ten years now. Sure, he was still a rake, a tease, a party animal, but his heart wasn't in it. He'd never really recovered from being stood up at the altar all those years ago. All in all, thought Lucy, behind his merry exterior, Bertie was a tragic figure. In fact, he'd been dogged by ill luck all his life.

For years before he was known as the Dishonourable

Bertie, he was known as Poor Bertie. Not officially, but that was how he was always referred to.

His father was Vincent Meredith III, a hugely wealthy American industrialist who had come to England during the fifties and fallen in love with Christina Lake, a doe-eyed debutante of immense beauty but little brain. They had a whirlwind courtship and a fairy-tale English wedding, after which Vincent decided to settle in London and further his British business interests. Sadly, the latter took up too much of his time, and the one thing that Christina craved was attention. With her looks and her exhibitionist tendencies, it wasn't hard to find, and she became the life and soul of the London social scene. Their mantelpiece was thick with invitations and inevitably Christina went unescorted. There was talk of if not affairs, then at least dalliances with any number of men. She had been a bombshell before her marriage but now, with a large disposable income at her fingertips, she dressed to kill, setting trends and then moving on, always the subject of gossip and the centre of attention, a breathtaking butterfly.

There was a slight hiatus in her socializing when Bertie was born, but she was soon back in the fray. Only this time her joie de vivre was bolstered up by a combination of pills and booze. Giving birth had messed up her system: she couldn't achieve her previous high without help, resulting in a number of faux pas. Unable to control her medication, she either went way over the top and became aggressive rather than outrageous, or collapsed and passed out.

Eventually some kind soul had a word with Vincent. His wife was becoming a laughing stock; people were no longer willing to make allowances. What had once been amusing behaviour was now painfully embarrassing. Vincent decided that the only answer was to remove Christina from the environment which provided her social life, and bought a massive pile in the Cotswold countryside, to which the Merediths decamped.

Christina wilted in the country. It held no interest for her. She didn't know a soul, didn't want to hunt, didn't want to play lady of the manor. Bertie remembered her drifting unhappily like a ghost around the house, smoking cigarette after cigarette. Sometimes she fell asleep on the sofa with one alight, and he would have to take it out of her hand, stubbing it out carefully in the fireplace. Life with his mother was a roller-coaster ride. Sometimes she didn't get up till lunchtime. Sometimes she didn't get up at all. But on one of her good days, she might button him up in his best coat and call a taxi to take them to the train station, where she would get them on the first train to Paddington. They'd go and spend the day at Harrods, where Bertie would be put in the care of one of the waiters in the restaurant and eat Knickerbocker Glories, while she tried on dress after dress. They'd rush home later, laden with carrier bags for her, and humbugs and liquorice from the Food Hall for him, just in time for her to hide her purchases in the wardrobe before Vincent got back, usually on the next train. For he was trying his very best to be attentive.

But there was nowhere for Christina to wear her pretty dresses.

It was a frosty morning, about ten o'clock, three days into the school holidays one Christmas, when Bertie had crept into her room with a tray of tea and shortbread, hoping that she'd wake up in a good mood and that he could persuade her to go and pick holly. Sometimes she was brilliant fun and would smother him in attention and it would be kisses and laughter all the way. And she'd been good so far this holiday. Plus Bertie had heard on the radio that it might snow. He loved the thought of his mother, wrapped up in one of her glorious furs, taking him tobogganing.

The room smelled close and fusty. The curtains were so heavy that it might as well be dead of night. He knew his father hadn't slept in here, as he'd seen him come out of one of the spare rooms earlier that morning, doing up his cufflinks. Bertie drew back one curtain very carefully, just enough to see what he was doing but not enough to dazzle Christina. He took in a sharp breath. The promised snow was falling, thick flakes that were absolutely, definitely sticking to the ground.

He tiptoed very quietly to the bed and balanced the tray on the bedside table. In doing so he knocked over a bottle, but it didn't matter – the bottle was empty so no damage done.

He leaned over to see if she was awake. She looked beautiful, her long lashes resting on her cheeks. But very pale.

'Mummy? Mummy! You'll never guess what!'

She wouldn't be cross with him for waking her. Not if it was snowing . . .

For the next few weeks, all the adults seemed to do was whisper in front of him. Should he go to the funeral? Where should he go on Christmas Day? Should he go back to school? And from then on, he was known as Poor Bertie. All he knew was that a light had gone out in his life. And that the smell of Chanel made him feel sick, sick, sick . . . He'd stolen a bottle from her bedroom, before it was cleared out, and when he wanted to remember her, he took off the lid and sniffed. It was as if she was there in the room with him. He could reach out and touch her curls, her lips . . .

Thirty years later, the smell of Chanel still haunted him. He'd scraped through school; there was no hope of him getting into a decent university. His father despaired of him and, wanting to go back to his native America, struck a deal with Bertie. He gave him the Dower House belonging to his Cotswold estate – the rest of which he sold off – twenty thousand pounds to invest in a business and a small annual income. That way his conscience was salved – whatever happened, Bertie had enough to live on – so Vincent flew back to Chicago with impunity.

To his credit, Bertie proved to be quite entrepreneurial. With the money his father had given him, he invested in a mobile disco with two turntables and a huge collection of records and made a packet DJing at society parties. The business grew and he ended up with two marquees which he hired out and a diary packed full of bookings which gave him access to a stream of pretty girls. By the end of the eighties he was pretty much partied out – cocaine, champagne and coitus uninterruptus. Most people were convinced that he'd end up killing himself. He never quite seemed to know when to stop. His driving licence had been taken away, he'd been banned from most pubs and clubs in London, even those that tolerated the most obnoxious behaviour. He seemed determined to burn himself out. And then one night he was hired to do a twenty-first for a stockbroker's daughter in Putney. Where he met the birthday girl's older sister and was knocked off his feet.

Tor Lyndhurst was jolly, sensible and pretty in a plump English rose sort of way, but with appalling milk-bottle legs and no dress sense to speak of – totally removed from Bertie's usual anorexic fashion victim. She was the sort of girl who'd never forget to pack a corkscrew on a picnic, who always wore white knickers because she thought black ones were rather slutty, who always posted her thank you letters exactly two days after a social occasion. But for all that, she was good fun and a great sport, tolerating appalling behaviour and high spirits without actually joining in herself.

She seemed the most unlikely person for Bertie to fall in love with. And he'd never fallen in love before. He'd told every woman he'd ever touched to expect nothing from him. And he was true to his word. He never phoned, never remembered a birthday or even a social engagement. He lived for the moment, and seemed to have no memory of anything that had gone on in the past. Whether that was through choice or drug abuse, no one could be sure. It didn't seem to harm his social life, though. When all was said and done, Bertie was amazing company. People wanted to be with him. And, of course, he was incredibly generous.

Perhaps it was because she was the total antithesis of his mother. Perhaps it was because she was the only girl who didn't look at him longingly and decide that she could change him. But Tor was the first girl Bertie ever telephoned to ask out on a date. The first girl to receive flowers from him.

She was certainly the first girl he'd ever asked to marry.

Tor kept Bertie at arm's length for months, knowing instinctively that he was trouble and utterly convinced that he would get bored of the novelty. But he didn't. His devotion grew and grew, and in the meantime, Tor laid down some ground rules. He wasn't to touch drugs for as long as he expected to remain with her. Drinking she didn't have a problem with, but he wasn't to drive whilst drunk. She wasn't a party-pooper, she insisted. It was merely a question of survival. To many people's amazement, Bertie cleaned up his act. To many people's annoyance, as well, because when he was charged with drink and drugs he tended to pick up bills, in bars and restaurants. It was a miraculous transformation.

And he spent more time at the Dower House. It was the prettiest little Strawberry Hill Gothick cottage, set in about two acres of grounds. It had been shut up for most of the time while Bertie rampaged around London, but now he opened it up again and was gratified at how charming it was. It had been furnished with antiques his father had sent over from the big house before he left for America; not the really valuable stuff, but some good pieces, some pretty paintings. Between them, he and Tor lovingly restored it, until Bertie found he preferred the Dower House to his flat in London and could never wait till the weekend to hit the A40.

It was Tor's idea for him to set up in reclamation. The nation was just beginning its obsession with renovation and doing up the Dower House had given Bertie a taste for hunting down authentic building materials. It was a business that went from strength to strength. Eventually he sub-let his Fulham flat and decamped permanently to the Cotswolds, striving to build up the business into something that would support a wife and, perhaps eventually, children. It proved to be right time, right place, and he had the knack, built up the contacts, developed a nose for sniffing out places on the verge of demolition and subsequently finding clients that were in need of bricks, tiles, gateposts, window frames. He secured himself the yard next to the railway station in Eldenbury and soon his stock was leaving the yard almost before it was unloaded from the fleet of trucks he'd purchased.

He took Tor up in a hot-air balloon to ask her to marry him. Incredibly corny, he knew, but Bertie had never made many romantic gestures before so he tended now to go over the top. She knew it was serious because he gave her his mother's engagement ring, a beautiful square-cut diamond, and he cried when she said yes, held on to her and promised her the world, everlasting love, babies, devotion, anything she wanted. She laughed and asked him to give up smoking. He tossed his packet of Dunhill over the side of the balloon.

Tor wasn't the sort of girl who liked a fuss. She knew what suited her and that she was the best person to do it. Most of the girls she knew had legions of beauticians and hairdressers on their wedding day, but she chose to do her make-up herself. Professionals always tried to push you into something you didn't want, like lip-liner and powder, which Tor found always added about ten years to her. She was naturally pretty; she didn't need much artifice. She just needed someone to help her put the pins in her hair before she put the veil on.

She sat at her dressing table for the last time as Miss Lyndhurst and admired her reflection. Bertie was going to love her underwear – a laced-up corset that was going to need pulling tighter than tight before she put on her dress. She'd had it specially made to measure to enhance her cleavage and minimize her waist. It killed, but it was only for a day. The most important day of her life.

Her mother knocked on the door. A parcel had arrived by Federal Express, addressed to the bride. Tor supposed it must be a present from someone who couldn't make it; she racked her brains but she couldn't think who. There was no clue. Just an oblong box, beautifully wrapped in gold tissue. Inside was a photo album covered in cream leather – a wedding album. Tor opened it and was puzzled to see there were already photos inside.

The first page bore a photo of Bertie smiling – she recognized his suit as the one he'd worn on his stag night. And sure enough, in black italic calligraphy someone had written on the fly page 'Bertie's stag night'. She thought it was a lovely idea – it must be from one of the other stags who'd seen fit to bring a camera and actually managed to stay vertical in order to take pictures.

There were pictures of all the boys at dinner.

Bertie giving a speech.

Bertie proposing a toast.

Bertie doing a line of coke . . .

The next picture was taken at a wider angle. Tor could see now that the line of coke was on someone's stomach. The next picture revealed that it belonged to a beautiful, stark naked girl. The next revealed yet another girl, poised beside Bertie, ready to do another line that had already been chopped up.

Tor dropped the album as if it was made of coals.

She looked in the mirror and realized that the next time she looked in it, she would still be Miss Lyndhurst. For the rest of her life, probably. She felt her heart break as she slipped out of her underwear and into her dressing gown, then called down to her mother.

Lucy thought back to the wedding day, more than ten years ago now. Bertie and James had long been friends. They'd been at prep school together and James had been appointed by the housemaster to keep an eye on Bertie when his mother had died, and James, being an honourable sort of chap even then, had been a stalwart. They mucked around on ponies together in the holidays when they were young, then hunted girls together throughout their adolescence. They were total opposites, with Bertie egging James on to be more daring, and James holding Bertie back from his wilder antics. They complemented each other beautifully.

When Bertie decamped to London, James often stayed with him; he shared his flat during his stint at Sotheby's and dropped by in later years whenever he was on a buying trip, often finding he didn't go back home to Honeycote for days. And now, their businesses were similar but not in direct competition, so they often helped each other out with tips and contacts, went off to auctions and country house sales together.

They'd all been invited to the wedding – James and Mickey and Lucy. It had been a beautiful day, the sunlight dancing on the Thames as they drove through Putney to the church.

Where they waited. And waited. And waited. Finally Tor's mother had arrived, pale with shock, and the silent word had been passed around. The wedding was off.

Lucy didn't think Bertie had ever really recovered. But it had been his own fault. He was drawn to trouble like a moth to a flame. He couldn't help himself and so he had paid the price. She didn't like to think what damage being jilted had done him. The life he led now was a mass of contradictions. He'd go off to London on binges for weeks on end and come back to the Cotswolds looking ravaged. Or he'd have wild parties at the Dower House, when his friends from London would come down and trash the place. Lucy didn't have to guess at what went on because Bertie shared a cleaning lady, Mrs Titcombe, with James, and she would report the damage back to him in wide-eyed outrage. The last straw had come when she'd found two people copulating on the billiard table one morning. Bertie had found it funny until she had refused to clean for him any longer.

Bertie also had a darker side. Often, after he'd partied for weeks on end, he would become a recluse, locking himself up in the Dower House, not coming out for days, not answering the phone even though it was obvious he was there. Lucy privately suspected these were the times when he went cold turkey. Bertie had never used drugs in front of her, but she was no fool. After all, there was an awful lot he probably wanted to forget. But it seemed he had just enough sense, just enough self-control, just enough will-power to pull himself back from the brink every now and again.

So, fond as she was of Bertie, Lucy didn't want him to set his sights on Ginny. Beneath his magnetic, seductive exterior were dark, murky waters, treacherously deep, ready to pull you under. It was Keith who deserved Ginny. Lovely, lovely Keith who needed the love of a good woman. The further Ginny could be kept from Bertie, the better.

Though that might be easier said than done.

'You insufferable, arrogant bloody pig!' Suzanna was torn between absolute fury and desperately trying not to laugh. To add to her frustration, Patrick was standing with his arms crossed, smirking at her.

'You know I'm right.'

They were in an enormous fabric warehouse, looking at a bolt of sun-coloured silk embroidered with bumble bees. Suzanna stamped her foot, knowing she was behaving like a brat.

'But I love it. And the bees can be the Honeycote Arms emblem – we could use it on the menus –'

Patrick shook his head definitely.

'Twee. Cotswoldy. Yuk.'

'Are you calling me tasteless?'

'No, I think you've just got carried away by some overpriced material that you'll get sick of in six months' time.'

Suzanna looked at him with narrowed eyes, realizing with absolute fury that of course he was right.

'So what do you think we should have, Mr Arbiter of Good Taste?'

'The one you chose first of all. The plain, simple, tasteful cotton that actually goes with the paint we've ordered.'

'We could have changed it.'

'Go with your first instincts.'

Suzanna relented, despite herself, knowing it was her

turn to back down. She and Patrick were gradually devising a way of working together. They both had strong opinions, but respect for each other, which sometimes made for a battle, but definitely an interesting life. They'd worked on sample menus, agonizing over whether to provide free nibbles before the start of a meal (they settled on a complimentary basket of home-made breads) and petits fours with coffee (Suzanna suggested Hershey's Kisses – they were delicious, perfect with coffee, stylish – and one less job for her to do). They'd also chosen a logo: simple, squat, bold capitals with slightly accentuated serifs for the pub's name, and a slightly less dramatic font to print up menus, wine lists and general information. Most importantly, but boringly, everything they had chosen was priced up, ready to be put into the pool with everything else to go before the progress meeting next week, when it was all going to be either rubber-stamped or thrown out. Keith had made it quite clear that he was going to be ruthless at this meeting – no sentiment, no argument – so Suzanna and Patrick had quickly learned how to prioritize, how to compromise, and were ready to put their heads on the chopping block for the few extravagances they felt were worth it.

They'd travelled the length and breadth of the county and beyond. Today they were on the outskirts of Oxford and had sourced tiles for the loos and bathrooms, light-fittings and, finally, curtain material. Suzanna had to admit her head was spinning. Of course, she felt a little guilty that she had the fun part while Barney was doing the donkey work, but actually making all the final decisions was quite daunting – you never knew what things would look like when they were finally pulled together.

She shoved the bumble bees back on the shelf with a sigh.

'Let's go and have lunch.'

Whenever they were out on the road, they tried to take in as many like-minded pubs as possible. Though they usually only grabbed soup or a sandwich, they had time to observe how things were run, to get ideas, to see where mistakes were being made. Today they found a place Suzanna had seen reviewed in one of the Sunday papers. They ordered risotto, a dish which Suzanna firmly believed gave you a measure of the chef's capabilities. Soggy, salty, stodgy was thumbs down. Today's was a pleasant surprise: firm, buttery and moist. Suzanna had perused the menu, making surreptitious notes and firing questions at the hapless waitress.

'For God's sake,' said Patrick. 'Relax. We're ahead of ourselves. We've done everything we need to today. Let's just enjoy ourselves for once.'

After a glass of wine, Suzanna found herself winding down. They chatted idly, with Patrick filling her in on village gossip, who the main players were in Honeycote, who was likely to cause trouble, who was likely to make a pass, who was a lush. He was very amusing, with a wicked wit and a powerful gift for describing personalities. Suzanna found herself increasingly curious about him, and his dreams and ambitions. He seemed almost too urbane for his surroundings; not the type to stay put in a tiny village like Honeycote for the rest of his life.

'So,' she said. 'What about you? Are you going to stay with the brewery for ever? Haven't you got the urge to travel, see a bit of the world? Or move to London?'

Patrick made a face.

'I absolutely loathe London. Always have done. I've never seen the point of it. It's dirty, there's nowhere to park, it's full of thieves and beggars and drug addicts . . .' He broke off to laugh at himself. 'I know I sound like an old fogey, but I just don't get it.'

He went on to explain how London reminded him of his mother Carola, Mickey's first wife, and the hideous early years of his life he'd spent living with her in hippy squalour, before Mickey had brought him back to Honeycote House. Once Mickey had married Lucy, Patrick's little life had been transformed to something resembling a small boy's heaven. Proper food, puppies, ponies, hide and seek. Then sisters: a proper family! Patrick had wanted to cling on to this paradise, always fearing he might be sent back to a world of lentils and hand-me-downs and the stench of patchouli. With the result that here he still was.

Suzanna forked up the last of her risotto thoughtfully.

'I suppose Honeycote is pretty idyllic. Why would anyone ever want to leave? And your family is fantastic – they've just got it so right.'

Patrick hesitated, not sure whether to tell her the truth. That life in Honeycote wasn't always what it seemed. That bad things happened. Why disillusion her? But then, he reasoned, it was only fair that she should know the history; have all the cards. They were all putting their arses on the line with the Honeycote Arms, and Patrick thought it should be a level playing field. So he told of the turbulent times Honeycote Ales had been through last year, his father's affair, how he'd smashed up Patrick's car and nearly killed himself into the bargain, how Patrick had feared that Lucy would never forgive Mickey, that everything would crumble and collapse around them, that the brewery would go bankrupt. Suzanna listened, wide-eyed with shock, amazed at the high drama, unable to believe that the people she'd met and admired could be capable of such outrageous behaviour.

'It just goes to show', said Patrick wrily, 'that people aren't always what they seem. Everyone's got secrets. Some darker than others.'

Suzanna picked up the dessert menu and studied it hard. She looked up with a smile.

'Raspberry bavarois,' she said decisively.

She came home later that afternoon to find Barney sprawled out on the sofa with Marmite on his lap, fast asleep. The smell of freshly-cut grass wafting in from outside explained his exhaustion: he'd spent the afternoon mowing the lawns, which had run amok with the alternate rain and sunshine they'd been having. The scene reminded her of when she used to come back from catering some social event on a Saturday. Barney would usually have fallen asleep in front of the rugby, but would always wake up protesting he had only just dropped off. Once she'd painted his toenails pink as he slept, just to prove to him that he was lost to the world.

She wondered whether to wake him now, but decided to let him sleep on. He hadn't been out gallivanting in pub restaurants, after all. Poor Barney had all the boring paperwork to deal with. They hadn't appreciated fully quite how many rules and regulations had to be complied with when kitting out a restaurant or a pub – the Health and Safety implications were infinite, and Barney was a great one for complying with rules rather than risk asking for trouble. At the end of the day his licence was going to depend on everything being followed to the letter; they didn't have time to stand arguing with some official who was going to enjoy exercising his power for the sake of it. As a result of which, it was Barney who had to breathe down everyone's neck, making sure they were as conscientious as he was. Mowing the lawn had probably seemed like light relief.

She thought how gorgeous he looked, his bare torso already turning brown from his afternoon in the sun, his stomach muscles still firm from the hours he'd spent at the gym. His hair was tousled, dirty blond; his jeans faded, one hole at the knee. Suzanna swallowed, wishing desperately that she had the nerve to wake him with a kiss; a kiss that could lead to more exciting things . . .

Instead, she went into the kitchen to try and recreate the sublime raspberry bavarois she'd had at lunch. She thought with a sigh that this was the only way she could express her emotions these days: through food. At this rate, Barney was going to end his days fat and celibate.

13

The morning of the point-to-point at the end of that week dawned damp and breezy but with the promise of sunshine. Keith was in his kitchen, preparing his picnic as carefully as a surgeon preparing to operate. The *Best Opera Album in the World . . . Ever* was on the CD player. His brand new picnic basket with the green gingham lining was sitting on the kitchen table. He'd removed all the crockery and cutlery and glasses the night before and put them through the dishwasher – he wanted everything pristine.

He opened up his fridge and removed his purchases from the day before. He'd been into Stratford – he much preferred it to Cheltenham, as it was smaller – to the specialist cheese shop, where he'd spent a delightful half hour browsing and tasting before deciding on a small selection. He'd gone on to Marks & Spencer for smoked salmon mousse, custard tarts and a selection of red grapes, pears and peaches, which he carefully washed and dried. He slid neoprene covers on to a couple of bottles of white burgundy to keep them cool, then added two bottles of elderflower cordial. Everything was complete, apart from a couple of fresh baguettes which he'd get from the post office. He closed the lid and did up the leather straps. The wicker creaked reassuringly, the clouds parted and sunshine streamed into the kitchen. Lesley Garrett yodelled triumphantly. Keith adjusted his cravat, checked his wallet for cash and found his car keys.

He'd got at least another hour to wait before half past eleven, when he'd arranged to pick up Ginny.

If his skirmish with the dating agency last year had taught him anything, it was to try and enjoy his own company. He'd figured it was all he was going to get until someone else came along. Now, miraculously, he thought perhaps someone had. As he sat at his breakfast bar, fingers drumming lightly on the granite worksurface, he determined to play it cool with Ginny; not show any hints of the neediness his previous dates had shown him. Nothing was more of a turn-off. Confident but casual, that was how he had to play it.

He looked at his watch. Five minutes had gone since he'd last looked. He could make a pot of coffee, but he knew it meant he'd need the loo again when he got to the point-to-point. He fetched the paper, but he couldn't take anything in.

Confident but casual. Who was he trying to kid?

Eventually the long hand dragged itself round the clock. At ten past eleven he loaded up the car: picnic basket, plastic-backed picnic rug, two extra blankets in case it was cold, umbrellas, two thermos flasks – one tea, one coffee – binoculars, Wellington boots, four folding chairs.

Twenty past eleven. It would take him five minutes to drive to Honeycote, three minutes to nip into the post office for bread. If he left now, he should be exactly on time. He turned the key in the ignition and the engine roared into life.

Ginny woke up on Saturday morning with a feeling of luxurious optimism that she was determined to wallow in. The sort of feeling you had when you knew all your exams were over and you could start enjoying yourself, because you'd done all your hard work and you deserved it. It had been a long time coming, this feeling. There had been times when she'd thought there was no way out of the gloom. She'd never been in the depths of despair, exactly, but there had been a tedious nothingness to life that made her feel tired and languid, as if everything was rather too much effort – and pointless to boot. Ho-hum-ish, she called it.

But now she'd turned a corner. She'd had an amazing week and, she had to admit, it was all down to her. All those articles she'd read in magazines about the power of positive thinking and grasping the nettle and meeting challenges head on weren't just clichés.

As soon as the twins had gone to college on Monday morning Ginny had written herself a list of life-changing bullet points. First, she'd walked down to the post office and solemnly handed over fifty pence for the privilege of displaying her poster in the window for a month – though it was pretty obvious that nothing was ever taken down and that it would be there in perpetuity. An advert for two lop-eared baby rabbits was dated eight months earlier. No doubt they'd had two more litters each by now. Ginny stuck her poster in as prominent a position as she could without incurring anyone else's wrath, and was encouraged by the nod of approval given to her by the woman behind the counter.

'They'll be queueing up, mark my words.'

Then she'd gone home and, instead of waiting for the phone to ring, had thrown out every item of clothing that made her feel fat, frumpy or that she hadn't worn for the past six months. She supposed she should have done it before she moved, but she hadn't had the courage then. Her clothing had been the only constant, a protective armour that she had been reluctant to shed. Now every pair of greying knickers, every misshapen T-shirt, every nasty pilling fleece was either binned or bundled up for the charity shop. Then she'd given herself a budget of two hundred pounds and went, not to Marks & Spencer where she usually ended up, but to Next. Capsule wardrobe, she told herself. She needed a Capsule Wardrobe, to go with her new life as Independent Business Woman with an Exciting Social Life and the Promise of Romance.

She'd bought two pairs of jeans – one dark blue Capri style with a little slit just above the ankle, and a more casual, faded pair. Then she added two fitted T-shirts – one white, one black – and a crisp, white shirt with three-quarter-length sleeves and mother of pearl buttons, which she'd remembered were key items in any woman's wardrobe.

On the sale rail, she'd found a denim-style jacket in pale blue suede. The assistant had pointed out a tiny mark on one of the pockets, which meant it was reduced to thirty pounds. Ginny tried it on and was amazed. She'd been afraid she might look a bit butch, like an extra from *Prisoner: Cell Block H*, but it made her look incredibly feminine. She turned up the collar and had to repress a squeal of excitement.

The purchase made her reckless and she went madly over-budget. A trip into Monsoon meant a long flowery skirt and a cream silk tunic sweater. She inevitably found herself drawn into Marks & Sparks out of habit, but where else did one buy undies? Three bras and nine pairs of matching knickers later, she completed her retail frenzy with a pair of tan suede loafers which she convinced herself would go with skirts or trousers and so were in fact an economy rather than a luxury.

She also bought a pair of tortoiseshell-rimmed sunglasses, and was amazed at the transformation. She looked almost glamorous. She pushed them up on top of her head and realized they were just what she needed while her hair was growing out. Better than any hairband.

Back at the barn she hung all her purchases on hangers and stood back to look at them. She did what she'd seen in the fashion magazines, and worked out by mixing and matching that she had more than a half-a-dozen brand-new different outfits. All for less than three hundred pounds. OK, so she'd gone fifty per cent over-budget. But when was the last time she'd splurged? David, after all, had bought an MG *and* a new house *and* a new surgery . . .

On Tuesday, she'd phoned James and Caroline to ask if there were still any puppies left. They invited her over to have a look straight away. There was chaos at Denham House, with Henry roaring for a feed, but the Liddiards dropped everything to welcome her. James clearly relished the opportunity to slip away from the mayhem and took her over to the garage.

'I still can't get used to it. I lived on my own for too long, I think. But I wouldn't swap it for the world.'

There were two left, a dog and a bitch. Ginny plucked the bitch from the basket and felt an immediate bond. The puppy nudged her affectionately, wedging her wet little snout under the crook of Ginny's arm and refusing to come out while her tail wagged furiously.

'What are you going to call her?' asked James.

'Hope,' answered Ginny, wondering if she'd sound daft bellowing that down the high street if the little dog ever got out. But she didn't care.

On Wednesday she'd made an appointment at the beauty salon in Eldenbury, where a pretty young girl called Kelly had assured her that leg waxing hurt a *little* bit, but it was definitely worth it and once she'd had it done she'd never go back to shaving. Ginny was ashamed when she revealed the state of her legs, positively woolly, but then she'd always just had a go every few days with David's razor, and now his razors weren't around any more . . . Well, she hadn't been interested enough in her appearance to invest in one of her own. And Kelly was right – initially the sharp tug of having your hairs ripped out at the roots was agony, but the incredible smoothness afterwards made her feel a million dollars. Kelly had insisted on doing her bikini-line as well. That had really hurt, but there was an almost masochistic pleasure in it. Ginny, being quite fair and not particularly hairy, had never really bothered about the few stray hairs that had peeped out of her knicker legs, but once they had gone she felt sleek, groomed, *cared* for . . . It had been a long time since she'd felt cared for.

Then Kelly had shaped her eyebrows and tinted her lashes, which suddenly gave her face definition. Kelly had also shown her how to pluck any stray hairs while following the natural line of her brows, and use an old mascara brush to smooth them into shape. Then she gave her a facial, sloughing off all the old, dead skin and giving her once dull complexion a warm, healthy glow. The difference in her appearance made Ginny realize how much she'd neglected herself over the years, and she scolded herself for letting herself go. She determined to visit the salon once a month no matter what, and made her next appointment before leaving.

By Friday, not only had she lost a couple of pounds courtesy of walking Hope, but she had six people definitely signed up for her ironing service. And here she was on Saturday morning, with the prospect of a day out in good company. Keith had phoned the night before, to make sure she was still coming and to tell her not to worry about bringing anything, just herself. And Hope.

She leaped out of bed, showered, then examined the weather outside before choosing her outfit from amongst her new purchases. She decided on the darker blue jeans, because they were stretchy and forgiving and made her look slim, with the white T-shirt and the suede jacket. She knew it was important not to look over-dressed but she didn't want to look a frump. And she was delighted to find that she didn't. Her bob had grown just long enough to tie back. She looked quite young and quite chic.

At that moment, all hell broke loose. She'd heard the phone ring, but one of the girls had answered it. Sasha burst into the bedroom, outraged, followed by Kitty.

'That was Dad. Faith's got a twinge in her little toe, so he can't come and pick us up.'

Ginny sighed. She'd hoped to have the two of them out of her hair for the day. Sasha was gearing up for a fully-fledged tantrum.

'I wanted to go shopping in Cheltenham.'

'You still can. I'll drop you at the bus stop.'

'I haven't got any money. Dad was going to give us some money.'

Ginny put both hands up in defence.

'Don't look at me. I haven't got any going spare. You've emptied me out. I've bought you both top-up cards for your mobiles *and* given you spending money –'

'You spent nearly three hundred quid on clothes this week. I found the receipts.'

Sasha was indignant. Ginny managed, despite inner rage, to respond mildly.

'It's the first time I've spent anything on myself for years. And I've got nothing left.'

'It's so unfair. We're stuck here in the middle of nowhere with no bloody money and nothing to bloody do –'

'Come with me.'

'What – to a horse thing?'

Sasha managed to make it sound like a morris dancing convention.

'Why not? The fresh air would do you good.'

Sasha rolled her eyes. As if that made the prospect any more attractive. But as the alternative was sitting in watching telly all afternoon, she reluctantly agreed. Kitty consoled her.

'There'll be loads of good-looking blokes there. All those jockeys –'

'Dwarves.'

'Amelia Locke reckons it's a great place to pull. And we can get pissed in the beer tent.'

'With what?'

Sasha looked beseechingly at her mother.

'OK, OK. You can have a tenner each. But don't come crying to me when there's nothing in the fridge next week.'

Exasperated, and wanting to try on her new sunglasses without an audience, just to make sure she didn't look ridiculous, Ginny shooed the girls out of her bedroom. Then she sat on the bed for a moment feeling a tiny bit deflated. Bugger David. He should know that even though the twins pretended to be all grown up and not need their daddy, that they looked forward to seeing him. Sasha especially. She wasn't his favourite as such, but she had always been very emotionally dependent on her father. He seemed able to cope with her mood swings and had the knack of bringing her down to earth when she went over the top, or snapping her out of it when she went into one of her sulks. Ginny, who was pretty straightforward, found it all rather baffling and too much like hard work.

She stood up decisively. She wasn't going to worry. Why should she feel guilty because David had let the girls down? Why should she let it spoil her day? Shit, as Sasha was so fond of saying, happens. Anyway, she'd given them a perfectly acceptable alternative. Point-to-points were a vital part of village social life. They were going to have to learn to join in.

Wow, thought Ginny. I'm getting tough in my middle age. Positively selfish. And why the hell not? She grinned with exhilaration at the freedom it gave her as she slid her sunglasses on to her nose. She gave herself an enigmatic smile and admired her profile. Very Jackie Kennedy. If Jackie Kennedy had been blonde.

Totally happy with her appearance for perhaps the first time in her life, she pushed the sunglasses on top of her head as she heard Keith's horn tooting outside and flashed herself a dazzlingly confident smile in the mirror. Calling the twins and picking up Hope's lead, she ran down the stairs to greet him.

At the point-to-point, legions of cars were squelching over the hillside to park in rows overlooking the course. The beer tent usually got its licence through the Honeycote Arms, but because the pub was in turmoil and Barney's name wasn't officially over the door yet, the landlord of one of the brewery's other pubs had obliged. It loomed huge and white, reigning over a flotilla of smaller tents and stalls whose merchandise seemed to get more and more diverse every year. The air was thick with the scent of frying donuts and roasting pork. Queues were already building up for the bouncy castle as desperate parents tried to entertain small children who were itching to be let off the lead. The clerk of the course struggled with the PA system, which spluttered and crackled and cut out at the most crucial moment, as it did every year.

The beer tent was already full of youngsters back for the Easter holidays intent on catching up with all their old friends, and Ginny was relieved when the twins happily disappeared inside without remonstrating. She and Keith slipped into the adjoining hospitality tent, where Honeycote Ales were distributing Pimms and beer and posh chipolata sausages on sticks to a legion of invited guests. Posters and leaflets announcing the impending reopening of the Honeycote Arms abounded. Keith winced.

'We've committed ourselves now. I hope we hit the opening date. We're going to look pretty daft if we don't.'

Ginny felt a bit shy as long-lost chums greeted each

other, but Mickey and Lucy were fantastic at introducing her. Keith confessed that he, too, had once been overwhelmed by their huge social circle, but admitted that after more than a year he no longer felt like the new boy. And when Caroline and James, with Henry in a very smart all-terrain pushchair, came over and greeted her, and made a huge fuss of Hope, she felt as if she was one of the gang.

Bottles of champagne began circulating and were poured into plastic glasses. The aim seemed to be to get as sloshed as one could as quickly as possible. Ginny thought she'd better restrain herself. Then she thought, what the hell? She was going to let her hair down. She was in the mood to celebrate. She held on tightly to Hope's lead with one hand – it was the puppy's first time out in public and she was thoroughly over-excited – and accepted a glass of bubbles off Mickey with the other. It was all people seemed to do in Honeycote, thought Ginny. Swig champagne. But she thought she could probably get used to it.

Suzanna and Barney arrived with Marmite on a lead, eyes wide with the new experience. As city dwellers they were bemused at everyone's utter determination to have great fun in the rain and the mud, not to mention the breeze that whistled through your coat. Kiplington Hill was probably the most exposed spot for miles. It had been a gruelling week: by Friday, Suzanna had to admit she was exhausted and Barney swore he didn't want to see another paintbrush as long as he lived, so they were both looking forward to a change of scene and a day out. As they wandered into the hospitality tent, they caught sight of

Ginny, already in there with Hope. The two puppies bounded up to each other and started a mock fight. Ginny greeted them effusively, thinking they looked as overwhelmed as she had felt when she arrived.

'Let me introduce you to the twins.'

Kitty and Sasha, bored of the beer tent already, had gatecrashed the Liddiards' tent but no one seemed to mind. Ginny beckoned them over. Barney couldn't help noticing every male pair of eyes in the tent following their advance. They were as leggy as the horses parading in the paddock. Kitty was in what looked like her grandmother's petticoat, a faux rabbit-skin gilet and vintage cowboy boots. Sasha had taken off her jumper and tied it round her waist, defiantly revealing a T-shirt with red handprints splattered across her breasts and underneath the slogan 'Pornstar'. Ginny shuddered but did her best to ignore it as she introduced the Blakes.

'This is Barney and Suzanna. They've taken over the village pub.'

Sasha's eyes lit up.

'Haven't got any jobs going, have you?'

Sasha had always been direct. She didn't believe in waiting until you were asked. Ginny exclaimed in delight.

'My God. What a brilliant idea! I don't know why I didn't think of it. The twins are always moaning they've got no money and nothing to do.'

Kitty didn't like to protest that actually, she didn't moan, but she was used to being tarred with the same brush as Sasha. Barney and Suzanna looked at each other.

'We're going to start recruiting this week,' admitted Barney. 'We need barmaids. And waitresses. If you're really interested, come and see us.'

'As long as we don't have to wear anything awful. And you don't fob us off with the minimum wage.' Sasha's tone was assertive.

The twins agreed to pop up to the pub during the week and have a formal interview, though it was obviously in the bag already. Barney had to suppress his glee. The girls were stunning, but not in a stereotypical busty barmaid way. He knew as well as anyone that it was a plus to have someone easy on the eye behind the bar. Not that he was sexist, just a realist. A pretty face and a sympathetic ear would lure in those harassed businessmen on their way home from work; encourage them to begin the ritual of a six-thirty pint every night. And two pretty faces would be even better, especially if they were identical. What a novelty! Though he'd have to make sure they were properly trained first. The one with the pornographic T-shirt looked as if she could be a bit of a handful. But they had two weeks to go – he was sure he could turn them round in that time.

Delighted, he left Suzanna swapping notes with Patrick and went off to the collecting ring to look at the runners in the next race before placing a bet. Not that he had a clue what he was looking for, but it made it more interesting than just sticking a pin on a name in the form guide.

Damien wasn't quite sure of the point of the point-to-point.

For a start, it was cold enough to freeze your tits off, but no one but him seemed to care. He couldn't drink much because he'd given Rick the day off and he was driving. Plus he was looking after Star. He'd castigated Nicole often enough for being drunk in charge. He could hardly be a hypocrite.

Anastasia had pleaded with him to go to the point-to-point, because her friend Emily was going, and a message had been got to him from Emily's parents to join them for a drink. When he'd got dressed, he had some image in his head of horse-racing being dressy – he'd seen Ascot and the Gold Cup on the telly – but now he realized that his champagne suede jacket and cream linen trousers were laughably wrong. Basically, pretty much everyone was in green. Green wax, green tweed, green cord, green wool, green wellies, green hats. And the essential accessory was a dog, preferably something small and rough-haired or a Labrador. Damien *knew* he should have had one of James Liddiard's puppies. Once again, he felt a bit of a knob, shining out in his best bib and tucker while everyone else looked as if they'd put on whatever they'd found on the floor that morning.

Compounding his discomfort was the fact that he loathed gambling. None of the people here seemed to have a clue how it could ruin your life. He remembered finding his mother crying in their kitchen, when his dad had lost a week's wages on a dead cert. Her wages. Not his. His dad didn't work. He could remember having to fetch him from the bookies. The stench of fags you could smell ten yards from the door. The way no one looked away from the screens when you walked in, until the race was over and they went to collect their winnings. Or not, as was usually the case.

Anastasia seemed to bump into people she knew from school every few steps. He'd been invited for a drink from the boot of one car already: a plastic beaker of lukewarm coffee. Everyone had seemed very friendly on the surface, but the trouble was Damien wasn't really sure how to engage in conversation with any of them. He had no straight answer for any normal question. He didn't want to discuss his marital status, his business, his plans, his prospects. As a result, he came across as shifty and evasive. For the life of him he couldn't think of a safe topic of conversation.

He didn't belong and that was the end of it.

He'd belonged in the tower block he'd grown up in all right. The grim, grey monstrosity on the outskirts of Bristol had threatened to imprison him for all of his life, the very walls taunting him that there was no way out. He'd been crap at school because the school was crap. You could have been a budding Shakespeare or Michelangelo and you'd never know because no one was interested in whether you could write or draw. They weren't even interested in whether you could breathe. The day he'd left those school gates, with their razor-wire topped spikes and peeling paint, he'd sworn to find a way out. A means of escape for him and his mum. He loved his mother and hated his father in equal proportion. He'd put his mother on a pedestal and his father in the gutter, if he could.

And he'd done it. He'd done it because he had nothing to lose. Slowly, gradually, bit by bit, he'd built his little empire. And he'd become somebody. A face. Tables appeared from nowhere in restaurants. Bottles of champagne materialized. He had respect.

In Bristol, anyway. Here, less than fifty miles away, he was nothing. People smiled, but their eyes looked straight through him. They asked questions, but they cared not a jot for the answer. To them, his address said it all. Common as muck. Never mind that he had enough cash in the bank to buy most of them out ten times over.

He was roused out of his self-pity by Anastasia shouting with glee. She'd found Emily and her parents, picnicking out of the back of their Discovery. The Davenports were quite clearly the real thing. Sarah hadn't a scrap of make-up; her mousy hair was shoved back in an Alice band; she was wearing jeans, wellies and a fleece. Tom was red-faced and jovial and similarly attired. They were obviously both quite happy with the fact that they looked dreadful. Everything was scruffy: them, the car, the pair of Jack Russells, the picnic. They greeted virtually everyone who walked past, most of them stopping for a chat or a drink or a cold sausage.

Tom pumped Damien's hand enthusiastically. Sarah thrust an empty ice-cream tub full of curling Marmite sandwiches at him.

'We've heard all about Star from Emily. They're the greatest chums. Star must come over and ride.'

'She'd love that.' Damien thought it would be rude not to take a sandwich, and discreetly picked out the dog hairs.

'Poo?' bellowed Tom, and Damien looked at him, startled. Tom held up a bottle of champagne by way of explanation.

'Only Tesco, but it's good stuff. I'm not a champagne snob, are you?'

Damien, who only ever drank Dom Perignon, denied that he was. One day he'd get to grips with it all, he thought wearily.

'So,' said Tom heartily, 'what's your line of business?'

Damien desperately wanted to say 'tarts', just for the look on Tom's face, but managed to stop himself.

'I'm in the restaurant trade. I'm hoping to open locally soon.'

'Not the Honeycote Arms?' ventured Tom. 'Thought that was the Liddiards' lot.'

Damien just smiled and popped the rest of the sandwich in his mouth to stop himself giving too much away, tempting though it was. He thought about the flyer he'd found on his windscreen. Just over two weeks until the grand opening of the Honeycote Arms. He'd wait until they were up and running before he knocked them off their feet. It was a bit like that game where you piled up little wooden bricks – he was going to pull out the key brick, the one at the very bottom, and watch the whole lot come tumbling down. Then he wouldn't feel the need to prove himself to these people: he'd have the respect he craved.

At the collecting ring, Keith was trying to explain to Ginny how to choose a horse, and failing.

'Actually,' he admitted, 'I haven't got much of a clue myself. I think it's probably a bit of a lottery.'

Ginny laughed, and referred to her form guide, then examined each horse carefully, admiring their gleaming flanks, the proud arched necks, the flared nostrils as they champed, quite literally, at the bit, ready for action. The jockeys on board looked impassive, which no doubt belied the nerves they must be feeling. To Ginny, the prospect looked horrific: hurling yourself round a race course at full pelt, leaping over jumps that brooked no argument – physically exhausting and mentally terrifying. Why would anyone want to do it?

As she didn't know what to look for in a potential winner, and the form was gobbledegook, it was going to be either the colour of the jockey's silks or the name of the horse that determined her choice. Maroon and grey hoops, pink with white spots, emerald green – nothing seemed to catch her attention or hold an omen.

Keith pointed a finger at Merry Divorcee.

'That one did well last time out, over similar ground.'

Ginny thought that, although she wasn't quite a divorcee yet, the name was pretty appropriate. She pulled a tenner out of her purse.

'Ten pounds to win,' she said quite definitely.

Barney was going to put his money on What's Your Poison. He thought that was a nicely ironic choice for a future landlord. He'd put five quid on it. What's more, he thought, if it won then the Honeycote Arms would be a success. He was pushing his way through the crowds of punters crowding round the tote when he felt a tap on his shoulder.

'You the new landlord at the Honeycote Arms?'

'Yes.'

An incredibly rough and work-worn hand thrust itself into his.

'Jonty Hobday. I wondered if you were looking for kitchen staff?'

'Well, yes.' Barney was bemused. This was turning into quite a recruitment drive. Jonty, it emerged, was the local farrier. He had a foxy, freckly face and the haircut that seemed to be de rigueur at the moment: a number-two crop all over. Years of working outside should have left their mark, but his face was surprisingly youthful – only his hands gave away the fact that he was the wrong side of thirty-five.

He'd been hit hard by the foot-and-mouth crisis the

year before last. Determined not to let it get the better of him, and with a young wife and two children to support, he'd taken himself off to evening classes and got himself a City and Guilds in catering, then got work in pubs locally for experience. He'd long had an interest in food and had entertained friends for years with his gastronomic feasts. His barbecues were legendary.

Although he might not have a great deal of official experience under his belt, Barney felt he was just right for the Honeycote Arms. He could learn a lot from Suzanna, while at the same time bringing his own enthusiasm to the table. By taking over as chef a couple of evenings a week, he'd gain valuable experience and have the opportunity to experiment himself. Mondays and Tuesdays, when the kitchens would be quiet, he could keep free for a select number of clients whose horses he would continue to shoe. And who better than a farrier to spread news of a new venture amongst the wealthy set?

They agreed that Jonty should come up to the pub during the week to discuss terms and meet Suzanna, but it was as good as a fait accompli. They shook hands, just as the commentator excitedly announced over the loudspeaker that What's Your Poison had romped home in first place. Even though he hadn't managed to put his fiver on, Barney felt it was an omen. He dragged Jonty off to the beer tent and bought them each a pint to celebrate.

He was so busy toasting himself that he didn't hear the clerk of the course announce that What's Your Poison had been disqualified for overuse of the whip, and that Merry Divorcee had come in first instead . . .

*

Mandy was trudging through rows and rows of cars in her wellies, sticking flyers under the windscreen wipers to announce the imminent reopening of the Honeycote Arms. The flyers had been Patrick's idea; an idea that had been much applauded by everyone, as the point-to-point was probably attended by ninety per cent of their target clientele. But if it was Patrick's idea, why did she have to be the one who had to spend the whole day trying not to fall over in the mud? Her father had pointed out as gently as he could that doing the PR for a small company meant you had to be hands-on. There was no one else to do it. So here she was, with two thousand A5 leaflets to get rid of.

What was really bothering her was Suzanna. She was in the Honeycote tent now, with everyone crowding round wanting to meet her; she seemed already to have achieved goddess status by dint of being both easy on the eye and a cook. Mandy told herself repeatedly not to feel threatened. Suzanna's husband Barney was gorgeous for a start, totally cuddly with his tousled blond hair and twinkly brown eyes. Yet Mandy was still unsettled by the amount of time Suzanna and Patrick had been spending together.

Even more unnerving was the fact that she couldn't bring herself to dislike Suzanna. She'd had a meeting with her the week before, to draw up a sample menu for the flyer and discuss catering for the hospitality tent. Suzanna had been so enthusiastic about it all and complimentary about everything Mandy had done – without sounding insincere – and had demanded her opinion on several issues: paint samples and curtain material, whether they should have linen or paper napkins, whether they should have background music and if so, what sort? Mandy had come away feeling that her opinion was valued, that she'd had an input – the very things her own boyfriend and father denied her. So, despite having been determined not to, Mandy had warmed to her charms. Which was why she was so worried. If even she'd been seduced, what hope did Patrick have?

She sighed and trudged on. She was just about to put a flyer under a Mini's wipers when the passenger got out. It was Rick. Kelly emerged from the driver's side and watched suspiciously as Rick went to greet her. Mandy was flustered. She'd spent the past week fantasizing about bumping into him, and here he was, where she least expected him. He kissed her warmly on the cheek.

'Hey. Good to see you.'

She stammered a greeting.

'I wouldn't have thought this was your scene.'

'You're kidding? Beer, birds and betting? Come and have a drink with me.'

Mandy shook her head. It was far, far too dangerous. And she didn't like the way Kelly was looking at her.

'I'm sorry – I've got to get rid of all of these.'

Rick looked at the flyers askance.

'You might as well dump them in the bin. That's where they'll end up.'

'I can't –'

'You're too conscientious.'

Mandy thought for a moment that he was going to offer to help, but she could see Kelly was anxious to get rid of her. He asked her to come out later instead – everyone was meeting up in Cheltenham to go clubbing. She said she'd think about it then, reluctantly, she watched him go. It took all her self-control not to run after him. Fuck the Honeycote Arms. She wasn't anyone's skivvy . . .

She checked herself. She shouldn't think like that. You didn't get anywhere by thinking you were too good to get your hands dirty. Patrick would think even less of her if she bailed out. She'd finish off the car park, then go and join him and mingle.

When it started to rain she was at the top end of the field, as far as she could be from the tent. By the time she got there, she was soaked to the skin. A roar of chatter hit her as she walked in. Suzanna and Patrick were surrounded by a little crowd of sycophants all, no doubt, hoping for an invitation to the opening night. No one seemed to notice her. Everyone was royally pissed. Even her father, who had his arm round Ginny and was looking as pleased as punch . . .

After his pint with Jonty, Barney went to find Suzanna and report back. She was talking to a young man with tight blond curls and a baby face. He looked about twelve, but was in fact twenty-seven.

'This is Toby. He's running a wine bar in Cheltenham but he wants a change.'

Toby was obviously a bear of very little brain but enormous good nature. Perfect as a second-in-command, thought Barney. He could leave him in charge on the quieter days, perhaps train him up to take over one of the other pubs as they became available. He had enough experience not to be a liability, but not a threat either.

Afterwards, he laughed with Suzanna at their apparently staffing the entire pub in a single swoop.

'I thought this was supposed to be our day off. I've done more work in two hours than I've done all week.'

'I suppose', said Suzanna, 'that's village life for you.'

She was as high as a kite from all the attention and good wishes and congratulations she'd received. Everyone was talking about the Honeycote Arms: no one could wait for it to open, all eager for a decent place to eat that didn't mean schlepping as far afield as Cheltenham or Stratford.

'We can't go wrong!' she told Barney, her eyes shining.

'It seems not,' he replied, and for the first time since they'd arrived in Honeycote he began to relax.

Sasha was doing her very best not to enjoy herself. She was gutted that her father had stood them up that morning. She was sure it was Faith kicking up an almighty fuss and he'd just given in for a quiet life. Sasha loathed Faith because she thought she was vile to her father. Sasha was very protective of her dad in her own way – even though it didn't stop her being vile to him herself. But that was her prerogative. Faith didn't have any right to treat Dad like a slave. Why did he put up with it?

So she stropped round the point-to-point with Kitty, until she clocked Patrick Liddiard and her eyes lit up.

'Now he', she declared to Kitty, 'is a top bit of knob.'

She started to walk determinedly in his direction.

Kitty grabbed her arm. 'You can't.'

'Watch me.'

Something in her sister's expression set off alarm bells in Kitty's head. She scrutinized her accusingly. 'You've taken something, haven't you?'

'For God's sake,' drawled Sasha. 'You didn't expect

me to get through this bloody circus without chemical assistance, did you?'

'Where did you get it?'

Sasha grinned. 'Midge gave it to me. Told me to save it for a rainy day.'

Kitty panicked inwardly. Her sister was a loose cannon at the best of times; even worse when bored. Add to this the prospect of her being loved up and she knew she was in for trouble. Sasha was attention-seeking, with a low boredom threshold. She'd also fallen in with a bit of a bad lot at college – thrill-seekers with a sex and drugs and rock and roll mentality, of whom Midge was the ringleader.

Kitty wasn't a prude, but she was a little more cautious than Sasha and felt responsible for her. She was going to have her work cut out for her this afternoon. By the look of the majority of the blokes in the beer tent, they weren't going to turn down any offer from Sasha. Kitty sighed. She'd spent her life trailing in her sister's wake trying to avert disaster. Today wasn't going to be any different.

Damien had been standing in the ice-cream queue for hours. He'd finally reached the end, and was presenting Star with a luminous lolly encrusted with multicoloured sprinkles, when he was greeted effusively by Rick. Behind him was Kelly. Damien's heart did a somersault. He tried to find his voice.

'I'm surprised to see you here,' he said eventually. And he was. He was still mystified as to why anyone would voluntarily stand in the freezing cold watching a load of horses chasing their tails.

'Mum and Dad always used to run the beer tent. We've

come every year since we can remember. It's a hard habit to break.' Rick lit a cigarette, with difficulty given the howling wind. 'Anyway, it's great pulling territory.'

Damien didn't think he'd seen anything worth pulling. All the girls so far had been vapid, blondish country types who'd looked right through him. Not his sort of girl at all.

Kelly, however, was a different story. She was bending down, talking to Star, admiring her Barbie wellies. Star solemnly showed her the Pocket Pony Damien had bought her. Kelly examined it very seriously and had an in-depth conversation about all the accessories that were available. Damien observed her from a distance while they talked. His memory hadn't betrayed him. She was so *very* pretty, her big blue eyes like saucers. A pert little arse, in very tight jeans covered in designer bleach stains. Silver platform trainers and a grey jacket with fake fur round the collar. And a Planet Hollywood baseball cap from which were escaping yellow curls. She stood up and smiled at Damien. Perfect white teeth. That was good. He had a thing about teeth.

'She's gorgeous, your daughter.'

Damien melted even more. Anyone who admired Anastasia shot straight into his good books. The clerk of the course announced the last race, sponsored by Honeycote Ales.

'Come on – let's go and watch.' Kelly held out her hand to Anastasia, who took it eagerly, and they both scampered off down the hill. Damien followed with Rick, unable to believe his good luck.

At the bottom of the hill by the rails, Kelly hoisted Anastasia up on to her shoulders as if she had known her all her life. Damien took advantage of the fact that everyone was watching the horses to watch Kelly, her wide smile, the animation in her face, her total absorption and lack of self-consciousness. He realized that, in her own way, she was as comfortable in her skin as the Davenports, and he envied her.

Damien didn't realize that Rick, who was no fool, was scrutinizing him in turn. Rick was interested in what he saw and couldn't believe that a light bulb hadn't appeared over his head. Damien and Kelly . . . Why the hell hadn't he thought of it before? They'd get on like a house on fire. He'd seen enough of Damien to know that he was good enough for his sister. That he would look after her and she after him. He knew that deep down all Kelly wanted was a home and a husband. He disregarded the fact that Damien already had a wife. He was pretty sure she'd been painted out of the picture, whoever she was.

And a courtship was just what Kelly needed. She was working far too hard at the moment, trying to get the salon established, having to do most of the appointments herself as she couldn't afford to employ much help yet. Compounding which was the fact that she was so good at her job, clients inevitably wanted her to treat them over anyone else – she was much in demand. And Rick knew, because he was living with her, that she wasn't having any fun during her time off. She was moping because she missed her parents dreadfully. She had always been both a mummy's and a daddy's girl – they hadn't spoilt her as such, but she had a lot of attention. And gave it back too.

A date with Damien would bring her out of herself. He'd pamper her; show her a good time. And it might well lead to something else . . .

Rick told himself to calm down. He was going a bit

too fast. But what sweet revenge that would be. He allowed himself a pleasurable glimpse into the future. A glimpse of Patrick Liddiard's face when he finally realized that Rick was screwing his girlfriend and that Kelly was marrying the new owner of the Honeycote Arms.

The tables would be turned all right.

The queue for the Portaloo had taken ten agonizing minutes. Kitty hadn't been able to persuade Sasha to come with her, so she'd left her with strict instructions not to move from the beer tent. But by the time she got back, Sasha had vanished.

I am not my sister's keeper, Kitty told herself repeatedly, before setting off with a sigh to scour the race course. The sun had come out again, lifting everyone's mood, which combined with the flowing alcohol made it feel almost like a festival. She picked her way through trashed picnics, scavenging dogs and abandoned children, until she finally and miraculously found her sister being lifted into the back of a battered black Land Rover Defender by a cheering trio of ruddy-faced young men in moleskin trousers and checked shirts, all delighted with their catch. When they saw Kitty their cheers redoubled. They were much the worse for wear – she saw one of them look at her very dubiously, then back at Sasha, clearly convinced he was seeing double.

She tried in vain to get Sasha to climb back down, but Sasha was up for a party.

'They'll probably lace your drink with the date-rape drug. You'll get gangbanged,' hissed Kitty.

'Well, I'll have had more fun than you, then,' said Sasha sweetly, and slid the window shut defiantly.

Kitty sighed, and watched as the boys got into the Land Rover and revved up, wheels spinning in the mud. She supposed they were nice enough blokes, though the amount of beer they'd swilled had turned them into virtual savages. As the car lumbered off, she saw a sticker on the back declaring YOUNG FARMERS DO IT IN THEIR WELLIES. Despite her disapproval, Kitty suppressed a smile. Sasha would wig out the next day when she realized. Sasha didn't do Young Farmers. They were not her type at all.

She trudged back to find her mother. Keith was pouring her tea out of a flask into a china cup he'd got out of his picnic basket. Everyone else was making do with polystyrene. Ginny's eyes were sparkling in a way Kitty hadn't seen for a long time.

'I had a win. Fifty-four pounds!'

'Cool. What are you going to spend it on?'

'I've spent it already.' She showed Kitty a very smart plaited leather collar and lead that she'd bought for Hope. 'Where's Sasha?'

'She went off with some friends.' Kitty didn't elaborate. If she hadn't been able to stop Sasha, Ginny wouldn't be able to either. There was no point in worrying her.

'Do you want to come out with us for supper?'

'No. Just drop me off at home. I'll look after Hope.'

She didn't miss the fleeting look of relief on Ginny's face, and couldn't help feeling a tiny bit hurt. Ginny put an arm round her and gave her a hug. Kitty leaned into her for a minute, enjoying the warmth. She wished she was little again and they were still a family. It was so weird, Dad and Faith. And now it looked like Mum and Keith.

Kitty tried not to mind. Mum deserved some fun. Dad had dumped on her big time. Kitty still didn't get it, why he'd gone off with Faith. They seemed to do nothing but argue. And Dad and Mum had never argued, not really.

Sex. It was all down to sex. Kitty decided she was going to put it off for as long as possible. Life was confusing enough. She wasn't going to piss on her mum's strawberry patch, though. If she wanted to get it on with Keith, Kitty wasn't going to cramp her style.

Caroline was exhausted from pushing Henry's chair up the hill. She finally arrived at the Portaloo and was trying to work out how to get the pushchair up the steps when Suzanna came down.

'Would you keep an eye on Henry for a second? I'm bursting.'

She didn't wait for a reply, just flew up the steps.

Suzanna knelt down by the pushchair and looked at Henry. He was wearing a beanie hat with ears on it, his ginger curls spilling out. He stared back at her balefully as only babies can. He was kicking one of his bare feet up and down. Playfully, she grabbed it and was rewarded with a rich chuckle. She dropped it and he started to kick, daring her to do it again. She wiggled her fingers.

'Ready . . . ?' Again she grabbed it. Again the rich chuckle.

This time she didn't drop it, just put his fat little foot up to her mouth and kissed it, then blew gently on his toes to tease him. His little face beamed with pleasure.

Caroline came back down the steps and Suzanna dropped Henry's foot and jumped back, guilty, startled.

Caroline might think she was gearing up for some sort of psychotic baby-snatching. Then she remembered that of course Caroline didn't know a thing.

So why was she looking at her so strangely, with a mixture of sorrow and sympathy and helplessness?

'It's OK,' said Caroline softly. 'I know. Barney told me.'

'Oh,' said Suzanna, flummoxed, and was infuriated when tears sprang into her eyes.

'Come here,' said Caroline, and gave her a hug. 'I think you're so brave,' she continued, almost crying herself. 'I'd die if anything happened to Henry. I can't imagine how awful it must be. But I'm sure it will get better.'

Suzanna felt herself enveloped in an enormous warmth that seemed to fill her with strength. It occurred to her it was the first time she'd shared her predicament with someone her own age; another mother. After Ollie died, she hadn't wanted to see the other mums from her antenatal group. And she was the first of her friends to have a baby, so none of them really understood. But Caroline did.

'Tell me to fuck off for interfering,' said Caroline, 'but I think you should tell people. You really should. Especially . . .' She wasn't sure whether to go on. 'Especially Patrick. I think you should tell him. You're working so closely with him; I think he should know.'

'I know,' said Suzanna. 'It's just so . . . hard.'

'Hard?' said Caroline. 'It's a nightmare. I really admire you. I think you're fantastic, coming here and starting a new life.'

'I'm not brave,' said Suzanna. 'I'm just a good actress.'

'If it was me,' said Caroline, 'I'd be in the nuthouse.

I'd be drunk from the minute I got up, swilling down Valium and Prozac and God knows what.' She smiled sheepishly. 'And I'm really sorry about my big gob the other night. Every time I think about what I said, I cringe.'

'It's not a problem. Honestly,' Suzanna insisted.

'That's another good reason for letting people know,' Caroline went on. 'They can't go sticking their foot in it then. And I think they'd appreciate you telling them. At the end of the day, people are pretty good. They want to help. But they can't if they don't know.'

'I'm not sure,' said Suzanna. 'I don't want people to make allowances.'

But as they made their way back to the hospitality tent, Suzanna wondered if perhaps Caroline was right. Perhaps, by not telling people, she was making it harder for herself, having to pretend all the time.

It was certainly making it harder for poor old Barney, because he was the only one she didn't have to pretend with, even though she tried desperately to keep it all inside.

After the last race, Damien, Kelly and Rick watched Lucy Liddiard, as Honeycote Ales' representative, present the trophy to the winner. She was very attractive, thought Damien, in pink pedal-pushers and a sloppy sweater, and looked as if she was used to handing out trophies every day of her life.

He caught Kelly looking tearful, and dared himself to put a hand on her shoulder.

'What's the matter?' he asked, genuinely concerned.

'Nothing. It's just that Mum would have loved this.

I tried to get them to come over for the day but they wouldn't. It's made me realize that they've really gone.'

Damien gave her a tentative squeeze, and she smiled at him gratefully. He felt his heart quicken at the connection, and for a wild moment he wanted to tell her that if he had his way, this time next year the Honeycote Arms would be his, and it would be him sponsoring the race. And her mum and dad would be guests of honour in the hospitality tent. For a split second he imagined Kelly, dressed in an Italian suit that they'd chosen together, giving out the cup . . .

But he didn't say anything. He didn't want to jinx his plans.

After the point-to-point, a big gang from Honeycote Ales went out for a Thai meal, some to celebrate their winnings, some to drown their sorrows. Mandy couldn't help feeling hurt when she saw Patrick sitting next to Suzanna. She wasn't sure if he'd done it deliberately or if it was just the way the seats had fallen. She told herself not to be silly and sat next to Mickey, who she was very fond of, so it didn't really matter. But there was still a part of her that wished she had the nerve to get up and go.

She didn't, of course. She went to the loo and texted Rick back from the cubicle to say she couldn't make it clubbing. Then she went back to the table and made a half-hearted effort to eat her green chicken curry. The only thing that warmed her soul was the fact that her father seemed to be getting on so well with his new escort. Mandy thought Ginny seemed very sweet, though she hadn't been as enamoured of her daughters, who looked like a barrel of monkeys. Luckily they hadn't come for the meal. Mandy knew her dad would have ended up paying for them. She could spot a freeloader when she saw one, and Sasha definitely – though perhaps not Kitty – was on the make.

Patrick obviously felt a pang of guilt after coffee because he offered to drive her home.

'I think your dad wants to be alone with Mrs Tait.' He stroked the small of her back, sliding up her shirt and massaging the base of her spine with his thumb. 'Let's go back to your place.'

Mandy snapped herself out of her mood. She had to admit that, however beastly Patrick had been over the past couple of weeks, he could always redeem himself when they made love. They went up to her bedroom, and he was surprisingly tender, kissing her all over until she was weak with anticipation. She took him in her hand, desperate to be taken. Perhaps he could screw the thoughts she'd been having out of her, the fantasies that were becoming slow torture. After all, it had once been Patrick she had dreamed about, Patrick who had been so out of reach. Funny, wasn't it, how once you'd got what you wanted you didn't want it any more. There'd been girls like that at school, who'd chased after boys for weeks then dropped them as soon as they'd got them. She'd always rather despised them for their fickle behaviour. And now here she was, behaving in exactly the same way. But as Patrick entered her, she gave a moan of pleasure and wondered why on earth she wanted anyone else. Patrick knew just what to do to her . . .

Suddenly they heard Keith's Land Cruiser coming in

the drive. Mandy pushed Patrick off, rolled out from under him and reached for her clothes in a panic. Patrick couldn't help laughing.

'For God's sake – what do you think he thinks we're doing up here? Playing chess?'

He tried to pull her back to him, but Mandy wriggled out from his grasp. She was always funny about screwing him when her father was around. Exasperated, Patrick pulled on his trousers and they went downstairs to have coffee with Keith, even though it was as plain as the nose on your face what they'd been up to.

After Patrick had gone, Mandy put on her pyjamas and went to bed. But she couldn't sleep. She was still turned on by what Patrick had been doing to her before they'd been interrupted. She did something she'd never done before. She slid her pyjama bottoms down and put an experimental finger between her legs. She nearly leaped with the shock of how good it felt. Tentatively, she explored the silky softness, like dipping into a jar of warm honey, enjoying the gentle warmth that slowly spread through her loins. She was in control and it felt fantastic. Wicked, but fantastic. Several times she brought herself to the edge and pulled back, teasing herself.

She knew what it was she wanted to do. She imagined Rick's body, imagined him sliding off that tight white T-shirt and those jeans, standing in front of her with that smooth skin, those taut muscles, that tattoo. Imagined him taking her, wordlessly, masterfully . . . Mandy arched her back and gasped in shock as she allowed his image to enter her, inadvertently crying out with the pleasure.

She lay back on her bed, panting. It had been like nothing she had ever felt before. Was it because she had been in control of her own pleasure? Or had the experience been fuelled by her fantasy?

She felt a stab of guilt. Did what she'd done count as being unfaithful? Shocked by her behaviour, Mandy tried to sleep. She'd always been such a nice girl.

14

Suzanna waited until the time was right before confessing the truth to Patrick. She'd given what Caroline had said to her a lot of thought and decided she had a point. She and Patrick had put so much trust in each other over the last couple of weeks, it wasn't fair to pull the wool over his eyes any longer.

They'd gone to an auction just outside Birmingham, which was selling off kitchen equipment from several bankrupt restaurants and pubs. Patrick tried to ignore the hidden warning implicit in this. They bid successfully for several essential items: a heavy-duty gas burner, a coldroom, a glasswasher and a dishwasher. It was barely used, all in gleaming condition, and they paid well under half what they would have paid normally. They arranged to have the items delivered, then went into the rather grotty bar adjoining the auction rooms for a celebratory drink. They sat down at a round-topped table with an egg sandwich and a gin and tonic each. Suzanna took a deep breath.

'I've got something to tell you.'

Patrick looked alarmed. It was obviously something big.

'You're not pregnant?'

'No.' She gave a little ironic laugh. 'Far from it. We . . . had a baby. Oliver. He died. It was a cot death; about two years ago. That's why we came here. To start again.'

Patrick looked away, shaken, totally at a loss for words.

After all he'd confided in her. He'd trusted Suzanna; told her things he'd never told anyone else. And she'd kept a bigger secret than any of that from him.

He was abrupt at first, hurt that she obviously hadn't trusted him.

'Why didn't you tell us? Right from the beginning?'

Suzanna managed to hold his accusing glare.

'There wasn't any space on the application form,' she said lightly.

'Don't be flippant. And there was.' He quoted directly. '*Are there any personal circumstances we should know about?*'

'I thought that meant like bankruptcy or contagious diseases.'

'No! It meant is there anything that we should take into consideration.'

She tipped her chin up defiantly.

'If you think we've come here under false pretences, we can fuck off.'

'Don't be so defensive. All I mean is we're a small family business, who would like to think we cared about our employees. You should have told us.'

'I don't think it's any of your business. Or relevant to how well we do our job.'

Patrick sighed.

'Suzanna – I don't want a fight. I'm only asking about it because I care. About you. Fuck the pub . . .'

She pulled one of his cigarettes roughly out of the packet and put it to her mouth with shaking hands. He flicked his Zippo and she held his wrist to steady the flame; the smell of paraffin made her stomach flip. She inhaled deeply, praying the cigarette would calm her, that her voice wouldn't shake.

'The whole point of coming here was to forget. I don't want to be reminded. I don't want sympathy and understanding. It's history. Over. Finished. So forget I told you. I just thought you should know. OK?'

Patrick looked at her. He couldn't believe that someone so full of life, so vibrant and creative, could have suffered so much tragedy. Over the past few weeks he'd come to respect and admire her so much. She was so full of ideas and certainty. So enthusiastic. So definite. But without being dogmatic. She knew what she wanted, but she got things done her way without being a brat or a bitch or a ballbreaker. And she could own up to her mistakes, with a smile. He'd learned a lot from her – mostly how to treat people, how to get what you wanted with charm rather than force. He thought he'd come to understand her but shit – he obviously didn't have a clue! She'd been walking round with a big gaping wound inside her and he'd had no idea.

He felt ashamed. He wanted to know the real Suzanna. He didn't want to work with a facade.

'What was he like?' His voice was gentle.

'He was a baby. He was six months old.'

She shrugged, as if that was it. Patrick said nothing, knowing she'd break the silence. She looked down at the table, picking the formica at the edge.

'He'd give me baby kisses, when he'd stick his mouth on my cheek and not move. He'd just learned to clap . . . Fuck it – I don't want to talk about this. This is personal, Patrick.'

She was angry. With herself. With Patrick. With Barney. With Ollie. With God, whoever he was, the bastard. Hot tears shimmered in her eyes; one escaped and started to slide down her cheek. Patrick reached out and gently removed it with his thumb, then put his hand over hers.

'Go on.'

And so she told him. Everything. About how Oliver had hated cheese and loved avocado. About her favourite romper suit with the frogs on, and how he'd lie on his tummy and stretch himself out with a big yawn. About his giggle when you blew raspberries on his bare skin.

And then she told him about that awful morning that had seemed like any other morning. How relieved she'd been that he'd slept through the night, because he'd had a bit of a snuffle the day before. How she'd gone to warm up his milk before waking him … Then the police, the doctor, the social services, the questions – and the complete lack of any answers. The funeral. The days afterwards when the phone rang and rang with people checking to see how she was.

And the ghastly nothingness, six or seven months after that, when the phone didn't ring any more, at least not so often, and she was supposed to cope, go back to something like normality when, really and truly, there didn't seem any point.

At the end of it all, Suzanna took in a big, shuddering breath and looked at Patrick.

'So that's why we're here.'

She smiled, but her chin was wobbling furiously.

'Hey,' said Patrick gently, and held out his arms. He held her tight as she sobbed, stroking her hair, wishing he could do something more to ease her pain, but he was only human. And eventually she stopped, pulled away from him half laughing and a bit self-conscious.

'Sorry. I didn't mean to do that. But you did ask.'

'I know. And I'm glad you told me.' He produced a white handkerchief. 'Your mascara's everywhere. Here.'

She stood still obediently, like a small child, while he wiped the black streaks from under her eyes. She sat back down on her bar stool and Patrick ordered them each a brandy.

'You know what? I feel better for telling you.' She frowned as she realized something. 'You're actually the first person I've ever told about it. Everyone else I know was around when it happened. I've never had to talk about it like that before, from scratch . . .'

She took a big gulp from her glass.

'The thing is, poor Barney doesn't always want to hear about it. It was his deal as much as mine, but he seems to be able to manage better. I don't know if he does, deep down . . .'

She managed a self-deprecating smile.

'I think I'm rather high maintenance, emotionally. I think there are times when Barney would like to tell me to shut the fuck up and get on with it, but he daren't.' She stubbed out her cigarette viciously in the foil ashtray. 'To be honest, there are times when I'd like to tell *myself* to shut the fuck up and get on with it.'

Patrick couldn't even begin to imagine what it must be like for Barney, to suffer a tragedy like that and have to support someone else through it. He could see how needy Suzanna must be; although in some ways she was incredibly strong – steely even, when she wanted to be – there was another part of her that must need constant bolstering. He didn't envy Barney one bit.

'Listen – any time you want to use me as a punchbag.

I don't mind. I'd rather you took it out on me. You and Barney must be under enough pressure.'

He almost regretted it as soon as he said it, because although he was quite good at women and emotions and mopping up tears and being supportive, he had enough on his plate at the moment without counselling Suzanna. But it was all part of the big picture, he supposed. The last thing he wanted was her falling apart. There was too much at stake.

Back in the games room that he was beginning to feel was his prison, Barney was surrounded by paperwork and feeling somewhat overwhelmed. Invoices and delivery notes were flooding in from all over the county; you could trace exactly where Suzanna and Patrick had been in the past couple of weeks. What they didn't seem to have with them was a calculator: the amounts were adding up to a terrifying sum. Barney felt cross, and rather like their father. He was going to have to give them a good telling off. He knew Suzanna was completely hopeless where money and budgeting were concerned, but he would have thought Patrick, as the brewery's representative and supposedly the one keeping a touch on the tiller, could have reined her in a bit.

But then he knew how easy it was to be swept away by Suzanna's enthusiasm, how utterly persuasive she could be. It wasn't that she was manipulative. It was just that, when she had a vision, you wanted to be part of it. Like the time she'd been made chairman of their street's millennium party. It had started off as a simple celebration with punch and sausages on sticks. By the time Suzanna had finished, it was a full-blown extravaganza with fancy dress and fireworks and a sit-down banquet with champagne flowing. No one had demurred; they had all been carried away by her plans, and as the price went up so did the ticket sales, until people were cancelling long-standing engagements in order not to miss out.

Clearly Patrick was unable to resist her siren-like charms either. Barney totted up the invoices that had come in so far and went first hot, then cold. They were more than halfway through the budget already; the bedrooms hadn't been touched, the builders hadn't been paid, nor the decorators. They had food to buy in, and included in the initial sum was the budget for the opening night, where Barney had hoped very much to have free drink. That was looking increasingly unlikely.

He was up to his eyes in payrolls, VAT, Health and Safety regulations and staff rotas. Quotes and price lists were coming in for everything from tablecloths to cooking oil, each of which he had to assess and then file in preferential order. It was almost as bad as being an accountant. He told himself not to become dispirited. It was bound to be hard work.

What he needed was something to take his mind off it all for a moment. Actually, what he probably needed was a drink, but Barney had made a private pact with himself that, if he was to be the landlord of a pub, he wasn't ever to seek solace from a bottle. It didn't mean that he wouldn't drink to be sociable, but a drink on his own – never.

He walked over to the ancient old upright piano that had been abandoned by the Bradleys. Or, by the look of it, their predecessors. He didn't think it had been touched for years; no doubt it had been an essential part of the pub twenty years or so back but it had long been put into retirement. Thinking it would be nice to reinstate it at some stage, Barney had found a piano tuner the week before in the *Yellow Pages*. He couldn't quite imagine the regulars of Honeycote standing round having a sing-song, but perhaps some discreet live piano music every now and again would be an attraction. He wouldn't be averse to tickling the old ivories himself, although perhaps that was a bit hammy.

The ball-park figure he was given over the phone had made him reel with shock, but he'd gone ahead and booked it all the same. He'd funded it out of his own pocket. A piano was just what he needed to relax. He'd been missing his music lately. He didn't know why. He hadn't picked up an instrument in all the time he'd been with Suzanna. She'd probably be surprised to hear him play. She knew he'd been in a band, but that had just been posey art college thrash. He'd actually got his grade eight piano. His mother had made sure of that. And now he suddenly felt enormously grateful to her. Parents forced you to do things, and it took you years and years to wonder why, then it suddenly dawned on you that they were right all along.

Barney felt a sudden pang as he wondered if he would ever be a parent himself again. He wanted to be, desperately. But Suzanna wasn't ready to consider that possibility yet; far from it. How long should he give her, he wondered, before he broached the subject?

He sat down gingerly on the piano stool, his hands hovering over the keys. He supposed it was like riding a bike – you never forgot the rudiments – but he was bound to be rusty. He pressed a couple of keys and was delighted to find the notes were crystal clear. The last time he'd tried it, a hideous sound had sprung out, like an outraged cat that had just been stepped on. The piano tuner had done his job, even if Barney had privately thought he could have bought a new piano for the price he'd charged.

His hands glided up and down the keys.

Suddenly he found he was enjoying it. He broke into one of his old favourites, 'Every Time We Say Goodbye'. He played it slowly, languorously, improvising around the melody. And as he played, he became aware of a voice, deep, rich and smoky, singing the lyrics, wrapping itself sensuously around his notes like a fur stole round a film star's neck. The sound sent an exquisite shiver down his spine, yet he daren't turn round for fear of spoiling the moment. They were in sync, in tune, in time, and it was almost perfection.

As the final notes died away, he turned. One of Ginny's twin daughters was standing there.

'That was fantastic,' he said, utterly in awe.

She shrugged, a bit embarrassed.

'You said to come up and see you. About waitressing.'

'Never mind about that. Has anyone ever told you what a wonderful voice you've got?'

'I know I can sing, I suppose.'

'Haven't you ever done anything with it? Joined a choir? Or a band?'

'I don't fancy singing hymns. And the only people I know with bands are total crap. They just play thrashy metal – they only know about three chords between them.'

'It's amazing,' said Barney.

She didn't seem to want to talk about it. She was far

more anxious about whether the job Barney had promised her was still on the go. 'Are you still looking for staff?'

Barney remembered being a teenager and being constantly broke.

'Of course. I was banking on you. And your sister.' He looked at her. 'Sorry – you must get really pissed off with people asking. But which one are you?'

She smiled.

'Kitty. I'm Kitty.'

Barney looked at her thoughtfully. He imagined her in a long velvet dress, with a camellia pinned in her hair. Him at the piano, her singing. Billie Holiday. Ella Fitzgerald. Nina Simone. They'd pack them in.

'Have you ever thought about singing live? We could do jazz evenings.'

She looked a bit panicky.

'I don't know. I've never sung in public.'

'You could, easily. You're good, you know. Really good.'

She didn't seem at all convinced, so Barney let it drop. If she was going to be working at the pub, there was plenty of time to talk her round. Anyway, it wasn't as if he had time to add in-house pianist to his list of duties.

After he got back from the auction, Patrick started thinking about Mandy. For some reason, Suzanna's revelation had unsettled him. It made him realize that things could seem all right on the surface, yet have a hideous fissure underneath. And it seemed an ominously long time since he and Mandy had spent any time together on their own. He decided to go over to Kiplington in the Healey and take Mandy out somewhere. He needed a good night out; to get away from the claustrophobic pressure of organizing the pub and just be a carefree young man out with his girlfriend for the night. They used to go out all the time, especially when Ned and Sophie had been around. Somehow when there were only two of you it was easier not to bother. But something inside Patrick told him that he should bother.

He turned off left down a little turning that was a short cut through to Kiplington; a single-track road that was rarely used. It led down a steep dip into a dingly-dell of a hamlet called Little Orwell, which basically consisted of a rambling old farm and a few workers' cottages that had seemed to stand still in time. Not even a postbox or a lamp-post gave any sign that this was the twenty-first century. The sweet smell of cows and may blossom filled the air. It was idyllic.

Patrick was surprised to see that one of the cottages was up for sale. Someone must have died. He slowed down as he approached it, then stopped. It was the tiniest little cottage, totally ramshackle, but utterly adorable. Curiosity overcame him, and he parked up on the road outside, then pushed through the wooden door in the wall that led into the garden adjoining the house. It was thoroughly overgrown, but even Patrick could see that the vestiges of a very pretty cottage garden were visible through the undergrowth, wild roses and clematis and lavender all tangled together.

He was amazed to find that the back door was unlocked. Inside it was ancient. The whole house was only one up, one down – no kitchen to speak of, only a stainless-steel sink and an old-fashioned range in what could just about be described as a utility room. And there was no bathroom – only a loo on the other side of a narrow passageway adjoining the coal shed.

Round, old-fashioned light switches, incredibly heavy to turn on and off. Peeling lino on some of the floors. Quarry tiles on others. Tiny cast-iron fireplaces. An over-whelming smell of damp. The last incumbent had obvi-ously died, probably of pneumonia given the living conditions. But as he pushed back the tattered rags that hung at the windows, a ray of early evening light flooded in, filling the little front room with a golden glow that disguised all its flaws. It had a wonderfully welcoming feel. It felt like . . . home, thought Patrick, who was not usually given to sentiment.

Patrick picked up his phone and dialled the estate agent's number displayed on the board outside.

'You've got a cottage up for auction in Little Orwell. What's the guide price?'

A hundred and forty thousand. A hundred and forty grand and you could hardly swing a cat by the tail. The place needed condemning. It needed bulldozing. But then, this was the Cotswolds. He was paying a premium for the waft of cow's muck.

Patrick thought about it seriously. It was about time he had a place of his own. He was nothing more than a glorified lodger at Honeycote House. A lodger who didn't actually pay any rent. He should be ashamed of himself really, but living there was so much easier than . . . than what? Getting off his arse and doing something about it?

He wasn't a boy any more. He was a man. And OK, so he would one day inherit Honeycote House, but both Mickey and Lucy were pretty healthy, if you didn't count Dad's accident. He could well be over fifty before it was his. He could hardly live there till then, like some namby-pamby mummy's boy in a cardigan, heating up a tin of mushroom soup for himself.

It could be, quite literally, their love nest. He and Mandy could spend weekends doing it up. They could move in together, if Mandy felt ready. Or they could wait until they got married. For somehow Patrick assumed that would happen, even though he hadn't asked her as yet. In the meantime, they didn't have any space that was their own – she was uptight about having sex in her own house, and not overkeen on it at Honeycote House either, even though Patrick assured her repeatedly that Mickey and Lucy were very broadminded. And she wasn't the sort of girl you shagged in the car.

He walked slowly round the house, embellishing his fantasy. He wanted to wake up in sheets they had chosen together; drink coffee out of mugs they'd bought; go into the garden and check on the progress of the roses they'd planted. He nearly laughed at himself and the picture of domestic bliss he was imagining. He'd paint in his pipe and slippers before you knew it. And a dog! They'd have to have a dog. He wondered if James had any puppies left . . .

He told himself to calm down and look again at Little Orwell Cottage objectively. For about the same price he could get a brand-new three-bedroomed house complete with fixtures and fittings that needed nothing doing to it. But this little house felt special. Patrick was surprised to feel butterflies, and a sharp stab of something that was even stronger than desire. He *had* to have it.

He shuddered at the thought, but he could sell the Healey and use it as a deposit. He'd get twenty grand for it, no problem. And a mortgage for the rest. Though he didn't have a clue how to get one or how much they cost or anything. Their old bank manager, Cowley, would have sorted this out for him, pulled a few strings, but he'd recently taken early retirement. He and his wife were touring the Scottish Highlands and looking forward to a meal at the Honeycote Arms, it had said in his last postcard.

James. He'd ask James. James was sensible, knew about money, wasn't going to start any heavy emotional black-mail family shit. And Patrick had always respected James's opinion. He didn't want to go to his father for advice: he loved his father dearly, but he had no illusions about his business acumen. Mickey still, at the tender age of forty-five, had the notion that money appeared out of nowhere whenever you needed it, and that although a vague attempt at working for a living was necessary in this day and age, it didn't do to work too hard.

As his uncle and his godfather, James had always been fond of Patrick, and had kept a distant but kindly eye on the boy without being too proactive. But since he and Caroline had had Henry, he was surprised to find his sense of responsibility to Patrick had increased, perhaps because now he was a father himself, he realized that Mickey had quite a few shortcomings and Patrick hadn't really been prepared for life and how tough it could be. James knew Mickey was no angel. His brother behaved appallingly and irresponsibly at times, and if James could now redress the balance, he would. He'd watched Patrick over the last year struggling to grow up and cope, and he thought he'd done pretty well, though his methods were sometimes unusual. After all, he could have turned out to be a feckless wastrel. So when Patrick came to him for advice on Little Orwell Cottage, he thought the boy needed a break and offered to lend him the money.

Patrick was horrified at first. He hoped James didn't think he'd gone to see him in the hopes of a sub. He'd just wanted his advice. James brushed away his fears.

'It's about time you got a place of your own. You're twenty-four. You need your own space. Somewhere to . . .'

'Get my leg over in peace,' said Patrick meaningfully.

James grinned. He might ooze cool English reserve, but he was a red-blooded male underneath it all.

'Absolutely. Anyway, the point is, if it's up for auction in a couple of weeks you're going to need cash. Which isn't a problem – I can lend it to you, then when you've got the place and it's in your name, you can take out a mortgage on it.'

'I'm not sure I'd be able to afford the repayments.'

Patrick had been on the Internet at the brewery. It was a whole new world to him, but he'd been on a few building society web sites and used their mortgage calculators. On what he was earning at the moment, he could afford the repayments on a hundred thousand max.

'Well,' said James. 'In that case, it's about time I told you about the Maze.'

He pronounced it to rhyme with vase. Patrick was puzzled.

'What's the Maze?'

'It's a painting. By Paul Maze. The one I gave you for your christening.'

Patrick nodded. The painting had hung in his bedroom

for as long as he could remember – a brightly-coloured, impressionistic Cornish seascape with jolly boats bobbing on the water. He loved it – when he was feeling pissed off he always imagined leaping into one of those boats and sailing off into the sunset, into another life.

'I've been waiting for the opportune moment to tell you. I got it for you at an auction for next to nothing, just after you were born. I had a hunch it would come good. If I'd known quite how good, I might not have handed it over to you in such a hurry. I'd have bought you a christening mug instead.' James gave a wry smile. Patrick wished he'd hurry up and get to the point. 'Anyway, as they say on the *Antiques Roadshow*, Paul Maze is very desirable. I reckon it would get anywhere between thirty and fifty grand at auction.'

Patrick was stunned.

'And it's hanging in my bedroom? Shit, James – you might have told me.'

'You're kidding, aren't you? What with everything that went on last year, I didn't want anyone knowing the answer was hanging on the wall in your bedroom. It's *your* legacy, that painting. For you to do what you want with.'

James didn't like to actually verbalize his fear that Mickey would have had it down off the wall and flogged it before you could say knife, so desperate had he been. It wasn't as if the painting could have saved the brewery, only put off the day of reckoning for a few weeks, so he didn't feel guilty about keeping it quiet.

'I can't sell it,' said Patrick. 'I love that painting.'

'Be realistic, Patrick. What would you rather have? A painting – or a house?'

'But it was a present. From you. A *christening* present. You don't sell your own christening presents.'

'It wouldn't bother me, I can assure you. I bought that for you as an investment. OK, it's a jolly nice picture. But what's the point of a painting if you haven't got a wall to hang it on?'

Patrick was deeply uncomfortable about the whole proposition, but James, who was enormously pragmatic, told him not to be sentimental. In the end, they agreed that James would buy the painting off him for thirty thousand and keep the difference when he sold it on in order to cover the interest on the rest of the loan for Little Orwell Cottage. Patrick couldn't stop thanking him and telling him how grateful he was.

'I just hope you'd do the same for Henry one day.'

'Well, of course. If I could,' said Patrick.

'What I mean', said James, 'is I'd like you to be god-father.'

Patrick was stunned. James carried on.

'Caroline and I have had endless debates about it. By rights, it should be Mickey I ask. But I've come to fatherhood so late, he's getting on a bit to be a godfather. So we decided you would be far better. And I know Mickey won't mind. In fact, I'm sure he'll be delighted.'

Patrick was choked, and accepted. He adored his little nephew Henry. He was never entirely sure what to do with him, as it was his first contact with a proper baby, but he was charmed by his giggles and wriggles and never forgot to bring an unsuitable chocolate rabbit for him to devour or a noisy wind-up toy that would drive Caroline to distraction.

When he drove away later, he wasn't sure what to feel.

Little Orwell Cottage was as good as his. He'd got a painting on his bedroom wall worth a small fortune. But the overwhelming feeling was one of pride. James thought enough of him to ask him to be godfather. He'd never imagined that; not in his wildest dreams.

15

A week before the opening night, the Honeycote Arms was due to have a dummy run. First thing in the morning, Barney and Suzanna ceremoniously stuck the sign with his name on it over the door. They stood back and admired the freshly-painted black letters, proclaiming Barney to be the licensee.

'I'm so proud of you,' said Suzanna, because she knew how hard he'd worked to get through all the red tape, the stringent tests, and he'd had to do it pretty much all on his own. He hadn't had a partner in crime like she had, and she was sure it was deadly dull, even though it was the sort of thing he was good at.

Barney gave a sheepish grin.

'It feels pretty good,' he admitted. 'I never dreamed I'd see my name over a door like that. Pity we can't bugger off somewhere and celebrate.'

'Don't tempt me,' said Suzanna. 'I've got so much to do I feel sick.'

'You do realize that this is it?' said Barney. 'That we're married to this place, as of next week. That our lives aren't going to be our own.'

'Wasn't that the whole idea?' she said lightly.

'You're quite happy we've done the right thing?'

Suzanna wrinkled her nose.

'Ask me tomorrow. I'll have a better idea then . . .'

*

That day was also Mandy's twentieth birthday. She woke up feeling unusually flat. Keith made a fuss of her at breakfast: he made her freshly-squeezed orange juice and a beautiful bowl of strawberries and blueberries with Greek yogurt. Propped against her glass was a funny card with a cheque in it. She was a bit disappointed. Keith was usually brilliant at presents – proper ones. She didn't really want money. It didn't mean anything. She remembered how he'd bought her Monkey the Christmas before last: the horse she'd always longed for. It was the best present she'd ever had.

Keith disappeared off to work before she was even dressed. It was a big day for the pub, he said. What about her, thought Mandy? It was a big day for her too. Keith saw that she looked a bit disconsolate.

'We'll make a night of it tonight. At least you'll be guaranteed a good meal.'

Mandy thought she might choke on anything Suzanna had cooked. But she didn't say anything.

When she got to the brewery, Patrick gave her a card – one which she recognized as the line kept in the village post office. It was cheap and naff. She'd rather he hadn't bothered. He did have the grace to apologize for not having had the time to get her a present.

'I'm really sorry. It's just been so chaotic. We'll go out and choose something, you and me. After the pub's opened.'

After the pub. That's where she always seemed to come these days. After the pub.

Mandy felt deeply hurt. She couldn't help being one of those people who considered birthdays important. She never forgot anyone else's. She always made a huge effort to get them a nice card, one that was relevant to them.

And a proper present. In unusual wrapping paper with ribbons and bows. It was, after all, the one day of the year when a person was supposed to feel special.

She didn't feel special today. It was quite clear where all the attention was being directed. To rub salt into her wounds, Elspeth spotted the card Patrick had given her and examined it very disparagingly. Mandy wished she'd chucked it straight in the bin.

Over at the pub, chaos reigned and tempers ran high. There were still workmen crawling all over the place finishing off little jobs, which seemed to get in the way of anything anyone wanted to do. In the end, it was obvious the dining room wasn't going to be ready, so as a contingency plan they put some old trestle tables up in the games room. Barney didn't know what they would have done without it – it had doubled up as a boardroom, training centre, office and common room.

Suzanna rose to the occasion when all the newly-appointed staff, including Kitty and Sasha, arrived for a briefing. She was incredibly clear about what she expected from them, and what they would get in return. They listened intently – even Sasha. Barney was impressed at how she managed to hold their attention.

'We're paying you well – over the odds – but for that we expect total dedication. You are part of the package people are buying into when they come here. I expect you, obviously, to be polite and attentive, but it goes beyond that. I want you to use your initiative. Anyone who goes blank when they're asked a question and has to go and refer to someone else isn't doing their research. I want you in here an hour before service starts. I want you to taste all the food so you can describe it from personal experience. I want you to understand why and how the menu works, know without referring to me or Jonty whether something can be altered.

'I want you to look customers in the eye. Refer to them by name – you should be able to work that out from the booking. Remember them when they come in next time. Be chatty, but not intrusive. Be enthusiastic, but not false. Helpful, but not interfering. Attentive, but not pushy. If they want to fill their own glasses up, leave them to it. You can tell if people want their own space or if they get off on being grovelled to. You need to be chameleons, adapting to the individual needs of each customer.'

She looked round. Everyone looked a bit daunted. She grinned.

'No need to panic. It'll come with experience. You just need to observe.'

She went on to demonstrate table etiquette: where they were to stand when taking orders; how to remember who had ordered what ('the last thing I want is my waiting staff to stand there asking *who's the guinea fowl?*'); how to check that a table was laid immaculately before anyone sat down; how to keep an attentive eye on a party's needs without interrupting to ask unnecessarily if everything is all right.

'I know this all sounds a bit anal, but it should come across as effortless. For me, the most important thing is that every customer should be *relaxed* . . . We've got fantastic surroundings, the food is down to me' – she pulled a funny little face – 'and if you do your job right, we'll get there.'

Everyone nodded solemnly, and as Suzanna spread her

hands to indicate her lecture was over, they broke into spontaneous applause.

At midday, Mandy's mobile bleeped. She had a text. A picture text with a birthday cake on it. From Rick. She phoned him straight away.

'How did you know?'

'Aha.' There was a teasing tone in his voice. He didn't tell her he'd looked at her driving licence when she'd gone to the loo last time they were out. 'What are you doing this afternoon?'

'Working, I suppose.'

'Bunk off. Come and meet me. I want to give you your present.'

Mandy thought about it. No one would notice. They were all too busy running round like headless chickens, getting ready for this evening. And why not? He was the only one who'd actually bothered to get her anything.

He led her through the backstreets until they came to a double-fronted shop. AMERICAN TATTOO PARLOUR, the sign proclaimed, and Mandy gave a horrified gasp as it dawned on her what Rick had in mind.

'I can't!'

'Yes, you can.' Rick took out a piece of paper with a Chinese character on it. 'Here. I chose it for you. M for Mandy. Just a small one. Right here.'

He slid up her T-shirt and touched her bare skin, just above the hip bone. She took a breath inwards. Half of her was totally turned on by the idea; the other was terrified. She shook her head, laughing. Rick spent the next five minutes doing his best to persuade her.

'A tiny, tiny one. It won't hurt, I promise. Col is brilliant – he's done all of us. Anyway, I'll hold your hand.'

She couldn't chicken out. It was so sweet of Rick to think of her. He'd chosen the design specially for her. He'd given more thought to her than anyone else had done. She smiled bravely.

'OK,' she said and, taking a deep breath, followed him inside.

When she came out of the parlour, Mandy was as high as a kite with the thrill and the wickedness of what she'd had done. It had hurt, despite Rick's reassurances, though in a funny way you got used to the pain. And it had been worth it. It looked fantastic, the black against her smooth skin – even though it was still a bit red and sore and would be for a few days. She had a bandage on it for the time being, and a tube of antiseptic cream to apply to make sure it didn't go septic.

'You'd better get back. Or everyone will be wondering where you are.'

Mandy didn't think she actually cared. If it hadn't been for her father, and the fact he'd be worried, she wouldn't have bothered. She sighed, and Rick knew, with no more than the gentlest of persuasion, that she'd run off into the sunset with him. But he wanted to be absolutely sure she was hooked when he closed in on her. It was still early days yet. He didn't want her having second thoughts and slipping through his fingers.

Rick took her back to her car. She thanked him again for the tattoo. She was so grateful, it was almost pathetic. He felt the tiniest twinge of guilt as he walked away and left her. He supposed it was a bit naughty, telling her it was an M when it was an R. He smiled to himself. He wondered how long it would take Patrick to find out his girlfriend had been as good as branded.

Mandy sat in her car after Rick had gone. Her head was spinning. Whenever he touched her, it was like being jump-started. And she couldn't take her eyes off him, his incredible golden skin that felt like silk velvet. She shut her eyes and fantasized for a moment, imagining the feel of his torso against her bare breasts. Then she stopped. She was torturing herself. He was just a mate. He hadn't made a move on her at all. She had to accept they were that all-time cliché: just good friends.

She looked down at the bandage covering her tattoo and felt a sudden rush of panic. What was going to happen when everyone found out? She couldn't keep it hidden for ever. She must be insane!

But then, it occurred to her, she'd probably do anything for Rick. Anything he asked . . .

At half past six that evening Suzanna realized with a jolt that this was the point at which she had to put her money where her mouth was. And it was a terrifying prospect. Although she'd worked in many, many kitchens, had catered hundreds of times for large amounts of people, somehow this was different. The success was so inextricably down to her – they could have a beautiful setting, attentive staff, a fabulous wine list, but if the food wasn't up to scratch, they could forget it.

They'd invited as many people along that they could trust, in case anything did go wrong. Mickey and Lucy, James and Caroline, Keith and Ginny, Jonty's wife, Toby's parents and the Liddiards' next-door neighbours, Ned's parents. They'd had a raffle at the brewery, four winners being awarded a meal for two. Graham Cowley, the brewery's former bank manager, and his wife had also been invited as a thank you for all the support he'd shown them over the years.

They were only running half a menu, as they didn't have a full house, but Suzanna wanted there to be a choice so the dress rehearsal was as realistic as possible. There would be no challenge in serving up the same dish to everyone. And it wasn't just for her benefit – the waiting staff had to be put through their paces. She had to see if her systems worked and if everyone had paid attention to her exacting demands.

So there was roasted guinea fowl in a creamy cider sauce, lamb shanks in a shiny redcurrant and wine glaze or fillets of beef with field mushrooms and shallots. And on each table were to be placed big dishes of dauphinois potatoes, a root vegetable purée, curly kale, carrots and fresh peas – all organic and locally grown, so fresh you could almost still taste the earth they'd been pulled out of.

It was chaos, because it was effectively one sitting, with everyone arriving at the same time. Because it was free, no one could complain, although some of the guests had fun trying to be the customer from hell.

The kitchen ran, amazingly, like clockwork. And once the last of the apricot bread and butter pudding had been scraped up by the dummy guests, Suzanna brought the remaining food out to be devoured by her hungry work-force. Barney opened legions of bottles of wine as fast as he could. The differential between staff and guests evaporated, and it turned into a drunken free-for-all.

Someone had brought along a karaoke machine and Barney plugged it into his PA system. No one needed much encouragement, and Caroline was first up to the mike. James cringed as she sang 'It's Raining Men', thanking God that she didn't attempt the Geri Halliwell splits sequence on the table – he wouldn't have put it past her to try. Then everyone listened in thrall as Kitty sang 'Killing Me Softly'. A reverent hush fell amongst the revellers.

'She should go on the next *Pop Idol*,' slurred someone.

'No way. She's better than that. She needs an agent or a manager . . .'

Barney couldn't take his eyes off her. He was utterly spellbound. And his mind was racing. There was no doubt about it – she had something special.

The air was thick was camaraderie and the smell of impending success – everyone was on a bit of a high. Kitty, Sasha and Jonty stood on the table, conducting everyone in a rousing chorus of 'We are the Champions'. Much wine had clearly been drunk, and no one was in control.

Before everything got too out of hand, Patrick stood up, banging his spoon on the table for attention.

'Ladies and gentleman, while you're all still compos mentis, there's just a little toast I'd like to propose. There's someone we've forgotten in all of this. If you could all just recharge your glasses . . .'

No one needed any encouragement and there was a mad scramble to top up their glasses from the bottles of champagne that had miraculously appeared. Mandy smiled. He'd remembered, after all. When she'd walked in, Patrick had barely acknowledged her, just scowled because she was a bit late.

'Where have you been?' he'd asked.

But he didn't actually wait for an answer. So she'd sat there, with her secret, wishing she was somewhere else.

Patrick raised his glass.

'I think you'll all agree that everyone worked their socks off this evening to make it special. But there's one person without whom none of this would have been possible. So I ask you to raise your glasses, please, to – the chef!'

'The chef!' everyone roared, turning to Suzanna, who was blushing and protesting and laughing at all the attention.

Mandy looked away, blinking rapidly, hoping that Elspeth wouldn't see how upset she was. The silly cow had asked her twice what she'd got for her birthday. The first time she'd wanted to punch her. The second time she wanted to pull up her top and show her Rick's tattoo. Oh God, if only she was with him now.

Twenty minutes later, Kitty found Sasha snogging Jonty Hobday in the corridor outside the loos. His wife Meggy, three months pregnant and already exhausted, had left after pudding, knowing it would be hours until Jonty finally staggered home. She was used to her husband's drink-sodden social life – all she could be grateful for was that he had an astonishing metabolism and never seemed to have a hangover.

Jonty saw Kitty and panicked, sloping off sheepishly into the men's toilet. Kitty marched up to her sister with her hands on her hips.

'What the hell are you doing?'

Sasha smirked.

'What does it look like?'

'For God's sake, Sasha – didn't you notice his wife at the dinner table? He's married!'

Sasha was silent. She obviously had no idea. Then she shrugged sulkily.

'Then bollock him. Not me. I'm a free agent.'

'Sorry, Sasha. But you shouldn't mess around with married men.'

'Why not?'

'Haven't you got a conscience? Haven't you got any morals?'

'What's the point of having those? No one else has. Dad hasn't – nothing very moral about running off with your hygienist. And look at Mum – flirting for England with anything in trousers –'

'She's just having a bit of fun.'

'Well, so am I.'

'Sorry, but there's a big difference. What do you think Jonty's wife would say if she found out?'

'It must be her fault in the first place. Otherwise he wouldn't be gagging for it. He probably hasn't had his leg over for months.'

'Oh yeah – well, how did she get pregnant then?'

For a second Sasha was silent. Kitty pointed at her.

'You see. You haven't got the full picture, have you? She's expecting number three.'

Sasha looked as if she'd been slapped. She looked away, and Kitty could tell she was trying not to cry. Then she turned on her sister defiantly.

'How the hell was I supposed to know? For God's sake, Kitty, don't stand there preaching to me like the bloody Virgin Mary. I don't tell you what to do.'

Kitty shook her head in despair and left Sasha to it.

Sasha watched her sister go then followed Jonty into the gents, where he was quaking in one of the cubicles. The doors hadn't been put on yet. Sasha pushed him against the wall and put her hands either side of his head, thrusting her groin against his with a smile that had been painted on her face by the devil himself.

'We can't! Not in here.'

'Why not?'

Jonty, terrified, felt himself shrivel to nothingness. He put his hands up to push her away. She rolled her eyes.

'You're all talk and no action. I thought farriers were supposed to be God's gift to women?'

'Really?'

Her eyes narrowed to slits.

'Why didn't you tell me you were married?'

Jonty looked cornered.

'I thought you knew. Everyone else does.'

Sasha tossed her head and stomped off. Jonty heaved a sigh of relief. He'd got a bit carried away for a minute there. He thought of his wife Meggy, curled up in bed by now, all soft and warm and plump, and felt a stab of guilt. He'd have to be careful in future.

Back in the games room, things were going from riotous to out of control. Everyone sensible, like Cowley the bank manager, had gone, and everyone else was up for it. Suzanna, hugely relieved that the evening had been an unqualified success, was drinking hard to catch up with everyone else. She knew it was a mistake, because she was out of practice, but she also knew it was her last chance to let her hair down for a long time. Plus she wanted her staff to know that she was human.

'Something Stupid' came on the karaoke and she leaped up, dragging Patrick protesting up on to the stage. By then everyone was singing along so loudly they were drowned out, but the two of them hammed it up for laughs.

Only Mandy wasn't particularly amused. Especially when Elspeth sidled up to her spitefully and said, 'Look good together, don't they?' How dare Patrick humiliate her like that in public? Elspeth was sniggering her socks off. Well, if he was so obsessed with Suzanna, she didn't need telling twice.

Sasha sat at the end of the table and got steadily drunk. Bloody Jonty. Even worse, bloody Kitty – who did she think she was? Getting all the attention with her singing, then daring to preach to her. It wasn't fair. She felt tears stinging the back of her eyes. Everything in her life was a total disaster. She hadn't told Mum she was about to get kicked off her course at college.

It was all Dad's fault. She'd phoned him earlier, hoping he'd wish her good luck for tonight. It might only be a waitressing job, but it was her first job, and weren't fathers supposed to give you moral support? She'd been terrified she might get an order wrong, or forget something. She hadn't, of course, but that didn't excuse the fact that her father had fobbed her off when she phoned, told her he had to go because Faith was complaining of Braxton Hicks' contractions, whatever the fuck they were. Terminal, hoped Sasha.

*

303

Ginny got home just before midnight. She couldn't remember when she'd last enjoyed herself so much. She flopped down on the sofa and allowed herself a rerun of the evening. The twins had turned out to be fantastic waitresses. The meal had been out of this world. And great fun. Ginny had been surprised to find she actually knew most of the people there, and the party atmosphere had been thoroughly infectious. Keith had asked her to the opening the following week. She'd already had an official invitation, of course, but it was nice to actually go *with* someone; not just be there as mother of the waiting staff.

It was incredible, she thought, how well they'd all settled in Honeycote. She'd worried that they'd feel isolated or bored, but nothing could be further from the truth. It almost felt as if they'd been there for ever. And her business was going great guns – she stifled a groan as she remembered the baskets waiting for her. She'd have a bit of a head tomorrow, but she'd have to tackle them. A huge glass of water and bed was the only answer.

As she went into the living room, she saw the answerphone flashing. Somehow, she knew that whatever she was about to hear was going to burst her bubble. She pressed play. David's voice leaped out at her.

'Ginny. I just thought you ought to know that the baby's arrived . . .' A bit of self-conscious throat-clearing . . . 'Five-hour labour, gas and air and pethidine *and* an epidural . . .' Good – I hope it hurt, thought Ginny spitefully '. . . Mother and baby doing well, eight pounds two ounces. And . . . um . . . we've called her Chelsea. Chelsea May.'

There was a desperate quality to his voice that was

304

begging her not to laugh. It obviously hadn't been his choice.

'Anyway, I just wondered if you could tell the girls. I know they're working tonight.' Another pause. A pause that he didn't know quite how to fill. He seemed to be struggling for words, as if he wanted to say something, but he just ended with an abrupt goodbye.

As she rewound the tape, Ginny felt overwhelmed with doubt. Bloody David. It was no thanks to him that everything was turning out for the best for her and the girls. It had all been so unnecessary. There'd been nothing wrong with the marriage she'd had, as far as she was concerned. She supposed that in the back of her mind was the hope that one day he'd admit he'd been wrong and come back to them.

But with the arrival of Chelsea, David had burned his bridges. He had his own living, breathing eight-pound-two-ounce ball and chain. There was no going back now.

Barney practically had to carry Suzanna up to bed. Luckily when she was drunk she just became very tactile, every-one's best friend. She'd been all over Patrick earlier, but Barney wasn't threatened. That was Suzanna. In fact, he was pleased to see her behaving like that; letting go and having fun.

She was definitely still in a party mood. She began a mock striptease, another one of her party tricks, giggling, slightly inept but nevertheless charming. Barney swal-lowed as her dress slid to the floor and she stepped out of it, turning round to unhook her bra, peeping at him over her shoulder as the straps slid down her shoulders. She sashayed towards him playfully, still in her strappy sandals, shaking her hair down over her shoulders. Her skin was creamy and luminous in the half-light, her eyes shining as she grabbed on to his lapels.

'Come on, you. Let's celebrate.'

Her meaning was quite clear. She tried to pull him back on to the bed, but he resisted. He didn't want it to be like this. Not the first time. He wanted her to be fully aware of what she was doing. He wasn't going to take advantage of her.

Despite her protests, and despite the fact it would have been easy for him to give in, Barney forced Suzanna into her nightshirt and tucked her in firmly. Within two minutes she was asleep. Barney smiled fondly. She was going to have a bitch of a hangover, but after tonight's success they both deserved a lie-in.

16

Like the calm before a storm, there was not a lot that either Suzanna or Barney could do the last weekend before they opened. The final glaze was being applied to the walls in the dining room, the plumber was fitting out the toilets, carpets were being laid in the guest bedrooms, their living quarters were finally – thank God! – being walloped out in magnolia emulsion. All the furniture and fixtures and fittings were waiting in the wings for the stage to be ready. But in the meantime, the best thing they could do was keep out of the way.

'Why don't you go up to your mum's for the weekend?' suggested Barney.

Suzanna thought about it. She'd only get frustrated if she hung around. She wasn't good at waiting for things to be finished. She was itching to put everything together.

Unspoken was the suggestion that they could do with a bit of time apart, and this was realistically the last chance they were going to have, at least for a while. Tempers had run high over the past week as panic had set in, when vital deliveries that had been promised hadn't materialized, when a pipe had burst in the upstairs loo ruining the paintwork in the bar below, when the cold-room Patrick and Suzanna had bought at auction had resolutely failed to get cold, forcing yet another last-minute purchase.

'I'll keep an eye on things here. You could go shopping with Sybilla – buy an outfit for Wednesday.'

'I thought you said we weren't to waste any more money?' Suzanna frowned, still stung because she'd got the blame for the dodgy fridge.

'Isn't that what credit cards are for?' Barney twinkled at her. Although he'd snipped them all up all those years ago, he knew Suzanna had a secret stash of store cards, and that the bills went to her mother's house.

Suzanna thought about it. Her mother would probably appreciate the visit. She knew Iris missed them dreadfully, though she would never admit it. She had a hectic social life, but they'd seen her at least twice a week when they'd lived in Twickenham, and there was nothing like the company of your own flesh and blood. She was coming up for the opening, but Suzanna knew it was unlikely she'd be able to bestow her attention on anyone that night. A cosy weekend with Iris and a bit of retail therapy with Sybilla sounded like just what she needed. It would be wonderful not to have the smell of paint and the sound of banging.

And sometimes, just sometimes, extricating yourself from a situation gave you a chance to think more clearly about it.

Barney watched Suzanna drive off in the Jeep on Saturday morning, and felt a bit like a teenager whose parents had gone away for the weekend. Not that he wanted to do anything wild, but the option was there.

He decided to walk down to the post office with Marmite, who insisted on terrorizing the tradesmen. He'd already eaten the plumber's lunch – well, what did he expect when he left tasty ham sandwiches on the windowsill? He'd go and get the Saturday *Times*, which Barney infinitely preferred to the Sunday edition, as you had a fighting chance of getting through it.

Kitty was in there buying milk and bread. Barney greeted her with a wide smile. He liked Kitty. She was going to be a great waitress. He wasn't so sure about Sasha – he suspected she was the type who'd dump soup in your lap given the tiniest hint of provocation. But Kitty was attentive and efficient.

'Thanks for all your hard work the other night. It went really well.'

'It was fun. I can't wait till Wednesday.'

'I can,' said Barney with meaning.

'You must be busy this weekend.'

'No. Not really. Suzanna's gone to her mum's and I'm twiddling my thumbs.'

'Snap. Mum's gone out with Keith and Sasha didn't come home last night.'

Kitty didn't voice her worst fear – that despite all warnings Sasha was in the throes of a torrid affair with Jonty – because she absolutely didn't approve and didn't think Barney would either. Sasha had suddenly undergone an about-face – having been resolutely anti what she called either pea-pickers or turnip-heads, she was now apparently dropping them for anything in trousers with a slight bucolic hint. The Young Farmers had obviously been the turning point.

Barney picked up a carton of orange juice thoughtfully and put it in his basket.

'Listen – do you fancy doing some recording? Just for a laugh? I've got all my old gear gathering dust at the pub. It would give us both something to do . . .'

Barney hoped desperately that this didn't sound like a corny chat-up line. It was a genuine invitation. And he was intrigued to hear what Kitty would sound like on tape.

To his pleasure, she looked delighted.

'That would be really cool. Are you sure you're not too busy?'

'Positive. I'll just take all this stuff home. I'll see you in about half an hour?'

Barney hurried back to the pub, delighted that he had something to do that would take his mind off things. On his own, he would have spent the day mithering about pricing policies and how much they'd been spending. And thinking about him and Suzanna . . .

Things weren't right. They were both resolutely avoiding the issue, because they were so busy. But they were operating almost like strangers. They fell asleep at night exhausted, without talking. It was as if the bed was five miles wide. That hadn't been his plan. Moving here was supposed to bring them together, not force them apart.

Then he placated himself. Perhaps when the pub was open, up and running and they knew where they were, they could relax and the tension would ease.

He took out his old TEAC PortaStudio from its case. It had cost him a fortune when he was seventeen; he remembered emptying out his post office savings account, selling his bike and doing a deal with his father for the last fifty pounds. He wondered how many hours of hopes and dreams he and his friends had recorded on it in his parents' garage, before they'd got their deal. Before everything had gone sour . . .

He wasn't going to dwell on it or he wouldn't be able to go ahead. Kitty had been so excited, and he didn't want to dampen her enthusiasm just because of his bad experiences. He cleaned the tape heads carefully with meths and a Q-tip. There was no reason the ancient piece of machinery wouldn't still work, though it was practically a collector's item. For the equivalent of what he'd paid for it, you could get an all-singing, all-dancing twenty-four-track computerized recording studio. But although Barney had kept up in theory with new technology by reading music magazines, he knew he'd be lost. Besides, he quite liked the hands-on, old way of doing things. It seemed more real, more pure to him. He miked up the piano with his trusty Shure microphones, replaced some dodgy strings on his bass and plugged it into his amp.

She arrived, in a pair of army camouflage dungarees over a lacy vest. And sang. She was incredibly unselfconscious. There was no pussyfooting, no beating about the bush. She went for it, while Barney busied himself, testing for levels, pushing buttons, moving microphones, sliding levers, until he thought he'd got the ambience just right.

Her voice was untrained, but incredibly powerful, and she seemed to have a natural ability to control it. They messed around with some jazzy, bluesy classics, with Barney improvising on the piano. They recorded a version of Nina Simone's 'Don't Smoke in Bed'. And Etta James's 'I'd Rather Go Blind'. They sounded great, but Barney hated cover versions. Anyone with half a voice and a few pieces of equipment could do it. There was no real challenge. And now he'd seen what Kitty was capable of, he wanted to push it further.

'Do you want to write a song?'

'I've never written one before.'

'I think we should try.'

'How?'

'Just ... do it. We think of a hook. Some notes or some lyrics to build it round. Some of the best songs are written in two minutes flat.'

Kitty looked unsure, but seemed happy to give it a go.

'I need a starting point. I can't just go into it cold.'

'OK. Try this.'

Barney picked out a clutch of notes on the piano – a haunting, winsome melody that he'd had in the back of his mind.

'Think of something to go round that.'

Kitty took up the challenge. She sat cross-legged on the windowsill for ten minutes, swigging her San Miguel, scribbling furiously, then crossing out, then sighing. Finally, she was satisfied.

The lyrics were slightly naive, but with a hint of darkness. Together they sat down and structured the lyrics around Barney's music. Kitty listened, rapt, as Barney showed her how to turn a basic idea into something special, how what you left out was as important as what you left in, how it should build, and also how to slip in the unexpected so that the song didn't become a cliché.

At last they were ready to record. It started gently, her voice skipping sweetly over and under the piano, lulling the listener into a false sense of security until the bass kicked in with no warning, as sudden and unexpected as a spurned lover appearing from nowhere with a knife. The music lurched into a terrifying crescendo, the lyrics dripping the pure vitriol of a woman scorned, spite oozing out of every syllable, while underneath the lower notes of the piano rumbled threateningly. Then almost as soon as it had begun, the maelstrom was over, like a mid-summer storm, the notes dwindling, dancing lightly on the edge of consciousness until they faded away.

> *If today was yesterday*
> *Tomorrow would never come*
> *I would not let them steal*
> *Another day from me*
> *Another day*
> *Day from me . . .*

It was magical. Barney knew it was good, because when you listened, you felt as if you'd heard it before. It insinuated its way into your soul. And his instinct never failed him.

'Now comes the boring bit, I'm afraid. I've got to mix it down.'

Kitty seemed quite happy to sit and listen while he played around with the sounds. Not many people realized how tedious the recording process could be – hundreds of takes, followed by hours of fiddling about with knobs in an attempt to get exactly the right sound. But Barney loved it. He had an idea in his head of exactly how something should be and was happy to persevere.

By eight o'clock that night, Barney had opened a bottle of Havana Club and drunk half of it. He remembered now, mixing down was always so much easier when you were pissed. By nine o'clock he'd sent Kitty out for cigarettes and smoked half of them. He hadn't smoked for five years. But God, it felt good. The whole process felt fantastic. The creative energy flowed through him, resuscitating his soul. Kitty sat patiently, listening, asking questions, never once looking bored.

In Iris's flat, Suzanna and her mother had shared a bowl of orecchiette with broccoli and Gorgonzola, and were sitting watching a video of *Chocolat*.

Suzanna felt incredibly relaxed. Getting away from the pub made her realize how exhausting and stressful the last few weeks had been. Living in turmoil, having to make decisions, the anticipation, wondering whether it would be a success or not. In the cosy confines of her mother's flat, she could forget all about it. And she could be herself. She didn't have to pretend everything was all right, keep control, make sure the smile didn't slip. She knew that if she wanted to weep, to rage at the unfairness of it all, that her mother wouldn't mind. And somehow, because she knew that she could, she didn't need to . . .

Iris gently removed the glass of wine from her hand and shook her awake. Suzanna stayed conscious long enough to make it into her old bedroom, where she pulled the covers up under her chin and slid back into sleep.

Iris looked down at her sleeping daughter. Something wasn't quite right, she knew it. Suzanna had told her about everything they'd achieved with great excitement; she'd fizzed and bubbled as she described the dress rehearsal that had gone so well the week before. But no matter how animated she was, Iris knew, with a mother's instinct, that there was something missing.

There was a deep ache in her heart. She wanted, with the desperate frustration that only a parent can feel, to make it all right again for Suzanna. And Barney – Iris adored Barney. They were so right together. Iris, a confirmed atheist, cursed God for what he'd done to them both. It made her feel better to have someone to blame, even if she didn't believe in him.

By two o'clock, Kitty had fallen asleep on an old sofa that Marmite usually used as a bed. Barney slipped upstairs and brought down their duvet to cover her over, and some pillows. He tucked one under her head, but she barely stirred. Then he carried on his work, with his headphones on.

The whole process brought the old days back to him. In the studio with the band, half pissed, a bit stoned, excited, arguing, buzzing, creating, collaborating, improvising, fighting. It was exhausting; it serrated your nerves; it was living on the edge, but there was nothing – nothing – like the high at the end. The experience had lain dormant in the depths of Barney's soul for all these years.

Somehow, naively perhaps, he'd hoped that working on the pub together would be a similar thrill; give him the edge he'd lacked for so long. But he and Suzanna weren't collaborating. They weren't really sharing the highs or the lows, the graft, the concept of bouncing off each other. They were working in parallel, very occasionally coming together.

Eventually, the first fingers of light through the window made him realize dawn was on its way. His eyes felt as if they were full of hot sand, but he was filled with excitement. He wanted to shake Kitty awake and share his excitement with her, but he didn't think she'd appreciate being woken. And he ought to have some sleep himself. He checked his watch – just after four. He could get in three hours; feel half human the next day.

He couldn't go upstairs and leave Kitty on her own. Anyway, the bedroom was filled with paint fumes. So he slipped on to the sofa next to her, pulled the other half of the duvet over him and folded up a spare pillow for his head. Marmite, asleep in the crook of Kitty's knees, shuffled over to his lap. Barney shut his eyes. He could see spools spinning in front of him; hear the jumbled notes tumbling through his consciousness.

In five minutes, he was fast asleep.

He woke at half seven with a crook in his neck. The duvet had slipped on to the floor and he was freezing cold. He was trying to work out where he was, and why, when Kitty came back into the room with Marmite. She smiled.

'He was desperate for the loo, poor little thing.'

Barney sat up, confused by the vision of Kitty in front of him, then remembered he'd been slaving over a hot mixing desk till dawn. He groaned, catching sight of the bottle of Havana Club taunting him, half empty.

'I need tea.'

'I've put the kettle on.' Kitty sat on the sofa next to him, tucking the duvet back round him. 'Did you finish it?'

Barney nodded.

'Do you want to hear it?'

'When you feel more human. You look like death.'

'Thanks!' Barney ruffled his hair and grimaced at the unfamiliar taste of stale cigarettes in his mouth. He pushed the duvet off and stood up tentatively. Not too bad, all things considered.

Half an hour later, when Barney had washed and drunk three cups of tea, he spooled back the tapes from the night before. They sat, almost in reverence, as he pressed play and the room was filled with sound: sound they had created together. It was the first time Barney had heard it at full volume. Listening on headphones had little impact.

He felt slightly ill. It would have been so much easier if it had been mediocre. But it wasn't. It was stunning. Breathtaking. Even though it was impossible for him to be objective, he knew instinctively he was on the brink of something big.

'Do you mind if I send this to someone I know? I've got a contact – I might be able to track him down.'

Kitty nodded. 'Sure.'

Barney wasn't sure whether to warn her that this was the final moment when she had complete control. That once Pandora's box was open, there was no going back. Did she want everything that was to follow? Was she strong enough? Was it a fantastic opportunity or a curse?

Barney thought about what it had done to him. It had, until he'd met Suzanna, destroyed his faith in human nature. He'd stifled his creativity for nearly twenty years, afraid of the consequences. It had made him bitter and cynical. Not on the surface: on the outside he was genial, affable, open-minded. But deep down inside he had fears and anxieties that he didn't unleash on anyone else; insecurities that he'd managed to bury.

Kitty was young and beautiful, and she had the voice of an angel with the devil inside. He wasn't sure if he wanted to be responsible for creating a monster. But more than anything, Barney couldn't bear the thought of wasted talent. Couldn't bear the thought of Kitty going to her grave without the chance to share her gift with the world and reap its rewards.

He felt a surge of something towards her – it wasn't

sexual, or paternal; he wasn't sure what it was. It was always weird, collaborating with someone in a creative process. It was so intense, so personal – turning your insides out in front of someone. It was, if anything, more intimate than sex.

Which was why, before Kitty left, he asked her not to mention it to anybody.

'Suzanna's not too keen on me doing musical stuff. She thinks it brings out the worst in me.'

This was a thumping great lie. His musical career had long been dead by the time Suzanna had come along. But Barney was feeling uncomfortable and unsure about what he'd done. Anyway, it didn't really do for your wife to know that you'd spent the night with a nineteen-year-old girl. People were so cynical these days. No one would believe that you could spend the hours between midnight and dawn alone in a room with someone and not get your leg over.

Barney put the mix-down carefully in its case and wrote on it 'Helicopter Launching Pad'. It meant nothing to him or anyone else. Which was why it wasn't likely to attract any attention.

After breakfast on Sunday, there was something that Suzanna knew she had to do. She got in the car and drove the three miles to the municipal cemetery where Oliver was buried. On the way she stopped off at a shop for flowers. Deep down, she thought it was a stupid, meaningless gesture, but she couldn't visit his grave and not leave some token. She chose sunflowers: bright, cheerful, jolly sunflowers that totally belied how she was feeling but that were, she felt, both childlike and masculine.

Clutching her bouquet, she walked along the wide, tree-lined path that ran down the middle of the cemetery. As municipal cemeteries went, it was quite attractive. And at least it was a sunny morning. On a grey, cloudy day it would have been insufferable, no matter how many attempts had been made to make it welcoming.

She came to Oliver's little stone. They'd agonized long and hard over what to have. There'd been a bewildering choice – stones in the shape of teddies or Thomas the Tank Engine. In the end, they'd settled upon something simple – a white stone with black lettering. 'In memory of our beloved son . . .' Their final choice had seemed almost irrelevant. They didn't need a gravestone to remember him by. It was a ritual; part of the process they had to go through.

She put her bunch of flowers down a little self-consciously. She was surprised how many people were there visiting. She supposed it was a Sunday-morning ritual for a lot of them. A visit to a parent or a husband or a wife. She wondered how many people were visiting their children, and how they had coped. How long, she wanted to ask them. How long before it stopped hurting?

But as she turned back to the grave, she noticed something. This time, it didn't seem to be hurting so much. She still felt sad – of course she did – but it was just a tight coldness in the bottom of her chest, not the asphyxiating panic usually brought on by seeing his name in black and white, and those pitiful dates, that pitifully short life.

A sudden thought occurred to her. It was the first time she had visited Oliver's grave without Barney. Perhaps that was the key? Perhaps it was Barney who reminded her too much of the past, too much of what they had had together; the life they had created. Barney who inadvertently kept opening that huge wound inside her, even though he did so much to try and heal it afterwards.

Did they realistically have a future together? She loved him, of course she did, but was that love ever going to be strong enough to fight the dark shadow that was always lurking? Perhaps their relationship was always going to be a facade? Was she always going to have to battle with herself to keep afloat, knowing that it was unfair on him to go under? Were they ever going to recapture their love as it had been at the beginning or was it always going to be marred by tragedy, with memories, with what could have been?

Somehow, coming back to Richmond had thrown everything into perspective. She'd passed so many of their old haunts and it had reminded her of their life together. Strangely, it evoked more happy memories than sad ones. Those mad, heady days when they had first fallen in love and done the ridiculous, soppy, crazy things that new lovers did. A picnic in Richmond Park when they had refused to be put off by the driving rain and had got soaked to the skin, then, because they knew nobody with any sense would be out, had made love under cover of the rhododendrons. The day they'd made fools of themselves ice-skating, doggedly holding hands and making their way tentatively round the edge while teenagers wove expertly in and out. The amazing barbecue they'd had in the tiny back garden of Barney's house, when they'd introduced their own friends to each other, and the neighbours had complained about the noise and then joined in . . .

They'd had a wonderful time. And Suzanna felt frustrated that they couldn't recapture the spirit of those days.

They still loved each other.

But it was different.

Could it ever be the same again?

Perhaps she shouldn't go back to Honeycote? Perhaps she should stay here; live with her mother for a while, then take steps to build a new life on her own. Without Barney, maybe she could be someone else. Not Suzanna Blake, bereaved mother, tragic figure, incomplete woman . . . And he could be free of the ball and chain that she seemed to have become. He'd find himself another girl quickly enough, someone without any emotional baggage, someone that would make him laugh, make his brown eyes twinkle. The twinkle that had drawn her to him in the first place. The twinkle that had gone out on that dreadful day.

Then she chastised herself. That was the coward's way out. They had too much together to walk away from each other now. She remembered all the leaflets and the counsellors. They'd all said the same thing. Give it time . . .

Eighteen months, two weeks and a day. Wasn't that long enough?

17

The day of the opening, both Barney and Suzanna woke at half past five, to glorious sunshine. Suzanna sat up in a panic and grabbed the list that was by her bed, wondering what she should do first. Barney took the list off her gently and told her to calm down.

'Lie there and do some of those deep breathing things they go on about. I'll bring you a cup of tea.'

Suzanna tried some meditation, tried to visualize a tropical beach or a cool green forest, but all she could see was millions of outraged guests wandering about wondering where the food was. Barney came back in with a tray, with tea and a tiny package wrapped in tissue paper. He handed it to her solemnly.

'This is to say good luck. And well done so far.'

Suzanna opened it. Inside was a tiny enamel box, in the shape of a strawberry; exquisitely detailed.

She clapped her hands in delight. It was the perfect present. The air around Honeycote was thick with the smell of strawberries from the surrounding fields. She'd spent all day yesterday making tartlet cases to hold the first of the crops. Then she grinned mischievously and put her hand under her pillow, drawing out a little parcel.

'You know what they say. Great minds think alike.'

Barney opened it, curious. Inside was another enamel box, this time shaped like a minute bundle of asparagus, the crop that had made the Vale of Evesham so famous.

They looked at each other in wonderment that their presents were so similar.

'Weird,' said Suzanna.

But she got up light of heart. It just went to show you, they did belong together after all.

Sybilla and Piers arrived at midday, throwing Suzanna into more panic, but Sybilla insisted they were here to help. Piers, who was taking a rare and much-appreciated day off, was looking redder-faced and longer-suffering than ever. Sybilla looked fabulous. Blooming, in a huge Brora cashmere sweater and leather maternity trousers. Suzanna smiled to herself. Only Sybilla could have found leather maternity trousers.

'I want a personal guided tour. Straight away.'

Suzanna tried to protest that she had mountains of things yet to do, but Sybilla insisted that as Suzanna now had two extra pairs of hands, she could afford ten minutes to show them round.

As much as they could, Barney and Suzanna had left the building to speak for itself. The lounge bar had kept its traditional feel, but was much lighter than before. The flagstones gleamed and the beams had been stripped of their black stain to reveal lighter coloured wood beneath. The walls were limewashed almost-ochre; hops had been hung over the bar and a huge blackboard listed bar snacks and wines available by the glass. A pair of distressed leather sofas faced each other across a stout, low coffee table smothered in the daily papers and up-to-date magazines: *Horse and Hound* and *Country Life* as well as *Vogue* and *Elle*. Barney was hoping to attract a clientele for elevenses: they would serve good coffee and tempting pastries to lure mums on their way back from the school run or people who worked from home and wanted a break. As well as the usual chairs and tables, and stools at the bar, there were a couple of high-backed settles in discreet corners for those who wanted a drink in privacy.

Barney went behind the bar and carefully poured himself and Piers an inaugural pint with a sense of ceremony. Then they went through into the dining room. Again, the flagstones and the beams had been revealed, but the overall atmosphere had much more impact.

Suzanna had to admit that the effect on the walls had been achieved by luck rather than judgement. She'd had an image in her head and no idea how to recreate it technically. She'd wanted to get away from the traditional red so favoured by dining rooms that it had become almost a cliché, yet she still loved the warmth and cosiness it brought; the way it acted as a perfect foil for candlelight and intimacy. She'd eventually hit upon a deep coral, a dead flat oil the colour of lobsters and scallops at their very richest, a glorious mix of dark pink and orange and red which, by the painstaking layering of different colours, had finally been perfect: vibrant in summer yet cosy in winter, a welcoming hue that should have been shocking yet felt absolutely right.

At the windows were hung simple blinds, wide ticking stripes of charcoal grey and cream on stout wooden poles with big fat acorn finials. The tables were farmhouse planks, stained dark and burnished until they shone, flanked by ladder-backed rush-seated chairs that had been chosen for their comfort more than their looks – it was important for customers to want to linger. The glasses were huge, as were the plates, just thick white china, flanked by black-handled bistro cutlery. On each table was a squat, square metal vase, stuffed with moss and cream roses tinged at the edge with the same coral as the paint on the walls.

Along one wall was a huge butcher's block, on which were to be displayed the desserts and cheeses, and a mammoth iron fruit bowl that overspilled with grapes, apples, pears, figs and oranges. Above that was an ornately carved wooden mirror that reflected the entire room. Wrought-iron sconces, softened with amber droplets, distributed a warm light that could be turned up or down from a switch on the wall, with the addition of fat church candles on each table and windowsill.

Two huge unframed canvases hung on opposing walls – one resembling a Dutch still life, an extravagant plateau de fruits de mer whose colours cleverly echoed that of the walls; the other a very impressionistic nude lolling on a chaise longue, a glass of wine in her hand. James had lent them from his gallery, happy for them to be hung there, and if a customer chose to buy one – which no doubt they would – another would be found to replace it.

The finishing touch was a rusty cast-iron pig with wings. As large as a cat, with its appreciative snout in the air like a Bisto twin, it was positioned by the till, the slot in its back waiting for tips.

Warm, rich, rustic, simple, stylish – it was an environment that enhanced rather than interfered with the senses. Because, as Suzanna had impressed upon her workforce, it was all about relaxation and enjoyment. They weren't striving for an elaborate award. Just a reputation for being somewhere that people could guarantee eating slightly better food than they could create in their own home, safe in the knowledge that nothing they asked for (within reason) would be too much trouble; that if they wanted a doggy bag or a taxi home or a digestive biscuit to dunk in their coffee, they would get it.

Sybilla gave a sigh of absolute contentment.

'It's utterly divine. Completely perfect. You are both absolute geniuses.'

Neither Barney nor Suzanna could wipe the grin off their face, as the memory was still fresh in their minds of total mayhem only three weeks previously, when it seemed as if order would never be restored in a million years.

They then showed their guests upstairs to the bed-rooms, which, explained Suzanna, had been a miracle in themselves, so low was the budget. But she had surpassed herself with her ingenuity.

Sea-grass matting was laid up the stairs, along the corridor and throughout all the bedrooms, which immediately gave a sense of uniformity and space. The walls were painted in a deliciously rich buttermilk which reflected the light. At a fabric warehouse she'd found reams of checked mulberry silk on sale for a ridiculous two pounds a metre – it had been, apparently, a cancelled order from a large hotel. There was just enough for floor-length unlined curtains and a bedcover in each room. To continue the colour scheme the architraves and skirting boards were picked out in a darker shade of damson, as well as the curtain poles, lamp stands and a job lot of cheap picture frames from the market. Suzanna had found some old fifties annuals in a second-hand bookshop and pulled out the comic strips, which she'd framed up and hung on the wall in order. The effect was nostalgic, quaint and very striking. She had trawled charity shops and bought up as many paperbacks that were in mint condition as she could find – Dick Francis, Agatha Christie, as well as some more intellectual tomes – to provide each room with a little bit of brain candy to make up for the fact that they couldn't afford to equip them with their own TVs just yet.

Everyone had agreed that white bathrooms were the best, and although they couldn't splash out on elaborate power showers they found the plainest suites they could. Piles of fluffy white towels were an absolute necessity. Pretty glass bottles were filled up with supermarket's own-brand bubble bath and shampoo, fresh candles were put into candlesticks and each bath was equipped with its own rubber duck.

In time, they could replace the polyester duvets with goosedown and the sheets with Egyptian cotton, install entertainment centres and satellite TV. In the meantime, the bedrooms were comfortable, and looked fresh and stylish and a little bit quirky. No one would exactly suspect the hand of Anoushka Hempel, but anyone fancying an illicit bonk or a romantic getaway in the Cotswolds would be perfectly satisfied.

Sybilla clapped her hands in delight, and even Piers, who rarely spoke or expressed an opinion chiefly because he wasn't allowed a word in edgeways when his wife was around, pumped Barney's hand in enthusiastic congratulations and kissed Suzanna on the cheek.

Sybilla chucked her overnight bag on their bed and rubbed her hands together.

'Right,' she declared. 'Show me what I can do. I can handle anything except raw liver.'

Suzanna gave her a big white pinny and got her to cut out pastry motifs to top the miniature pies she'd made. They were samples of what they were going to be serving in the bar. They wanted to keep the bar menu as simple as possible so as to concentrate on the restaurant, and Suzanna had hit upon the idea of a range of pies which she hoped would soon create a dedicated following. Pies were easy to prepare, easy to serve and everyone liked them. She'd even devised a 'Vale of Evesham' pie for vegetarians, crammed with peas and asparagus and purple sprouting broccoli in a local blue cheese sauce.

She gave Sybilla the templates – fish for the fish pie, rooster heads for the chicken and asparagus, and cow horns for the beef in Honeycote Ale – and left her to get on with it while she worked through her checklist.

At six o'clock that evening, as Sybilla rubbed shimmering, sparkly body lotion on to her back and arms, Suzanna shivered with excitement. She'd resolutely decided to be glamorous tonight, as it was probably one of the few chances her future customers were going to get to see her tarted up. Henceforth she was going to be chained to the stove in her chef's whites and rubber clogs. So she'd chosen a pale blue Ghost dress, floaty and asymmetric, and sandals with a single silver-beaded strap across the front.

'You look beautiful,' moaned Sybilla, who'd also gone for Ghost, but black.

'So do you,' said Suzanna, and kissed her friend. It had been fun having her around. She'd missed female company lately. Not that she went as far as sharing any of her dilemmas with Sybilla, but somehow the sense of expectation was greater with a girl. She was in a party mood. She took a slug of the champagne Sybilla insisted they have while they got ready, even though neither of them had made much inroad into it. But it had given them a sense of occasion nevertheless.

'I'm nervous,' she said.

'You've got no reason to be,' said Sybilla. 'It's going to be a huge success. Piers is seriously impressed. And not much impresses him, I can tell you. What time's kick-off?'

'The invitation said seven,' replied Suzanna, looking at her watch, 'but I don't suppose anyone will get here till nine. If they come at all.'

She couldn't have been more wrong. By twenty-five past seven, Barney had to close the doors to any more guests until people started leaving.

It was heaving! Absolutely everyone who had been invited had come, even the vicar. All the old regulars, everyone from the brewery, people that Barney and Suzanna recognized from the village, including batty Coral from the post office, and hordes of people from the point-to-point. Some had dressed up for the occasion, some had come straight from work, whether it be in the fields or in an office. Some had just fallen off the train from London. From sixteen to sixty, every age was represented. And they were all quite determined to enjoy themselves.

There was cava, Pimms and, of course, Honeycote Ale flowing on tap. For canapés, there were the little mini pies, as well as crostini topped with smoked trout, goat's cheese or air-dried ham, all locally produced. And beautiful flat baskets filled with quails' eggs and asparagus and tiny salt-encrusted new potatoes to dip in a bowl of saffron sauce. And strawberry tartlets. Suzanna had planned to fill the freezer with the leftovers, but at this rate there wasn't going to be a single crumb left.

Damien hadn't been able to resist going to the opening. Thick, glossy invitations had arrived for all the residents of Honeycote Grove, who, with their wads of money, would obviously be target clientele. He'd welcomed the opportunity to go and have a look at his future investment first hand. He'd been so busy over the past couple of weeks, tying up all the loose ends with Marco Dinari, but he was now a free agent. It was time to focus on his next conquest.

He also allowed himself to think about Kelly. He'd banished her to the back of his mind temporarily, knowing that he would be too preoccupied to concentrate on her properly, for this was one relationship that he didn't want to screw up.

He asked Rick, super-casually, if he'd ask Kelly if he could take her up on her offer to babysit. The message came back that she would be delighted.

'She'll be glad of the extra cash. She's saving up for her own place. She can't stand sharing with me any longer.'

It was true. Poor Kelly. She was working all the hours God gave at her salon. Then she insisted on coming home and doing the housework, cooking Rick a proper meal and doing his washing, even though he told her repeatedly not to bother. She was so like his mum it wasn't true. And she would be so ideal for Damien. He was doing a valiant job as a single father, but it was obvious he needed a woman about the place. When he stood in the kitchen he always looked a bit panicky. And Kelly would adore Honeycote Grove; she'd keep it as clean as a new pin.

Kelly was indeed delighted with the prospect. She'd got home from the salon at six, showered and changed into a pink fleece and tracksuit trousers. She didn't blow-dry her hair for once, just left it to dry naturally and tied it up in a butterfly clip. When she saw Damien, she couldn't help wishing she'd made a tiny bit more effort. She'd forgotten how gorgeous he was. Not that he'd be interested in someone like her. And anyway, you couldn't turn up to babysit in lurex and stilettos. He might as well see her at her worst. The only way was up then.

He was incredibly courteous. Showed her where everything was; told her to help herself to anything she wanted from the fridge and to be firm with Anastasia about bedtime.

'I won't be late,' he promised.

He wasn't going to stay long. Just enough to get the lie of the land. He didn't want to make himself too conspicuous, or get too close. The better you knew people, the harder it was to shaft them.

Anyway, he wanted to get back, so he could talk to Kelly. Get to know her. Maybe even tentatively ask her out. Though he wasn't sure if he had the courage quite yet.

Sybilla had to go to the loo. Again. The baby was perched right on her bladder and she couldn't stop peeing.

The ladies' loos had been another of Suzanna's inspirational labours of love thrown together on the cheap.

The walls were painted a soft bluey-purple, the colour of butterfly wings; the louvred doors on the three cubicles were painted lavender with glass doorknobs – Suzanna had spent hours making sure no one could peep through the slats while someone was having a wee, and had been happy that unless you were a real pervert you were unlikely to be able to catch a glimpse. A row of Venetian-style boudoir mirrors hung over the sinks, which had been sunk into a slab of marble from Bertie's reclamation yard. The illusion of luxury was granted by bottles of hand lotion on an old Singer sewing machine they'd topped with the remaining marble, and a vase of fresh freesias.

Sybilla admired her friend's handiwork. It infuriated her that Suzanna had the knack of pulling things together without paying through the nose, or making it look like a bad episode of *Changing Rooms*. She thought of her own house in Richmond and shuddered at the bills Piers footed, yet still the decor was never quite right. It felt too *done*. There was no doubt about it, Suzanna had talent oozing out of every pore. Sybilla was immensely proud of her friend's achievements.

There was something not quite right, though. She sensed Suzanna was jumpy, and it wasn't just first-night nerves. If she didn't know her better, she'd have said she was coked out of her brain. But Suzanna didn't do that kind of thing, she was pretty sure. Well, she never had done in London, and Sybilla doubted it was the sort of thing you got lured into in the depths of the Gloucester-shire countryside, despite what the tabloids hinted about the young prince's recreational activities.

She washed her hands, checked her bump in the mirror for signs of growth since earlier that evening, touched up her lippy and went off to find Piers who, it had to be said, was enjoying himself enormously. He was even talking about getting a weekend cottage in the Cotswolds. She was just heading down the corridor when she saw a couple up ahead. She stopped dead when she realized it was Patrick and Suzanna. They were very close, heads together. She shut her eyes. She didn't want to see what might happen next.

But curiosity got the better of her, and she opened her lids just wide enough to see them kiss. Not a full tongue snog, granted. But not a meaningless peck on the cheek either.

'Right, young lady,' she muttered to herself grimly. 'We're going to have words, you and me.'

Damien had heard rumours via Rick via Mandy, that the Honeycote Arms had gone substantially over budget. Which wasn't really all that surprising – there was a rule that refits always took longer and cost more than you ever accounted for, no matter how realistic your estimates. But that was good – the further they were in debt, the less he'd have to do to fuck them over.

Annoyingly, thought Damien, he could smell success in the air. The place was rammed. OK, so most people were happy to turn out to the opening of an envelope if there was a sniff of a free drink, but he had to admit that the atmosphere inside the pub was infectious. It was very stylish, but not in the least off-putting, which gave it a broad appeal. And the wide range of people that had turned up proved that: young, old, trendy, conventional, wealthy, ordinary, townies, countryfolk – and they all looked comfortable rubbing shoulders with each other.

Damien wasn't used to this concept. All of his establishments had a very specific target clientele: either young, style-conscious urban types or dirty old businessmen, both of whom he knew how to divest of their spare cash.

He spent the evening usefully, doing a bit of judicious snooping. There were so many people in the place, so much going on, so much being drunk, that nobody noticed him accidentally wandering into the kitchens and having a nose round, quickly assimilating the names of their chief suppliers. A quick phone call to intimate they were bad payers would soon foul up their credit. The odd extra order here and there over the next few months would screw their accounts up. A customer with salmonella – he thought he could arrange that, together with the threat of a lawsuit. Rumours of food poisoning were always the kiss of death in the catering trade.

He looked at Barney and Suzanna, who were circulating amongst their guests, both looking ecstatic, high as kites. For a moment, Damien couldn't help feeling a little niggle of guilt, which was rather unusual for him. He told himself it was a dog-eat-dog world; that you had to play dirty to get what you wanted. The Blakes were naive if they thought it was just a question of shoving a decent bit of grub on to a plate and having pretty waitresses. Nevertheless, he couldn't help feeling rather like a bully swiping someone's sweets in the playground. Perhaps he was going soft?

He was just wondering whether to jack in the whole plan, when Patrick Liddiard barged past him, giving him barely a sideways glance, nearly knocking the glass out of his hand. Damien felt his resolve refuel. Fuck you, you arrogant bastard, he thought. You're going to remember me all right. For the rest of your days.

He wandered out into the car park to make a call on his mobile. It was chaos: everyone had parked like complete prats. The first thing he'd do when it was his, he thought, was introduce valet parking. And a limo service. He crunched his way over the gravel to a darkened corner, away from the babble of voices inside.

'Pebbles? It's Damien here. I've got a little job for you. Just wondered if any of your boys fancied a day out in the country . . . ?'

A few minutes later and the deal was done.

Suzanna was taking deep breaths to calm herself down. She told herself it was because she was nervous about the opening; sort of stage fright. But she knew jolly well that, although she was a little apprehensive, that wasn't what was causing her insides to whirl like a Catherine wheel.

It was Patrick.

When she'd seen him arrive that evening, her heart had given a little leap of joy. He looked devastating, in a deconstructed linen suit, grey with the thinnest raspberry stripe. She'd slid her arms inside his jacket, put her hands on his waist, and he hadn't stopped her. It wasn't the sort of gesture you could misinterpret. It was unmistakably intimate. As their lips met, the feeling had hit her, suddenly and unexpectedly; a feeling that she remembered from long ago. What was alarming was it wasn't lust, not as such. It was deeper, more subtle than that.

Shit, thought Suzanna. She remembered what it was now. It was the feeling you had when you first fell in love.

The feeling that fleeting strangers in your deepest dreams sometimes gave you. The most intense feeling in the world. The feeling that you never wanted to end but that sadly, inevitably did, because it had such a short shelf-life; became, when the novelty wore off, diluted by familiarity and routine and duty.

The feeling she'd been remembering at Oliver's graveside the week before. The feeling she so desperately wanted to recapture with Barney. Only now it had materialized unexpectedly somewhere else.

She stepped outside for a moment to take in the realization. The nicotiana Barney had planted outside the French doors were in their full evening scent, but combined with the lavender and the heat made her feel slightly ill. How the hell could this have happened? She tried to look at it logically, rationally. She still loved Barney, of course she did. She always would. But as she'd realized in the cemetery, with him she could never be her real self again. Barney brought with him the baggage of guilt and fear and regret and despair.

But Patrick. Patrick brought hope . . .

Inside, Patrick was thinking that perhaps he shouldn't have kissed Suzanna quite like that.

All in all, he was quite a kissy sort of person. He kissed people all the time. Friends. Relatives. Lucy. Sophie and Georgina. People he socialized with. In the circles he moved in, a kiss was a meaningless gesture. A fleeting meeting of mouths didn't really amount to much.

So why was he worried? He told himself the kiss had been a symbol of their mutual self-congratulation. It was one of those mad moments when two people who'd worked hard together became close. They were just . . . recognizing each other's worth.

But it had gone on a fraction too long. And it had been definitely, definitely on the lips. It was the sort of kiss that, under a different set of circumstances, would have led to other things. He'd felt her start to melt into him, which was when the warning bells had clanged in his head. Suzanna was fragile, damaged, needy. He mustn't give her the wrong signals.

He reflected how much he'd changed over the past few months. Not so long ago, he would have thought nothing of a quick leg-over with anyone who was up for it. He'd learned a big lesson from his father, whose inability to keep it zipped up had nearly cost them the whole brewery. He wasn't going to let that happen again.

Giving Suzanna one would be asking for trouble, when they'd worked so hard to bring it all together. Anyway, he liked Barney. He wasn't going to screw another man's wife behind his back, not when he had genuine respect for him.

Patrick smiled to himself. He was becoming honourable in his old age. What with the impending mortgage, and impending godfatherhood as well, he was in danger of becoming positively grown up.

He went off to find Mandy. She looked fantastic, in a black dress and high heels, her hair long and shiny. She was talking to the editor of the local county magazine, professional as ever. He suddenly felt a stab of guilt that she'd been somewhat sidelined over the past few weeks. She'd kept her head down and stayed out of the way. He went over and joined her.

She gave him a look that was odd. Wary? Accusing?

He wasn't sure. Shit – she hadn't seen him kiss Suzanna, had she? He hoped not. Even though it had meant nothing.

On her fifth trip to relieve her bladder, Sybilla finally cornered Suzanna in the loos. 'Right, young lady.'

Suzanna looked at her with wide, innocent eyes.

'What?'

'What is it with young Master Shagworthy?'

'What are you talking about?'

'Patrick. I've seen the way you look at him.'

'Sybilla – he's a colleague. We've been working closely together –'

'A bit too closely, if you ask me.'

'I'm married; he's got a girlfriend; I haven't had time to shag him, even if I wanted to. Which I don't. For a start, he's nearly ten years younger than me.'

'Who said anything about shagging?'

'I thought that's what you were implying.'

'So you've thought about it, then?'

'No!'

Suzanna hoped she sounded convincing. Sybilla pointed a perfectly manicured finger at her.

'If you screw things up with Barney, don't come crying to me. You've been warned.'

That was the trouble with Sybilla. She was terrifyingly perceptive. But not actually psychic. Suzanna realized with a jolt that if she'd sussed her out within hours of arriving in Honeycote, other people weren't going to be too far behind.

Sybilla carried relentlessly on. She was like a dog with a bone.

'I know you too well. You're not going to find happiness by running away, Suzanna. For God's sake, when are you going to face up to it?' Suzanna shrank back from Sybilla's piercing gaze. 'You've got no idea what you and Barney have achieved, have you? It's completely amazing. You've done all this, the two of you. You've pulled it all together. It's fantastic. Just don't, please, please don't, fuck it all up because you're a coward. Because you're an ostrich, and because you think falling in love with a *boy* ten years younger than you' – that was spiteful, but she had to be spiteful – 'is going to help you forget Ollie and make it all right. Because it isn't. It's going to make it ten million times worse in the long run. Trust me.'

Sybilla turned on her spiky heels, elegantly for one in her state, and stalked back inside, leaving Suzanna in semi-shock. For a second she felt furious – how dare Sybilla talk to her like that, make those assumptions? Then she realized that every word she had spoken was the truth. Sybilla might be a silly, superficial cow a lot of the time, but she had a deadly perspicacity, and she shot straight from the hip.

She was right. Patrick was ten years younger than her. And he had a girlfriend. And she had a husband. Any little sparkle between them she felt – or imagined she felt – was just the idle fancy of an emotionally unstable, pretty nearly middle-aged woman. What on earth would he see in her anyway?

Mandy worked the room like a true professional. She wanted to show them all how good she was at PR, that in fact she was better than any of them at charming journalists and editors and people that mattered. So they'd all be sorry when she fucked off . . .

'What's in a kiss?' she kept asking herself. Mandy had been retouching her lipgloss, when Suzanna's pregnant friend from London had left the cloakroom. She'd seen Suzanna and Patrick in the mirror, and their lips meet, just as the door closed behind Sybilla. The two of them had gone on to resolutely ignore each other all evening. Which, thought Mandy, was as much a sign of guilt as anything.

She seethed inwardly, and went on to greet the restaurant critic of the *Eldenbury Advertiser*.

'I do hope you'll come and give us a review,' she smiled. 'Please contact me if you want to book a table. Unless you prefer to come anonymously.'

The critic leered, making it pretty clear that what he wanted was dinner with Mandy. She smiled graciously and moved on to charm the vicar.

Ginny was waiting for Keith to fetch her a drink when she felt a finger slowly and deliberately tracing its way down her spine. She didn't need to turn round to know who it belonged to. She lit up like a string of fairy lights. She swallowed as Bertie buried his face in her neck teasingly.

'You look fucking gorgeous. They do rooms here, don't they?'

Ginny tried and failed to look stern, but couldn't take the smile off her face. The smell of his cologne, as scents are so cruelly wont to do, brought back the memory of that doorstep kiss with a frightening clarity. She tried to keep her tone light, but came over as arch.

'I haven't seen you for a long time.'

'I've been in France. I go every year for a couple of weeks. Go racing. Bit of buying. Bit of selling. You know the sort of thing.'

Yes, thought Ginny. I can imagine. He was looking . . . divine. He was in cricket whites, slightly rumpled, hair dishevelled – as if he'd walked straight off the pitch, which well he might. You couldn't be sure with Bertie. He was such a poseur, he might just be wearing them because he knew he looked utterly irresistible.

'How's the ironing going?'

He was scoffing the canapés as if he hadn't eaten for a week.

'Actually, I've got you to thank for that. It's doing incredibly well.'

He stopped in amazement.

'You don't mean you really went ahead with it?'

'I certainly did.'

Ginny felt proud. She was, as she predicted, clearing a couple of hundred pounds a week and it wasn't really eating into her spare time. She could do fifty quid listening to *Woman's Hour*. It was hardly work at all.

'Well, that's great. I've got absolutely piles of laundry after being away. I'll bring it round to you tomorrow.'

He gave her a dazzling smile, patted her on the shoulder and disappeared off to greet a friend. Ginny felt rather flat when he'd gone. He'd flirted with her one second, overtly propositioned her, then treated her like a skivvy the next. She sighed. She was just too old to cope with a helter-skelter every time they met.

As Keith came over with another glass of Pimms, she felt awash with fondness. Keith was reliable. He wasn't a roller-coaster ride. He was . . . safe. She sipped her drink and looked around, absorbing the atmosphere. There was no doubt the pub was going to be a roaring success. And she felt proud that Kitty and Sasha were the hit of the evening. They were playing on the fact that they were identical for once. They'd both tied their hair back into a plait, bound at the bottom like a horse's tail, with black ribbon tied in a big, fat bow. They wore black jeans, white pumps and the black T-shirts Barney had had made up for all the staff, inscribed with the pub's name in white across their chest. Snow-white aprons that reached nearly to the floor were tied round their waists. In line with the house rules they wore no jewellery, no nail varnish, and just subtle make-up – a sweep of mascara and rosy pink lipgloss on their full lips. They worked tirelessly all evening, filling glasses and passing canapés, answering questions, taking bookings, calling Jim the Taxi for people who'd overdone it on the complimentary booze.

The noise was monumental, like a West End bar on a Friday night, not a remote pub out in the sticks.

Ginny congratulated Keith. 'You must be so relieved.'

'Well, yes,' he admitted. 'There were a few hairy moments. But I knew they'd do it. I've got a great team. Now it's all over, I think I might treat myself to a break. A long weekend in Paris or somewhere?' He looked at her almost for approval.

'Sounds lovely,' murmured Ginny. She wasn't quite sure what he was saying. Was he suggesting they both go? She could certainly cope with a weekend away, but wasn't sure about the implications. Presumably a weekend in Paris did not mean single bedrooms and meeting up for brioches in the hotel dining room. Was Keith hinting that their relationship went up a gear? For some reason this made her start to panic. She decided the easiest thing to do was change the subject.

'I hope the neighbours won't complain about the noise.'

'I don't suppose it will be like this every night. And they shouldn't moan – if this is a success, it will push the value of their property up. That's all anybody seems to care about these days.'

He didn't seem to mind that her reception to his invitation had been lukewarm. Ginny needed to be very clear in her head about where she stood, before she went dashing off on Eurostar to the George V with Sasha's fake Louis Vuitton holdall.

Kelly and Anastasia had a wonderful evening together. A real girlie time. Kelly had given her a proper manicure and had painted her fingernails and toenails sparkly silver, then tied her hair up into a French pleat. Then she'd taken her up to her bedroom and read her *Angelina Ballerina*.

The little girl put her arms round her neck and hugged her hard.

'Will you come again?'

Kelly didn't like to make promises she couldn't keep.

'We'll see.'

She sat with Anastasia until the little girl was fast asleep. Then she went back downstairs. The lounge was amazing. An enormous U-shaped leather settee, with steel legs – a bit minimalist for Kelly's liking, but it was actually very comfy. A champagne carpet, incredibly soft. And a flat TV screen the size of a small house. A row of DVDs in alphabetical order sat on a chrome shelf next to it. Kelly picked out *Pretty Woman* – it was her most favourite film ever. She prodded the remote, trying to get the machine to work, and got the fright of her life when the curtains closed instead.

Foiled by the high-tech equipment and not wanting to break it, she amused herself looking around for evidence of Star's mother, but there was none. No photos. No stuff that could conceivably belong to a woman. She wasn't snooping, just curious. Rick hadn't really given her any details about Damien's private life. But Star couldn't have appeared out of nowhere.

The phone rang, making her jump out of her skin. She thought she'd better answer it, in case it was Damien checking up on her.

'Hello?'

A husky, slightly slurred voice on the other end responded after a confused pause.

'Who the fuck are you?'

'I'm the babysitter.'

'Yes, of course you are.' There was a cynical chuckle. 'Well, this does put an interesting light on things. Tell him I called, will you?'

The phone went dead. Kelly put the receiver down her end thoughtfully. The woman hadn't left her name. But then, she didn't really need to. Kelly knew the bitter tones of an ex-wife when she heard one.

When Damien got home, Kelly gave him a bottle of nail-varnish remover.

'I painted Star's nails. They probably won't like it at school, so you can take it off with this.' She grinned. 'I didn't think you'd have any in the house.'

'Was she good?'

'Ever so. She's lovely. You're very lucky.'

Damien felt proud. And he was grateful to Kelly. It was nice for Anastasia to have a woman about the place. Someone soft and caring, who'd take an interest in her. Not like her bitch of a mother.

'Would you like a drink before you go?'

Kelly hesitated. She was knackered. She'd got one of her most demanding clients in first thing in the morning. But Damien was looking at her anxiously. He obviously wanted a bit of company. And this was an opportunity too good to miss. She knew she was only the babysitter, but stranger things had happened. Look at *Pretty Woman* . . .

'Go on then. I'll have a cup of tea.' She sat down on a chrome bar stool. 'How was the opening?'

'Packed. Looks like it's going to be a success.'

Kelly's face gave nothing away. And Damien didn't let on that he knew about her one-time relationship with Patrick. He'd seen the boy there, lapping up all the glory. Never mind. He'd be able to surprise her soon.

They shared a pot of tea, and Damien listened while she chattered about her salon, about how the girls she employed drove her mad because they were sloppy, didn't do things the way she wanted, thought nothing of bunking off when they had a hangover. Damien admired her. She was a grafter and he had respect for that. He had tried to give her thirty quid for babysitting, but she'd insisted that was far too much. Even twenty was overdoing it.

'I haven't exactly had to do much. And it was nice to get out of the flat.'

'If you won't let me pay you, I won't be able to ask you again.'

'I'll babysit for Star any time.'

The problem with that, thought Damien, was the only reason he was likely to want to go out was with Kelly. He didn't quite have the nerve to ask her out; it was early days yet. He'd get her to babysit a couple more times, even if it meant going to sit in his car somewhere for a couple of hours. Then he could come back and chat to her, get to know her.

As Damien walked Kelly out to her car, she turned.

'By the way, somebody phoned for you. A woman. She didn't leave her name.' She paused. 'But she didn't sound very happy about me being there.'

Damien smiled at her reassuringly.

'A man's got to have a social life, hasn't he?'

He shut Kelly's door, then pressed the remote. As the gates to Honeycote Grove opened, and the security lights came on, Kelly smiled to herself as she drove her little car out. She could get used to this lifestyle, no problem.

Damien watched her leave, then waited until he was quite sure the gates were shut again. Fuck. If Nicole had got his number, then she wouldn't be very far behind. He'd have to be very careful. Very careful indeed.

After the party Keith dropped Ginny off home. The twins were helping clear up; they'd walk back together later. Gentleman that he was, he saw her right to the door.

'Perhaps we could go somewhere quieter next time. Actually have a conversation,' he joked.

'That would be lovely.'

'Friday night, maybe? I'll give you a ring.'

'Great.'

Ginny wondered if she should ask him in for coffee, but she knew the barn was in a bit of a state. Not that it should matter, but it did.

Keith leaned forward to kiss her goodnight. She turned her head imperceptibly to the side, so he got her on the corner of the mouth. He lingered a second too long and drew back to assess the look in her eyes. Ginny looked away hastily with a little smile and stepped back.

'Good night, then.'

Keith tried very hard not to look hurt and smiled bravely. He lifted a hand in farewell.

'Good night.'

As she watched his retreating back, Ginny bit her lip. Why hadn't she let Keith kiss her? He was so lovely; treated her like an absolute princess. She'd kissed Bertie all right, and he'd treated her like a slut.

That was the problem. Bertie. Just when she thought she'd got him out of her system and forgotten him, he'd turned up again, confusing her. If he hadn't gone and turned her inside out she'd have been quite happy to ask Keith in, she knew she would. But now all she could think about was that warm finger tracing its way down her spine . . .

If she kissed Keith, that meant commitment. And that meant she'd have to repel any advance Bertie made quite firmly. Not that he was going to make an advance. Or was he?

Ginny tried to pull herself together. She'd just have to make sure she wasn't in when he dropped his ironing off. If he dropped his ironing off. When had he said? Tomorrow? Oh God, she couldn't bear it. It was just like being a teenager again.

It was gone half past one before peace reigned once more at the Honeycote Arms. Everything was washed and gleaming and put away ready for the first day of trading tomorrow. The staff had all been thanked and paid a few quid extra for good will, and had gone home. Barney's parents and Iris and Sybilla and Piers had gone upstairs to bed. Barney and Suzanna, who'd hardly drunk all evening, sat down with a bottle of champagne to toast their incredible success. It had gone better than either of them had dreamed. Cars had been parked all the way down the high street. It had been standing room only inside the pub. The restaurant was booked three weekends in advance.

'We did it.'

'We did.'

They grinned and clanked glasses, drinking a toast to each other. Then Barney put his glass down and looked into Suzanna's eyes. She met them and smiled. He pulled her into his arms and she nestled into him. He kissed the top of her head, then led her upstairs by the hand.

But Suzanna couldn't do it. She couldn't make love to Barney while she was thinking about Patrick. It was too tacky for words. She tried to banish Patrick's image from her mind and concentrate. But she couldn't summon up the magic.

Barney felt her tense beneath him; sensed her reluctance. Almost her revulsion. Abruptly, he rolled off her and sat on the edge of the bed, his head in his hands.

'What is it?' Suzanna looked confused.

'If it's that much of an ordeal', he said with gritted teeth, 'then forget it.'

He threw back the duvet and got back into bed, pulling the covers over him. Horrifed, Suzanna tried to tug them off him.

'Barney!'

He turned and snarled at her.

'It's OK. I'm not going to make you do anything you don't want to.'

Suzanna felt filled with shame. What was wrong with her? Why couldn't she make love to Barney? It wasn't just because of Patrick. She could have shut her eyes and pretended; fantasized. People did it all the time.

Suddenly, she realized. It was because she was afraid; afraid that if they made love she'd get pregnant again. Even if they were careful, there was always still a chance. And she didn't think she could face it: the guilt, the betrayal of Ollie. And the fear, the terrible gut-wrenching fear of it happening all over again.

Hours after Suzanna had gone to sleep, Barney lay seething. All the support he gave her, all the love, the time, the patience, the care . . . He was only human. He was a bloke, for God's sake. How long was he expected to go without sex? He understood that it might be an ordeal for her. But they were husband and wife. He wanted to make love to her. He didn't think he was asking too much. Or maybe he was? Was he a monster for wanting sex? It had been over eighteen months. Even after Oliver had been born, they'd been at it after three weeks. But after he'd died . . . nothing. Just the big freeze. He wasn't even sure if he was capable any more. He'd had the odd furtle with himself, when the urge had got more than he could bear, but he didn't really like doing it. Anyway, it wasn't just about sex. It was about feeling close to someone, that wonderful togetherness . . .

It wasn't going to bloody happen.

He couldn't believe that they'd got so far. On the surface, they'd built a new life for themselves. The pub was on track – he didn't think the endless praise they'd received that evening was hollow. They lived in a beautiful village, with friendly neighbours; they had a tailor-made social life. Even Marmite was perfect. Why couldn't they make it work?

Beneath the surface it was all a sham. He felt hurt that he obviously repelled Suzanna so much. And he didn't think he could live in a marriage without physical love. It had once been such an important part of their relationship. Did that make him shallow?

At least it had made his mind up about one thing. Barney had been agonizing over whether to send off Kitty's demo all week. He'd managed to track down his old manager, who was still working for the same company. It had only taken a phone call to get his e-mail address. He'd even transferred the track on to his computer so he could send it as an attachment. But something had been holding him back. It was a can of worms that he wasn't sure he wanted to open.

But now? Bugger it – he didn't care any more. He'd e-mail it to Jez first thing in the morning.

18

The next day, because she knew that otherwise she would jump every time the doorbell rang or the phone went, Ginny took the twins into Cheltenham to buy something for baby Chelsea – or Arsenal, as Sasha insisted on calling her. It was odd watching her daughters cooing over little romper suits and matching hats for their half-sister. The half-sister that was no relation whatsoever to Ginny. She tried not to feel excluded when they piled up the presents in Baby Monsoon – pink ballet slippers with rosebuds on the front, a dear little angora cardigan, a T-shirt embroidered with flowers, a tiny floppy rabbit for her to clutch in one fist. The bill was whopping. At least four baskets of ironing.

Two of which, as she had feared, expected, hoped, dreamed, were waiting just inside the porch when she got back that afternoon, with a hastily scrawled note in extrovert black italics: 'When you're ready. Bxx.'

She resolutely ignored them for the rest of the day, because she knew once she'd done them she would have to contact him.

On Friday morning the twins left for college, and Ginny felt extraordinarily flat. David was picking them up that afternoon and taking them back to Cheltenham to see the baby, and they were going to stay the night. Though Sasha kept insisting if she looked anything like her mother, Chelsea would be the ugliest baby on the planet,

Ginny knew they were excited, and it made her feel more out of the picture than ever.

She decided to tackle Bertie's ironing. If she left it any longer, she would look unprofessional: she prided herself on a forty-eight-hour turn-around, and she wasn't going to let Bertie think she couldn't manage. He might, after all, prove a valuable customer. A basket a week at twenty quid was not to be sneezed at.

She felt like a bit of a pervert going through his laundry. Even though she had permission, it still felt like snooping. And it was a sensual experience. The clothes were all beautiful, in fabrics that were delicious to the touch: Sea Island cotton and poplin and silk. All absolute buggers to iron, of course. But Ginny enjoyed her task, especially when she came to his Liberty lawn boxer shorts at the bottom. It was most disconcerting, trying to be professional about ironing a man's undergarments when you couldn't stop fantasizing about what went inside them. But then Ginny suspected that was exactly why he'd put them in there. Out of sheer mischief, because he knew the effect it would have on her.

She sprinkled them liberally with lavender water, let her iron glide over the creases until they were as crisp and immaculate as the day he'd bought them, then folded them neatly on top of the other clothes.

By ten o'clock, she'd finished. She decided to drive by the Dower House and drop it off. Then she'd have the rest of the day to do whatever she liked. Convincing herself he'd be out, she put on the stonewashed cornflower-blue sweatshirt that she knew full well brought out the colour of her eyes and pinched some of Sasha's raspberry lipgloss.

*

Bertie was wrenched from his sleep by the sound of Ginny's Shogun coming down his drive. Shit! She was bringing back his ironing. He shot out of bed, pulling on a shirt and jeans and managing to brush his teeth before he went to answer the door. Luckily he was the type who suited not having a shave – it made him look even more piratical and attractive. Still, he was cross with himself. He'd meant to get some order into the place before she'd arrived, but he'd become engrossed in a Nicolas Cage action adventure movie the night before and had then gone straight to bed, resolving to get up early. But his curtains were so heavy that daylight never filtered through into his bedroom, and at half past ten he was still unconscious.

She looked sweet, bright-eyed and bushy-tailed with some sugary pink lipgloss on that made her look about twelve, clutching her Mrs Tiggywinkle basket.

'I'm just making coffee. Come and join me.' She protested, as he knew she would, but Bertie insisted. He didn't know why, but he felt like the wicked wolf in some fairy tale, luring the innocent maiden inside.

Too late, he remembered just what a hideous state the house was in. He and some friends had trashed the place the weekend before he'd gone to France two weeks ago. He'd been knackered by the time he'd arrived back at the Dower House earlier in the week; had spent the last two days at work taking delivery of everything he'd picked up on his trip. He'd been meaning to have a bit of a clear up this coming weekend. Bugger Mrs Titcombe for being so narrow-minded. It wasn't as if anyone had asked to screw her on the billiard table. He really would have to get round to finding someone else.

He saw Ginny looking up at a stag's head in the hallway. Someone's G-string was hanging ceremoniously off one of its antlers. Bertie hastily led her through into the kitchen, which he soon realized was a mistake. Ruminants bedecked with scanty underwear were nothing compared to the squalour that lay inside. In the unforgiving sunshine of a glorious May morning, it looked like a Camden squat. The cats were up on the counter, tails curled like question marks, starving hungry. They'd already licked clean every plate and bowl they could find. Bertie hastily found a box of Go Cat and shook some out on to the floor.

God, he was never going to get her into bed now. The filth was a total turn-off, and Bertie could see Ginny was horrified but trying to pretend not to be. 'Coffee?' he asked, not quite daring to meet her eye. No one in their right mind would drink out of any receptacle that had come out of this kitchen without first being vaccinated for tetanus, cholera and hepatitis at the very least.

'It's a bit of a mess, isn't it?' he said, lamely. She struggled to know what to say.

'Um, I've seen worse.'

'Have you?' he said hopefully. She tried not to laugh.

'When I was a district nurse in the backstreets of Birmingham.'

Bertie was offended.

'I've been away. And my cleaner left me – I haven't got round to getting another one . . .' Bertie trailed off. There was no excuse. He was a complete and utter slob. He gave her a winning smile. 'I don't suppose you'd give me a hand?'

She looked totally affronted, and Bertie backtracked hastily.

'I mean, just point me in the right direction. I haven't got a clue where to start.'

'It's not exactly rocket science.'

He picked up her hands in his, rubbing his thumbs over her knuckles in a rough gesture that made her quite weak at the knees. He grinned at her beseechingly.

'Two pairs of hands would be better than one, don't you think? And then we could have lunch.'

Despite herself, Ginny felt herself melting, even though she knew this was always how he got his way. But hell – what was the alternative? More ironing? She knew damn well she'd only come here this morning in the hopes of seeing him. She was hardly going to turn down his offer.

'Go on, then,' she grinned.

'What?'

'Show me where the Hoover is.'

Delighted, he took her through into the utility room and showed her the upright Hoover that had been a part of the house ever since he could remember. There was a canvas bag on the side that swelled up as soon as you turned it on. The accompanying noise was deafening. Ginny looked at it in disbelief.

'This should be in a museum. Haven't you heard of a Dyson?'

'Mrs Titcombe never complained.'

A hunt for cleaning things unearthed some smelly old dishcloths, a rancid mop and a half-empty bottle of bleach.

'I'll nip to the supermarket, shall I?' suggested Bertie.

'Do you know what to get?'

He looked a bit unsure. Ginny pulled out a chair at the

kitchen table and sat down, hunting among the debris for the back of an envelope. Bertie produced a pen from inside his jacket, which was straddling the back of another chair. She wrote him a list, then explained how he would have to insert a pound into a curious device on the shopping trolley which would allow it to be released from its chains, warned him not to join the shortest queue because it would be the nine items or less checkout and there would be a riot if he had more, and gave him her loyalty card so she could have the points added on. He looked utterly baffled, but seemed quite cheerful at the prospect.

Bertie found the supermarket, parked, and followed Ginny's instructions on how to extricate a trolley from its mates. He cruised up and down the aisles, intrigued. He watched in horror as a young woman battled with her trolley, which was laden with a mass of writhing limbs: a tiny baby with a globule of snot bubbling from one nostril, an enraged toddler screaming next to it and a grubby-faced urchin hitching a ride on the end, lobbing every brightly-coloured box within arm's reach on to their pile of shopping, which consisted of ready meals, oven chips and tins. Bertie watched, fascinated, as their mother plugged the toddler's mouth with a dummy, swiped the head of the three-year-old, wiped the baby's nose, extricated all the unwanted items from the basket and still managed to steer her trolley in a straight line, which was more than Bertie could. He reflected that this must be real life, that the nightmare she was undergoing probably wouldn't end when she got home, that there would probably be some slob of a husband waiting for her in a stained vest who'd give her a good clout if she forgot his lottery ticket.

Eventually he found the cleaning agents aisle. He remembered the days when his mother was still alive; when he used to help the woman that did. She carried with her an all-purpose tin of Vim that did for sinks, floors, loos and work surfaces. Now he was faced with a dazzling array of products, in any number of strengths, flavours, easi-pour, easi-grip, non-drip, no-run, refill, April-fresh, lemon zest, anti-bacterial, disinfectant, anti-fungal, antiseptic, de-scaling, de-moulding, non-scratch – the list went ever on. He cruised up and down for a while before getting out his phone and dialling home. Ginny answered, breathless.

'I've been stripping the beds.'

Bertie shuddered to think what she might have found, then got on with the task in hand.

'I'm completely flummoxed. What smell do we want to go for? I'd like to think there was some sort of continuity. I mean, do I plump for a zesty lemon freshness? Or a waft of alpine meadow? Or a sort of piney undertone?'

'Lemon, definitely. Everything else smells like an old lady's knicker drawer. Stick to citrus flavours. You can't go wrong.'

Bertie loved the way that Ginny knew, and was so definite. He set to filling up the trolley. Soon he had bleach, under-rim cleaner, bath-cleaner, tap-scourer, oven-cleaner, washing powder, fabric conditioner, dish-washer powder, furniture polish, air freshener, fridge-cleaner, floor-cleaner, packets of dishclothes, dusters, scourers and a funny metallic thing that promised miracles, a new mop and bucket, and two pairs of rubber gloves.

The phone had rung three times on his way round. Once for light bulbs – three screw-fitting 60-watt, five bayonet-fitting 100-watt, pearl effect. Once for candles. And loo paper, luxury white Andrex, twelve-pack.

Finding a counter that was spit-roasting chickens, Bertie remembered his promise to treat her to lunch, so he bought one, adding a French stick, a packet of rocket and some vine-ripened tomatoes. Bertie couldn't cook but after years of living out of delicatessens he knew what to buy. He didn't need to get wine. The cellar was groaning.

By the time he got back Ginny was in the utility room sorting out piles of sheets and pillow cases and towels. She immediately put the first lot on for a boil wash, the implication being that all his linen harboured disease-ridden germs that needed obliterating. And it probably did.

The house was filled with fresh air; every window had been thrown open and the odour of stale fags and cats that had lingered there before was gradually fading. Bertie dutifully retrieved every empty glass and cup from around the house, emptied all the ashtrays, picked up all the papers and magazines, then filled up his boot with empty bottles and took them off for recycling. In the car park by the Scout hut in the village, he enjoyed posting the bottles in one by one and listening to the satisfying smash. It had been a very therapeutic morning.

By three o'clock, the house was sparkling like a new pin. Light flooded in through the now clean windows. Most of the curtains had been taken down and put into a pile to be taken to the dry-cleaners. Rows of sheets and towels were drying in the sunshine outside.

Bertie insisted they stop and have something to eat. Ginny accused him of being a lightweight – she forced him to go through all the piles of junk mail and unopened correspondence that were variously littered about the house and have a ruthless chuck-out before they were allowed to stop.

Then he opened a succulent bottle of Puligny-Montrachet while Ginny laid the Pembroke table in the kitchen – Bertie was surprised at what a nice little piece it was, and felt ashamed to have covered it in his bachelor debris for so long. With his bone china and sparkling Waterford glasses, and a vase of early roses that he'd plucked from the garden, Bertie suddenly felt proud of his home.

He'd abused it, ever since he'd lost Tor. He'd had no respect for the beauty of some of the furnishings which had been left over from the big house, that his father had insisted he have. He should know better than anyone their worth and intrinsic value, but he was a spoilt little boy, putting his feet up on the sofas and leaving coffee cups on the mahogany. It had taken Ginny to make him stand back and appreciate it. None of his London friends gave a toss – used to grand surroundings themselves, they were glad of the chance to be able to behave as appallingly as they wished and not face the consequences. They thought it was a hoot to act like savages, taking their lead from their host, squashing out fag butts in their saucers with considered insouciance. Because Bertie always served tea in proper cups and saucers. It was all he had.

Ginny was glad to sit down, and was astonished at how hungry she was, until she realized how long it had been since her bowl of cornflakes that morning. They ripped the chicken apart with their bare hands, pulled off chunks of French bread which they slathered in unsalted butter then topped with thick slices of tomato. A simple feast, but one which tasted fantastic after all their hard work. And Bertie was surprised at how appreciative Ginny was of the wine, letting it roll around her tongue and savouring every last drop. He drew the cork on the second bottle he'd had the foresight to put in the fridge, then popped another one in to chill just in case.

They chatted comfortably, and Ginny told him how happy she was in Honeycote and how well the business was going already. Bertie was horrified when she told him she'd actually had to turn work away.

'You should get some outworkers. In fact, you should do that anyway. Put your prices up and get someone else to do the hard work. Just cream the profit off for yourself.'

'I couldn't do that.'

'That's what I do. I've got someone running the reclamation yard for me, doing the graft. I just do the bits I want, the buying and so on.'

'You make it sound so easy.'

'It is easy!'

Ginny didn't look sure. He picked up her hand.

'I think what you need is a holiday.'

She protested that she had only just started working.

'It doesn't matter. You've had a traumatic time of it lately. You've gone out of your way to make life easy for everyone except yourself. You deserve a treat. I've got some friends with a place in the Dordogne. I've got an open invitation. It's right on the river, surrounded by walnut trees.'

Ginny wasn't at all sure. Either how far the invitation

extended, or what to say. But it was very nice, being made a fuss of, as Bertie topped her glass up again and produced a box of profiteroles.

By four, Ginny was positively tipsy and remembered with horror she was supposed to be meeting up with Keith later that evening. She couldn't see him now! What on earth would he think? She was hardly capable of stringing two sensible words together.

She'd better phone him, before he went ahead and booked a table or something. She kept telling herself it had only been a casual arrangement; an 'if you're not doing anything else' sort of a thing. Well, she was doing something else. While Bertie wandered off to find another bottle of wine, she surreptitiously pulled her phone out of her bag.

Keith was browsing in Austin Reed. It had been so long since he'd worn a suit that when he came to look at his ties he'd found them all boring and unimaginative, plus they reminded him of all the occasions on which he'd worn them in his former life. He needed a new tie to go with this new beginning.

He was disproportionately excited about this evening. Originally, he'd thought he and Ginny could go for supper at the Honeycote Arms, to show a bit of loyalty as well as enjoy the food, and do a bit of clandestine market research. But a contact of his had left a message on his answerphone that morning, offering him last-minute tickets to *Romeo and Juliet* at the Birmingham Royal Ballet. He'd hesitated, not knowing if it was Ginny's scene or not, then reasoned you'd have to be mad to pass up the opportunity. It wasn't like forcing someone to sit through a heavy, obscure opera or a lesser-known Shakespeare play. It had had rave reviews and the tickets were like gold dust. It was, he decided, a romantic gesture without being too presumptuous.

He was very anxious to get things right at this stage in the proceedings. He looked at his watch and decided he would phone her at four to tell her. That would give her an hour to get ready – he didn't think Ginny was the sort to need any longer; a judgement that was not a criticism – and he could pick her up at five. That would leave enough time to drive into Birmingham and sneak in a couple of glasses of wine and some tapas at a little place he knew, to fend off their hunger till dinner afterwards.

He'd just chosen a splendid navy silk tie with a discreet yellow spot, and was queuing to pay, when his mobile went. It was Ginny. She sounded dreadful; her voice was rather thick and subdued.

'I'm sorry. I feel rotten. I'm coming down with something. Do you mind if we call this evening off? I just want to go to bed . . .'

Keith's heart plummeted to the bottom of his boots.

'No. Of course not. You get yourself better. It doesn't matter. I didn't have anything special planned.'

No point in making her feel worse about letting him down. Or making himself look a prat. Keith tried to be philosophical, but the taste of disappointment was more bitter than he remembered as he rather sadly put the tie back without paying for it.

He went out into the street. He passed a chemist and an idea struck him. He'd put together a little get-well gift basket for her – some Lemsips, some Lucozade, some of those scented wipes to mop her brow if she had a fever. She'd sounded very sorry for herself and there was nothing worse than being poorly on your own. He'd drop it off on the way home.

Ginny dropped the phone back in her handbag, leaned her elbow on the table and rested her head in her hand. She was, she knew, utterly plastered but in the nicest possible way. She still knew what she was doing, but she felt totally free, floating on a little cloud with no inhibitions.

Bertie looked at her with mock gravity.

'You look exhausted.'

'I am.'

'I think what you need is a Bertie special.'

She raised a querying eyebrow.

'A what?'

'A massage. To soothe your aching muscles.'

Ginny gulped. She knew this was the moment; the moment she had fantasized about though she would never admit it to anyone, not even herself. She knew she should stop right now, that what she should do was ask for a nice cup of tea to sober her up.

But then she'd never know, would she?

Keith pulled up outside Tinker's Barn. He lifted up the basket carefully, slipped out of the car and went up to the front door. He tapped gently on the knocker. He'd just give her the basket, see if there was anything she wanted. There was nothing worse than feeling rotten and wishing desperately for something you really couldn't be bothered to get yourself.

He waited, then knocked again a little louder. There was still no reply. Perhaps she was fast asleep in bed and couldn't hear. Well, he wouldn't disturb her. He left the basket in the porch, scribbling a get-well wish on the back of one of his business cards and tucking it underneath.

Then he got back in his car and drove home. He'd see if Mandy and Patrick wanted to go to the ballet. If not, he wouldn't bother. He wasn't going to drive all the way to Birmingham on his own.

Bertie ordered Ginny on to the chaise longue in the drawing room and gave her a feather pillow. The linen was still crisp and fresh from where it had been dried outside on the line. She buried her face in it while he put Roxy Music on the CD player.

'Take off your top.'

'What?'

'How can I give you a massage otherwise? Don't be silly.'

'This is such a bad idea.'

'Rubbish. It's purely therapeutic. I give all my friends massages after we've been skiing. I'm not called Magic Fingers for nothing.'

Obediently, Ginny took off her sweatshirt and lay back down as quickly as she could so he couldn't see anything. She tensed as he unhooked her bra, then told herself not to be so uptight. Of course it needed to come off. She wriggled out of it as discreetly as she could, then clamped her arms by her sides in case one of her boobs betrayed her and decided to pop out. She wasn't that drunk.

She gasped as he dripped ice-cold lotion on to her back, then began to rub it in with long, strong fingers.

He certainly knew what he was doing. She could feel all the little knots in her back and her shoulders dissolving; little spots of tension that had developed from all the ironing. She could feel herself drifting away on a cloud of Puligny-Montrachet, Bryan Ferry singing sweet nothings in her ears. She was so relaxed that she didn't protest when gradually his hands crept lower and lower, down to the base of her spine, and then lower, till he hooked his fingers into the sides of her jeans and slid them off in one smooth, expert movement . . . along with her pants. Ginny tensed with self-consciousness at first, but when he hadn't burst out laughing at her cellulite or commented on her saddlebags, she relaxed. He traced little tiny patterns on her buttocks with his fingertips that made her nerve endings tingle. She shivered with delight, never knowing quite what to expect next, lost in the luxury of this undivided attention, attention she wasn't used to.

Eventually, his hands slid down to the tops of her legs and parted them. Ginny swallowed hard with expectation. Her veins were by now throbbing sweetly: she felt sure he could hear the pulse that was pounding inside her. Feather-light, he stroked the inside of her thighs, running his thumbs along her bikini-line – thankfully still smooth – until she nearly screamed with the frustration. She wanted him to touch her – there – desperately. It was more desperate than any need she'd ever felt – the need for food, or water, or air. She gave a pleading whimper.

He turned her over and looked into her eyes with a wicked smile: 'What? What is it you want?'

She couldn't speak – couldn't say it. She'd never asked for anything sexually. What was she supposed to say? Suddenly she gave a gasp. A light finger had brushed the top of her clitoris – barely perceptible, so fleeting she couldn't have been sure he'd actually made contact if it hadn't been for the shockwaves it sent through her. He laughed with pleasure at her pleasure. He'd relented. He was no longer teasing her, and she gave herself up.

She didn't know what to focus on. His fingers inside her. Or his fingers on her. He was playing her like a virtuoso plays a violin – just the right amount of pressure here, a light touch there, then a pause, an agonizing pause that only increased the pleasure when he started again. As she floated away on the sensations he was giving her, she felt she was someone else. An Egyptian princess being anointed by her slaves; a damsel no longer in distress, at one with her rescuer. She was in a world of her own, a world that she alone was the centre of.

She'd always enjoyed sex with David. It had always been . . . nice, she supposed was the word. She'd always enjoyed the warmth and the closeness. And she'd always climaxed – or she'd thought she had. At least, there'd usually been a warm, whooshy feeling in her tummy at some point. And if she'd suspected that there might be a little more to it than that, given that entire multimillion-pound industries were based on the pursuit of that supposed ecstasy, she'd never felt the need to seek it.

This, however, was different.

Suddenly, all the sensations she'd been experiencing joined up, from her breasts to her loins to the tips of her fingers. A white hot current shot through her, shattering her into millions of tiny particles, glittery snowflakes of ecstasy replacing the blood in her veins. At the height of the intensity, she thought she couldn't bear any more; that she might die from the extreme pleasure. In the depths of her consciousness, she thought perhaps she was already in heaven.

Before her tremors had died away, she felt Bertie slide into her. With long, firm, confident strokes, he recharged her, and the feelings began again, deeper, more subtle, less intense but still exquisite, and this time she found having him inside her gave it another dimension. Instinctively she pulled him to her, wrapping her arms around him in her need to become part of him, in her need to share the experience, wondering how you could feel so close to someone you barely knew.

In a flash, she understood. If this was what David had gone to Faith for, if she'd been able to supply him with this sort of experience, then it all made sense. You'd give up everything for this. If there was any point to life, thought Ginny as she gasped for breath, then surely this was it.

That evening, Damien was having his weekly meeting with his managers at the bar in Cheltenham when his mobile rang. He snatched it up. It was Kelly, who was babysitting for Anastasia. He'd been planning to cook her a meal when he got back. Steak and salad; something simple that didn't look as if he'd given it too much thought. Which of course he had.

'What is it?' There was panic in his voice, because he knew Kelly would only phone in an emergency.

'There's a woman at the gates. She won't go away – she keeps on ringing the bell.'

Damien's heart was in his mouth.

'I'll be right back. Just take the entryphone off the hook. Does she know Star's there?'

'No. I said I was the cleaner.'

'Good girl.' That's what he liked so much about Kelly. She used her initiative and didn't ask too many questions. He stood up and looked at his managers.

'Got to go. I'll call by tomorrow. Phone me if there's any problems.'

The two of them nodded. They were good blokes. He paid them well, because he didn't want them to walk. And he knew they wouldn't have their fingers in the till, because he made sure his reputation went before him. They knew he'd have their fingers chopped off without asking any questions.

He put his foot down all the way back to Honeycote. He knew it had to be Nicole trying to get in, but his heart still sank into his boots when he saw her. He thanked God that no one else had come in or out of the compound in the time it had taken him to drive home. She'd have sweet-talked her way in, he was sure of it.

He parked outside the gates, hiding the remote control in his pocket so he could get back in later. She was leaning against a beaten-up old Ford Sierra with different-coloured panels. Inside, it had furry seat covers and Damien could smell the sickly air-freshener that was doing battle in vain against the stale smell of cigarettes.

Her companion was sitting in the driver's seat with his legs out of the car, obviously ready to leap to his feet at the first sign of trouble. He was anywhere between thirty-five and fifty-five, with pock-marked skin, greasy swept-back hair and a distrustful, foxy gaze. Each ear was pierced, with a silver skull hanging from a ring. Damien knew he was scum, lowlife – the type that would do anything for a pitiful amount of cash. Which was, of course, what made him potentially dangerous. He'd have to be careful. He might have a gun. He'd certainly have a knife.

Was this how low she'd sunk?

If he hadn't known it was Nicole, he wouldn't have recognized her. Would certainly never have looked at her twice. How could he ever have thought her beautiful? She was so thin, so wasted, and her nose looked huge against her ravaged sunken cheeks. Her eyes were spiteful slits, eyes that he could have once drowned himself in. She looked, he thought, like the picture of Baba Yaga in the story book he'd read to Anastasia the other night.

She dropped her fag on the ground. He could smell the cheap tobacco on her breath. It repulsed him. He hated smoking. She looked at him defiantly as he approached.

'I suppose you thought I'd never find you. Well, you're not that clever.'

Her companion gave a self-satisfied grin. It was obviously him that had run them to ground. Damien shrugged and smiled, feigning insouciance.

'The only thing I'm surprised about is you didn't find me sooner.'

Nicole scowled in annoyance.

'I want to see Anastasia.'

'You can't. She's staying over at a friend's.' Nicole looked suspicious and Damien stood his ground. 'You can wait here till she comes back, but you might be moved on. As you can imagine, the residents of Honeycote aren't too keen on loiterers.'

She looked mockingly in at his house.

'You have done well.'

'You could have had it too, Nicole. It was your choice.'

She smirked.

'You're going to drop her like a hot potato when you find out what I've come to tell you.'

'And what's that?'

There was a gleam of triumph in her eyes as she delivered her death blow. It was the only sign of animation he'd seen in her face since she'd arrived.

'She's not yours.'

Damien laughed.

'Nice try.'

'She's not. She's the spitting image of me. There's not a single drop of blood in her body that belongs to you.'

Damien made a supreme effort to hide the tremble in his voice.

'We'll have a test done.'

'Just what I was going to suggest. Then you'll have the proof. And then we'll see what the court says.'

Damien felt winded. As if she'd punched him full on in the stomach without warning. But a voice in his head told him to keep his cool. She was goading him. It was a trap. No doubt she had a hidden camera ready for when he swung the first punch. Ready for the judge.

'And you won't have a leg to stand on. If she's not actually yours, there's not a judge in the land who would give you custody.' She wiggled her bony fingers at him in a taunting farewell. 'Be in touch.'

She jumped into the Sierra and the car sped off with a screech of tyres.

Damien didn't make it back to his car before he threw up, retching and retching until there was nothing left in his stomach. In the back of his mind he thought he'd better clear it up before any of the other residents caught sight of it. It was strange how in times of total panic one could be so practical. And it made him realize how far he'd come. Where he'd been brought up, a pool of vomit wouldn't merit a second glance.

At the Hippodrome in Birmingham, Keith settled into his seat, trying to relax and enjoy himself. Mandy had been sweet: she'd immediately suggested they go to the ballet together. She obviously realized how disappointed he was at being stood up, and thought it would take his mind off it. Better than sitting at home moping.

Romeo and Juliet were enacting the balcony scene. The ballerina looked so tiny, her seeming fragility belying the strength that allowed the graceful movements that were well beyond the physical capabilities of most people. She fluttered and shimmered before her lover.

Next to Keith, tears were streaming down Mandy's face. The love between them was so tangible, so strong, so passionate, so right. It was like another presence on the stage. Finally the lovers kissed and Mandy buried her face in her hands. What luxury, to be so sure. She herself was torn in two, not knowing which way to turn, and seeing the star-crossed pair so certain of their commitment twisted the knife in her heart.

Rick had texted her earlier, about going surfing that weekend. She'd put Patrick to the test, and asked if they could go out for the day together. He'd hesitated before saying no; he had far too much to do at the Honeycote Arms.

He'd made her mind up for her.

*

Later, as they lay in his freshly-made bed in a sweat-drenched post-coital tangle, Bertie kissed Ginny's bare shoulder and demanded, 'Marry me.'

'Don't be ridiculous,' answered Ginny tartly.

'Please. You're everything I've ever wanted.'

'What – someone that will do all your dirty work? Clean for you and screw you, you mean?'

She was only teasing, but he was concerned that she shouldn't think that.

'No. You make me feel safe. You feel like you'd always be there.'

'You make me sound like your mother.'

There was a short silence. She didn't know. She couldn't know or she wouldn't have said it.

'I never did anything like that with my mother, I can assure you.'

Bertie hooked his arm round her waist and pulled her to him. She was so comfortable, nestling up in the crook of someone else's body. 'There is just one other problem,' she murmured in answer to his proposal. 'I'm actually still married to someone else.'

But Bertie was already snoring gently. And moments later Ginny too dozed off on a little cloud of bliss, images of the day sliding through her mind, mops and dusters and mind-blowing orgasms . . .

Keith took Mandy to Bank after the ballet, a huge, bustling glass-fronted restaurant that was buzzing with life. As the car made its way up Broad Street, Mandy found herself thinking how much Rick would love it here. Everywhere you looked people were in party mode. There was an infinite number of bars and clubs to choose from: vodka bars, Irish bars, Australian bars, retro bars, salsa bars. Music spilled out on to the street. Outside one restaurant was a gaudily-dressed fire-eater. Legions of scantily-clad girls prowled the pavements in gangs, laughing and talking on their phones and flirting with strangers. It was a million miles away from Honeycote – and yet less than an hour's drive.

Mandy realized Rick was right. She didn't have a clue about the real world. If this was Birmingham, then what was further afield?

In the restaurant, Keith put down his fork with a sigh.

'Mandy, love – is anything the matter? You don't seem yourself.'

She looked down at her plate. The Dover sole was perfectly cooked in lemon butter, but she couldn't face it. She shook her head emphatically. So emphatically it was obvious she was lying.

'I'm fine. I'm just . . . tired.'

'Maybe you need a break. Have a little holiday. Get on the Internet, book yourself something.'

Her father was so kind, so concerned. Mandy felt herself about to dissolve into tears. Keith put a hand on hers.

'Hey . . .'

'I'm so confused, Dad.' She couldn't elaborate. Couldn't confide in him. He'd be shocked.

'Just follow your heart, love. I know you'll do the right thing.' He paused. 'I'll always be here for you, you know that.'

He trusted her so much. She didn't deserve his concern. He'd be furious if he knew what she was about to do.

*

On the journey back, Keith slowed down at Tinker's Barn as he went past, wondering how Ginny was. He peered towards the front door, and saw his basket still inside the porch. She must be still in bed, and hadn't ventured outside. He was concerned. She must really be ill. She might need a doctor.

Another thought occurred to him. One that he didn't like much.

Perhaps she hadn't actually been at home when she phoned him.

Keith put his foot down and headed back to Kiplington, trying to ignore the horrid little stab of humiliation that was digging him just below the ribs. It was far worse than the disappointment he'd felt earlier, when Ginny had phoned him to say she was unwell. Now he realized that he'd been passed over; that she'd had a better invitation. He supposed he'd been optimistic to think that their relationship might work. He remembered how he'd had a little daydream, about them being an item, a couple, and hosting dinner parties at Keeper's Cottage. Not dinner parties like Lucy and Mickey had – he could never hope to have their style, their élan – but it would have been nice to have been on the social circuit; to have people saying 'We're going to Keith and Ginny's tonight,' and perhaps looking forward to it.

That wasn't going to happen. Keith contemplated the future gloomily and decided he wasn't going to bother putting himself through the torture any longer. He thought ruefully that perhaps he should try and find a partner on the Internet. A Russian bride, or Thai – apparently they devoted themselves to making their husbands happy, waited on them hand, foot and finger.

But that wasn't what he wanted. He was a giver, not a taker. Sod it, he thought. Why had he driven past and looked? He could have been at home asleep in blissful ignorance by now.

He turned and looked at Mandy fast asleep in the front seat next to him. She was still the only thing that mattered. If things didn't work out with Ginny, if the Honeycote Arms was a disaster, if the whole bloody brewery went bust, it didn't matter. As long as Mandy was happy. He wished desperately that he knew what to do to put a smile back on her face.

Damien had never known such pain. Such fear. Such uncertainty. If the bitch had wanted to make him suffer, she'd certainly succeeded. He'd hustled a somewhat bewildered Kelly out of the house, wanting to be alone with Nicole's dreadful revelation. And when Anastasia padded in wearing her pyjamas with the little pink stars all over them, all ready for bed, he held her warm little body so tightly she protested.

One moment he was able to convince himself that of course Nicole was talking nonsense. And the next his heart would give a lurch as he realized that she could be speaking the truth. If Anastasia had been sired by some-one else, no matter who he was he was unlikely to have been as wealthy as Damien. Anastasia would have been Nicole's ticket to the life she craved. Only now, when they'd reached the end of the road in their negotiations, was she willing to give up her weapon in order to hurt him, out of spite.

As he tucked his daughter in that night, he analysed her every feature, her every mannerism, searching in vain for a similarity between them. Physically, she was emphatically Nicole, from her colouring down to her bone structure – her dark curls, her pale skin, her sooty lashes and her eyes the colour of Coca-Cola. Personality-wise, she was just herself. She could be bossy and assertive when she wanted to be, but she wasn't demanding as such; never had a tantrum when things didn't go her way, but listened to reason. She would just give the smallest pout of disapproval. She was loving, giving, affectionate – would bring him glasses of juice full to the brim and a handful of biscuits when she thought he needed refreshment, without being asked. Every picture she painted at school, every model she made, every sticky, squashy fairy cake or biscuit was proudly presented to him.

He waited until she was fast asleep, then slipped into his study. It was immaculate, as if no one had ever set foot in there, but then Damien was meticulous about filing: everything was slipped into a colour-coded file and stored in the beech-fronted cabinet.

He sat in front of the computer, heart thudding as he turned it on and the screen-saver swirled into life in front of him. He connected to the Internet and called up his favourite search engine. His hands hovered uncertainly over the keys. He wasn't sure what to type in. Eventually he made a decision and typed in 'paternity test'.

Hundreds of possible web sites came up. He didn't suppose he was the first person ever to face this particular dilemma, but he was amazed that there was a huge industry supplying what were, in effect, home DNA tests, for those with a sneaking suspicion that their children had in fact been fathered by the milkman, or had been presented with a demand for financial support for offspring they were sure they couldn't have fathered.

He read through everything carefully. The procedure seemed straightforward and painless, involving a simple swabbing of the inside of the mouth with a Q-tip. The only complication seemed to be that if a sample wasn't available from the mother, then the test might not be so conclusive. Damien couldn't imagine Nicole opening wide and providing him with a gobbet of saliva, and he certainly didn't want to alert her to what he was doing

He trawled through what felt like hundreds of web sites until he found one that seemed efficient and bona fide and quick. The test itself wouldn't stand up in a court of law, but at this moment Damien was only seeking reassurance for himself. He applied for the kit on-line, typing in his credit card details and asking for the express service. The kit should arrive with him by courier the next day, with the results within two working days. She had to be his. What the hell had he done to deserve this?

He stopped short as he suddenly realized something. This was, in fact, exactly what he deserved! He'd made his money exploiting women, for God's sake! What was that saying? An eye for an eye? Perhaps taking Anastasia away was just punishment for all those souls he had tarnished, all those sixteen-year-olds who'd leaped at the chance to dance in his clubs, only to discover the horrible, seedy truth. She was the price he was going to have to pay.

And now, even though he'd moved on from all of that, he wasn't behaving any better, with his bully-boy plan to destroy the Honeycote Arms. Just so he could have it for himself. Just so he could impress everyone. Just so he could play the big I Am.

He was getting his just deserts all right. Who on earth

did he think he was? He might think he had moved on and purged himself, but in fact what he was planning – the sabotage, the hostile takeover bid, the vain attempt to prove he was one up on everyone else – was even more despicable than his previous dabblings. How could he hope to prove he was better than everyone else, when in fact he was probably what they had thought he was all along: a small-time petty criminal-cum-gangster, with a chip on his shoulder.

He told himself it was partly for Kelly: revenge for the way she and her parents had been treated by the Liddiards. But what would she say if she knew the truth? She wouldn't be impressed in the least. Kelly was honest and true to herself. She was happy with who she was. She didn't need to prove herself, not like he did. And she'd never felt the need to get revenge; she didn't seem to hold anything against Patrick or his father. So why did Damien feel the need to go charging in and give them their come-uppance? Because Patrick had called him a pimp and sneered at his car? Perhaps Patrick hadn't been so far from the truth . . .

Why couldn't he be comfortable in his own skin? Why did he have this brash need to show off how big, how clever, how rich he was? How he could pull a fast one? Why on earth did he think people would like him more and accept him, just because he owned the Honeycote Arms? It wouldn't change the person he was underneath at all. Bitter, cynical, greedy, insecure, hard-bitten . . .

No! thought Damien. That wasn't what he wanted to be. It might be what he had become, through circumstance, because of the cards life had dealt him, because of the way he'd been treated. But it wasn't what he wanted to be at all. He wanted a simple life, a happy life. He wanted to be a good father to Anastasia – he thought he was a good father to her already, but he wanted to be someone she could be proud of, not someone who had skeletons and secrets and a dark past. And he wanted a healthy, happy, trusting relationship, to provide Anastasia with a secure environment.

Assuming, of course, she was his and he still had that choice.

Damien had never been superstitious before. He'd never felt the need to avoid cracks in pavements, was happy to walk under ladders, didn't panic if he broke a mirror. He believed that you made your own luck. But now, he wasn't prepared to take the risk.

He had to turn his back on everything he had done. He had to undo all the evil things he had done. And everything he was about to do. He had to turn over a new leaf. If he did, Anastasia would be his. He rushed to his phone.

'Pebbles? It's Damien. Listen – that deal we had – I want you to call your boys off. Forget I even said anything.'

There was a pause and sucking in of breath through teeth.

'No can do, mate. The orders have gone out.'

'Well, surely you can cancel it?'

'No. I put the word out to my man, see. He sorts it, anonymously. So it can't ever be traced back to you, see.'

'There must be some way?'

'You know the rules, Damien. You shouldn't strike a deal if you want to go back on it.'

'Can you just tell them – no rough stuff? No violence.'

'I told you. It's out of my hands. The boys have got their money. They'll do their job, like they were asked.'

Damien put the phone down, hands trembling. That was the trouble with going straight to people who you knew would do the job. They did it, no messing. They had no truck with people who changed their minds.

19

Anyone watching Mandy pack for the weekend might have thought it was strange that all that was going into her rucksack were jeans, T-shirts and shorts, plus a swimming costume and two bikinis. Very odd, given that she was going to spend the weekend in London with an old school friend.

'It's Libby's birthday. She's having a girls' weekend. We're going to go shopping. And clubbing,' she explained to Patrick, who had no objection. In fact, he was relieved. He'd been wondering how to keep her out of the way during the auction.

'I'm debriefing with Suzanna this morning,' he covered.

Huh, thought Mandy. Yet more proof of his increasing uninterest in her and his obsession with Mrs Blake. At least that was what she convinced herself.

Keith was delighted, and glad that she seemed able to snap herself out of her gloom of the night before. She had to get away and have her own space and a bit of fun. It might be just what she needed to bring her out of herself. He dropped her at Eldenbury station to get the train to Paddington and slipped her a couple of hundred quid.

'Have some fun. Get yourself something nice.' Mandy didn't really need spoiling, but Keith's marriage had led him to believe that what made women happy was money, and it was a hard mindset to lose.

All it made Mandy feel was guilty. She waited for his car to disappear before buying a ticket to Evesham — totally in the opposite direction for Paddington — and nipping over the bridge to platform two. She lurked in the waiting room, praying that she would see nobody she knew, and leaped on to the train when it arrived, looking anxiously over her shoulder all the while. She was, she decided, no good at deception, and thanked God it hadn't been Patrick who had taken her to the station. She would never have been able to go through with it.

She didn't like lying to him. But then, she reasoned, if he'd given her the attention she felt she deserved, she wouldn't be asking herself if indeed there was more to life. She felt unsettled and insecure. Not just about her relationship with Patrick, but about her entire future. It would be only too easy to settle down into a cosy existence in Honeycote, perhaps become the next Mrs Liddiard. It was very idyllic, on the surface. But would she be missing out, by settling for the soft option?

The train pulled into the station at Evesham and she jumped off. With her head down and a baseball cap pulled over her eyes, she went out into the car park and scanned it anxiously. He was there, sitting astride his bike. Her stomach gave a lurch. He hadn't seen her yet. There was still time to bottle out, turn round and jump on the next train home. It was an enormous risk, and Mandy wasn't used to living dangerously. But the whole point of the exercise was to push herself and see what she was missing.

Her pulse quickened as she strode decisively through the car park towards him, and as he smiled at her, lazily, just with one corner of his mouth, she knew she'd made the right decision. She took the helmet he held out to her, slung her leg over the saddle and nestled into him. As the bike roared through the car park and out on to the main road, heads inevitably turned, but by now Mandy wasn't worrying about being seen. The speed, the closeness of Rick's body and the anticipation of the weekend ahead gave her an incredible rush that was worth going to the gallows for.

Ginny woke the next morning with a thundering headache and a boiling torrent of guilt roaring through her veins. Bertie was out for the count. She slid very carefully out from under his proprietorial clasp. She couldn't see her clothes anywhere. She wrapped a towel round her for decency and went in search. Eventually she found the trail of evidence: her bra and knickers were hanging over the side of the chaise longue, on which she vaguely remembered being stretched out.

She scrambled into them hastily. She found her car keys, trying not to think about the fact that she was bound to still be too pissed to drive. She'd seen at least three empty bottles on her search, but she didn't care. She had to get away, back to the peace and solitude of her own bed and some sort of sanity. She scooped up Hope, not quite able to meet her eye. She couldn't explain to the little dog why she'd been housed in Bertie's scullery overnight and had to have cat food for supper. She thought about leaving a note for Bertie, but didn't have a clue what to write. Thanks for a fantastic shag?

By some miracle she got back to the barn safely and let Hope out of the boot. She could barely walk up the path; her legs had been like jelly in the car. She'd hardly had the strength to use the pedals. Giddy with lack of sleep, she thanked God that the twins had stayed the night at David's. She couldn't have stood their questioning. She wouldn't have been able to fob them off. She had 'rogered senseless' written all over her. She fumbled to get her keys into the lock and pushed open the door. Stumbling inside, something on the floor of the porch caught her eye. It was a little gift basket full of soothing items. Attached to it was a note: 'Wishing you a speedy recovery. Keith.'

She picked up the basket with shaking hands. What the hell was she thinking of? She was being courted by the kindest, sweetest, most thoughtful man she'd ever met; a man who'd shown her the utmost consideration. And she'd repaid him by spending the night having rampant sex with the most notoriously unstable, unfaithful, unsuitable man in the county – probably the country.

Not only that, but Keith must now know she had been lying to him on the phone the night before, for she obviously hadn't been in when he came round to drop off his gift.

She couldn't think about it. She had to have a shower. No, a bath, to wash away her aches, her bruises, her guilt. Her hip bones were bruised where Bertie's had dug into hers. She was covered in rashes: on her cheeks, where his five o'clock shadow had chafed her. And her inner thighs . . . She shuddered with the memory, wanting to shut it out, but at the same time wanting to relive every agonizingly ecstatic moment.

She poured half a box of Radox under the taps, then slid into the punishingly hot water. All she craved was a fresh pair of pyjamas, her own sheets and sleep.

Sleep that would help her escape from her torment; sweet, healing oblivion from which she hoped, desperately, she would wake with an answer and some sort of absolution.

Was it a crime? She hadn't plighted her troth to Keith, or whatever you called it. They weren't an official item. But what constituted official?

No matter how hard she tried, Ginny couldn't really justify what she'd done. However she explained it to herself, it just wasn't very nice. And Ginny had always been just that. Nice.

Eventually the bath became cold and the tank was drained of hot water. She climbed out of her cocoon and put on her dressing gown; her pink towelling dressing gown that was twelve years old but she couldn't bear to throw away because it was big and cuddly and made her feel safe.

A banging on the front door made her jump out of her skin. Whoever it was, she didn't want to answer it. It might be Keith, demanding to know where she'd been the night before – though she knew he'd never ask. Or it might be Bertie . . .

She couldn't hide. Her car was there: whoever it was knew she was in, because they were persisting. She took a quick look in the mirror, but couldn't meet herself in the eye, then hurried downstairs.

It wasn't Keith. Or Bertie. It was David, with a small, howling bundle of rage and a desperate expression.

'I've just dropped the twins off at the pub for their lunchtime shift,' he explained. Then rather desperately, holding up the baby: 'I don't know what to do. I can't get her to take her bottle.'

Life was weird, thought Ginny.

'Chelsea, I presume,' she said, and stood aside to let the two of them in.

Fifteen minutes later, she had managed to establish some sort of order. She'd discovered that David was trying to feed the week-old Chelsea stone-cold milk straight from the fridge.

'Faith says she's got to learn. She says there's no reason on earth why babies need their bottle warm. It's a question of getting used to it.'

Faith had, apparently, gone shopping with her mother to buy some new clothes. For herself.

'She won't touch her maternity stuff now. And she can't quite get into her pre-pregnancy clothes,' explained David, who'd been left in sole care. Faith seemed to think that, as he'd already raised two perfectly healthy daughters, he could manage on his own. But he was in total despair. The car seat was a mystery. He hadn't even attempted to unfold the pram-cum-pushchair-cum-stroller. The changing bag was full of all sorts of mysterious items that he couldn't identify.

Ginny warmed the bottle in a jugful of boiling water, then sat with Chelsea in her lap while the little baby sucked contentedly. She turned to talk to David to see he'd fallen asleep on the sofa. He'd been up all night, apparently, even though he'd done a day's work at the surgery. Surely that wasn't fair, thought Ginny indignantly, then wondered why she was sticking up for him. He'd made his bed – if he didn't get to lie in it, then that was his problem.

She popped the baby on her shoulder and paced round the living room, rubbing her back until the required little burp. It was almost as if it was yesterday that she'd done the same for her girls. She could tell by the sudden dead weight that Chelsea had gone off to sleep, just like her dad.

Patrick arrived in good time at the Star and Garter Hotel on Saturday morning. The auction was to begin at midday – to the minute, the details had said rather sternly. There were several lots being sold off: a couple of pony paddocks, a building plot, a bungalow with an agricultural covenant and a cluster of barns for conversion. Little Orwell Cottage was the last to come under the hammer. He was given a bidding number – fifty-five. He'd tried to see some omen in this allocation, but couldn't.

He went to the bar and got himself a drink. Just half a pint. He didn't want his judgement going all over the shop. He recalled James's advice. James, who had been to more auctions than anyone he knew had had hot dinners, and had made a successful living out of it. Enough to finance this venture, anyway. He impressed upon Patrick that the important thing was not to get emotional; to look upon it as a business proposition, to fix a top price in your head and not to go beyond it for any reason whatsoever. *Whatsoever.*

Patrick was determined to heed his advice. They'd taken a long hard look at the economics: even done out to the highest specification, the cottage was too tiny to ever command much over two hundred thousand. There was no scope for extension to the sides or the back – it was an end-of-terrace that backed on to someone else's land, with only a pocket hanky at the side for a garden.

So Patrick's top price was a hundred and fifty. He just had to hope and pray that no one else had set their heart on it.

James had offered to come with him. But somehow Patrick didn't want his uncle there holding his hand. This was something he had to do on his own. He took his seat and watched the room filling up with people, and whiled away the time trying to second-guess their reason for being there. The auctioneer in his owlish glasses was self-explanatory, as were his minions, who immediately began busying themselves with paperwork, looking self-important. A trio of farmers, who looked as if they'd been called away in the middle of milking, were no doubt curious about the prices that the barns were going to reach, with a view to selling off their own surplus farm buildings. A young, cocky-looking lad, sporting construction boots and clutching a tiny mobile phone, was probably a builder looking for development opportunities and with cash in his pocket. A couple of suited types looked like professionals being sent to bid on someone else's behalf.

Then a mousy-looking girl came in, late twenties, with a navy round-neck jumper, floral skirt and obligatory pearls and hair band. She had the details of Little Orwell Cottage in her hand. She sat down nervously, eyes darting round the room. And Patrick knew instinctively that here was his opposition. That she had fallen in love with Little Orwell Cottage too. That she'd already worked out which Designers Guild fabric she was going to have for the curtains in the sitting room. Moments later she was joined by a pink-faced bloke of about her own age. The socking great sapphire on her left hand told Patrick they must be engaged to be married, and had Little Orwell earmarked as their first home.

Well, dream on, he thought. They weren't fucking having it. It was his. His and Mandy's.

When David woke up with a start half an hour later, Ginny was looking down at Chelsea with a strange expression.

'I was just wondering', she said, 'if you'd rather she'd been a boy.'

David looked horrified.

'Of course not! What an awful thing to say.'

Ginny shrugged.

'I just wondered if you'd always secretly wanted a boy. And you left me because I couldn't ever give you one.'

'No. No! The girls were always all I'd ever wanted.'

'I see. It was just me that wasn't.'

Guilt and tiredness were making Ginny carpish and self-pitying. How dare David waltz in here, dump his love-child on her lap and go off to sleep?

'That's not fair –'

'Excuse me?' Ginny felt every right to be outraged. 'I don't think you know the meaning of fair. I don't think it was particularly *fair* of you to run off with someone half my age. When the only thing I was guilty of was cooking and cleaning and ironing and bringing up your daughters and doing your filing and paying your bills and all the things to do with your business that you found beneath you –'

'You never said you were unhappy.'

Ginny took in a deep breath.

'I wasn't. I was quite happy doing all of those things. It was you, obviously, that was unhappy.'

David looked very shamefaced.

'No, Ginny. I wasn't. Looking back I think what I was is a tiny bit bored. And Faith came along and brought back some adrenalin into my life. Gave me a reason to look in the mirror. All very shallow, I know . . .'

'Sex. It was about sex, wasn't it?'

After her night with Bertie, Ginny now understood. She recalled a moment, at the height of her ecstasy, when she'd genuinely thought that was the only thing that mattered. It was an incredible, all-consuming, all-powerful feeling. She wondered what would have happened if the tables had been turned. If, instead of David meeting Faith, she had met Bertie and been unable to resist. Would it have been her telling David she was sorry, that their marriage was over because she'd found sexual gratification . . .

David was talking.

'I was never unhappy with you, Ginny. I loved you. And I still do. In fact . . .' He swallowed, and his mouth twisted into a wry smile. 'I wouldn't blame you if you came at me with a carving knife, but I'd like to try again.'

Ginny looked at him in disbelief.

'Don't tell me you're really serious. Don't tell me you've thought it through.'

'I miss my girls. I miss the fun we all used to have. They're always on their guard when they come to me. Faith . . . inhibits them.'

'What about Faith? What does she think about all of this?'

'She's got no rights. We're not married. I'll support Chelsea, of course. And I'll buy her out of the house. It would mean us living in Cheltenham, because of the surgery . . .'

'David. You can't do this to me.'

'Think about it, Ginny. We can rebuild our life. Better than ever before. You're free now the twins are at college. You can do what you like – not other people's bloody ironing.'

He gestured dismissively at the empty baskets.

'I like my ironing!'

'For heaven's sake. You've got a good brain, woman. Use it.'

'What about Chelsea? How can we rebuild our life with a baby in tow?'

'Faith's got her down for full-time nursery as soon as she's six weeks. I'd only have her at weekends. Or every other weekend.'

Ginny raised her eyebrows. She knew Faith's type. Any excuse to dump Chelsea and run.

'And how are you planning to buy her out?'

David didn't quite meet Ginny's eye.

'You've still got your share of the house, haven't you?'

Ginny gasped. He was serious. To have thought it through to this extent. A wave of light-headedness came over her; too much bed and not enough sleep, as the old saying went.

'I can't deal with this, David.'

'Ginny . . .'

He came towards her, with his arms outstretched. Shit. He was going to kiss her. And for a moment it was very tempting. To fall into his familiar arms. After all, she'd never actually fallen out of love with him. Not officially. After he'd left, she'd trained herself not to care, but she'd never really convinced even herself.

She tried to picture their life. The twins would love to live in Cheltenham – they'd both be finished at the college in Evesham this summer. It was a lively town: lots to do and see. If they joined forces, life could be easy again. She thought of the knickers hanging on the line in the tiny bathroom upstairs – they took ages to dry. There wasn't room in the kitchen for a dryer and Ginny didn't like hanging them on the rotary line outside as it was too close to the road for comfort. She didn't like the thought of passers-by inspecting their smalls, and possibly being tempted to pinch them.

Then she thought to herself – hang on a minute! She hadn't struggled for the past few months to build a new life for her and the twins, only to capitulate at David's whim. They'd got a lovely new home, they'd settled into the village, the girls each had a job which they seemed to love and seemed to be good at – even Sasha! – and they'd made a host of new friends. Added to that, Ginny had discovered that, far from being the mousey little house-wife she'd thought she was, she was very eligible indeed. Last night had been proof enough of that.

As if on cue, the telephone shrilled indignantly, vying for attention. Flustered, she snatched it up, moving to the other side of the room, as far out of David's earshot as she could manage. She panicked when she heard a voice, as rich and as dark as a Columbian coffee bean.

'You ran off. I wanted to bring you breakfast.'

'I can't talk. I've got someone here.'

Chelsea gave an indignant howl.

'I'm not even going to ask,' said Bertie.

'Don't,' said Ginny. In a minute, she thought, I might wake up, and everything will be back to normal.

'I love you.'

'Don't toy with me, Bertie,' she replied, a trifle harshly. 'I'm tired of being picked up and put down at other people's convenience, for their own amusement.'

'That's not what you think, is it?' Bertie sounded hurt.

'Yes, I do, actually,' she replied. 'So can you give me a bit of space? I'm a bit confused at the moment . . .'

'Is that a don't call me, I'll call you sort of a thing?'

'Yes,' she said and hung up.

David looked at her questioningly.

'You look a bit . . . flustered.'

'Just a tricky client,' she assured him. Which wasn't a total lie. But the pinkness of her cheeks told David that he wasn't the only one in the running.

The wait for Little Orwell Cottage to come under the hammer seemed interminable to Patrick, but eventually, at twenty past one, the time arrived. The room had thinned out a little bit, but most people seemed to stay on. Patrick prayed that it was because they had nothing better to do on a Saturday than watch other people part with their money.

'And here we have a delightful farmworker's cottage; ripe for renovation. *Very* desirable.' The auctioneer looked round sternly, in case anyone should disagree with his diagnosis, and opened the bidding. It began briskly, slowing down once it went over a hundred and thirty-five, until eventually it was down to Patrick, the young builder and the mousy girl and her pink fiancé.

At a hundred and forty the builder dropped out, obviously seeing any hope of a profit margin evaporate into thin air. Patrick kept on bidding, impassive, unemotional, trying not to flicker every time the bids went up by another thousand. Forty-eight. Forty-nine.

It was down to him. He put up his card for his last bid – a hundred and fifty – hoping and praying that his counter-bidders had the same ceiling. He thought they probably did. Pinky was looking even pinker and little droplets of sweat had appeared on his forehead. It didn't look as if he was going to top Patrick.

He watched the Mouse put a pleading hand on her fiancé's arm. Big limpid eyes gazed into his. Pinky gave a frown of irritation, indicating they'd reached their limit.

'Going once.' The auctioneer, satisfied that there were no more bids, was about to close the sale. It was down to Patrick.

The Mouse leaned into Pinky's ear and whispered urgently. Patrick could see her simultaneously digging him in the ribs with her elbow. Pinky looked pained. He, too, obviously knew the golden rule.

'Going twice . . .'

The Mouse shot Pinky a look of pure evil. The prospect of facing her wrath was clearly too terrifying, and Pinky thrust his card defiantly in the air.

'A hundred and fifty-one. I'm bid a hundred and fifty-one. Do I hear a hundred and fifty-two?' The auctioneer, enjoying the drama of the moment, looked around the room.

Fuck, thought Patrick. This was the point at which he was supposed to bow out gracefully. But then he thought – what the hell? For the sake of another two grand . . . He'd bloody kick himself if the Mouse and Pinky got it for a hundred and fifty-one. So he put up his card coolly and casually, holding it between two fingers as if the whole carry-on was too boring for words.

The auctioneer recognized his bid and the Mouse looked round indignantly. She gave another furious dig with her elbow and the long-suffering Pinky matched his bid. A hundred and fifty-three.

Right, thought Patrick. This was war. If he couldn't have Little Orwell Cottage, then he'd bloody well make sure Pinky and the Mouse paid over the odds for it. He stuck his legs out in front of him, crossed his arms and languidly raised his card into the air once more, as if he really had better things to do with his time.

When David had gone, after she'd patiently shown him how to strap Chelsea into her car seat safely, Ginny sat down on the sofa with a sigh.

What on earth was happening to her? She was being wooed by no less than three men. It was completely and utterly preposterous. How on earth was she supposed to choose?

In fact, did she have to?

Because the more Ginny thought about it, the more she thought she didn't want to rush into anything. Not a serious relationship, in any case. She wanted the chance to get herself back on her feet, establish herself, decide who she was, before she committed herself again. There was no point in wasting twenty years on one marriage then hurling yourself into the next relationship before you'd even got over it and worked out what you wanted.

Her head was whirling. Why was life so complicated? Because there was too much choice, that was why. On the television. In the supermarket. The likes of her mother, she thought, had had it easy. OK, life might have been rather humdrum. But at least it had been safe and predictable. Other than dithering between whether to have cling peaches or pear halves for pudding, Ginny didn't think her mother had ever had to make a really important decision. There wasn't a lot to be said for being a millennium woman. You were accountable every bloody step of the way.

Well, she wasn't going to be forced into making any decisions. She decided that what she really needed to do was take it easy this weekend. It had been a mad social whirl recently and she thought she'd like a nice domesticated couple of days, slobbing about the house with no make-up on, and perhaps spending some time with the girls. They could go to the movies or something.

She did have to do one thing first. She had to apologize to Keith. He didn't deserve to be treated like that. She dialled his number and, coward that she was, was thankful when his answerphone clicked in.

'Keith – it's Ginny. I've got an apology to make. I behaved appallingly towards you yesterday. The truth is, I was a bit down in the dumps and had a bit too much to drink at a friend's. I didn't think I'd be a very good dinner date. But I must apologize for fibbing. And thank you so much for the basket – it was lovely . . .'

Hoping he'd be mollified, she took the phone off the hook, put on her grey flannel pyjamas and took to her bed, knowing that she could sleep in peace for at least three hours before the twins finished their shift at the pub.

*

As they began the dizzying descent down into Woola-combe, Mandy gripped on even tighter as Rick took the hairpin bends. They passed a clutch of hotels, whose developers must have been dishing out backhanders left, right and centre, so unattractive was their architecture. But then she gave a gasp as the sea came into view; crashing surf fronted by a magnificent blonde beach. Because it was still only May, and the forecast had been gloomy, there were scarcely any visitors, just the usual crowd of intrepid surfers who tipped up whatever the weather. And because of that, there was a sense of smug glee amongst those who had made the effort as the dazzling sunshine brazenly contradicted the weather report.

They followed the coast road, climbing higher and higher, the view becoming ever more dramatic, until they reached the entrance to the campsite. As far as Mandy could see, it was just a field. In the distance she could make out a breeze-block building which apparently housed the loos and showers. Rick found where his mates were pitched – their tents were up but empty.

'They've obviously hit the beach already. Let's get the tent up and then we can join them.'

He started pulling stuff out of the panniers. The tent was packed tightly into a small sausage-shaped bag. 'It's a two-man tent. Or one man, one woman. No ensuite, I'm afraid. Or central heating. It's all pretty basic,' he grinned, 'but as we won't be spending much time here, it doesn't matter.'

Mandy tried not to think too much about being in such close proximity to him for an entire night as she followed his instructions and valiantly drove the pegs into the ground. She racked her brains, but she didn't think she'd ever been in a tent before. She'd only ever done four- or five-star hotels, hotels that were fairly anonymous and alike in their provision of fluffy white towels and complimentary shower caps. It was definitely going to be a weekend of firsts.

They spent the afternoon on the beach at Croyde, the surfing Mecca: miles and miles of golden sand, with the sea an irresistible playground filled with bodies. They hired boards and wetsuits, and for two hours they frolicked in the surf. Rick was incredibly patient, showing her how to wait for the opportune moment to ride the wave. She'd never laughed so much. She'd never had so much fun, even if she hadn't quite managed to get the hang of it.

By five o'clock Mandy was exhausted and starting to get cold. She went back on to the beach and dried off, put on some warm clothes, then sat with her arms wrapped round her knees and watched as Rick and his friends got down to some serious surfing. For more than an hour she feasted her eyes on his physique, as he rode the waves like some sort of Greek legend.

All too soon they were enjoying the very last moments of daylight, and sat with a crowd of his friends sharing a few beers and cigarettes as the sun went down. She was introduced to endless people, who all greeted her as if they'd known her all their lives.

Once the sun had finally gone it was off to a local bar for more beer and tequila and pool. Nobody seemed to worry about food, but Mandy didn't care. She was far too full of adrenalin to eat. She'd had a wonderful day. Exhilarating yet relaxing. She'd tested her physical limits, but found it had unwound her to an incredible extent. The sun had warmed her through to the marrow of her bones, which ached with a delicious tiredness. She could still taste the salt of the sea on her lips, her skin, her hair.

Eventually they were all kicked out of the bar and they wandered back to the campsite. She slithered inside the tent and lay on top of her sleeping bag, arms behind her head, waiting for Rick to come back from having a pee. She let her thoughts wander lazily, images scudding before her closed eyes like clouds across a sky, with no particular direction. Chilled wasn't the word. She supposed the beer had helped, and a couple of drags on the spliff that had been passed round. She had no worries, not a care in the world. She hadn't thought about Patrick all day. She'd almost drifted off when Rick reappeared, startling her.

'Are you warm enough?'

Mandy nodded. Rick zipped up the tent and crawled into his sleeping bag.

'You should sleep like a log tonight. All that sea air.' He smiled, and leaned over to kiss her. She shut her eyes, ready for the incredible fullness of his lips on hers.

But they merely brushed her cheek. Then he stroked her head, a rough but caring gesture, and turned away.

'Night.' He burrowed down and, folding up his sweat-shirt for a pillow, nestled in for the night.

Mandy was incredulous. Was that it? Were they really just mates? Had he brought her here just to teach her how to surf? Was she just someone for him to show off to? Didn't he fancy her? Had there been a point at which he'd decided she wasn't for him? Was it because she hadn't got the hang of surfing quickly enough? Was she too fat? Too thin? Too boring? Was he gay? Was she supposed to make the first move? Or had she misinterpreted the reason for the trip? After all, men and women could be friends without shagging. All his surfing friends seemed to muck in together – although there were some couples that were obviously items, there was an easy, non-sexual camaraderie between all of them, a bond between people who clearly just wanted to have fun.

Was she wrong to want sex with him? Well, yes, of course she was, because she was already spoken for. She was betraying Patrick. But in her mind this weekend was supposed to be a test. This was an unexpected twist, however. She'd assumed, somehow, that sleeping together would be a natural progression for her and Rick, with no obstacles in the way. She'd come down with that expectation.

Now she felt filled with desolation. She unzipped her sleeping bag and got in. The feeling of relaxation she'd had earlier had totally dissipated. Anxiety and doubt flooded back through her. And she felt cold. Longing for the warmth of the body that lay so tantalizingly close to hers, she hugged herself until she finally fell asleep.

It might have consoled her to know that, next to her, Rick was in torment, too. He'd thought it was going to be so easy. He thought he'd be able to screw her without a conscience. He was the king of casual sex, after all. Ricky No Strings, one girl had called him.

So why the hell couldn't he go through with it?

A hundred and fifty-eight thousand pounds. James was going to absolutely kill him, for flagrantly ignoring his advice. But Patrick didn't care. What was another eight grand, in the scheme of things? He'd find it somehow.

He'd signed the paperwork with a shaking hand and driven home as high as a kite. He didn't tell anyone about his purchase. He wanted Mandy to be the first to know.

That night, he could barely get to sleep for excitement. He couldn't wait for Mandy to get back the next day. He thought of texting her on her mobile, then told himself to be patient. He'd drive her out to see it the next night. He tried to imagine the look on her face. She'd absolutely love it, he knew she would.

20

On Sunday morning Mandy woke up filled with resolution. Despite having difficulty getting to sleep the previous evening, the sun and the sea had awarded her a
good night's rest, and she decided optimistically that
today was going to be on her terms. She slid out of the
tent and went to find the loo. Then wished she hadn't.
The campsite might be a picturesque location but it hadn't
been chosen for its amenities. And most of the people
who'd made their way here the night before had clearly
missed their aim. She managed to brush her teeth in the
sink and wash her face in cold water, but she didn't risk
the shower, which looked as if it was encrusted with
verruca possibilities. Never mind, she thought. She'd
spent so much time in the sea yesterday, she wasn't exactly
dirty. Then she got on her mobile. By nine o'clock she
was satisfied. She slid back into the tent and tickled Rick
under the chin.

'Wakey wakey.'

He sat up, confused and gorgeous, his skin already
tanned the colour of toffee. Mandy wished fervently that
he'd hurry up and put his top on.

'Come on, you. Today's on my terms. We're going
riding.'

It was worth it for the look on his face. But it was the
perfect revenge. Yesterday she'd felt so uncoordinated,
as if she would never master the art of surfing, while Rick

rode the waves as if he owned them. Now it was her turn. She'd found the number of the local riding stables and had booked them in for a ride across the dunes.

The stables weren't far, and they were quickly kitted out with boots and safety helmets. Then the young girl that was going to escort them led out their horses. Mandy was on a nice-looking grey, fine-legged and eager to go. She thought of Monkey at home. Keith had promised to throw him some hay and top up his water. She felt a tiny little pang of guilt at duping her father. This wasn't exactly how he'd imagined she'd be spending his money . . .

Rick's horse was a big, fat coloured mare with staring blue eyes and white lashes. Possibly the least attractive animal Mandy had ever laid eyes on. She stifled a giggle as Rick surveyed the horse in horror. The girl defended the animal stoutly.

'This is Patsy. No more dangerous than sitting on the sofa in your own front room. And just as comfy. She'll look after you.'

Rick looked doubtful, but climbed on to the mounting block and hoisted himself on to Patsy's broad back. Their escort leaped on to a game little chestnut and led them off down the lane.

Mandy had to admit that Rick took to riding quite well. There was nothing more levelling than putting a novice on a horse; nothing like it for turning an otherwise lithe and streamlined human into a sack of potatoes. But the girl had been right – Patsy was as comfy as a sofa, and even when she broke into a trot Rick seemed to manage.

They rode through the village, the clopping of hooves on tarmac the only sound as it was still fairly early Sunday morning. Even the most avid surfers were still sleeping off the excesses of the night before. Then they left the road and cut across to the dunes, the horses happy to go at a gentle, ambling pace, so they could enjoy the incredible beauty of their surroundings. The long grass rustled softly in the early morning breeze; the horses kicked up the sand and in the distance the sea made its way tentatively inwards along the shore.

All the while, Mandy looked longingly at the beach. Their escort, seeing she was an experienced rider, relented. She was given permission to gallop back to their starting point along the sands, while Rick was escorted back across the dunes at a more sedate pace.

As she headed towards the water's edge, Mandy could feel her horse's muscles bunching up underneath her in anticipation. He was looking forward to the thrill as much as she was. She could feel butterflies in her tummy – she knew once she'd let go there would be no stopping him.

'Easy, boy. Easy.' She kept him under control until the moment when she wanted him to go, when they became as one. He danced on the spot in frustration as she gathered up her reins, then kicked him on. Flat out for the entire length of the beach, she leaned over his neck, urging him on, the ultimate freedom, the ultimate partnership. Better, thought Mandy defiantly, than sex.

She came back to Rick at a sitting trot, eyes shining, and he looked at her with a renewed respect. He trusted the waves, understood how they worked, was happy to ride them. Never, in a million years, could he trust half a ton of muscled sinew that had a mind of its own. But Mandy, it seemed, didn't give it a second thought.

Touché, he thought admiringly, as they returned to the

stables and he slid off his mount, wincing in agony as his feet hit the ground.

Barney and Suzanna dragged themselves reluctantly from their beds as late as they could on Sunday morning. They were both running on empty. The success of the opening night had ensured a constant stream of diners and drinkers that first weekend. The restaurant had been full to bursting, with those who hadn't booked unable to get a table on spec. Adrenalin got them through it; only Sunday lunchtime to go and they could relax. They were due to have the evening off. Toby was going to look after the bar with one of the barmaids, Melissa, and the dining room was closed. However, it didn't look as though they were going to be collapsing in an exhausted heap full of mutual self-congratulation and elated relief. They were each feeling tense with guilt, the little secrets they were hiding from each other needling their consciences. It wasn't long before they were bickering like overtired toddlers about a series of mishaps that had occurred in the dining room the night before. Mishaps that hadn't actually ruined anyone's evening, but that needed ironing out. Being tired and defensive, neither of them wanted to take the blame.

'I'm stuck in the kitchen. I don't see how I can be held responsible for a waitress not knowing guinea fowl from corn-fed chicken.' Suzanna regretted the carping tone of her voice, but she was filled with nerves. Lunch was fully booked, and the ovens had proved temperamental at best over the past few days.

Barney clenched his fists in frustration.

'Suzanna – I can't go on like this much longer.'

'Neither can I,' she snapped back.

Barney put his head in his hands, then looked up.

'Maybe this was a mistake. Maybe we're not cut out for this. It's making us both miserable.' As he spoke, Barney knew that it wasn't the pub that was making them miserable; that they really hadn't given it a chance. But it was easier to displace the blame than address the real issues that lay unresolved between them, like sharks basking in shallow waters. 'Perhaps we should just forget it.'

'Yes. Maybe we should.' She spoke with a quiet, measured menace that struck a chill into Barney's heart. She walked out of the room and he punched the wall with frustration.

He was going to get tough. Why should he constantly sacrifice himself in the hopes that their marriage was going to repair itself? If he didn't put himself first, he was going to be left with nothing when it all fell apart. Then he felt overwhelmed with sadness. They should be enjoying this. He and Suzanna should be slipping away quietly this evening to congratulate themselves. He imagined a riverside walk in Stratford, a quiet supper, then home to bed for a much deserved night's sleep, preceded, of course, by sleepy, contented love-making.

Dream on, he thought gloomily. That wasn't going to happen. It was each man for himself.

Mandy lay on the beach that afternoon and thought she never wanted the day to end.

She was stretched out on her towel in her bikini – she'd undone the straps and tucked them out of sight in the hopes that the sun might eradicate the tell-tale white mark from the day before. She protected her tattoo with factor fifty sun cream, as the tattooist had told her. She was pleased with how good it looked – it had been much admired. It occurred to her Patrick still hadn't seen it; she hadn't had to explain. They hadn't had sex for . . . days. Weeks. Which just went to show how little interest he had in her.

She banished Patrick from her mind, and tried to remember the last time she'd felt like this, if ever. Totally relaxed. Not a care in the world. She was so chilled she wasn't even thinking about the fact that soon this dream would be over.

Rick came out of the sea, and she watched him wander back up the beach, his board tucked under his arm. He flopped down beside her, lying at right angles to her, then lay his head on her stomach as if it was a pillow.

The two of them lay there, eyes shut, half dozing in the sunshine as the sounds of life around them continued – shrieks of laughter as people made the most of the last of the weekend. Someone had brought a ghetto blaster and the strains of Crazytown's 'Butterfly' danced across the beach. The jangling lead guitar sent shivers up and down Mandy's spine; the suggestive lyrics made her squirm with longing. She was in torment, the warmth of Rick's head on her stomach was melting her . . . More than anything, she wanted him to turn over, brush his lips against her bare skin. But she knew for some reason that wasn't going to happen. She wondered what was holding him back. She was pretty sure he found her attractive; there were moments when their eyes had met, when his hand had lingered for longer than necessary on her, and there had been a definite frisson. But something was stopping him. She wondered if he had a girlfriend already that he hadn't admitted to. Or if he'd been badly treated and had sworn to himself to keep away from women. Either way, she wasn't going to humiliate herself by making the first move. All she could do was lie there and fantasize. She thought she might scream with frustration, boil over with desire, when suddenly he leaped to his feet.

'It's time we went. The forecast said rain. I don't like driving the bike when it's wet.'

Startled, Mandy looked up at the sky. It was relentlessly blue. Not a cloud to be seen.

What she didn't know was that it had taken all Rick's self-control not to roll over and kiss Mandy. But he knew that the moment his lips touched her skin, he would be lost. He had to let her go. He couldn't look her in the eye as he gathered up their stuff and strode off, angry with himself for letting her get to him.

Thankfully, the restaurant was incredibly busy for Sunday lunch, which left neither Barney nor Suzanna much time to brood on their argument.

Suzanna didn't allow her mood to spill over into her cooking; she had always had the ability to absorb herself totally in her work. There were only three of them in the kitchen: she and Jonty, and a little kitchen porter called Lee, who had been at catering college with Jonty. Between them they were perfectly choreographed, instinctively knowing which moves to make as they slaved, quite literally, over a hot stove for two solid hours. The menu was simple: Gloucester Old Spot pork or Welsh Marches lamb, with all the traditional accompaniments. Suzanna was elated to get the measure of the ovens at last, and achieved the crunchiest of roast potatoes. There was much idle banter between them as they worked, with the odd insult traded between the two blokes. They didn't quite dare award Suzanna the same irreverence. They'd privately agreed she was a fit-looking bird, but needed treating with respect. And in return, she treated them with respect; always had time to ask nicely and said thank you, which was unusual in a kitchen. They hoped it wasn't just a honeymoon period.

When the very last plate of rhubarb crumble and custard had gone out, Suzanna ran upstairs, tore off her whites and shoved them in the laundry basket, then pulled on her jeans without even stopping to shower. Without a word of explanation she ran past Barney, who was trying to look modest as a group of well-oiled diners congratulated him on the pub's success. She jumped into the Jeep and started up the engine, not caring that she left a hideous tyre mark through the freshly-laid Cotswold chippings on the car park.

Without slowing down she pulled her mobile phone out of her bag and pressed Patrick's number. She didn't bother with pleasantries like hello.

'I need to see you.'

Patrick was at Little Orwell Cottage, admiring his purchase. It wasn't technically his yet, but he couldn't wait for the formalities. The sign outside didn't even have a sold sticker on it, but he'd gone to make a list of everything that needed doing. A list that was getting alarmingly longer.

'I'm viewing a house,' he told Suzanna. 'For a friend. Come and have a look.'

He gave her directions.

'I'll be there in five minutes,' she said.

Patrick hung up, mildly concerned that she seemed upset about something, but he was too caught up in his surroundings to dwell on it. He was sure he and Mandy would be happy here. OK, they'd had a rough few weeks while he'd been under stress, but now it looked as though the pub was on course and he could take his foot off the throttle. Summer was on its way. He imagined happy, sun-drenched evenings sanding floorboards and painting walls, stopping for a couple of little bottles of beer on a rug in the garden, perhaps making love while the birds chirped and the bees hummed and the scent of honey-suckle drifted on the breeze.

It was the perfect house for them. And maybe, one day, a baby. Babies hadn't been part of Patrick's big picture until now, but he'd seen what fatherhood had done to his uncle. With Henry's arrival, James had taken on another dimension. He was almost a different person, bursting with pride and love and fulfilment. Patrick wanted to fast-track to that stage. He didn't want another twenty years of bachelordom and meaningless if pleasurable leg-overs.

Because he did love Mandy. Even if he had been a bit of a grumpy shit over the past few weeks. She'd arrived just in time to save him from himself, to save him from a lifetime of cynical affairs and meaningless dalliances. She'd taught him that you could respect and cherish another human being and that it didn't make you weak and vulnerable. Most importantly, she'd taught him to relax and be himself, not feel he had something to prove all the time.

Not that he'd relaxed much lately. Or her, for that matter. They had both been as tense as piano strings with each other. Never mind – perhaps a weekend apart had given their relationship the breathing space it needed to forge ahead. They had such a bright future together. She was going to be so amazed. Patrick imagined driving her out to the little cottage, putting his hands over her eyes until she was at the garden gate, then letting her see . . .

Suzanna appeared in the doorway like a ghost, interrupting his reverie. Her face was pale, her eyes enormous and glassy, dark shadows underneath.

'You look knackered,' said Patrick, concerned.

'I am. I didn't get to bed till two. I've just done Sunday lunch for thirty-five.'

She looked around but there was nowhere to sit. She slumped on the floor, leaning her back against the wall and putting her head in her hands in despair.

'I can't carry on like this.'

Alarmed, Patrick knelt down beside her, patting her shoulder in what he hoped was a supportive manner.

'It'll get easier. Once you've got into a routine – you can offload on to Jonty a bit more. We can recruit some more staff.'

'It's not that,' said Suzanna.

'Then what?'

Her fierce gaze seemed to burn a hole right through him with its intensity.

'I think I'm falling in love with you,' she said.

Fuck, thought Patrick. He hadn't expected that.

'What?'

'When I'm with you, I forget. I'm a new person. There

411

seems to be – some point to it all. I've tried to pretend it's not happening. But ever since the opening evening . . .'

She grabbed his arms. Their eyes locked and for a moment he couldn't tear his gaze away from hers. She pulled him towards her and he didn't resist. She shut her eyes and their lips met in the gentlest, most tentative kiss. Suzanna felt a swirl of emotions wrapping itself round her head and her heart. It felt so right. She felt like Sleeping Beauty, coming to life again after being asleep for so many years, as a delicious, life-giving warmth zinged through her veins.

As her response became more passionate, an alarm bell suddenly rang in Patrick's head and he cursed himself for his weakness. He'd fallen into one of his own bloody traps again. Vain little sod that he was, he could never resist the lure of a pretty woman and an open invitation. But this wasn't a silly, stolen little kiss that could be brushed to one side, like so many kisses he'd had in the past. He pushed her away roughly.

'It's no good, Suzanna. It won't work.'

She looked at him in outrage that would have been comical in any other circumstance.

'Shit, Patrick. You're my chance. You've made me feel alive again. I've been like a zombie for the past eighteen months. I might as well be dead –'

He looked at her sharply. He hoped she wasn't going to make any serious threats. He thought desperately for a way out. He'd known there was a thread between them, but not that things would accelerate so fast and come to a head. The trouble was, there was no denying the attraction. If it hadn't been for Suzanna's fragile emotional state, he would certainly have risked a bonk, making sure she knew the deal first. But this was incredibly dangerous.

'Suzanna – think about this rationally. Maybe it's not surprising you feel like this. You've had a tough time lately, and we've spent a lot of time together. We get on, incredibly well. Maybe, given a different set of circumstances . . . I mean, it's not that I don't find you attractive, of course I do . . .'

For God's sake, he thought to himself. Stop waffling and cut to the chase.

'You belong with Barney.'

'Do I?' She looked incredibly sad for a moment. 'I did. Once. But I don't think I'm making him very happy any more.'

'You still love him, don't you?'

'Of course I do. But not . . . in the same way. Like a friend, I suppose. And I don't want to hurt him. But do I have to spend the rest of my life with him, both of us miserable? If one of us has got the chance for happiness, shouldn't we take it?' She laughed bitterly. 'I mean, neither of us could be more unhappy than we already are, so what difference would it make?'

'Hang on a minute. It's not just you we're talking about here.' Patrick felt a surge of anger and allowed himself to be sharp with her. 'Look at the big picture. There's me and Mandy too . . .'

'She'd get over it.' Suzanna knew she sounded harsh, but she was desperate.

'And there's a pretty big knock-on. What would happen to the pub? You and Barney couldn't go on running it. And we've ploughed a shedload of money into it. We can't risk that going down the drain.'

Suzanna looked at him.

'I see,' she said quietly, but with an underlying menace that Patrick knew meant trouble. 'At the end of the day, this is all about money, is it?'

Patrick took a deep breath. OK, she was going to think he was a mercenary bastard, but he was wise enough to know that it was the only weapon he had.

'Yes. It's my arse on the line with the Honeycote Arms. If I upset the apple-cart, not to mention Mandy, then Keith Sherwyn will pull out. I can't take that risk. I can't do that to my family.'

'I shall walk out anyway.'

'You can't. You've got to make it work. We've all invested too much. You as much as anyone. You walk away and you'll blow it for everyone.'

'Just tell me what the point is?' She glared at him belligerently. 'If we were given sixty-eight Michelin stars, if we were fully booked till the next millennium, it wouldn't make me any happier.'

Patrick sighed. She was being incredibly naive. How could he make her realize that all he would be was an emotional sticking plaster, a temporary dab of antiseptic on her wounds? Wounds that would continue to fester; that he could never hope to heal because he would never understand what she'd gone through. Sure, if he succumbed to her they'd have fun to begin with. They'd have great sex, because Patrick always made sure the sex was great. But it wouldn't be long, he knew, before the novelty wore off, and her fears and worries came back to haunt her. And there wouldn't be enough depth to their relationship to withstand that.

'There can't be anything between us, Suzanna. You're

clutching at straws. OK, so you think things are better when you're with me – but that's only because I'm a novelty. You don't know me.' He gave a self-deprecating smirk. 'You've only had the good side.'

She was about to protest, tell him that anything was possible, but he cut her off and aimed straight for her heart. 'I might as well tell you the truth. I bought this house yesterday. We're going to live here together, Mandy and me. I'm going to ask her to marry me . . .'

She crumpled visibly before his very eyes. He couldn't bear to look. She seemed so small, like a little girl. She looked around the room, imagining, he supposed, him and Mandy making their little home. She gave a wan smile.

'It's lovely. I'm sure you'll be very happy here.'

'I'm sorry.'

And he was. He thought a lot of Suzanna. No doubt they could have had something together. But they couldn't possibly build a relationship on the crumbled ruins of other people's lives. She needed love, and Patrick firmly believed that the only one capable of giving her that was Barney. He had faith in Barney. It was just a shame that Suzanna, who was so embroiled in a morass of mixed and powerful emotions, didn't.

'I'd better go,' she said matter-of-factly.

Patrick didn't really know what else he could say to help. He gave her a hug, as brotherly a hug as he could manage, because he didn't want to come across as cold.

'Listen,' he said. 'Try and make it work with Barney. I'm not just saying that because of the pub. I'm saying that because . . . I think the world of you, and I think that's who you belong with. I really do.'

'You don't know', she whispered, 'what it's like.'

They were very close, heads together, a warm current flowing backwards and forwards between them. Patrick cradled her head in his hands, massaging her temples lightly with his thumbs.

'It's in here,' he said gently. 'You've got the power in here. You can do it. I know you can.'

Rick and Mandy were walking back along the coastal path. They stood for a moment on the cliff's edge before turning into the little gate that led to the campsite. The sun was beginning a gradual descent, seemingly as reluctant to leave as they were.

Mandy felt very small and powerless. The waves down below were pounding and crashing. Only the birds were free from the lure of the rocks below: they circled overhead, mewling their taunts, unaffected by that overwhelming desire to jump that seems to come upon humans when faced with a vertiginous drop.

Mandy turned to Rick to find him looking down at her with a strange expression in his eyes.

'What?' she faltered. 'What is it?'

He answered only with a kiss. It seemed to go on for ever, but still it wasn't enough, she'd waited so long. She licked the salt from his lips, ran her hands through his curls, pressed her body against his. Their tongues entwined, dancing, probing, exploring; a languorous pastiche of love-making that left Mandy quite faint. If merely kissing him made her feel like this . . .

Suddenly Rick broke away and started to walk back along the path. Mandy ran after him.

'What's the matter?'

'It's time we went. I don't like riding the bike in the dark.'

'It was the rain a minute ago.'

'Whatever.'

Mandy pulled on his arm, desperate for him to stop and explain.

'Rick, please. I don't understand . . .'

He answered roughly.

'I never touch anything that isn't mine. You don't belong to me. You belong to Patrick.' He smiled a bitter, twisted smile. 'Call me old-fashioned, but I don't like the taste of forbidden fruit.'

They got back to the campsite just before four and packed up the tent, only speaking when necessary. As they were strapping their things on to the bike, fat raindrops started to fall. Rick had been right after all. He gave Mandy a waterproof to put on over her clothes.

The drive home was horrible, totally different from the ride down, which had been exhilarating and full of a sense of expectation. Mandy felt exhausted from the emotional and physical turmoil. The urge to go to sleep was overwhelming, but you couldn't fall asleep on the back of a bike. So she fought to stay awake, with only her thoughts for distraction. Every mile they covered was a mile nearer decisions she didn't want to have to make, and she was confused.

Just past Bristol, Rick pulled into a service station.

'I need caffeine. I'm knackered.'

The service station was a harsh slice of reality. The lights were hideously bright and a pall of fag smoke hung in the air of the foyer. Gaming machines thudded and squawked and bleeped. They queued up in silence to pay for their food, then scoured the room for a table without dirty plates and used ashtrays.

The coffee was weak; so diluted it was unlikely to do anything to raise Rick's energy levels. Mandy had two bites of a chicken salad sandwich and pushed it away – it was over-refrigerated and the lettuce had gone brown at the edges.

Rick seemed to have drifted away somewhere and become rather distant. He wasn't unpleasant – he asked if he could finish her sandwich, then offered her a finger of his KitKat – but a barrier had come down. He seemed almost a stranger. The magic had gone and somehow she couldn't find the way to ask him . . .

Ask him what if . . .

Ask him what if she and Patrick were finished. What then?

21

By late Sunday afternoon, Bertie couldn't bear waiting for the phone to ring any longer. He'd patiently read the *Sunday Times* from cover to cover, drinking coffee out of his sparkling bone china, made himself a sandwich for lunch, then lolled in his hammock for an hour. By half four he'd reached screaming pitch, so he drove over to Honeycote House, where he found Lucy lying on a rug on the lawn in her bikini, writing to Sophie. He flopped down next to her.

'I need you to do me a favour.'

'Mmm?' Lucy was concentrating on her letter, only half listening.

'I want you to organize a tennis match. And invite Ginny.'

Lucy's eyes flickered towards him in amusement.

'And you, I suppose?'

'Of course. No point otherwise.' He smiled winningly. 'Please?'

'Bertie – you can't play tennis on our court. With the best will in the world, it needs thousands spending on it. Thousands we don't happen to have. So much as I would love to help . . .'

Lucy bent her head and continued her concerted scribbling. Bertie lay on one side watching her, his head resting in one hand. She made a charming picture as she chewed the end of her pen thoughtfully. She looked half her age, her body as slender and as toned as any twenty-year-old, her tortoiseshell curls escaping from their ribbon.

Bertie had often wondered about Lucy. Was she really as angelic as she seemed, as she was rumoured to be? Bertie didn't think it was possible. He didn't believe her claim of the other night, that she'd only ever slept with Mickey. If it was true, Bertie thought it was a crime. Besides, he had his suspicions about Lucy and James. He'd seen looks pass between them on occasion, looks that went beyond the companionship shared between a brother- and sister-in-law. He wondered if she was corruptible. He tugged playfully at the string of her bikini top until it came open.

'You'll get a line.'

Lucy didn't bat an eyelid. The top still covered her modesty, just. Encouraged by her lack of resistance, Bertie traced his fingers lightly down her spine. In the drowsy heat of the afternoon sun, it was a delicious moment filled with promise. As he danced his fingertips over her skin, he held his breath, a smile of mischief playing on his lips.

The trouble was, Bertie didn't have a conscience. He'd gone forty years without ever needing one. No one had ever been in a position to reprimand him: his mother had indulged or ignored him, his father just ignored him. He'd had no respect for authority at school. He'd only really ever worked for himself. There'd been no one on hand throughout his life to teach him right from wrong. So even though his head was stuffed with romantic notions about a life of bliss with Ginny, he would have thought nothing of pleasuring Lucy Liddiard in the privacy of her own garden. If she'd shown the slightest inclination, that was. Bertie wasn't in the habit of actually forcing himself upon women, though it wasn't all that often that they resisted his advances.

Lucy, however, was made of sterner stuff than most. By this time his fingers had reached the waistband of her bikini bottoms.

'Bertie,' she murmured, rather wearily. 'Fuck off. If you want something to do with your hands, go and make a cup of tea.'

Bertie headed off towards the kitchen obediently. Nothing ventured, nothing gained, he thought.

Lucy shook her head in exasperation, thanking God that Sophie was thousands of miles away and that Georgina was hopefully still too young to attract Bertie's attention. He was incorrigible. Once again, she hoped against hope that Ginny hadn't succumbed to his charms. No matter how well-intentioned Bertie believed himself to be, it would end in tears.

Barney, against his better judgement and in total defiance of all his own rules, had spent the rest of the afternoon getting pissed as soon as the pub was closed. He'd started off sharing a bottle of wine with Jonty. They'd had a drunken, philosophical conversation about the minefields of marriage, both agreeing that you couldn't win. Jonty was bemoaning Meggy's hormonal hysteria and her complaints that he was never at home to help her with the children.

'She moaned when I was a farrier because I was out all hours, and now she's moaning because I'm a chef. I can't help it if my hours are antisocial – that's when people want to eat!'

Privately, Barney thought he'd be in for less grief if he went straight home after his shift without staying on to get drunk, but he didn't say anything. He knew Jonty was a bit of a lad, but part of him sympathized. Sometimes the demands upon men were too great, and the only answer was a session with your mates. It was what had kept the brewing industry afloat for all these centuries.

When Jonty had finally dragged himself away, Barney carried on, rather ill-advisedly. He found the bottle of Havana Club that he'd half drunk the night he'd recorded with Kitty, and poured himself a substantial slug. On top of the wine, it provided him with a little cloak of protection against the memory of his row with Suzanna. His row? Drink convinced him that it had been her bloody row. He hadn't wanted an argument but she'd been determined. Another thing, he and Jonty had agreed, that women were so good at.

He flicked on his computer to check his e-mails, then froze. Still stung from his rejection the night of the opening, he'd sent an MP3 file of his recording with Kitty to his old manager. He'd told himself he'd never hear back, but there was an answer from Jez already. Bloody hell. He hadn't expected that. His hand hovered over the mouse and he clicked on 'Open'.

Twenty minutes later Barney, in a drunken elated blur, trotted out of the pub. He had to see Kitty – tell her what had happened. Jez's reply had merely said 'Wow!' and left his mobile number. Barney had called him before he'd had time to think. They'd had a brief, businesslike conversation, with Barney trying his best to sound sober. They arranged to meet the next day at Jez's office in Soho.

He staggered down the high street in the direction of Tinker's Barn. When he got there, he was glad to see Ginny's car wasn't there. He liked Ginny, but he wanted to see Kitty on her own to break the amazing news to her. He didn't want to share the moment with anyone else. It was their moment of glory. He grabbed the twisted ring of iron on the front door and rapped hard, praying she'd be in. He didn't know where he'd go if she wasn't. He couldn't bear the thought of going back to the Honeycote Arms.

By some miraculous twist of fate, she was in. She came to the door, still damp from her bath, a red silk kimono around her and her hair wrapped up in a towel. Whatever she'd been bathing in smelled absolutely delicious, like the bottom of a child's sweetie bag – Refreshers and jelly babies and parma violets all mixed together. Barney leaned drunkenly against the door jamb. He wasn't sure how his words were going to come out: they were muddled enough in his brain. Could they make it to his mouth? He gave what he hoped was a charming smile, to cover up his inebriation.

'We've got something to celebrate . . .' He stumbled over the doorstep. 'Got anything to drink?'

'Don't you think you've had enough?' she smiled, watching him lurch over to the sofa.

'No such thing as enough.'

She pulled open the fridge and found a half-bottle of white wine. She poured each of them a glass, then walked over to Barney.

'Here. It's probably filthy – Mum's no connoisseur –'

'Don't care.'

He put out his hand and she guided the glass into it.

She sipped her drink demurely as Barney downed his in one.

'So – what is it we're celebrating?'

'I managed to track Jez down. I sent him what we'd done. He works for a big record company. He loved it. He thinks you're mind-blowing . . .'

She sat down to digest the news, looking at him, puzzled. She didn't seem able to take it in.

'What?'

Barney realized he wasn't being all that coherent.

'Our demo. The track we recorded. He played it and he loved it.'

'Shit.' Her eyes were as wide as saucers. 'I don't believe it. That's amazing.' She paused. 'What does it mean, exactly?'

'I'm going to go and meet him tomorrow. See what he's got in mind. If he's that keen – other people will be too. We don't have to jump straight into bed with Jez. We can just use him as a sounding board.'

'Barney – that's fantastic.'

She came and put her arms round him. And kissed him. Just a little peck.

'Thanks.'

Then she looked into his eyes, her own eyes sparkling, and kissed him again. Only this time he felt her body pressing up against his, her little cat's tongue probing open his lips and her warm hands sliding up under his T-shirt. The sweet, sugary scent of her warm skin taunted him; haunted him. He groaned a groan of despair, hopelessness and unrequited lust that came from the very depths of his soul. He felt her fingers stroke his neck and started at the intimacy. It was so long since he'd been touched; so long since he had felt anything remotely resembling affection. He nuzzled his way in further, not wanting to express his feelings verbally, just wanting to immerse himself in her softness.

He could feel her breasts under the silk of her gown. He put out a tentative hand to cup one and felt her nipple stiffen under his touch. She let out a little whimper of pleasure. Without taking her lips from his she tugged at the belt of her gown until it undid. It fell open, revealing nothing underneath but a minute pair of pants. She was urging him on, her lips everywhere, her thighs parting as she pulled him to her, her hands on his back, nails digging in.

He was lost. There was no going back. He was amazed to find that everything was still in working order, after all that time, not to mention after all that booze. The sex was frantic, passionate. An onlooker would have found it hard to decide who was the more desperate. Each of them was totally lost in the physical pleasure, barely aware of each other, ruled by their needs.

'Oh my God,' groaned Barney as the long-forgotten sensation swept over him, sweet as it ever had been. She sat up, cheeks flushed, her hair now drying into its familiar snaky curls. She looked like some pre-Raphaelite nymphet, cheeks flushed, eyes shining.

'We shouldn't be doing this,' said Barney, lying on his back exhausted.

'Why not?' She leaned over him, her hair tickling his chest. 'I think it's just what we deserve, after all that hard work.'

She was positively purring, rubbing herself over him. God, she was wild. She was kissing his chest, trailing her hair all over him, working her way downwards. He'd have to be inhuman to resist, he told himself. Never mind the fact that he hadn't had sex for eighteen months, no man in the universe could turn this down. It didn't make him weak. It didn't make him evil. Oh God . . . As she took him in her mouth, he panicked inwardly. This could be embarrassing. But, unbelievably, within moments he was ready again. Happy with her handiwork, she slithered back up his body and pulled him on top of her.

As he plunged back into her with gay abandon – may as well be hung for a sheep as a lamb – he caught sight of her discarded knickers on the floor next to him. Tiny, pink, with a logo on the front – 'Little Miss Naughty' . . .

Suzanna sat in a car park overlooking Broadway Hill until the sun finally slipped down over the horizon.

She knew that the time had come when she had to make a decision, once and for all. Patrick's words went round and round in her head, and the more she thought about what he'd said the more she realized he was right. He'd been an infatuation; a straw she had clutched at because she'd been too much of a coward to do things the hard way. The right way. She looked at the bare facts as objectively as she could. Two things were very obvious.

Oliver wasn't going to come back, ever, and nothing she did was ever going to change that.

And she and Barney had too much together to be apart.

She remembered their first morning in Honeycote, when they'd woken up with such hope. And everything they'd achieved had exceeded their wildest dreams. They'd kept within the deadline and hadn't gone wildly over budget. The Honeycote Arms was an unqualified success, after just three days. The praise and the compliments they'd had heaped on them told her that; the bookings they'd already had confirmed it. It was an incredible achievement.

And then she remembered the pact they'd made. That it was all to be done in memory of Oliver, as a tribute to him. Is that what Ollie would have wanted – a tribute that had cost them their marriage? She thought not.

She pulled her cardigan round her. It wasn't cold, but she was shivering. She was afraid. The time had come for her to face up to what she knew was the only answer, if she and Barney were going to come out of this with their marriage intact.

She had to have another baby.

Deep down she had always known that this was what she had to do. She just hadn't had the strength to face up to it before. Even now, she wasn't sure she was quite ready. But at least she was able to consider it as an option. Until now, it had seemed an impossibility. The wounds were too raw. The guilt was too fresh.

The problem was, she and Barney had been floundering without a purpose. They'd made the mistake of thinking the Honeycote Arms could be a distraction from their grief. But all along they'd been kidding themselves; avoiding the solution. She supposed she was being unfair: having another child wasn't a decision that could be made lightly. It had to be made at the right time. For some it might be straight away; for others, never. But now, Suzanna thought she was nearly ready.

She decided she would give herself three months. Three months to get her head round the idea and build herself up, both physically and emotionally. Three months to detox, give up drinking and smoking and start taking her folic acid. Three months to cement their success at the Honeycote Arms, and train up Jonty, so that he could pick up the reins whenever necessary.

And three months to build up her relationship again with Barney.

Maybe they could buy a little house. She didn't really like the idea of living over the shop permanently, and a pub wasn't really the right environment for a child. There were plenty of gingerbread houses along the high street in Honeycote. They could sell their place in Twickenham. They'd be able to afford something quite decent. And although it would be tough being a working mum, there were enough people around to give them support. And Iris. She thought how thrilled her mother would be. Iris had never broached the subject with her daughter, but Suzanna thought it wouldn't be fair to deny her the chance of another grandchild. Maybe it would even give Iris the impetus to move down here too. The prospect filled her with a warm glow: the thought of her own little family flourishing in Honeycote, being part of the community. Belonging. Capturing that sense of warmth she'd felt so strongly at Honeycote House, only for themselves . . .

The sun had set completely by the time Suzanna started up her car engine. And this time when she shivered, it wasn't with fear, but excitement. And she found she wasn't frightened any more.

Filled with a sudden sense of urgency, vaguely aware that they might be interrupted at any moment by Kitty's mother, which even in his drunken state he knew wasn't advisable, Barney was tugging his clothes back on clumsily. Watched by a laughing pair of eyes, he felt rising panic.

'We shouldn't have done that.'

'Why not?' She seemed unashamed and defiant. Barney prayed she was only teasing.

'Listen,' he slurred. 'You mustn't tell anyone about this.'

'Of course not.'

'No one. Not even your sister.'

'Definitely not my sister. She'd only be jealous.'

Barney was anxious to clear the air.

'I didn't mean to take advantage.'

She ran an affectionate finger down the side of his cheek.

'Don't worry. You didn't. I'm big enough to know what I'm doing.' She kissed him reassuringly. 'If it makes you feel happier, it never happened.'

Barney smiled at her gratefully.

'I'll let you know what happens tomorrow. But we might have to wait for the right moment to talk. Not at the pub. I'll . . . contact you.' He was making this sound more like subterfuge than was necessary, but in the dim recesses of Barney's brain there was a little voice telling him that this situation could have its tricky moments, and he was anxious to avoid trouble.

But as he tottered out of Tinker's Barn and made his way back to the Honeycote Arms, he was amazed to discover that he didn't feel guilty. Not in the least. He'd technically been unfaithful. Twice. And all he could think was he didn't know why he'd waited so long.

*

Behind him, Sasha gently shut the door and leaned against it, bursting into gales of laughter. She couldn't believe that Barney had walked straight into her trap. She giggled at the thought of Kitty's whiter-than-white image now being soiled. That would teach her to be so bloody judgemental; always spoiling Sasha's fun with her puritanical admonishments. She chortled at the thought of the chaos that would be unleashed.

Her mobile bleeped. There was a text from Jonty. He was in the pub. Did she fancy meeting up?

Huh, she thought. He didn't want to buy her a drink, she was sure of that. He was getting too eager. He'd have to realize that any action he was going to get was on her terms. She texted him back to say she was washing her hair. Which wasn't a lie. It had dried into wild snaky curls like Kitty's and it was going to take her bloody ages to straighten it. And anyway, two men in one night was too much even for Sasha.

Keith came to pick Mandy up from the station where Rick had dropped her earlier. She had to go through the same rigmarole of making sure she waited on the London side so as not to arouse suspicion. Deception was so exhausting, but then she wouldn't have to go through these charades much longer.

In the car, she gave Keith a very brief outline of her weekend in London, remembering that the best thing when you were lying was to say as little as possible. Over-elaboration always caught you out.

'By the way,' said Keith, 'Patrick phoned. He said he was going to pop round, if you weren't back too late.'

'Did he?'

Mandy felt a little flutter of panic. She wasn't sure if she was ready for what she had to say. But there wasn't ever going to be a good time. She'd just have to bite the bullet. As the country lanes slipped by, Mandy looked ahead and kept telling herself to keep calm and think of the reward.

It was nearly closing time again when Suzanna finally drove back to the Honeycote Arms. She realized it was the first time she had driven up to it as a potential punter. She had to admit it looked wonderfully inviting. The sign was welcoming: cream with black writing, subtly highlighted in gold leaf and discreetly lit. Stout whitewashed bollards had been placed along the front of the parking area, with garlands of spiky black chains hung between each one. The stone was glowing from the uplighters that had just come on. Conical bushes in square terracotta pots flanked the door.

She drove in more sedately than she had driven out, noticing with a prick to her conscience the marks her tyres had made in the gravel. She'd rake them over in the morning. She drove round the back to park and was amazed to find it was difficult to get a space. For a Sunday night, it was incredibly busy.

She walked in through the lounge bar. Toby and Melissa were serving. There was a mixed bunch of customers: a group of young lads, some older couples who looked as if they were on their way back from a day out, a couple of men enjoying a last moment of relaxation before they set off for the City next morning. Jonty was there too, with some of his mates. He gave Suzanna a wave and came over before she could escape.

'People keep asking if we're doing food. We're going to have to. It's turning good money away.'

Suzanna smiled.

'If you don't mind working Sunday nights.'

Jonty shrugged good-naturedly.

'It's all money, isn't it? I'm going to need as much as I can get when number three arrives.' He hoped that would placate Meggy. She hadn't been entirely thrilled when he'd come home for his tea and then gone straight out again. Choir practice, he'd told her, not expecting her to believe it.

Suzanna went to check how things were with Toby, who reported brisk business and seemed delighted. She felt chastened. How could she have been such a selfish pig? All these people wanted the Honeycote Arms to be a success, and had pride in what they were doing. Who did she think she was, jeopardizing it all because she didn't have the courage? Well, all that had changed.

'Have you seen Barney?' she asked.

'He went out earlier. He got back about half an hour ago. I think he's upstairs,' replied Toby cautiously, thinking it best not to mention he'd been four sheets to the wind.

Suzanna went into the cloakroom to check her appearance before she went upstairs. She'd gone out after cooking lunch without a scrap of make-up, and realized she looked pretty wrung-out. She dragged a comb through her hair and put on some mascara and lipgloss, then grinned at her reflection. This was crazy: she was almost nervous about going upstairs to see her own husband. But the thought of what she wanted to tell him was giving her butterflies.

She knew he'd think it was a good idea. She felt sure it

was something he'd often wanted to broach with her, but had held back, knowing the time wasn't yet right. She thought back over what a good father he'd always been. He'd been very hands-on, without being too nauseatingly new-mannish about it. He'd loved giving Ollie his bath; he'd been happy to do bedtime on the days when Suzanna had been catering in the evening.

Not that it was going to be easy. There would be all sorts of emotions to deal with. Getting pregnant wasn't always easy for a start. Then the hormone thing would kick in. And it would be strange if they weren't anxious, over-protective. But they had each other. They'd get through it.

She walked out of the cloakroom and through the bar, wondering if she should take a bottle of champagne upstairs with her. Yes, she decided. She was going to go on a strict detox diet as of tomorrow, and if anything needed celebrating it was this.

Bursting with pride and excitement, Patrick arrived at Keeper's Cottage just after half ten. He knew it was late, but when Mandy and Keith heard his news, they would understand.

He waited in the hall as Mandy came down the stairs to greet him. She looked totally different. She was glowing golden, with a few freckles coming out on her nose. Her hair was in loose plaits, like an Indian squaw. She was in khaki shorts and a little vest with CUBA written on the front. Barefoot and no make-up. Patrick was puzzled. Somehow he'd expected her to come back from her weekend even more polished, surrounded by carrier bags, looking like an 'It' girl. He kissed her.

'You look brown.'

'We went to Libby's gym. They've got one of those high-speed tanning cabs.'

Patrick nodded, happy to believe her.

'Listen. I made a radical decision while you were away.'

'Did you?' Mandy tried to keep her voice steady.

'It's been a tough few months. We haven't had much time for each other. It made me realize, maybe it's time . . .'

He wasn't quite sure how to phrase it, but Mandy interrupted.

'We had a break?'

'What?'

He looked up in shock. Mandy ploughed on.

'It's OK. I was thinking the same thing myself.'

Patrick was speechless. Mandy went on to explain.

'I want to get away for a while. Away from the brewery and the Honeycote Arms and Dad and . . .'

'Me?' asked Patrick flatly.

'Maybe not for ever,' said Mandy miserably. 'But I'm finding it really hard to figure out what I want at the moment. All I do know is, I'm not happy.'

Patrick's eyes hardened.

'I'm sorry it's not good enough for you. I'm sorry we haven't had enough time to give you all the attention you need, but we've all been under a lot of pressure.'

'It's not that.'

'Then what is it?'

She didn't reply. She couldn't. He stepped forward, grasping her arms.

'Is there someone else?'

She hesitated for a moment before lying. Well, it wasn't lying. Technically there wasn't anyone else, yet.

'No . . . Of course not.'

His fingers were digging into her flesh. Mandy was frightened. Patrick could be so fierce sometimes. Never to her, but then she'd never tried to dump him before.

'I just . . . need to find out who I am.'

'What?' Patrick's sneer was derisive, and rightly so. Mandy floundered as she sought for the right words to explain her predicament, something that didn't sound quite so flaky. Never in a million years would Patrick be able to relate to a journey of self-discovery. It was probably a reaction to his own mother, who had dropped him like a hot potato when he was small, in exchange for the chance of hitting the hippy trail in India. He'd been suspicious of anything remotely spiritual ever since. Mandy tried to explain her dilemma in terms he could relate to.

'I'm just extensions of everyone else in Honeycote. I haven't got my own identity. I don't make my own decisions, not really. I feel like . . . nobody. I want to go somewhere where I wake up in the morning and I decide what's going to happen. I want . . . choices. I want to know who I really am. I need to find my . . . niche.'

She was horrified that she'd used her mother's word. Patrick was staring at her hard. She stepped back with guilt, feeling sure that he could see the imprints left by Rick's kisses upon her skin. He knew. She was sure he knew. But he couldn't. Could he? She soldiered on with her explanation.

'Everything happened so fast last year. And everyone else seems to be happy with where they are and what they are doing. I'm just . . . not sure. I can't help it if that's how I feel. I'm sorry . . .'

She trailed off rather lamely, and looked to him for understanding.

'So – where are you going? To find this magical answer?'

Mandy realized she hadn't given any thought whatsoever to the practicalities of her plan.

'I don't know yet.'

He picked up a strand of her hair and rubbed it between his fingers. It was like straw; the sun and the sea had dried it out. He dropped the strand as if it was contaminated and walked out of the room.

Patrick saw Mandy's shoes by the door as he left. Something made him pick one up. As a trickle of sand fell out on to the doormat, he reflected that the last time he'd been to South Kensington, there hadn't been any beaches.

Suzanna crept into the bedroom. The bedside lamp was still on. Barney was fast asleep. She kicked off her shoes and sat on the bed next to him.

'Barns? Are you awake?'

He struggled to open his eyes. He looked at her, but it was as if he couldn't see her, the emotionless stare of a dead fish. She caught the smell of booze on his breath. A top note of wine, and underlying it a stronger spirit – she didn't know what.

'Fuck off,' he said flatly, and fell back into a drunken slumber.

Suzanna was shocked. She didn't think Barney had ever said that to her before. She lay on the bed beside him, staring up at the ceiling, willing him to come to, willing his invective to have just been part of some silly dream, willing him to see her and smile and reach out his arm for her to snuggle into.

But he didn't.

Her heart sank like a stone. She'd pushed him too far; asked too much of him too many times. She'd had so many needs, but forgotten that he had needs of his own. He'd finally cracked under the strain. She'd broken him.

A single hot tear squeezed itself from her eye.

She was too late. Too bloody late.

22

The next morning, Mandy waited till her father had gone off to work, which he always did at a quarter to eight promptly. She was usually at least an hour behind him, so he didn't think it strange that she wasn't ready in her usual trouser suit as they shared a quick pot of coffee. Mandy didn't mention what had happened between her and Patrick last night. She wanted to make sure all her plans were in place before she dropped any bombshells. She didn't want anyone trying to talk her out of anything, after all.

As soon as Keith drove off, she pulled on her jeans and a T-shirt, jumped in her car and drove to Eldenbury. She put on the Crazytown CD that had been playing on the beach the day before. It reminded her of the heavenly heat, Rick's head on her stomach, the wicked thoughts she'd had. A little frisson of excitement shot through her. He'd have her now she was free of Patrick. She knew he wanted her. And although she felt guilty about Patrick, the thrill of the unknown was a stronger motivation. Was she selfish? Maybe. But then, you had to be in this life, if you didn't want to trail round in someone else's wake, be at their beck and call. And Patrick would survive. He'd find someone else soon enough.

She parked on the high street and bounded up the stairs to Rick's flat. The smell of last night's sesame oil still hung thick in the air from the Chinese takeaway downstairs. She rapped on the door, dancing up and down with impatience. The door opened. Mandy's face dropped when she saw it was Kelly, still bleary with sleep.

'Is Rick in?'

Kelly opened the door a little wider.

'You'd better come in.'

Mandy followed her into the kitchen. Kelly went over to the sink and filled the kettle.

'Is he still in bed?'

Kelly flicked the switch and turned to face her.

'He's gone.'

'Gone?' Mandy frowned. 'To work, you mean?'

Kelly sighed with the weight of the information she had to impart. 'Mandy, he's gone. He packed everything up last night and went off on his bike this morning.'

'He can't have. I only saw him last night.'

'He's always been impulsive. I don't know where he gets it from.'

'Impulsive?' Mandy didn't think that was quite the word. 'But he didn't say anything. Not a word. I was with him all weekend and he didn't say a word.'

'That's typical of Rick, I'm afraid.'

'I don't understand.'

Kelly looked at her with sympathy.

'Were things starting to get . . . serious between you?'

'Yes . . . no. I don't know. I thought maybe . . . that's why I came here. To talk to him.'

'Look – the trouble with Rick is there's no room for anyone else in his life. He's a free spirit. He always does a bunk when things start to get heavy. Believe me, I've sat here and picked up the pieces often enough.'

Mandy sat down on the sofa, shell-shocked, trying to take in what Kelly was telling her. Of course, she was probably laying it on with a trowel and loving every minute of it. In her eyes, it was probably a great payback for Mandy stealing Patrick off her in the first place. Not that Mandy had actively stolen him. She'd never realized he was already spoken for.

She thought she knew the truth. Rick hadn't done a bunk to get away from her. He'd done a bunk because he thought they couldn't be together. He hadn't known that she was prepared to give up Patrick for him. And now she was too late.

She sat there, numb with shock, as Kelly pressed a cup of tea into her hands. Mandy took it wordlessly.

Rick had gone. Goodness knows where. And she'd dumped Patrick for him. In the space of twenty-four hours, in the hopes of taking control of her destiny, she'd made a complete and utter mess of her life.

Rick drove his bike through the centre of Honeycote, enjoying the slightly outraged stares as the vehicle throbbed its way through the postcard perfection. This wasn't Harley-Davidson territory by any stretch of the imagination. But never mind. Soon he'd be back in North Devon, where it would be admired and envied. He'd been offered a job over the weekend, hiring out wetsuits and boogie boards, maybe doing a bit of teaching. He hadn't thought he'd wanted it at the time, but things had changed. He'd phoned late last night: the job was his if he wanted it.

But first he had to go and tell Damien he wasn't going to work for him any more. He was sorry. Damien had been a good boss, more than generous, and he hadn't made too many demands on Rick. But he couldn't stay around any more. After what had happened yesterday, he'd got to cut loose.

For Rick had come dangerously close to falling in love for the first time, and he didn't like it. He knew getting involved with Mandy would only end in tears. It would involve her in too many decisions and sacrifices that she would end up regretting, and that he wasn't prepared to force her into. He'd asked Kelly the night before if she thought he was a coward, and she'd said no, he was very noble, and one day the right girl would come along with no strings attached.

He worried that perhaps he was going soft, letting Mandy get to him. That last moment at the cliff's edge, he'd never wanted anyone like that before in his life. And Rick didn't do love. It wasn't his style. What was the point, when ultimately it could only end in either boredom or heartbreak? Instead, he went for high-octane bursts of lust; little turbocharged encounters that were hugely pleasurable but never had a chance to reach his soul.

More than anything, if he had succumbed to Mandy, he couldn't have lived with the fear that one day she would find out that the whole thing, originally, had been a set-up. That he'd been trying to lure her away from Patrick out of a desire for revenge. Because the truth would be bound to come out eventually. It had a nasty habit of doing that, in Rick's experience.

He'd packed up his stuff the night before. It hadn't taken very long. Rick wasn't into stuff. Kelly, bless her, had washed his clothes from the weekend, and dried them. He'd held her tight before he left, feeling guilty that he was leaving her in the lurch, but she'd told him not to be daft. She'd cope. They were both copers.

He arrived at Honeycote Grove and pressed the intercom. Damien answered, sounding very abrupt.

'It's Rick. I need to talk to you.'

The gates swung open, almost reluctantly, and Rick drove up the drive. Damien came to the front door. He looked dreadful, as if he hadn't slept. His clothes, very unusually for him, were crumpled. His hair hadn't been washed. But there was something about his body language that said 'Don't ask'. So Rick didn't. He just told him he couldn't work for him any more.

Damien didn't seem bothered that he was going. It was almost as if he hadn't taken the information in. All he seemed worried about was that Rick never repeated anything they'd discussed about the Honeycote Arms and him taking it over.

Rick looked affronted. Confidential meant confidential, didn't it? And he'd always been able to keep his gob shut. That way people told you things.

'Course not. Strictly between you and me.'

Relieved and grateful, Damien counted out some notes from a wad of cash and handed them to Rick as his final payment.

'There's a bit extra. Have a drink for me when you get there.'

'Cheers.'

It was only when Rick got back on his bike and looked more closely at the roll of notes that he realized how important discretion was to Damien. He wondered what was up with him: he looked really stressed. Really jumpy.

Rick shrugged and shoved the money in his pocket. Maybe he'd been on a coke binge all weekend or something. Right now, it wasn't his problem. He could be on the beach by lunchtime if he got his skates on.

That morning, Barney had done his very best to ignore the spectacular headache that was inevitable after white wine, rum and infidelity. He told Suzanna he was going to London for the day to see a wine merchant: they'd been having problems with their supplier. She didn't seem bothered. She was very subdued. He didn't remember her coming in the night before. She didn't apologize for yesterday's argument, so neither did he.

He got on the train at Eldenbury, along with all the regular commuters. The carriage buzzed with people hitting their mobile phones, setting up meetings for the week, comparing notes, discussing deals and takeovers and sackings with no apparent regard for confidentiality. Unable to face coffee yet, he leaned back in his seat, feeling like total shite, heavy-headed and light-headed in turn. He shut his eyes to watch the edited highlights from the night before run through his mind. Him and Kitty. Him and Kitty and maybe, after today, a recording deal. Him and Kitty and a recording deal and a new life ... Was that what he wanted?

For a moment he indulged in a fantasy involving six figures and a tour, followed by a hit album. It wasn't impossible. Kitty was fantastic; he'd written a great song. He contemplated the chaos that would occur if that was the outcome of today's meeting with Jez. What would happen to the pub? What would happen to his contract with Honeycote Ales? Would they sue? He allowed himself a little smile. It wouldn't matter if they did. He'd be a rock and roll star.

He didn't ask himself what would happen to his marriage. He didn't want to think about it, so he concentrated on falling into a troubled sleep.

He woke with a start five minutes outside Paddington, when the conductor announced their imminent arrival. He had a trickle of dribble coming out of one corner of his mouth. He wiped it away hastily and went to buy a packet of Extra Strong Mints and a Coke. Then he found a cab and asked the driver to drop him on Tottenham Court Road so he could wander through the maze of Soho streets until he got to the record company.

He breathed in deeply. After the relentlessly fresh air in Honeycote, it felt good to breathe in filth and fumes. He almost got a hit off it. He walked through the little streets, looking in all the windows: shops specializing in all manner of things – film posters, vinyl records, an off-licence with a staggering display of absinthe, the usual sex shops which had their mind-boggling products proudly on display, sushi bars with plastic seafood. He felt almost over-stimulated, assaulted by so many images.

He arrived at the office at five to eleven – uncoolly early, but he didn't care. The place had certainly smartened up since he'd last been here. Then the walls had been painted black and pink with tattered posters, the reception desk littered with empty cans of Red Stripe and ashtrays. Now he felt sure lighting up a cigarette would be frowned upon; the receptionist looked sleek behind her curved maple desk with its state-of-the-art phone system.

Jez came down to reception to greet him personally. Barney was amazed at his transformation – he'd obviously undergone a serious make-over. He'd always had shockingly bad teeth, but now he displayed a dazzling row of pearly-white porcelain. Gone also was the misguided New Romantic look, which Jez had always got slightly wrong, and in its place was a well-cut suit with a black T-shirt underneath. The ponytail, too, had been sacrificed. In fact, if it hadn't been for the rather effeminate giggle, Barney wouldn't have recognized him.

He greeted Barney with much over-enthusiastic back-slapping and hand-shaking, which Barney went along with. He'd always considered Jez a bit of a prat, but he had a certain thick-skinned enthusiasm and dogged determination that got things done. Together, they went up to his office, which in itself was evidence of his success. There were plush carpets, an enormous desk and leather seating banked all the way round the edge. Chrome-framed album covers lined the walls. In the old days, Jez had been surrounded by piles of demo cassettes and fanzines and begging letters and draft contracts. Now his desk was clear, apart from an ominously blank notepad and pen.

Jez steepled his fingers and looked at Barney gravely.

'I don't mind telling you', he began, 'that I am majorly, seriously excited. This is what I've been waiting for. Everyone's falling over themselves to find the next Dido.' He picked up a remote control. 'Let's listen.'

He played the demo Barney had sent him through the sound system he'd got rigged up in his office. There was no doubt about it – she was spine-shiveringly good, and it sounded fantastic on the expensive speakers.

'So. Do you reckon this girl could do it? Could she handle it?'

'Can anyone?' Barney threw him a cynical smile. Jez picked up his pen.

'Describe.'

Barney shrugged.

'Pretty – very. Unusual. Good bone structure. Sort of . . . kittenish. And a bit quirky. She's got her own style. Romantic. Looks as if she's been in the dressing-up box.'

'Not too Björk, I hope. No dead swans?'

Barney shook his head.

'Tits?'

Barney thought of Kitty's small, round breasts. How perfectly they'd fitted into his hands. Her nipples that had turned hard with desire under his lips –

'I've got no idea,' he said primly.

Jez laughed nastily. 'Don't try and tell me you're not shagging her.'

Barney looked indignant. 'No, I'm not.' He might have shagged her, but he wasn't *shagging* her. There was a difference.

'Oh yeah. I forgot. You're a happily married man.'

Jez managed to make it sound as if no such thing existed.

'So tell me, Barney. How do you see yourself fitting into the picture?'

Barney was immediately on his guard. He didn't like Jez's tone of voice. The slight sneer that had always made him itch to punch him on the nose. It was all coming back to him now.

'I hadn't really thought about it.'

'Because I'm going to make it plain to you from the start. If we're going to deal with this girl, we want a clean package. A solo artist. Not a young girl with a middle-aged Svengali attached to her.'

Barney sat back in his chair, shocked by Jez's bluntness.

'No need to be offended. We can do a deal. An introduction fee.'

Barney crossed his arms.

'And a publishing deal, of course. I take it you wrote that track? It's got you written all over it and it's fucking good. We'll need more of the same. But don't get any ideas about this being a duo.'

He looked Barney up and down disparagingly. Barney wished for a moment he'd made more of an effort than jeans and a suede jacket, but he hadn't wanted to arouse any suspicion when he left Honeycote. Jez was looking at him as if he was wearing bicycle clips and socks with sandals.

'Because you're not exactly an icon, are you? It would have been all right if you'd stayed in the industry. Blokes over thirty-five can still hack it if they're legends in their own lifetime. Like . . . New Order, for example. But you'd be starting from scratch, or as good as. It would be, frankly, embarrassing. Stick her on *Top Of The Pops* with you and they'd think you were her dad.'

'I'd forgotten what an arsehole you are.' Barney got up to go. He held up a hand in sarcastic farewell. 'Adios.'

Jez didn't flinch.

'Don't be an arsehole yourself, Barney. I've got the demo. How long do you think it's going to take me to find her?' Jez grinned. 'In fact – what a fantastic idea. I'll get this sent out to every radio station in the country. We'll have a nationwide search.' He gestured with his hands. '*Where's Kitty*? We'll have it fly-posted everywhere – on the tube, at every bus station, outside every club . . . She'll be famous before she's even started. Brilliant. *Pop Idol* in reverse – the star's already born; we've just got to find out where she is . . .'

Barney felt quite ill. Jez was right. It was a completely brilliant idea, and he'd played right into his hands. But one thing was for sure. He wanted nothing more to do with it. He hadn't felt that feeling for so long – that feeling of rage mixed with fear; that feeling of knowing you were being exploited yet desperately wanting to realize your dreams. Dreams that someone else had control of.

Jez did have the grace to look a little contrite.

'I'm sorry, Barney. But you know me. I tell it like it is. I always have done. That's why I'm still here.'

He was right about that. He still remembered Jez coming to see him to tell him he was off the tour, that the band was going on without him. He gave a resigned sigh.

'If you're really interested, I'll talk to her. See what she wants to do. It's up to her.'

'Tell her to get in touch. No promises, mind. I'd want to stick her in a studio, put her through her paces. Then we'll see.'

Jez saw him back down to reception. As Barney was about to go through the smoked-glass doors, he put a hand on his shoulder to stop him.

'I just want to tell you, Barney. That band were nothing without you. I don't mind admitting it was the biggest mistake of my career, kicking you off the tour. But that's rock and roll, as they say.'

448

Was that supposed to be a consolation, Barney wondered, as he made his way out into the stifling Soho hubbub. The hubbub that had seemed so exciting and stimulating when he arrived, but that now threatened to choke him with its fumes and increased his headache tenfold.

Having spent the morning in torment, Patrick made his way to the Honeycote Arms. He had to get out of the brewery: if Elspeth gave him one more curious gaze, brought him one more cup of coffee or simpered over him once more, he would kill her. And he wanted to see Suzanna. He couldn't think who else to talk to, even though it was rather ironic that she was the one person he could think of who would understand the agony of unrequited love. He didn't think she'd mind him crying on her shoulder. They hadn't parted enemies.

Suzanna was horrified by his appearance. He told her flatly what had happened, that Mandy had dumped him, and was gratified when she took him in her arms and hugged him, a big, all-enveloping, comforting embrace for which he was very grateful but that nearly made him cry.

'Come on. You need something to eat.'

Suzanna got them some carrot and sweet potato soup from the kitchen, and some crusty rolls, and they sat at a table. Marmite sat at their feet, hoping for the odd morsel to drop his way. Patrick struggled to swallow anything. His insides were churning. He put his spoon down in defeat.

'Shit, Suzanna. What am I supposed to do now? It was my mistake, I suppose. I went charging ahead with everything, had it all mapped out, just assuming it was what Mandy wanted too.'

Suzanna shook her head in amused disbelief.

'Ironic, isn't it? We all seem to want something we can't have.' She laughed, a trifle hysterically.

'I'm glad you can laugh.' Patrick wasn't able to see the funny side yet.

'Sorry.' She put her hand over his. 'I really am, Patrick.' She paused for a moment. 'If it's any consolation, I think it's too late for me and Barney. I think I might have blown it.'

They both dwelt in silence for a moment on their respective plights. Patrick looked up with a smile.

'If Barney kicks you out, I've got a room going spare. I'm going to need a lodger to pay the mortgage.'

He hadn't addressed that one yet. He'd only got a few days to find the money. And secretly, in the back of his mind, he'd been hoping that Keith might bail him out, once he knew that Patrick and Mandy were engaged. Hah! Fat chance of that now. He'd have to go grovelling to his relations instead. Sell his car, probably. What a mess.

The door to the lounge bar opened – they'd forgotten to lock up. Two men came in. Stocky, dressed in jeans and black leather bomber jackets. Not the usual Honeycote Arms clients. Patrick stood up.

'I'm awfully sorry – we're closed.'

The men didn't stop. They carried on till they were right by the table.

'We open again at six –'

Patrick stopped. Something wasn't quite right. The taller of the two held his hand up, as if to tell him to be quiet.

450

'We don't want a drink. We want cash.'

Suzanna was surprised to find herself calm. She stood up and fixed them with a charming but firm smile.

'It's all in the safe, I'm afraid. We haven't got the combination.'

This was true. Only Barney knew the number. The takings for the entire weekend were sitting in the safe, waiting for him to take them to the bank.

'Bollocks.' The shorter one turned to Patrick. 'You're the gaffer. You must know it.'

'I'm not the gaffer. I don't have a clue –'

'Then maybe this will remind you.'

One of them produced a baseball bat from behind his back and brandished it threateningly. Instead of being frightened, Suzanna felt filled with fury – how dare they march in here like this?

'Look – he's not my husband. He doesn't know the combination. We've got no way of getting in, OK? So just piss off.'

'So where is he then? Your husband?'

'I don't know. London. He won't be back till . . . tomorrow.'

'You'd better phone him, then.'

The thug reached over the bar and picked up the pub handset, tossing it to Suzanna. He gave her a look that said he meant it.

With trembling hands, she punched out Barney's mobile number. A warning hand grabbed her wrist before she could put the phone to her ear.

'Remember, no funny stuff. Don't try and warn him. Just get the number.'

Something in his cold eyes told Suzanna he meant

business. She nodded wordlessly and put the phone to her ear, listening to the ringing tone.

Barney jumped out of the cab at Paddington and made his way into the station. He eyes sought out Eldenbury on the timetable. Platform six. Shit – the train was about to go. He could see them closing the barrier. He ran for it as his phone began to trill. He ignored it – he'd miss the train if he answered it. He rushed past the guard without showing him his ticket and pulled open the door of the carriage just as the last whistle went.

Suzanna hung up the phone and shook her head.

'He's not answering. He's probably in a meeting or something.'

The thug looked agitated.

'Bloody well try him again.'

Hearing the bloke's harsh tones to his mistress, Marmite came rushing forwards with a little warning growl.

'Shut up, mutt.'

A huge booted foot drew back and kicked out, catching the little dog square in the chest and sending him flying through the air.

'You bastard!' Suzanna flew at the man in a rage.

'For God's sake, Suzanna – just sit down!'

But Patrick's warning was too late. The bloke reached round and grabbed her by the hair, pulling her round, then put a burly arm across her to pin her to his chest. She was screaming and struggling.

'Shut up, bitch.'

'Leave her alone!'

With a superhuman effort, Patrick pushed the table

aside and lunged across the room to Suzanna's defence, but suddenly found his chin connecting with something cold and hard. The baseball bat. There was a sickening crunch. There goes my nose, thought Patrick, as he flew backwards through the air, and his head hit the limestone floor with an ominous smack.

Barney fell into an empty seat with relief. He pulled his phone out of his pocket to see who'd rung. It was the pub's number. He put it back into his pocket. They'd ring again if it was important.

His hangover had dissipated, just leaving him totally knackered, and he didn't have the adrenalin he'd had on the journey up. It was the slow train and the miles seemed to drag by. He hadn't had time to buy a paper or a magazine. He was left with nothing but his thoughts for entertainment.

He'd been an idiot to think even for a minute that picking up where he'd left off all those years ago was going to be a remote possibility. In just one meeting, that had lasted barely an hour, he remembered all the shit that went with it, the constant insecurity and battling to keep one's place in the pecking order. Thanks Jez, he thought ruefully. You've done me a favour.

Trouble was, what he was going back to wasn't any more enticing. For a start, he had Kitty to face. He was going to have to be very gentle with her, but he thought she'd understand. They had no future together. There was, after all, only one woman he'd ever loved.

Suzanna. The words of an old Clash song went through his head – should he stay or should he go? Of course, it wasn't a serious question. He wasn't going to walk out on Honeycote Ales. But he and Suzanna had to make a decision.

The way he saw it, they had three choices. They could carry on as they were, running on parallel lines, slowly destroying each other. But that would ultimately spell disaster. A pub depended on the chemistry of the people running it. It wouldn't take long before people detected a rift between them, souring the atmosphere.

They could admit defeat and set each other free by going their separate ways. But Barney felt that way everyone lost: him, Suzanna, Honeycote Ales, all the people that had contributed to what was on its way to being a success.

The third option was to sit down and try and make a proper go of it. Talk everything through, in practical and emotional terms – the past, the present, the future. It would be painful, but they couldn't run away from that. Surely it would be worth it? And they shouldn't discuss it in the light of an argument, but when they both felt calm and strong. The trolley went past with some rather unappetizing cans of beer, and for a moment Barney was tempted. But he thought not.

If he was going to have the final showdown with Suzanna, then he'd better do it sober.

Mandy sat in the travel agents in Cheltenham biting the side of her nails with impatience as the girl tried endless permutations on the computer before finally coming up with a convoluted timetable of planes and stopovers that would, God willing, have her in Sydney by Friday. She slid her credit card over the table top decisively.

It was what she should have done all along. She should

have gone to Australia with Sophie and Ned on day one. She would have saved herself and Patrick so much pain. She couldn't go back to him now, not after what she had done. She couldn't expect forgiveness.

This would be a new beginning. The start of life on her own, without anyone else to influence it. She'd see new places, meet new people, open her mind, take some risks. Then, once she'd lived a little, maybe she'd feel equipped to make decisions about the rest of her life.

Her father would understand, she was sure. And she was happy that she could leave him on his own now. He seemed very keen on Ginny. Mandy was pretty sure they were going to be an item and the last thing she wanted was to cramp her father's style by being a gooseberry in her own home.

Barney took a taxi back from the station. As the cab drew up outside the Honeycote Arms, the driver woke him from another snatched moment of sleep.

'Looks like something's up.'

Barney was instantly alert. He looked out of the window and saw three police cars and an ambulance in his car park. He shot out of the cab without a backward glance and made for the door, where a young policeman blocked his way.

'What's going on?'

'Excuse me, sir. Could you tell me who you are?'

'I'm the landlord here. Where's my wife? Where's my fucking wife?'

Barney pushed past him into the lounge, his heart racing. There were tables overturned, a smashed chair. He looked round wildly.

'Suzanna?'

'Barney!'

She was there, thank God. Sitting at a table with a young policeman, being interviewed. She stood up. She looked incredibly pale, her freckles standing out in stark relief. The policeman explained.

'There was a hold-up. Unfortunately the other young man didn't escape so lightly. He's had to go to hospital. Concussion. Broken nose.'

'Who? Toby?'

The policeman referred to his notebook.

'Patrick Liddiard. He should be all right. And they didn't get anything, sir.'

'Never mind about that.' Barney strode over to Suzanna. 'Are you all right?'

She nodded and tried to speak, but suddenly she began trembling. It was as if the sight of Barney had suddenly brought the shock home to her. She wanted to throw herself into his arms, feel his strength around her, the strength that had got her through so much agony. But she'd gone overdrawn; she feared he had nothing left for her. For a moment, they just stood and looked at each other. Barney turned to the officer in charge.

'Do you really have to do this now?'

'Best to take the details while the memory's still fresh, sir.'

'Could I have five minutes with my wife? I'd just like to know she's all right.'

'Certainly, sir.'

They went through into the dining room, which was spookily empty but all laid up for dinner that evening. Barney looked at her as if he was looking at her for the first time. Which in some ways he was.

'My God,' he said slowly. 'I'm so sorry I wasn't here. I'm so sorry I wasn't here to protect you.' A sudden realization came over him. 'You could have been killed.'

'It's OK. I'm OK.'

Guilt overwhelmed him. Guilt at what had happened and what could have happened, while he'd been feeding his own ego. To his horror, tears started sliding down his face. He grabbed her and pulled her to him, big choking sobs getting in the way of what he wanted to say.

'I love you. You've got to know that. Whatever happens to us, I love you.'

Suzanna clenched her teeth. She wasn't going to cry. She was going to be strong for him, so she could see through her resolution. She managed a whisper.

'I thought . . . I thought maybe you'd gone for good. I thought I'd pushed you too far. You wouldn't answer the phone . . .'

'I thought you didn't love me. I thought you'd had enough.'

Suzanna shook her head.

'Barney, I . . .'

His heart gave a lurch. She was struggling to say something. Was this it? Was she going to say it was all over?

'I want another baby.'

Barney stood stock-still. Joy pumped through his veins at what he was hearing, but he couldn't move for the shock. Suzanna looked at him anxiously.

'Barney?'

Ten minutes later, they were interrupted in the throes of a passionate embrace by a pink-faced policeman clearing his throat.

'Excuse me. I just wondered if you were ready to

resume your interview, Miss. And there's a taxi driver outside wondering about his fare . . .'

Mandy was packing. She had all her stuff out all over the bed, desperately trying to figure out what she'd be needing for her new life. She put in one cream trouser suit, that she could accessorize and mix with different T-shirts, in case she decided to try and get a proper job. The rest was casual stuff — she would leave all her smart clothing behind. She surveyed the rail for a moment, admiring the Jasper Conran and French Connection she'd accumulated. She wouldn't be needing any of that on the beach.

Her mobile rang. It was her father. She'd been into the brewery that morning to sort out her paperwork and file everything that needed filing, putting it into order so that her replacement would find things easy. If they even bothered to replace her. Maybe Elspeth would finally get her wish.

She answered the phone cautiously.

'Mandy, love. Where are you?'

He sounded agitated.

'At home.' She paused. She was going to have to tell him before she left. She wasn't that much of a coward. And she thought he'd understand. Hadn't he said, that night at the ballet? Hadn't he told her to follow her heart? 'Dad —'

He cut her off.

'I'll come and get you.'

'What is it?'

'It's Patrick. There's been a hold-up at the pub. He's in hospital. I'll be five minutes.'

He hung up. Mandy stood still for a moment in shock, her mind racing.

She had to get the last train out of Eldenbury tonight. She was due on the first plane out of Heathrow in the morning. She looked at her watch. There'd be time. She'd just make sure Patrick was all right, and then she'd go.

Keith collected Mandy from Keeper's Cottage and drove her to Evesham hospital. He explained what had happened: the police had alerted the brewery straight away. It was obvious her father didn't know what had gone on between her and Patrick. She didn't tell him. Now was not the time.

Keith dropped her at the door while he went to find a parking space, and she was directed to the ward. Suzanna was just coming out. She looked at Mandy with a hostile glare.

'You've bothered to turn up, then?'

Mandy didn't know what to say. Suzanna ploughed on. 'You've broken his heart. You know that, don't you?'

Mandy bristled.

'I'd have thought *you'd* be pleased.'

'What?'

'Isn't that what you wanted? To have him for yourself?' Filled with fear and panic, Mandy could feel her voice rising hysterically. 'He wasn't interested in me any more. I bet he was glad to get rid of me. So that you two could be together.'

Suzanna looked at her in horror.

'Mandy,' she said gently. 'I think you've got it all wrong. Patrick thinks the world of you.'

'He couldn't wait to get rid of me half the time. He

certainly couldn't wait to see the back of me this weekend.'

'Didn't he tell you why?'

Mandy blinked.

'What do you mean?'

'He bought you a house. He bought you a house and he was going to ask you to marry him.' Suzanna looked at Mandy sternly. 'But you never gave him a chance.'

Mandy sank down weakly on to the nearest seat.

'A house?' she asked, rather stupidly.

'It's beautiful. He showed it to me.' Suzanna sat down next to her. 'Mandy, if Patrick and I spent a lot of time together recently, it's because we had to. There's nothing between us, I promise you. I wouldn't want you to go and do anything rash.'

'Of course not,' said Mandy, thinking you couldn't get more rash than booking a one-way ticket to Australia. 'I just needed . . . a bit of time to think.'

'I'm sure he'll understand. It's been a difficult few weeks for everyone.'

Mandy walked into Patrick's room. He looked incredibly young, tucked up under the sheets, as pale as chalk against the blue-black of his hair. He looked at her like a dog that had been kicked, not sure if it was going to be kicked again.

'What are you doing here?' His voice was gruff.

She picked up his hand and held it tightly.

'I came to see if you were all right . . .'

Patrick looked away, out of the window for a moment.

'What does it look like?' He paused. 'They've broken my fucking nose.'

Mandy put her fingers up to touch his beautiful face. The bruised cheekbones, the swollen eyes.

'Last night ... I'm sorry. But everything I said was true. I'm so confused. I need to get my head round everything.'

'I was going to ask you to marry me.'

Mandy looked down at her nails. She'd chewed them to the quick since yesterday.

'Do you still want to?'

'That's up to you. The offer's there.'

His voice was full of hurt pride. It must have taken him a lot to say it. How could she have got him so wrong? How could she have thought he didn't care about her? It would be so easy to say yes ...

But Mandy knew that would be wrong. That half the reason they'd got to this stage was because she still wasn't sure about who she was and what she wanted. She needed to find out more about herself, why she'd succumbed to temptation, why she was frustrated and at times insecure. She wasn't going to get those answers in Honeycote. She took a deep breath.

'I can't say yes, Patrick. I can't say yes, but I'm not saying no. I'm going away. I'm going to Australia to see Sophie and Ned. I need some space and some time.'

Patrick shut his eyes. The painkillers didn't dull the pain in his heart. Mandy leaned forward and he could smell her scent.

'If you can wait. Just a little while. Then I can give you an answer ...'

Damien had been sitting in the house all day. He hadn't let Anastasia go to school. He couldn't let her out of his sight, not until he knew for certain either way and could take action. He'd phoned the company to speed up the process: the DNA test had arrived by courier on Saturday. He'd sent it back by courier that morning, and they'd promised him the results within twenty-four hours. It had cost him, but he didn't care. Anything that curtailed the agony he was in.

In the meantime, he was like a cat on hot bricks. Adding to his uncertainty was the fact that he couldn't be sure what Nicole's next move might be. So when the phone went at six o'clock that evening, he jumped out of his skin.

'Damien? It's Pebbles. Your job's been done. It all went a bit pear-shaped.'

'What do you mean, pear-shaped?'

'I know you said no violence. But one of them managed to get in the way of a baseball bat. You know how these things happen. It goes with the territory.'

Shit, thought Damien. Shit shit shit.

'Are they OK?'

'Don't know. No one stayed around to find out. Understandably. Just wanted to let you know the job had been done. Call it . . . after-sales service.'

There was a chuckle and the phone went dead.

Damien felt ill. What kind of a wanker was he, with his smash and grab mentality, thinking he could have whatever he wanted? He was no better than Nicole, with her scheming, manipulative ways. He was a thug. OK, so he didn't actually wield the baseball bat himself, but didn't that make it worse? The blokes he had hired, albeit indirectly, probably needed the cash. They probably didn't have any other way of making a living. Whereas he had it all, but still wanted more. He was a greedy megalomaniac with the morals of a snake.

It was all very well for him to have made resolutions. But it was too late for him to change. What goes around, comes around, thought Damien.

The letter was due tomorrow. Registered post. And he knew damn well the answer he deserved. The only thing he had left was prayer.

23

Sasha woke up on Tuesday morning and knew it was one of those days when she didn't want to get up. She often had days like this. She usually managed to fob her mother off by saying it was a migraine or period pains, spacing the excuses out so as not to arouse suspicion. Some days there just didn't seem to be any fucking point and this was one of them.

News of yesterday's hold-up had flown through the village, even though the brewery was desperately trying to keep it quiet. Baseball-bat-wielding thugs weren't exactly good for business. Sasha wasn't overly concerned about the hold-up itself. They were a fact of modern-day life.

But suddenly, in the light of the drama, what she'd done to Barney didn't seem very funny any more. In fact, she felt sick with shame. Every time she tried to blank it out of her mind, the images of her quite literally dropping her knickers came back to haunt her. And she couldn't face Kitty. Sweet, kind Kitty who'd just brought her up a cup of tea, so she'd had to pretend to be asleep.

She wondered what had made her into such a thrill-seeker. Such an attention-seeker. As a child, everyone had always exclaimed how naughty she was and what an angel Kitty was. Well, was it so surprising, then, that she'd turned out like she had? It was a self-fulfilling prophecy.

Plus life had been pretty shit lately. Sasha had been devastated when her father had left, though she'd pretended it was no big deal – everyone came from a broken home, didn't they? She hated Faith with a vengeance and resented her for taking her mother's place. On several occasions she'd fantasized about pushing Faith down the sweeping staircase she'd wheedled out of her father, killing her and hopefully the cuckoo of a foetus she had in her big fat stomach. Now Sasha had seen Chelsea she couldn't think of her in quite the same ruthless terms. She was still jealous, though. Hideously jealous that this blob, albeit a cute one, was robbing her of her father's time, attention and money. Just wait, she'd whispered to Chelsea once as she held her in her arms. Just wait till your daddy tires of you, when something better comes along, just like he did with me.

So was it any wonder that she got her kicks by playing with other people's minds, messing up their lives? But Sasha was gradually coming to realize that it was doing her no good whatsoever. Her self-esteem was plummeting lower and lower. She was horrid to her mother and Kitty. She was leading Jonty Hobday a merry dance, teasing him and taunting him. And as for what she'd done to Barney . . .

Not that he knew yet. She was going to have to go to him and confess. For all her faults, Sasha was quite a brave little soul. Even as a child, she'd always owned up to her misdemeanours.

But not yet. Kitty was just off to college. She had the day to think over how she was going to tackle this one without coming off too badly. It was unlikely that Barney would try to contact Kitty throughout the course of the day, or so she hoped.

Ginny came in, anxious.

'Is it one of your heads?'

Sasha nodded. Ginny sat down on the bed next to her and put a cool, soothing hand on her forehead.

'Mum,' she said in a very small voice, 'have you ever done anything you were ashamed of? Something you really regret?'

There was a moment while Ginny considered her reply.

'I've done lots of things I wished I hadn't,' she answered. 'But I don't see the point in regretting things. They make you the person you are.'

Sasha considered this for some time, then realized it was no comfort at all. Because she didn't want to be the person she was.

Kitty decided to call in at the pub on her way to college. She was appalled at what had happened the day before, and wanted to make sure Barney and Suzanna were all right.

She found Barney in the cellar, cleaning out his pipes. He started when he saw her. Kitty supposed it was understandable. You would be jumpy after a hold-up.

'Kitty!'

'I just came to see if you were all right. After yesterday. It was terrible . . .'

'Um . . . yes. Everyone's fine. Well, Patrick's a bit of a mess, but he should be out of hospital today.'

'And Suzanna?'

'Having a lie-in. But she should be OK. Um . . . Kitty?'

Kitty looked at Barney. He looked . . . she couldn't quite put her finger on it. Guilty? Worried? Awkward, certainly. He'd backed right up against the wall, as if he was trying to get away from her.

'Barney – I just wanted to say. About the demo – don't worry about sending it off yet.'

'What?'

He looked utterly blank. He must have forgotten his promise. Kitty felt a bit of an idiot.

'You said you were going to send it to someone. Someone you knew. But it doesn't matter. Not yet. I don't think I'm ready.'

Barney felt for a moment as if time was standing still, or as if he'd stepped into some parallel universe where he hadn't quite caught up with reality. A hideous realization was creeping up on him, one he didn't want to confront . . .

Kitty carried on explaining.

'I've got exams over the next couple of months. Mum will freak if I don't get them this time. And if anything does come of it, I want to be ready. I want to have time to write some songs, get my head around the whole thing.'

Barney was feeling faintly sick. He had to find a way to make sure.

'Um – Kitty. Sunday – you didn't work here Sunday night, did you?' He smiled weakly.

'Sunday? No – me and Mum went to the movies.'

She was looking at him with a perplexed expression. Barney felt he had to explain.

'It's OK. I'm just trying to work out the payslips. I realized I hadn't filled in the staff rotas properly.'

'Oh.'

Barney tried to gather himself together, to look as if he was in control just for a moment.

'Don't worry about the demo. I'll keep it on hold.

I'll – er – see you later in the week, yeah? Thanks for coming by.'

He turned back to washing out his pipes, hoping she'd get the hint. Which she did.

As soon as she'd gone, Barney leaned back against the cellar wall with a groan. Kitty didn't have a clue – she didn't know about his meeting with Jez; didn't know how ecstatic he'd been about her singing.

Which could only mean one thing. He hadn't slept with her. He'd slept with Sasha. Conniving, manipulative, evil little monkey. What a fool he'd been! He should have realized. Should have clicked that Kitty couldn't possibly have been the predatory, man-eating tigress who'd taken advantage of him. Practically raped him, if he looked back on it.

What the hell was he going to do? Sasha wasn't the type to just let it lie. She was bound to use it to her own end. She was a potential bunny-boiler if ever he'd met one. He imagined her sitting in her room, laughing her head off, planning the next twist to the plot.

Barney thought he might be sick. He'd been worried enough about smoothing things over with Kitty, who was a reasonable girl. But Sasha – Sasha was a maniac!

Jesus. Just when he'd got everything sorted with Suzanna.

Tuesdays were Kelly's day off. They tended to be quiet, and she needed one day to sort through the salon's paperwork, do her ordering and have a bit of time to herself. All she needed to do was pop into the salon and make sure Eloise and Pam were coping and she had the rest of the day to do what she wanted.

Rick had phoned her the night before. He'd got there safely; he was sharing a room with a mate in Croyde until he found his own place and was starting work the next day. She thought about what he said just before he hung up. He'd told her to give Damien a call. He reckoned he needed some company. Kelly was unsure. She was only his babysitter, after all.

She supposed she could drive over to Ross-on-Wye to see her parents, but that wasn't the sort of company she wanted. She weighed things up in her mind for a few moments, then picked up the phone.

Damien answered almost immediately. He sounded wary; strained.

'Damien? It's Kelly.'

The relief in his voice was palpable. 'Kelly.'

She wasn't sure what to say next, but she carried on regardless. Like Rick had said, she had nothing to lose.

'I was just phoning . . . I've got the day off . . . I wondered . . . Do you want to do something?'

'Can you come over?' Kelly was surprised at the speed of his reply. 'There's something I need you to do for me.'

Barney was in agony when Suzanna refused to stay in bed and recuperate from the traumas of the day before. The doctor had been quite concerned about her, as Barney had discreetly indicated that she was in a fragile emotional state as it was. He'd muttered about counselling and victim support and post-traumatic stress disorder, and had told Barney to get straight back in touch if he thought she needed anything to help her sleep.

But Suzanna seemed to be in an extraordinarily robust and cheerful mood, and insisted she was well enough to do lunch. Barney swore to himself. He'd relied on her being incapacitated for at least the rest of the afternoon while he sorted out the mess that was his life.

He didn't know what to do. Whether to find Sasha and confront her. Or go to Suzanna and confess. Put his hands up and make a clean breast of it.

Barney groaned in despair. It wasn't as if there was anyone he could turn to for advice.

When Damien answered the door to Kelly he was as white as a sheet. Anastasia was watching *The Borrowers* on DVD. Kelly wondered if she was poorly: why wasn't she at school?

He was holding an envelope in his hand. He ushered her into the kitchen, out of Anastasia's earshot.

'That woman who was here the other night. It was my wife. My ex-wife. Nicole.'

Kelly nodded. She'd guessed as much.

'She told me . . . Anastasia wasn't mine. I've had a test done.'

He held up the envelope.

'A paternity test. The answer's in here. They've just sent it by bike.' His face crumpled. His hands were shaking. 'I can't bear to open it.'

Kelly was horrified.

'Of course she's yours. Anyone can see that.'

'But she looks so like Nicole . . .'

Kelly shook her head emphatically. 'I know she's dark, and you're fair. But there's lots of you in her. I can see it. There's no way she's not yours.'

Damien thrust the envelope at her.

'Just open it, will you? Tell me what it says.'

Without even thinking about the consequences of the information she might have to impart, Kelly tore open the envelope and pulled out a headed letter. She scanned the contents, a frown appearing between her perfectly plucked brows.

'I think . . .'

She had to make sure. The letter was made up of so much legal jargon, so much on-the-fence beating about the bush, as well as a number of statistics and percentages, that she couldn't be sure what it was saying. She read through it again.

Damien thought his heart was going to stop. Kelly looked up at him.

'I *think* it says she's yours.'

She handed him the letter. The words danced before his eyes as he tried to decipher them.

Eventually he crushed the paper in his hands. He pulled Kelly towards him and folded her tightly in his arms. He was going to break down and cry, but he didn't care.

Anastasia was his. The letter said it was 99.9 per cent certain, which was good enough for him. Hot tears fell on to Kelly's curls, but she didn't seem to mind a bit. In fact, she'd put her arm around his neck and was hugging him tightly, reassuring him. Eventually, his sobs subsided.

'I'm sorry.'

'That's OK. I just can't believe your wife did that to you. What a bitch.'

'You don't know Nicole,' said Damien ruefully. He realized he'd never known her either. He could never have dreamed of the depths to which she'd stooped. He was going to have to be a lot more careful second time around, especially as he had Anastasia to think about. He couldn't afford to make another mistake.

Though he didn't think Kelly was going to be a mistake. Unless she was an even better actress than Nicole had been. He didn't think you could fake the affection she seemed to have for Anastasia. And Rick had told him a lot about his sister over the past few weeks, enough for Damien to know she was a perfectionist and house-proud, that she never bore a grudge for long, that she never forgot birthdays or to take videos back to the video shop, that she didn't drink much but it didn't matter because she knew how to have a laugh without getting pissed, and that she was a dutiful daughter and a doting sister. All ticks in the right boxes as far as he was concerned.

'Will you come out for lunch with us?' he asked, rather abruptly. He wasn't used to showing his emotions like that.

'I'd love to. But I'd better go home and get changed.'

Damien looked at her. She was in jeans and a pink off-the-shoulder sweatshirt. She looked adorable. He thought back to Nicole and how she would have been gussied up in Prada and Patrick Cox. How that once would have been important to him.

'No, don't,' he said. 'You look great.'

24

James parked his car at the front of the Dower House and let himself in through the front door. Bertie never locked the place; it was always open house. People wandered in and out as they liked. It was incredible that the place had never been ransacked.

Something wasn't quite right. James sniffed as he entered the hallway. It smelled ... of polish. And there was a vase of fresh flowers on the hall table. And the usual huge pile of boots and shoes you had to kick to one side wasn't there. He ventured through into the kitchen and realized that the strains of Vivaldi's 'Four Seasons' were wafting through from the drawing room. Very strange. Bertie hated classical music. Vivaldi was a bit populist for James, who actually listened to Radio 3 a lot of the time, only turning to Classic FM if things got too heavy and Wagnerian. But Bertie always retuned his radio to Virgin if they went anywhere in the car together. His usual taste was firmly planted in either Oasis, the Rolling Stones or Crowded House. Something was definitely up.

Perhaps he'd rented the place out. Got in some agency to clean the place out and decided to go for holiday lets. James was hurt. He knew Bertie did things on impulse, but that was a big decision. If he'd decided to decamp back to Fulham, he could have told him.

But no – he had to be here. His Audi estate had been

parked outside. James looked around the kitchen. It was immaculate. One thing was for sure. He'd either got himself a cleaner, or a woman.

'Coffee?'

He turned to see Bertie in the doorway, looking incredibly crisp and clean, in a dusky pink polo shirt and chinos, his hair freshly washed and curling over his collar.

'Lovely,' said James, intrigued. He didn't think Bertie had offered him coffee ever in his life. Vodka, yes. Champagne, yes. A spliff, yes. He watched as he made real coffee and was intrigued to see the china sparkling. Bertie's cups were usually ringed with stains.

'What on earth's going on?'

'I'm in love,' said Bertie, simply. 'I've just got to be very patient and wait.'

'What for?' said James cynically. 'For her to leave her husband? Or to leave school?' Bertie's track record was littered with married women and schoolgirls.

'No. For her to realize she's in love with me.'

'Oh.' This was very unusual. Bertie was more often trying to beat off his conquests – he usually came down to the Cotswolds to hide from them until their ardour had died down. 'Well, come on. Fill me in. What's so different this time?'

'She's made me realize what a complete and utter waste of space I am. She makes me feel – safe. She doesn't make me feel like running away. Metaphorically, of course.'

'So who is this angel in disguise?'

'Ginny Tait.'

James put his coffee cup down slowly.

'You are joking.'

'She's gorgeous. Wonderful.'

'She's certainly a bloody miracle worker if she's made you clean up your act like this. But she's far too old for you.'

'A couple of years older, perhaps. But that doesn't matter. Not at our time of life.'

'Bertie, you've got nothing in common!'

'How do you know?'

'Come off it. She's hardly going to feel comfortable with your coke-fuelled, champagne-swilling, hard-living bachelor-boy lifestyle. Have you taken her on your ritual Saturday night tour of all the bars in Fulham, culminating in a group vomit? Does she want to share a bath with you and a few close personal friends? Does she enjoy a good game of strip billiards?'

Bertie waved away James's thumbnail sketch of some of his more lurid escapades.

'OK, so I've got a bit of a dodgy past –'

'Past?' James looked dubious. 'You're never going to change. The words leopard and spots spring to mind. The novelty of pairing up with some saintly, sweet, clean-living creature will wear off the minute temptation steps into your path. And then what? Mrs Tait ends up as another casualty of Bertie's quest for gratification. Just like Tor did.'

Bertie looked at him oddly. James carried on.

'Ginny's very vulnerable. She's only just got back on her feet since her husband left her. She's not a plaything, you know.'

'You're very protective of her.'

'Someone's got to look out for your victims. You're like a vampire where women are concerned, Bertie.'

Bertie didn't retaliate. He walked over to the window

and looked outside for a moment. He admired the lawn, which he had cut last night. Immaculate green stripes. It had been immensely therapeutic. He didn't know why he had never bothered before.

He turned back to James.

'It was you, wasn't it?'

He spoke flatly. James looked blank. He carried on.

'I've spent ten years wondering who was sick enough to send that album to Tor. I always thought it was some girl I'd dumped who'd never got over it.' Bertie looked at James and sneered. 'I should have guessed. It should have been obvious, shouldn't it? My best man. The only one in the stag party sober enough to take photos.'

James didn't deny it. His expression didn't flicker. Instead, he reached out for one of Bertie's cigarettes. He usually only indulged in cigars, but this was heavy. He blew out a heavy plume of smoke and started to explain.

'I had this very same conversation with you ten years ago, before your wedding day, but you didn't listen then. The whole thing was like watching some bloody awful soap opera, waiting for the predictable ending. I was doing you a *favour*. I certainly did Tor a favour. I couldn't sit there and watch you destroy her; marry her and then go off with the first bit of skirt that took your fancy. Because you would have –'

Bertie opened his mouth to protest, but James put up a hand to stop him.

'What about the pictures that didn't go in the album? The tequila girl. Or should I say girls? That was a record, even for you.'

'You're telling me you've never fucked anyone you shouldn't have?'

476

'Not the week before my wedding. And generally speaking, not someone whose name I didn't know. And her best friend.'

'It meant nothing. They meant nothing!'

'That's precisely my point, Bertie.' James's voice was patient, calm. 'It's the very fact that you don't see anything wrong in it. I'm afraid that's not how other people see it. And until you understand that . . .'

Bertie knew he didn't have a leg to stand on. And that James was right. And that he'd done the right thing all those years ago. Bertie had always blamed the sender of the album for destroying what he and Tor had. But, in fact, he only had himself to blame.

'You can't think very much of me.'

'On the contrary, I think a great deal of you. A great deal.'

Bertie looked puzzled. James grinned.

'I don't think you're very good husband material. But as a mate, you're all right.' He stubbed out the cigarette. 'Actually, I came to ask if you'd be Henry's godfather.'

Bertie couldn't have been more shocked if James had proposed marriage.

'What? After everything you've just said – you want me to be responsible for Henry's spiritual and moral welfare?'

'Oh no. I've got Patrick doing that. You're to be the naughty godfather. The one who teaches him about gambling, how to double-declutch, how to tell Burgundy from Beaujolais . . .'

Bertie's face broke into a wreath of smiles.

'The one who gets him his first Parisian hooker?'

James shuddered slightly, but managed a nod.

'Something like that.'

'So what do I do about Ginny?'

James tried to sound as kind as he could.

'For God's sake, Bertie. Just find someone that can cope with your lifestyle. Whatever your romantic notions about turning over a new leaf, you're not going to change. Not now.'

Damien took Kelly and Anastasia to the Petit Blanc in Cheltenham. He'd overheard Coral in the post office confiding to anyone who would listen that Patrick was going to be all right, so now he felt high on relief. He was fairly certain the police weren't going to get anywhere with their enquiries. He ordered champagne, and cursed Rick for going off just when he really needed a driver.

They had a wonderful lunch. The bubbles put sparkles in Kelly's eyes as she described her life to him. How she wanted to expand the salon and find herself a proper flat.

'And you? What are your plans?'

He thought about his murky past. The hideous scheming of the past few weeks, which – unbeknownst to her – had involved her brother. Somehow, miraculously, he'd got away with it. Now he had a chance to atone, build a new life on clean bricks. Put greed to one side and concentrate on . . .

Love, he decided. Love of his daughter, the daughter he now knew was his. And maybe . . .

'I don't want to rush into anything just yet,' he said softly.

It seemed an interminable wait for Sasha until Barney eventually went to the gents. She emerged from her hiding place and slipped in behind him, locking the door, praying that none of the other customers would want to use the toilet for the next five minutes.

He looked up, startled, mid pee.

'Jesus! What the hell are you doing here?'

'I had to talk to you.'

He zipped himself up as hastily as he could. As soon as she met his gaze, she knew this wasn't confession time. She was going to be lucky to get out of here alive. He bore down on her with a cold rage.

'For God's sake, Sasha – why? It was an evil thing to do.'

She put the heels of her hands in her eyes to stop herself crying.

'I know. I know. It's just – I've had a shit time. Dad's run off with the redhead from hell – he doesn't care about me any more. Mum's being pursued by every eligible bachelor in Gloucestershire and hasn't got time. Everyone thinks Kitty's so fucking wonderful and sings like an angel. Jonty doesn't care me – he just wants to get his end away because his wife's up the duff and won't have sex –'

She put a guilty hand to her mouth.

'Oops. You're not supposed to know about that. Just erase that bit from your mind, will you?'

Barney brushed the remark away.

'None of that gives you the right to do what you did.'

'I know.' A little spark of Sasha's spirit flared up. 'But it's the only perk you get when you're a twin. All your life you spend being compared or mistaken. It's bloody tedious. So when you turned up and thought I was Kitty, I couldn't resist . . .'

Barney shook his head in incredulity. Sasha put her hands on her hips.

'And hang on a minute. I'm not the only guilty party here. You're the one that went ahead and shagged my supposed sister. And you're married. I'm a free agent. I might have screwed you under false pretences, but I wasn't being unfaithful.'

Barney panicked. She had more than a point. He thought he'd better get off her case. He'd got a lot more to lose than she had.

'OK. Listen. Let's have a deal. Neither of us are going to look too good if this gets out. So it never happened.'

Sasha put her head to one side, considering. She grinned.

'Only if you admit that you enjoyed it.'

Exasperated, Barney went to mock throttle her. She pushed him away, laughing.

Suddenly there was a furious knocking on the loo door. Sasha became very serious. She put her face up close to his.

'OK. It never happened.'

She turned and, unlocking the door, walked away very quickly.

Barney followed, rather sheepishly, giving an apologetic shrug to the bemused customer waiting outside.

As Sasha made her way back down the high street, she thought for the millionth time in her life that it wasn't fair. She wondered sadly if she'd ever find someone like Barney: someone cute and cuddly who you could occasionally entice into a bit of wickedness, but who would always be there. Someone who was essentially good. You came into this world good or bad, and Sasha was certain she was bad. And it was very tiring. You were constantly having to try and extricate yourself from the evil you'd done; it was a permanent damage-limitation exercise. How much easier to have been born Kitty . . .

Sasha tossed her head and told herself it would be boring to be a little goody two-shoes. She decided to cadge a lift into Evesham and go and get bombed. Her mate Midge had got some draw that he said was a total trip, and Sasha reckoned that was just what she needed to forget the last couple of days.

That evening, Ginny was curled up on the sofa, reading a novel she'd been meaning to read for ages, luxuriating in the silence and sipping a glass of wine. Kitty was at work; Sasha was out somewhere. She felt thoroughly relaxed. She'd had a wonderful weekend doing absolutely nothing but please herself.

At nine thirty, the phone rang. Ginny hated it when the phone rang late. It used to mean people with abscesses. Now it could only mean trouble.

She was right. Sasha's voice came down the line. It sounded very tiny. Very far away.

'Mum. I've been busted. I need you to come to the station in Evesham.'

There'd been a load of them in a café, apparently, when the police had decided to do a raid. Ginny tried her very best to sound calm, a nervous reaction to how frightened Sasha sounded. She'd never heard her like that before. What did this mean? Prison? A court case? Would she have to stay the night, or would she be released? Ginny didn't have a clue. She didn't know how to handle the procedure; how to deal with the police. Who could she phone?

Not David. He'd go berserk and only make matters worse. He had zero tolerance on drugs, Ginny knew. She herself didn't condone it, but she was a realist. Experimenting was part of growing up. So she made sure the twins were well-informed, and told them a few cautionary tales of people who'd ended up in the casualty ward where she'd done her training as a result of drug abuse.

She thought fleetingly of Bertie, but wasn't convinced he'd deal with the situation with the gravity it deserved. She had no proof, but he was no stranger to drugs, she was sure.

Keith. She'd phone Keith. He'd know exactly what to do.

Keith was wonderful, and took immediate total control of the situation. Within ten minutes he arrived at her door in the Land Cruiser.

'Get in,' he ordered, calm and authoritative. As he drove towards Evesham, he made several calls on his mobile until he got in touch with the solicitor he wanted. Ginny sat by meekly as he rapped out questions and took in the answers, then ordered the solicitor to stand by in case he was needed.

He swept into the police station with Ginny close behind, demanding to see the most senior officer in charge. He wasn't remotely intimidated, whereas Ginny knew she would have been submissively meek, and probably taken all the blame for her daughter's wayward behaviour.

Keith soon satisfied himself that Sasha hadn't actually

been in possession of anything, so wasn't being held. She emerged looking remarkably sheepish. Keith grabbed her firmly by the scruff of the neck, before she got any ideas about slipping off with the rest of her mates who'd been released.

'Right, young lady. In the car.'

Ginny sat by as, unabashed, he gave Sasha a serious talking to.

'I don't know how you've got the nerve to put your mother through that. You've got no thought for anyone but yourself. Don't you understand the implications? You're lucky you got off with just a warning. You wouldn't get very far in life with a record, I can tell you.' He turned to give her a look that said he meant it. 'You're lucky I'm not going to sack you from the Honeycote Arms for a start. I won't tolerate drug users on my staff.'

Sasha, amazingly, kept quiet and looked suitably chastened. Ginny didn't think anyone had spoken like that to her before.

Keith drove them both back to Honeycote with nobody daring to squeak. But as soon as they had arrived in the warmth and safety of Tinker's Barn, he turned from nasty cop to nice cop.

'Right,' he said. 'I think we need a bit of light relief after that. I'm going to get us all a Chinese takeaway.'

Ginny was pleased that she wasn't going to have to spend the rest of the evening alone with Sasha, and examine her own shortcomings. Rationally, she knew that she was a good mother and that she'd done a good job of bringing the girls up. But it was only natural to blame yourself when they did something silly. What if? If only? Should have. Shouldn't have. Though thankfully Sasha's escapade hadn't come to anything. Better to be picked up from the police station than the hospital. And maybe it would teach her a lesson.

Sasha slunk upstairs to get changed while Ginny set the table for supper. She found bowls and chopsticks, soy sauce and paper napkins, then lit some little tea lights round the room to give it some atmosphere.

Sasha came back down, soberly dressed in jeans and a grey cardigan, not displaying her usual flamboyant style. Mother and daughter looked at each other, neither quite sure what to say.

'I'm sorry, Mum,' croaked Sasha, and threw herself into her mother's arms. 'I'm sorry I'm such a stupid cow. I can't do anything right. I bet you hate me!'

'Darling, of course I don't!' Ginny hugged her daughter tightly. Keith's lecture had obviously hit home. 'I just wish you'd think a bit more, that's all.'

'Don't you wish I was more like Kitty?'

'No, I don't,' said Ginny stoutly. 'That would be ... boring.' She hoped by saying it she wasn't being disloyal to Kitty, but Sasha obviously needed a boost. The two of them were both having a little weep, mixed with laughter, when Keith arrived back with the Chinese, and with Kitty behind him, having finished her shift at the pub.

The meal was, surprisingly, after everything that had happened, great fun. After a couple of glasses of wine everyone relaxed. Sasha became her old self again, but instead of demanding attention by being confrontational she was actually quite amusing. She looked almost happy, thought Ginny, and wondered why.

As she looked round, she thought she knew the answer. There might only be the four of them, but it felt like a family, sitting round the table, enjoying a meal, sharing experiences, having fun. She watched as Keith insisted Sasha had the last spring roll, and Sasha insisted on cutting it in half to share with him.

At nearly midnight, Keith announced reluctantly that he had to go. Ginny saw him to the door. Unnoticed by her, Sasha and Kitty had slipped away discreetly.

'Thank you so much for this evening. I don't know what I'd have done without you.'

He smiled kindly.

'No problem. I enjoyed it. I was feeling rather sorry for myself, anyway. Mandy left for Australia this morning. It's going to be strange without her.'

Impulsively, Ginny reached up on her tiptoes and kissed him. Full on the lips. A kiss that was full of promise. She gave him a mischievous smile.

'I would ask you to stay', she said, 'but I think Sasha needs me tonight.'

It took Keith a second to recover and realize what she was saying.

'No. Quite right.'

'But if you're not doing anything later in the week . . . maybe we could go out?'

His smile lit up his whole face and Ginny thought what a nice face it was, a trustworthy face, and one she could grow very fond of given time.

As he went back down the path to his car, Keith felt the urge to leap in the air and click his heels together in glee. He decided that probably wasn't wise. But in his head he did a merry dance of triumph all the way home.

*

After service that night, Barney went to extricate his wife from the kitchen. He'd got a bottle of chilled white wine and two glasses. She was busy swabbing down the surfaces.

'Come on. That'll wait till morning.'

'I've nearly finished. I can't leave it dirty.'

Suzanna's idea of dirty was most people's idea of sparkling clean. Barney grabbed her firmly by the hand and led her upstairs to their bedroom, where he poured them each a glass of wine.

'I think we need to talk everything over,' he said firmly. 'But before we start, I want to tell you that I love you. And admire you. And respect you. More than anything in the world.'

Suzanna looked at him. She took a thoughtful sip of her wine. He was so big. So kind. So strong. And so . . .

Suddenly she put her glass down. She walked over to him and took his out of his hand. Then she leaned forward and kissed him. Hungrily. Passionately. Barney didn't even have time to be shocked. He responded with equal passion. Within moments, their clothes had tumbled to the floor. Warm skin met warm skin. Lips, tongues and fingers bestowed caresses that woke in each of them a wild need to show that their love was stronger than their grief. Fear melted away as they came together to kill the dark spirit that had threatened to destroy them.

Afterwards, Suzanna sat up with a smile, her hair tousled, her skin slick with sweat, her eyes huge with exhilaration.

'Jesus,' she breathed, overwhelmed by the tidal wave of bliss that had washed over her. 'That was the best ever.'

The ghost was gone.

25

It was a boiling hot August day, the sort of day that made people say no one would bother going abroad if you could rely on the weather being like this in England. Everyone who had planted hanging baskets or containers was cursing at having to spend so much time watering. Some had given up.

Even the flower arrangements in the little church at Honeycote were starting to wilt in protest. Caroline, riddled with nerves, was furious that the florist had fobbed them off with blooms that were less than fresh, and threatened to cancel the very substantial cheque she'd given her, but James calmed her down. Nothing was capable of withstanding this heat. Henry was doing his best, looking perfectly splendid in the Liddiard christening gown. Patrick had worn it, and James and Mickey before him, and the silk was now yellowing and worn right through in places. But Lucy had very carefully sewn up the tears with tiny stitches, as Caroline hadn't ever so much as threaded a needle, and they both agreed it was so much nicer to christen your baby in an heirloom than spend money on some awful frilly, white monstrosity.

At the instruction from the vicar, Patrick stood up and made his way to the font. The card he'd been given with the words printed on it shook slightly in his hands. Bertie took his place beside him in a white linen trouser suit, rakish as ever but somehow more wholesome than usual, less as if he'd spent the night languishing in an opium den. His girlfriend was in the congregation, too. Erica. A cool, Greta Scacchi-like blonde, she was in a floaty tea-coloured silk dress, with hundreds of silver bangles up each arm and beaded slippers. A white Zimbabwean who had fled to England when things had got sticky on her family's game reserve, she was more than a match for Bertie. Anything he got up to was nothing compared to the drama she'd already experienced in her twenty-four years. She had her own company, organizing riding safaris to countries in Africa that were less dogged by political upheaval than her own. She could shoot a charging rhino from fifty paces; break a wild horse; fly a plane. Bertie didn't phase her in the least – he was firmly under her thumb. And he clearly worshipped her. He seemed to be settling down at last.

They were all growing up, thought Patrick. Poor Henry. He was the one with it all in front of him: the potential minefields that life presented to you. Then he grinned. Henry would be all right. He had Patrick and Bertie looking out for him. He couldn't go wrong.

He thought about the e-mail he'd received that morning, from Mandy. She absolutely couldn't wait to see him, she'd said. She was counting the days. Patrick felt in his pocket for the ticket that Keith had presented him with the day before. A ticket to Australia – return, Keith had pointed out mock-sternly. It was a reward for all his hard work. Incredibly, since its opening in May, the pub's profits had doubled each month and looked set to rise even further.

Patrick was hoping against hope that this long-awaited

holiday would result in him bringing Mandy back home. Home being the operative word – he'd done little this summer but work on the pub, then go straight to Little Orwell Cottage, which was now almost worthy of a feature in *House and Garden*. He couldn't wait for Mandy to see it, and put her own imprint on the place. Patrick knew he'd done a good job, but he wanted to wake up and feel it was *their* home, not just his . . .

Inside the Honeycote Arms, Damien and Kelly and Anastasia were finishing lunch. Anastasia was scraping up the last of some home-made vanilla ice cream which had been, to her delight, served with star-shaped shortbread biscuits. Damien and Kelly were lingering over coffee, surrounded by pieces of paper on which they were doing calculations.

Damien was in the process of buying a local manor house, Barton Court. It belonged, apparently, to the man who had backed Kelly's salon, who was now living with his wife in Portugal. He wanted to get shot of his old house so he could increase his sun-drenched property portfolio. The garden centre adjoining the house had been sold off as a separate enterprise, but Barton Court itself was perfect for what Damien and Kelly had in mind.

A day spa. An absolutely top-of-the-range, unashamedly luxurious and self-indulgent day spa, where you could wrap yourself in seaweed from head to toe, enjoy ayurvedic massages and hot-stone treatments and thalassotherapy. And all sorts of cosmetic enhancements of the kind that were becoming increasingly popular, the ones that stopped the ageing process in its tracks. Kelly was going to manage it: she'd sold her interest in the salon in Eldenbury for a nice profit. And although it wasn't quite – *quite* – the fulfilment of Damien's ultimate dream, it was well on the way. And anyway, contentment was dulling his ambition.

He thought about the past couple of months and the person he had now become. Since he'd followed his resolution, to be true to himself and not try and be something he wasn't or what he thought people wanted him to be, he'd felt more comfortable in his own skin. He'd become accepted. He was now on first-name terms with Coral in the post office, who'd been so snotty to him when he first arrived. She even saved him his copy of the *Mail* each day. He and Kelly had been to Anastasia's end-of-term concert at school and had mixed freely with the other parents. Emily's Mum and Dad had asked them to a barbecue. Damien had brought Dom Perignon, because that was what he liked and what he wanted to bring, and he no longer cared what anyone thought. He didn't have to.

True love meant not having to prove yourself . . .

There had been a bit of a cloud on the horizon. A cloud which, if you looked hard enough, had had a silver lining, although Damien would never have actually wished death on Nicole.

She'd had an overdose. One of her brothers had called him on his mobile. Barry was the best of a bad bunch who'd realized not only the severity of the situation but also the fact that, of any of her feckless relations, Damien was the one person likely to be able to create order out of the chaos.

He got to Bristol Royal Infirmary twenty minutes too late. He'd steeled himself to look at her lifeless body and had been shocked. If he'd thought she looked bad the last time he saw her, she'd deteriorated tenfold since then. Heroin, Barry told him bitterly, and all Damien wanted to know was why? Barry hadn't blamed him, had just shrugged and said but for the grace of God went the whole fecking family. It was a well-travelled path when you lived in the arse-end of Bristol, surrounded by the sort of scum and lowlifes who were happy to bring you down with them.

'I couldn't have done anything to help her,' said Damien desperately. 'She didn't want to know.'

'I know she didn't,' said Barry. 'All Nicole ever wanted to do was escape. She should have known heroin wasn't the way out.' He put his hand on Damien's shoulder. It wasn't quite affectionate, but it was a gesture of recognition. 'You were her only chance. I don't know why she fucked it up.'

'Neither do I,' said Damien, and felt sick. Was there a point at which he should have put his foot down? Paid her more attention? Been more sympathetic? Less sympathetic? But no – he remembered the nights he'd spent racking his brains as to how to make her happy. She was flawed. Rotten to the core. And he hoped fervently that Anastasia wouldn't inherit any of those genes that promised nothing but eternal unrest, a constant quest for something that was never going to happen, a quest that ultimately ended in self-destruction.

All he could do to counteract it was surround his daughter with love, give her the strength of character and self-esteem that would allow her to enjoy life as it was and not think that gratification was always round the next corner. It was a huge responsibility and a daunting task, and having failed with Nicole, Damien occasionally had a crisis of confidence. But he thought, with Kelly at his side, he'd be able to manage. She was extraordinary. She treated Anastasia as a proper person, had time for her, was interested in her, had incredible patience – yet never spoiled her somehow, as she was very firm about things like table manners and bedtimes.

She'd be a fantastic stepmother, Damien found himself thinking, as he watched her show Anastasia how to put her spoon neatly on her plate when she'd finished and wipe her mouth with her napkin.

And perhaps, one day, a mummy in her own right.

In the kitchen, Suzanna was putting the finishing touches to the christening tea. Jonty had taken care of lunch in order to free her up. It was incredibly hot in the kitchen, a combination of a blazing August afternoon and the fact that the cookers had been going full blast for over two hours. It was making Suzanna long for a cool shower and a lie-down, but that was out of the question. Instead, she filled a glass with iced water and pressed it to her head for a moment before drinking it.

As well as cucumber sandwiches and miniature scones with jam and cream, she had iced hundreds of pastel-topped fairy cakes with Henry's initials – HJL – a labour of love which she swore she would never repeat. Not for anyone.

The cake itself was a triumph. She'd made an enormous square devil's food cake, dense and moist and chocolatey, then covered it carefully with smooth, white frosting.

Around the edges she had fashioned dozens of tiny frolicking bunny rabbits out of icing, thrown into relief by little blades of green grass and the odd flower. Because it was so detailed, it was just on the right side of good taste.

Satisfied that it was perfect, she re-covered it with a damp tea cloth to stop it drying out too much before carrying it out on its silver tray. She double-checked all the food. Everything seemed to swim slightly before her eyes in the haze. She tried to open a window, but it made no difference. The air outside was as hot. A couple of waitresses came in to get the plates, ready to pass round. Suzanna waved a hand at the scones and sandwiches and rushed to the cloakroom.

Upstairs, Kitty and Sasha were putting the final touches to their outfits, bickering over eyeliner and lipgloss. They were both in slithery little pink velvet dresses that showed off the tans they'd spent hours perfecting in the tiny garden at Tinker's Barn, much to the shock of people passing as they went brazenly topless.

They were singing at Henry Liddiard's christening, outside on the patio, with Barney on a ridiculous grand piano they'd hired for the occasion. It had occurred to Sasha, somewhere along the line, that if she and Kitty were identical, she should be able to sing as well as her. It was just that she'd never really tried. They'd experimented one night, after a bottle of Martini, and been astounded by the results, laughing with glee at the fact they could harmonize, duelling with their voices, and the result was amazing.

And so Double Trouble was born. With Barney's help,

they produced a sample CD and within weeks they'd secured bookings singing at weddings and parties, as well as a regular slot on Sunday nights at the pub, which had proved to be a real crowd-puller. They sang mostly well-known jazz classics, but also more up-to-date songs that they put their own twist to, moving effortlessly from romantic ballads to more raunchy covers.

And Barney's contact from London was coming down to see them soon. He'd made them think about it long and hard before contacting Jez and didn't pull any punches when he described to them what might be ahead. They talked it over and decided that no one could make them do anything they didn't want, so it was worth the risk.

And Ginny had backed them all the way. Ginny, who had very coyly come to them the week before with an announcement. Their lease was up in a month's time, she said. She could renew it, of course. But Keith had asked her to move in with him. There would be room for both the girls in his house, and they would be more than welcome. But if they didn't want to, if they thought it was a terrible idea, then they'd all stay in Tinker's Barn. It was entirely up to them . . .

They were moving in the following week.

Barney was ushering everyone outside for the toast. He'd worked tirelessly over the past month making sure the garden was on a par with the interior of the pub, and although it wasn't mature yet, it still looked magnificent, with pots of white geraniums and marguerites interspersed with the lavender and nicotiana he'd planted earlier. A Rambling Rector was starting to insinuate itself tentatively across the brickwork. Cream parasols and awnings shielded the guests from the blazing sun. Everywhere he looked there were beautiful people wafting about in silk and linen. Even Henry looked as if some casting director had spent months scouring the country for the perfect child, with his riot of ginger curls and freckled nose. Champagne circulated freely: no doubt everyone would regret it later, but for the time being it flowed like water.

It was, apparently, time for the cake and speeches. Everyone gathered round expectantly. Barney took his place at the piano and began the opening notes of a serenade to Henry. And as Kitty and Sasha began to sing 'My Baby's Got Blue Eyes', even the most cynical guests felt tears pricking their lids. There was no doubt about it: the girls were fantastic.

As the notes finally faded away and everyone had a good old dab with their hankies, Suzanna carried the cake out to the waiting crowds, who broke into spontaneous applause when they saw it. It was only James's quick thinking that averted a disaster when he saw her sway. Being the gentleman that he was, he caught Suzanna rather than the cake as she fell to the ground in a dead faint.

She came to, ten minutes later, in her bedroom. There was a fan blowing delicious cool air on to her. Barney was sitting on the bed, looking at her anxiously.

'The doctor's on his way.'

She managed a smile.

'There's no need,' she said. 'I know exactly what's the matter.'

She struggled to sit up. Barney was alarmed.

'For *our* christening', she said defiantly, 'I'm getting someone else to do the bloody catering.'

Then she lay back on the pillow and fell fast asleep.

2 for the price of 1
Weekend
Leisure Break

Why not get away from it all with a weekend break at a great price?

We have teamed up with Ramada Jarvis Hotels [UK] and Jury's Doyle Hotels [ROI], each with a range of leisure facilities, to give you and a friend two nights for the price of one.

To take up this offer, simply cut out the token opposite and send it with a stamped, addressed envelope to: Making Hay Leisure Breaks Offer, MKM House, Manchester M16 OXX. You will be sent a Leisure Breaks voucher and hotel brochure within 28 days.

If you have any queries about how this promotion works, please call our Helpline on 0161 877 1113 (lines open 9.00am – 5.30pm, calls charged at standard rate).

READERS' TOKEN

2 for the price of 1*

Weekend
Leisure Break

Offer open to UK & ROI residents 18+.
Claim by 01/04/04. Bookings valid until 01/06/04.

*Minimum 2 night stay

Token - cash redemption value 0.01p

TERMS AND CONDITIONS:

1. All promotional instructions form part of these terms and conditions.

2. Offer open to UK & ROI residents aged 18 and over.

3. Closing date for claims 01/04/04. Bookings valid until 01/06/04.

4. There is no limit to the amount of claims you may make however each claim must be accompanied by the required token that appears within MAKING HAY.

5. The 2 for the price of 1 Leisure Break voucher entitles two people sharing a twin or double room to two consecutive nights stay for the price of one based on the hotels' standard tariff rate. The Ramada Jarvis rates include breakfast.

6. The offer excludes Bank Holiday weekends, special events and the Christmas and New Year period. All hotels may require weekend stays. Any additional restrictions are detailed within the brochure. The offer cannot be used in conjunction with any other promotional offer.

7. Bookings are subject to promotional room availability.

8. Only original tokens will be accepted.

9. The promoter and MKM accept no responsibility for claims lost, damaged or delayed in the post.

10. There is no cash alternative to this offer.

11. Offer applies to new bookings only. One voucher per booking. Group bookings may not be taken. Full terms and conditions appear on the brochure.

12. This promotion is administered on behalf of the promoter, Penguin Group [UK], 80 Strand, London WC2R ORL by MKM Marketing & Promotions Ltd, MKM House, Warwick Road, Old Trafford, Manchester M16 OXX.

Honeycote

VERONICA HENRY

The Liddiards have lived at Honeycote House for generations. But all that might be about to change . . .

Mickey Liddiard adores his wife, Lucy. So why is he cheating on her with Kay? He knows it's wrong, but he can't help himself.

Mickey's brother James has been in love with Lucy since the day he met her. He can't betray his brother – but he's not going to stop the truth coming out.

Kay only married Lawrence Oakley for his money, and he knows it. But is it Mickey who holds the key to her happiness?

Just some of the praise for Veronica Henry's riveting début:

'The book I've enjoyed most this year has to be *Honeycote*. It's always a joy to discover a new writer whose work you love, and this is pure pleasure from start to finish' Jill Mansell

'Long, entangled and irresistible, it is so right for a suitcase' *The Bookseller*

'Billed as the new Jilly Cooper . . . an enjoyable, lusty début novel' *Woman's Own*

'A picturesque Cotswold village, an ancient family business under threat, love triangles, deceit, broken hearts and guilt . . . the multiple, intertwining storylines are equally engrossing and, all in all, this is an ideal, undemanding, entertaining read' *Time Out*

'Veronica Henry's début has all the ingredients of a good summer read . . . plenty of sex, scandal and shenanigans' *Hello!*